COLD THREAT

ELLIE KLINE SERIES: BOOK THREE

MARY STONE

DONNA BERDEL

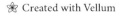 Created with Vellum

Mary Stone

To my husband.

Thank you for taking care of our home and its many inhabitants while I follow this silly dream of mine.

Donna Berdel

First, a big thank you to Mary Stone for taking a chance on me by collaborating on this story. I'm honored and indebted!And, of course, to my husband. Thank you for being you. You're my rock.

DESCRIPTION

Monsters hide in the dark until it's time to feed.

Puppets. Toys. That's all his captives are to him. He's the master, the one in complete control, and he's planning on recreating the night he kidnapped Ellie when she was fifteen.

Ellie Kline's life has never been the same since that night thirteen years ago. Now a detective in the Cold Case Division of Charleston Police Department, she's compiled a mountain of evidence against a dirty detective, revealing betrayal within the department. Determined to reveal the truth, Ellie enlists the help of her best friend, CPD file clerk Jillian Reed, to help her prove she's not just paranoid.

But as the anniversary of the day she escaped a serial killer nears, the murderous villain is coming to finish what he started. She beat him once before, and when he takes someone close to her, she has to hope she can outplay him again.

This time, she's not a child. And the master is only a man.

An enthralling game of puppet and prey, Cold Threat is the third book of the Ellie Kline Series that will make you want to check in the shadows for monsters.

1

Thirteen Years Ago…
    Whistling a happy tune, Anderson Duncan paused in the parking lot and turned his face up to be warmed by the sun.

Taking a deep breath of fragrant Charleston air, he continued to the front of the building where his therapist kept an office. He held the door open for a woman coming out of the building, frowned when she didn't thank him, and walked through the entrance, determined to not let a thankless bitch ruin his day.

A short drive from his own workplace, the small psychiatric practice specialized in treating compulsive behavior and intrusive thoughts, of which Anderson suffered from both. *Used* to suffer from, he told himself, whistling again.

Used to.

He was better now. Much better. Thanks to a magic pill and the good doctor located in this building.

His shoes squeaked on the polished floor with each step, the sound echoing off the vaulted ceiling above. He'd come to think of this particular tone of squeak as the sound of mental health. Even after a long day at work, Anderson was excited for his weekly session. He had news to share, and he just knew his doctor would be very proud of what he'd accomplished.

There was no one at the front desk, so Anderson checked the hall. The tiny light above the doctor's office door was green, indicating he could enter without interrupting another patient in session. At the door, he turned the handle and opened it without knocking—he was expected, after all. He froze as his gaze landed on a young man sitting beside the doctor.

He'd made a mistake. He should have knocked. The doctor wouldn't be pleased.

Worry circled Anderson's mind, the questions picking up speed before the doctor inclined his head in the briefest of greetings. The stranger said nothing. Did nothing. It was as if he were made from stone.

Anderson needed to go. Flee. Run away from this awkward scene. An awkward scene of his own making. He was such a fool.

No!

He was supposed to be here, he reminded himself. Not this other man.

Giving himself a mental shake followed by a deep, cleansing breath he practiced every day, Anderson flashed the pair a bright smile as he pushed the door open a few inches more. "Good afternoon, gentlemen."

"You're rather chipper this afternoon, Anderson," the doctor said, his mouth a thin line. "How was your day?"

"Amazing," he blurted, glancing at the other man who still hadn't moved. "I implemented some of the changes you suggested, then I confronted the coworker who has been undermining me. I feel like I've had a breakthrough. Standing up for myself is almost intoxicating." He checked his watch, preparing to stand up for himself just a little more. "In fact, I have to leave our session a little early today, but don't worry, I'll still pay the full price. It's worth it."

The doctor's mouth ticked at each corner. "The fee is a flat one, but may I ask why you have to leave early today? They haven't roped you into working overtime on a Friday?"

"No. Ellora in accounting is leaving the company, and they're throwing her a party at the office." He gave a half snort, half laugh. "What can I say, I wanted to see her off personally."

The doctor's bland expression didn't change. "I hope you're not letting your animosity toward Ellora color your excitement?"

Although he hadn't been invited in, Anderson took two full steps into the room. "Actually, ever since I started coming to therapy, things have changed for me. I haven't forgiven her for mocking me in front of our colleagues and acting like OCD made me incapable of doing my job." His heart started hammering at the memory, but he took a deep, cleansing breath, just as the doctor had taught him.

"And how does that make you feel?"

Anderson lifted his chin, immensely proud of himself. "I feel more in control of my compulsions, and I've made positive changes in my life. She doesn't bother me the way she did. To be honest, proving that she's wrong about me and showing everyone in the office that I'm capable and driven despite my challenges has been the best kind of revenge."

"I'm glad to hear it."

"I have you to thank, doctor. She nearly broke me with her constant ridicule. We'd be in a meeting, and I would catch her using her thumb to count off silently on her fingers, just like I do...like I *did*." His smile grew wide, his heart feeling like it might explode with gratitude. "Doctor, I can't thank you enough for everything you've done for me. If you ever need anything at all, please don't hesitate to ask."

"I'm glad you feel that way." The doctor gestured toward the blond man seated near the desk. "Of course, you noticed my assistant here."

Anderson nodded in greeting. "I did."

"He's doing an internship with me, and I was hoping you would allow him to sit in."

Anderson's gaze shifted from the doctor to the strange man and back, tension becoming a ball in the pit of his stomach. "I…um, I don't know if I'm the best patient to observe."

"What did we decide about self-depreciation?" the doctor asked in a firm voice, his expression gentle. Reassuring.

Anderson couldn't help it. He tapped his thumb on his pinky finger—one tap, two taps, three taps, four taps. Then his ring finger, counting each tap until he reached the number four at his index finger. Immediately, he started again.

One, two, three, four.

One, two, three, four.

Behind his desk, the doctor waited patiently for Anderson to stop the compulsion.

The intern was less patient, fidgeting in his seat, glancing at the doctor a couple of times, obviously wondering what the holdup was.

Anderson blinked and shook his head, forcing his fingers open to stop the endless counting. Air hissed through his clenched teeth as he took a slow, measured breath. "I'm fine with him observing."

"Excellent." The doctor brushed a bit of lint off his suit and turned to the intern. "Anderson really is the perfect subject for this. Take notes. You'll want to remember everything you learn today."

The intern nodded, reaching out to pick up a pen from

the silver cup in the center of the desk. He grimaced, fingertips shaking as he struggled to grab the tip of the pen closest to him.

The doctor's bemused smile held a touch of cruelty Anderson wasn't expecting. Anderson caught his thumb stretching toward his pinky, balled his hands into fists, and took a step forward.

The intern froze and eyed Anderson.

Anderson stuck out his hand. "It's nice to meet you. I didn't catch your name."

"You can call him Ernest."

Ernest stood and took Anderson's hand, then winced and quickly pulled away, clutching at a spot on his chest. "Sorry. It's a pleasure to meet you, and I appreciate the opportunity to observe your session."

"Are you injured?"

Ernest took a step back and waved his hand in front of him. "It's nothing."

The intern opened his mouth to say something more, but the doctor interrupted him. "Just an unfortunate incident with a patient a few weeks back. It's a hazard of psychiatry when you work inpatient."

Anderson frowned. "Oh, that sounds scary."

"More frustrating than anything. Ernest and I had to postpone some of our work, which threw us off schedule." The doctor smiled. "You know how that is."

"I do."

"Speaking of schedules, shall we start? Ernest, there's an audio recorder in my bottom drawer if you'd rather take notes that way."

Ernest retrieved the recorder and moved his rolling office chair out of the way so he was close enough to observe Anderson and the doctor without interfering.

The doctor cleared his throat, forcing Anderson's attention back in his direction. "Are you ready?"

Anderson sat down on the couch and nodded.

"Excellent."

Using a small remote, the doctor dimmed the lights until only a single, recessed light above them lit the room.

The intern faded into the shadows, his outline visible but indistinct. With a pale, shaking hand, Ernest set the voice recorder on the desk, angling it until the microphone was pointed in his direction.

Panic welled in the pit of Anderson's belly, and his thumb itched to start counting. Licking his lips, he cleared his throat, thumb poised and ready. "I'm not comfortable recording this."

The doctor's face remained calm. "This is how it needs to be done." His voice was low, steady to the point of monotony. "If you truly wish to heal, you need to be willing to give up control."

"I'm really uncomfortable."

"Change is uncomfortable," the doctor said in a flat tone, unbothered by Anderson's protests.

His thumb twitched toward his pinky. "I don't want to lose control."

"Control is an illusion." When the corner of Anderson's lip twitched, the doctor tilted his head. "Have you been taking your medication?"

"Yes."

The scratching of the doctor's pen on the yellow notepad paper set Anderson's teeth on edge. His thumb flexed, fingers ready.

"I see your fingers twitching. Are you sure you've been taking the medication as prescribed?"

"Every day at the same time." He had an alarm set to the minute.

"And how many do you have left?"

"Two."

The doctor checked the calendar on his desk and made a tsking sound. "You should have four left. What happened?"

"I dropped the bottle and couldn't find two."

The doctor became motionless, his expression indifferent, but his sharp words didn't match his demeanor. "That was careless of you."

Deeply ashamed, Anderson lowered his head. "I'm sorry. I tried to refill it at the pharmacy, but the pharmacist couldn't find any information on my prescription." He retrieved the small yellow bottle from his jacket pocket, shaking it to prove there were only two pills left.

"It's a proprietary formula not yet available to the general public."

Anderson's spine stiffened, alarm forcing his thumb against his pinky. "Has it been cleared by the FDA?"

The doctor's eyes bore into him. "How well did the FDA-cleared medications you've been on before work?"

"They didn't." Anderson leaned back into the couch cushion, letting out a deep sigh. "I'm sorry, you're right. Ever since I started taking it, I feel better. I've even become more assertive at work. Just like you said I would be." He perked up when he remembered his news, his chest swelling with pride. "I'm up for a promotion. I've been at the firm ten years, and I finally took a chance." He glanced down at the small container of pills in the palm of his hand and shook his head. "Who knew something so small could completely change my life?"

"It's amazing what one can do with a little push." The doctor leaned forward and held out his hand for the bottle. Reluctantly, Anderson handed it over. "When did you take your last dose?"

"Right before I got in my car to drive here."

An arched eyebrow was the only emotion the doctor had shown since he'd dimmed the lights a few minutes before. "And you were fifteen minutes away, correct?"

Anderson blinked, surprised the doctor had that information. He nodded.

The doctor smiled, and Anderson relaxed under the silent approval the gesture created. "That makes sense. It starts to take effect between twenty and thirty minutes later. You'll start feeling it soon." Tucking the bottle into his own pocket, the doctor clicked his pen.

Anderson moved to the edge of the couch, his jaw twitching. "Why did you keep my medication?"

"You don't need it right now."

"But I *do* need it." His thumb itched, bending at the knuckle. "I can't stop my compulsions without it."

"I'll return it when we're finished." The doctor glanced to the side, reminding Anderson that the intern sat just outside the circle of light, silently watching from the shadows.

He shuddered. "Why is he here again?"

"He's learning. Are you feeling anxious, Anderson?"

"A little."

"You've had an eventful day."

Anderson nodded, thumb waving, the urge to count so strong that his throat constricted. He licked his lips and swallowed hard. When the doctor's eyes lowered and settled on Anderson's hand, he locked his thumb joint, ashamed. "Why isn't the medication working?"

"You've had an eventful day, like I said." The doctor reached into his pocket, pills clicking against each other inside the plastic cylinder. He opened the lid and shook out one pill, handing it to Anderson. "Have another."

Anderson stared at the pill in his hand. The doctor motioned to the intern, who stood quickly, shuffling deeper into the shadows. He returned with a water bottle from the mini fridge, twisted the cap off, and handed it to Anderson. Holding the pill in one hand and the water in the other, Anderson was frozen by uncertainty. "Is it safe to take two on the same day?"

"Absolutely. You want relief, don't you?"

Nodding, Anderson regarded the tiny white pill, jaw working as he grappled with his choices. He could take a second pill and hope the doctor was right, or he could suffer in silence the way he had for years.

"What the hell," he muttered finally, popping the pill into his mouth and chasing it with a swallow of water. He pursed his lips, turning the water bottle to the side to read the label. "Is this flavored?"

"There's a hint of cucumber and mint or some trendy nonsense like that." Another small smile shifted the doctor's expression. "Do you like it?"

Anderson took another drink, not stopping until the bottle was empty. "It's delicious."

"I'll make sure to keep it in stock. Now, shall we begin?"

"Sure."

The doctor set aside the pen and steepled his hands, watching him with interest. "You were saying when you walked in that you'd had a successful day. Was the rest of the week positive as well?"

Anderson nodded and blinked as the edges of his vision went fuzzy for an instant before sharpening. "Overall, it's been one of my best weeks. I've felt almost invincible."

"And the suicidal ideation?"

Anderson stiffened, casting his gaze toward the intern before shooting the doctor a look of betrayal. "That was almost a year ago. I don't know why we need to talk about that now."

"Establishing a baseline to measure progress is an important part of the process."

Anderson scratched his itchy palm, blinking again as his vision went out of focus. The right corner of his lip twitched upward. "I haven't thought about killing myself since I started treatment, no." The doctor's pen scratched over the paper, making him want to clamp his teeth together. He scratched his palm again as sweat dampened his underarms. "Is it hot in here?"

"The temperature is the same as usual. Are you feeling hot?"

His shoulder flexed and relaxed, almost on its own. "Yes."

"It will pass." The doctor tilted his head to the side, a dreamy smile settling over thin lips. "What about intrusive thoughts? Have they been as loud as before?"

"They're almost gone." He flinched, glancing down to see that his hands were clenched so tight, his nails dug into his palms. He tried to open his fist, but his fingers only twitched. "Something is wrong."

"When those thoughts do intrude, are they the same as before? Do you see yourself jumping out a window?"

Anderson's head lifted, his eyes narrowing as he divided his attention between the doctor and his hands. "Not anymore, no."

"Look at me, Anderson. Give me your full attention."

Anderson blinked, and his eyes focused on the distinguished man only a few feet away. "Yes, Doctor."

"Can you feel the wind whipping through your hair as you plummet to the earth?"

"It would be hard to breathe. The wind would rush at me so fast it would be difficult to draw a breath." Anderson clamped his mouth shut, a moan locked in his throat. "I don't know where that came from."

"Where would you do it, Anderson?"

"At work." Anderson's shoulder jumped, his fingernails digging deeper into his palm. "The balcony looks over the courtyard." He swayed in his seat, blinking his eyes rapidly to clear them of the vision, but it was as if he were staring down at the inner courtyard at work. "There's a fountain there. Four stories down."

"Ellora would be shocked."

Anderson's vision disappeared, turning gray before the room became clear again. He nodded. "Ellora would be shocked."

"She always said you were all talk, no action."

"All talk, no action." His voice echoed in his ears. Distant and flat.

The words turned into Ellora's words, leaving his mouth in her high-pitched tone. "All talk, no action."

The clock on the wall ticked off the seconds. One, two, three, four. One, two, three, four.

"Ellora would be shocked," Anderson repeated, his voice his own once again.

"Anderson, are you counting?"

One, two, three, four.

One, two, three, four.

He looked down at his fingers, but they were invisible. Gone.

"I feel weird." The words were little more than a whisper. "Something is wrong."

"Don't let your illness lie to you. You're safe here. You're safe."

Anderson surrendered to the heaviness in his eyelids and let them flutter closed. Inhaling deeply through his nose, he nodded slowly, just once. When he opened his eyes, the room had grown darker than before. Still sitting across from him, the doctor's gaze was intent. Anderson's compulsive urges faded in response. "I'm safe here."

"The party is starting soon. You should go. Show Ellora that you're a man of action."

"A man of action." Anderson shook his head, blinking rapidly. Wiping a hand over his face, he gasped when the room shifted out of focus, then snapped back into place with painful detail. "What was in that pill?"

The doctor chuckled. "The pill was your standard prescription." He took an orange bottle out of his pocket and handed it to Anderson.

"This bottle is orange." Anderson turned it over in his hand, counting the pills. There were four.

"The bottle has your name on it. It is your medicine, Anderson."

Anderson frowned, tilting the bottle to one side, then the other. "There are too many in here."

"How did you like that water?"

Anderson swayed with the beat of the ticking clock. "It was good."

The doctor turned to the shadow in the darkness, just outside the circle of light. "Water is a much better delivery system. A little flavoring and it's undetectable."

"Who are you talking to?" Anderson asked.

"My intern." The doctor stood and motioned toward the door. "You need to go. The party is starting."

"The party is starting."

The doctor's gaze met his, unwavering and filled with pride. "Show them you're a man of action."

"A man of action."

"They'll know Ellora drove you to it. They'll know what kind of monster she is."

Anderson laughed, the sound coming out like a cackle. "She'll be so embarrassed."

"She said you're sick, that you need help. Show her who you really are."

"Yes, Doctor."

"Go. Don't disappoint me, Anderson."

Anderson scowled, offended that the doctor would ever think he would disappoint him. "Yes, Doctor."

Anderson stood, car keys already out and in his hand. His eyes closed for an instant, and he was somehow in the parking lot, starting the engine. Damn, he was good. The radio played softly, the low, pleasantly familiar notes skipping forward in the song with reckless abandon.

Time skipped with the music, and he was exiting the freeway, coasting to a stop. The song had changed, the warm harmonies of a full string quartet giving way to a piano concerto.

Floating on the memory of the music, his hand was on the door to his building. The symphony was gone, replaced by humming that followed his every step. It echoed in the hall where the elevator waited, its mouth yawning wide, light bursting from inside it.

Anderson hesitated, but only for a moment. He didn't remember the elevator looking so much like a monster rising from the depths of Hell.

Man of action.

As the doors slid open, metal scraping as they shuddered along the warped track, Anderson was surprised that the monster hadn't swallowed him whole. Forcing his eyes to stay open, he carefully placed one foot in front of the other and wound his way through the long hallway that led to McBride Industries. The double doors were propped open, the afterhours party already in full swing.

Ellora stood just inside the doors that led to a wide balcony that encircled the inner courtyard on all four sides. Four. Four fingers. Four stories down to the fountain.

How eloquent.

What wasn't eloquent were the party decorations. Balloons with storks and babies all over the blue and pink.

He blinked in surprise. Was the retirement party over, a baby shower taking its place?

He didn't care.

He cared about one thing. Being a man of action.

Marching forward, Anderson walked up behind the brunette and snagged the champagne glass from her hand. This was his, now. His and no others.

Ellora's mouth formed a shocked o as she turned. "Hey! Anderson, what the hell are you doing?"

He downed the entire drink in one quick gulp. It wasn't champagne at all. Sparkling apple juice maybe? He didn't care. He cared about only thing.

"You're going to be surprised."

Ellora's face was a mixture of disgust and unease. "What are you talking about?"

"I'm a man of action."

He grabbed her wrist, yanking the petite woman forward and through the double glass doors. He stopped only long enough to wedge a heavy metal chair against the door between them and his fellow employees. It wouldn't buy him a lot of time, but he didn't need much.

"What are you—"

He whirled on her and squeezed her arm so hard he could feel the bone pressing into his palm. "You mocked me and called me names. You drove me to it. I'm a man of action, Ellora."

"Stop! You're not making sense." She twisted her arm in his grasp, trying to pull away, but Anderson dug his fingers deeper into her skin. "You're hurting me."

He took a step toward the railing, pulling her with him. She stumbled in her ridiculous heels.

"The wind will take your breath away. You'll move so fast you won't be able to draw air into your lungs."

"Anderson, stop!" Her voice was more of a screech. "What are you doing?"

"The party is starting." Another step closer. "It's your party, Ellora. Your going away party."

Her face contorted as she began to cry, struggling anew against his iron grip. "Please don't do this, Anderson. They lied to you. This isn't a going away party. It's a baby shower. I'm pregnant."

Even better. The devil's spawn would never darken this world.

Anderson grinned. "It's a going away party now."

On the other side of the glass door, panicked voices rose, their words jumbled, too many people talking at once for Anderson to clearly understand.

"You made me miserable, Ellora. Mocking me."

She was crying hard now. "Anderson, please."

He pulled her the rest of the way, reached the railing, and peered down at the fountain. "It's off-center."

"What?" She sniffled, her arm going slack as she followed his gaze.

Behind them, someone was banging a chair against the glass. The chair he'd wedged under the door's handles moved an inch, the metal against concrete screeching through the air.

"The fountain. It's closer to this side than the others. A fountain that big should've been easy to center."

Her frightened blue eyes widened, and she tried to pull her arm back from his grip once again. "You're scaring me."

"You're going to be surprised. All those times you said I'd be better off dead. You're going to see. I'm a man of action."

"I never said that, Anderson. *Never.*" Her body shook with tremors, and her bottom lip quivered, but she still managed a reassuring smile. "I think you need to see a doctor. You need help."

The hate for her that Anderson had learned to chomp down on for so long rose up, making his head hurt. He leaned in close, whispering in her ear, as the shouts of their coworkers grew more frantic by the second. "I did see a doctor."

The metal legs of the chair screeched again, and people's shouts grew a little bit louder. He was running out of time.

"Anderson, you're sick. You need help. Please, let me go." The vitriol in Ellora's voice drew him back into the fog, where there was just the two of them.

His lips turned up in a slow smile. "You'll be so embarrassed."

Show them you're a man of action.

"I said, let me go." She was clawing at him now. "Can you hear me?"

"I hear you, Doctor."

"What are you—"

"They're going to know what kind of monster you are." He snaked his arm around her waist, which was much more protruded than he remembered—the spawn—and lifted her.

As he did, he saw a friendly face on the other side of the glass. Brianna looked terrified. Her fear bounced off him. "Help me," he mouthed, just as Ellora's elbow caught him on the side of his head.

What had he been thinking?

He was a man of action.

Renewed in his mission, he lifted the struggling woman higher.

Her legs kicked at the air as she screamed.

Hands grasped at his shoulders. The railing.

Grappling.

Catching hold.

She screamed again, loud and high. A scream of absolute terror.

Good.

Smiling, he plucked her hands free of the railing, and with an ease that surprised him, flung her over and into the wide expanse of air.

Her scream was cut off seconds later by the gratifying thud of her body hitting the concrete edge of the fountain's reservoir. Cut short, her voice was now silent, but Anderson was already climbing onto the railing, balancing on the beam with his arms out for balance.

He smiled as he looked down at her twisted body, half in the water, half out. Her hair floated around her, giving the illusion that she was still alive.

He knew better.

Shouts rose behind him, but the only words he could hear clearly came from the inside.

Go. Don't disappoint me, Anderson.

"Yes, Doctor." He bent his knees and flung himself forward, jumping as far out as he could, aiming for the middle of the off-center fountain, arms out in a graceful swan dive. He smiled as he took a deep, calming breath.

I was wrong. You can *breathe on the way down.*

It was his last thought before his head broke the surface of the shallow water.

Then the world went dark, and Ellora couldn't hurt him anymore.

2

T oday...

DETECTIVE ELLIE KLINE adjusted the vent on the passenger side of her boyfriend's Cayenne, turning the warm air so it hit her bare shoulders. She wrapped the soft turquoise shawl tighter around her arms until it hid the scar from where Tucker Penland's bullet had grazed her skin.

That was a night she wouldn't soon forget, one that had turned out well after she found his hostage, Valerie Price, and they beat him at his own game of hunting humans as prey. She shivered again, though this time it had nothing to do with the temperature.

She caught Nick watching her and flashed him a quick smile. "I'll be so happy when it's spring."

Nick Greene smiled back. "Only a few days left."

She gave a decidedly unladylike snort and pulled the shawl closer. "Just because the calendar says spring officially starts in March doesn't mean I'm buying it." Sighing, she took in the majestic old buildings with hand-carved details as they passed through Charleston's historic district, each as unique as the next. "I was meant to be a summer baby."

She'd had a hell of a winter, having witnessed the man she held responsible for allowing her own kidnapper to remain free blow his brains out. Not to mention she'd been under suspicion for his death until it was ruled a suicide.

Being put on leave from the Charleston Police Department for having witnessed Detective Roy Jones's self-destruction and also for being shot by a serial killer—or nicked by the bullet of one—might've been procedure, but for her, there was nothing worse. A break was the last thing she needed, with so many cold cases waiting. So many families who wouldn't know what happened to their loved ones until she cracked the case. And the evidence locker was full of cases, so many that she'd often been tempted to haul in a cot and camp out there.

Still, she'd promised herself this night out. This one night away, where she could forget the horrors humans wreaked upon one another before she began to make her way back to some semblance of normalcy.

Nick chuckled, the soft tick of the blinker syncing with the flashing green arrow as he took the next left. "I don't think that's how it works. And if you want to get technical, March fifteenth means you're a winter baby. So, not even close."

Ellie rolled her eyes at him, but their shared laughter filled her with warmth. "It's my twenty-eighth birthday. Let me have this one."

He pulled the car to the curb in front of an upscale Italian restaurant and leaned over, planting a quick kiss on her cheek before leveling his piercing blue eyes on her. "Anything you want. It's your day."

"I'm going to hold you to that."

He arched an eyebrow, but before he could ask what she meant, the valet was opening her door and offering a hand to help her out. She gave Nick a pointed glance over her shoulder as she stepped out of the warmth of the car and into the brisk evening air.

"I don't remember them having valet. I guess business is good." She shrugged, smoothing down her skirt, and Nick was by her side a moment later, holding his arm out for her. She took it, resting her head on his shoulder. He looked so handsome in his suit, the fine black material setting off his perfect hair. "It's been so long since we've been to Villa Dianna. I'm glad you mentioned it."

"I thought you could use a night out. I know you've been under a lot of stress at work and then on leave." He stopped and turned toward her, concern etching deep lines into his face. "I want you to have one night where you're not looking over your shoulder or worrying about the next case. Since you won't let me take you on a vacation, a night out on the town is the next best thing."

She shook her head, ready to deny she'd been struggling, but his jaw clenched, and she relented. "You're right. Things are…" She paused, searching for the right word and enunciating it in a sarcastic voice. "Intense. Very intense, answering the tip line."

"We'll talk about that later. Right now, let's just have a nice, relaxing evening."

She frowned but allowed him to tug her forward. "Okay. It's not getting any warmer out here."

He chuckled as the host opened the double doors and welcomed them in and out of the cold. The restaurant beyond was dark, the foyer lit by a single candle.

Ellie turned to Nick, lips parted in question, and the lights suddenly flicked on. Loud voices echoed off the walls, making her jump. "Surprise!"

Her family was gathered in the dining room, which was decorated lavishly with purple orchids, silver streamers, and a large chocolate fountain in the middle of the room surrounded by every shade of fruit imaginable. Tucked in the back corner opposite the kitchen, a string quartet played an upbeat yet soft refrain of "Happy Birthday."

Nick's lips were warm against her ear when he leaned in to be heard over the applause that welcomed her. "Happy birthday."

Helen Kline was the first to welcome her, arms flung wide and a brilliant smile on her ageless face. Bright red lips kissed Ellie's cheek as her mother squeezed her tight, but she knew from experience that there would be no trace of color left behind on her skin.

Dan Jr. pushed their father, Daniel, forward in his wheelchair. Before Ellie could bend down to hug him, he waved her away and stood, folding her into a bearhug that was stronger than it had been in a long time. Ellie's chest swelled, and her throat stung with happy tears. Just a few months had passed since Daniel Kline's successful heart transplant, but every day was better than the last.

"You look beautiful, sweetheart."

"Thanks, Daddy."

Daniel's eyes shown at the endearment as he sat back down in the wheelchair and let Dan Jr. wheel him to the head of the long table set up in the middle of the room.

Wes stepped forward, his green eyes, so much like Ellie's, were alight with mischief. The youngest of her three brothers, they were the closest both in age and temperament, not to mention looks, with both of them unmissable in a crowd due to their brightly colored auburn hair. Helen Kline had desperately wanted a second daughter, but a young, raucous Wes had cured her of any desire to have more children by the time he was two. Ellie adored him.

"I have a feeling you had something to do with this," she teased.

He shrugged, flashing the trademark smile that made him adored by Charleston's debutants. "I may have wrangled Jillian into helping me make sure you were available this evening. Then, of course, there's Nick, who's always up for a good surprise."

Ellie scanned the small crowd at the mention of her friend and coworker's name. A man she didn't know caught her attention. Clad in a dark suit, he stood well away from the other guests, his eyes in constant motion. When he caught her watching him, he nodded gravely.

"Wes, is that man a guard?" She kept her voice quiet so only her brother could hear.

Jaw tightening, her brother nodded. "Ever since you convinced Mom that your kidnapping was not a failed ransom attempt, she's been hypervigilant. They hired guards for the party."

"How many?"

"I have no idea, but I've already counted four, plus the men in the front working 'valet.'" The last word came with a dramatic air quote that had Ellie rolling her eyes. "I also overheard her talking to Dad about hiring twenty-four-hour security for your apartment building." He smirked, knowing she would hate that.

Ellie cringed. "She knows that Jillian and I are both armed, right?"

"Like that's going to stop her." He turned his palms up, shaking his head, laughing off the subject like he did with most stressful things in life. "Don't worry about that right now. It's a party. Enjoy your special day, and we'll go over that later."

"You're right," she muttered. Still, she ran her gaze over

the gathering, looking for others she didn't know. And more importantly, those she did.

Jillian Reed stood off to the side with Jacob Garcia, her former partner. Separated from the rest of the partygoers, it was clear they were outsiders doing their best not to look out of place. Ellie patted her brother's arm and excused herself, hurrying to the back of the room. Jacob held a flute of champagne, his brown eyes soft and relaxed.

"I'm glad you two could make it." Ellie motioned toward Wes, elbowing Jillian playfully. "I hear you and my brother were scheming."

Jillian's light-colored skin flushed the softest shade of pink as she shrugged one shoulder. The pretty evidence clerk had transformed into Ellie's best friend when she'd been tossed into the police precinct's basement to work on cold cases back in the fall. "Someone had to make sure you got out and had a good time. Especially on your birthday."

Movement along the back wall caught Ellie's attention, and she stiffened.

Jillian held up her hand before Ellie could ask. "It's okay. According to your brother, the guestlist is a little more selective than usual."

Jacob nodded his agreement. "Wes made us swear not to tell Chief Johnson and Captain Browning about the party."

"Aside from Nick, Jacob and I were the only ones invited that aren't family." Jillian frowned. "It's safer this way, but I heard your last party was epic."

Ellie scoffed, snagging a flute of champagne from a passing waiter. "That's how my family does these things. If it's not extra, my mom isn't happy." She pursed her lips and nodded. "I'm glad they're taking this seriously. With everything that's going on with Valerie, and not knowing who is behind the website where my...kidnap video was posted, I'd rather not have the entire town here." She downed half the glass.

The video was actually a snuff film, meant to end in two deaths. Only Ellie had gotten away. Survived. And she'd be damned if she stopped before she found the woman she had ordered to be killed.

Kill the bitch. The words still rang in her ears.

"It looks more like a wedding reception than a birthday." Jillian held up a simple black gift bag with a pink ribbon tying the handle closed. Jillian's initials were written on a tag in neat cursive with a silver marker. "I have to say, this is the first time I've been to a birthday party where I *received* a gift and brought nothing."

"Have you opened it yet?"

Jillian bit her bottom lip. "Would it be rude if I took a peek?"

"Not at all."

"It's a charm bracelet." Jillian lowered her voice to a dramatic whisper. "The expensive kind."

Jacob cleared his throat, crossing his arms. "That's real pretty and all, but I want to talk about something a little less flashy. Arthur Fink. Any headway on his case?"

Fink. The bastard's name suited the man to a T.

A pervert to his very core, Ellie had arrested the asshole a month ago after discovering that he was a top-tier client for a human trafficking ring.

Ellie shook her head, taking a sip from her glass. "I miss you too, partner." Jacob had been the only partner she'd ever had to not desert her because of her...rambunctious style of police work. Not even after she jumped off a bridge. "His lawyer has him in protective custody, and he's working on a deal."

Jillian's hazel eyes narrowed. "Am I the only one who

thinks that prick is going to walk away without serving a day in jail?"

"I've wondered the same thing, but at least for now, he's behind bars." Ellie lifted the glass to her lips and took another sip, letting the alcohol hit her bloodstream and soothe her raw nerves. "In solitary, with constant supervision, which is not much different than what he did to Valerie Price for nearly two years. *If* he gets released before the trial, he'll have officers assigned to him round the clock. Not the justice he deserves, but no matter what happens, life as he knows it is over."

Jacob set his empty glass on a nearby table. "How is Valerie? Did you visit her today?"

"I see her at least once a day. She's doing a lot better than the doctors expected after being on death's door from sepsis, not to mention being malnourished and being traumatized. She'll be released from the hospital soon, and she's going a little stir-crazy." Ellie glanced around the room, stepped closer to Jacob and Jillian, and lowered her voice. "We'll talk about it later. Mom's on her way over here, and you know how she gets when she catches us talking shop."

Jacob laughed, stopping abruptly as his eyes focused over Ellie's shoulder. "Mrs. Kline. It's a pleasure to see you." He stepped forward and took her hand, kissing the back of it with the grace of an aristocrat. "Thank you for inviting us to this lovely celebration."

Helen Kline beamed. "Thank you for coming." She squeezed Jacob's hand affectionately, then she glided from Jacob to Jillian, hugging her tight. "I'm glad you could come, dear." Still holding on to Jillian's hands, she turned her gaze to Ellie. "Jillian, if you don't mind, I'd like to speak to my daughter alone for a moment."

Jillian nodded as Jacob hooked an arm around her, and

they blended into the crowd, heads close as he made a comment that made her laugh.

Ellie prepared herself for one of her mother's well-intentioned lectures, so when Helen Kline reached into her purse and handed her an envelope with nothing but a smile, she was shocked almost speechless. "What's this?"

"Eleanor, I was racking my brain, trying to figure out what to get our only daughter for her birthday. You have everything, and you've never asked for anything more, so it was hard to come up with a gift without asking you outright."

"I have everything I could ever want, Mom. You don't have to give me a thing."

"I thought you would say that very thing, but then I had an epiphany." She motioned to the envelope. "It's cash for Valerie Price." When Ellie opened her mouth to protest, Helen cut her off. "It's not much, but enough for someone about to start a new life. I thought you might prefer a gift in your honor, to Valerie, instead of something for yourself."

Ellie's lips dropped open as tears filled her eyes.

Helen waved her hand in the air between them before Ellie could say anything. "Your father and I are still struggling with your career choice, but it's obvious that this is your true calling, no matter what life we'd envisioned for you. You've grown so much since you became a detective at Charleston Police Department, and we don't tell you enough how proud we are of you. Not only for saving that poor woman but for ignoring your detractors and following your heart *and* your head."

"Mom, I—"

Helen's bottom lip quivered delicately as she lifted a hand. "Eleanor, I believe with my whole heart that poor woman wouldn't be alive today without you, and after being held captive for so long..." Helen's voice broke, emotion clearly overwhelming her. She dragged in a shuddering breath to calm herself and lifted her chin. "Well, let's just say the poor dear will need a little help to get back on her feet."

"I don't know what to say." Ellie threw her arms around her mother and pulled her close. When she could finally speak, her voice was just above a whisper. "Thank you."

"No. Thank you, darling. For always showing me that there's more than one way to bring light to this world." When Helen pulled away, her brown eyes glimmered with unshed tears. "This world deserves more people like you." Helen hugged Ellie again and sighed, her gentle laugh like tinkling chimes on the wind. "Looks like our private moment is over." She gestured to the center table where Daniel Kline sat, flanked by Ellie's brothers, an empty seat saved for Helen. "They're beginning to serve dinner. We'll talk more later, but I wanted you to have this."

Ellie nodded and tucked the envelope into her small clutch just as Nick arrived to escort her to her seat.

When Helen walked away to join her husband, Nick leaned in close. "What was that about?" He chuckled, stealing a quick kiss. "Is she still trying to convince you to give up police work for something more noble?"

"No." Ellie shook her head, watching her mother place a loving hand on her dad's shoulder. "She was telling me how proud she is."

Nick arched an eyebrow. "Well, that might be the biggest surprise of the night."

"You're telling me."

He took her hand and gave it a little tug. "Your party awaits. Here's hoping the rest of the night is just as wonderful."

NICK TWIRLED the last strand of handmade fettuccini onto his fork, swirling it in the thick garlic cream sauce before bringing it to his lips and savoring the last bite.

Ellie set her fork down and picked up her wine glass, throwing her head back and downing the last drops of red wine. Her lashes fluttered, and her lips turned up into a satisfied smile as she held the empty glass up for the waiter to fill. He rushed forward, careful not to splash the crimson liquid as he poured. When the waiter handed the glass back, Ellie swirled the wine gently in the glass, inhaled, and sipped. Glancing over, she caught Nick watching her and grinned. "It's my birthday."

Nick shrugged. "No judgment. I just enjoy watching you let loose every once in a while."

Ellie felt a niggle of guilt. "It has been a while since we've been out."

"Too long." He stood and held his hand out to her. "The band's been playing all night, but the dance floor's still empty. What do you say we get this party started?"

She chuckled, placing her hand in his and letting him lead her into the center of the room. He spun her once, her turquoise dress shimmering as the generous skirt floated on the air. His breath caught when she stepped into his embrace, her nearness setting his heart racing.

They'd grown up together, dated since she'd graduated high school, yet she still took his breath away. Wrapping his arms around her, he pulled her close until she rested her head on his shoulder, one hand on his chest. They swayed to the sweet melody as the lights dimmed slightly, and the guests scattered about the large dining area faded into the background.

"Happy birthday," he whispered.

"Thank you." Poised and confident on the dance floor, she

followed his lead with effortless grace when he stepped back to spin her again. "Tonight was exactly what I needed."

He flashed her a wry grin. "Does that mean you're not mad that I brought you here under false pretenses?"

"I'm always game for a surprise."

He raised his eyebrows, giving her a disbelieving look. "I'll file that information away for another time."

The band flowed into the next song seamlessly. Couples fell into step around them, one at a time. Nick motioned with his chin, drawing Ellie's attention to her parents entering the dance floor.

Ellie sighed. "Their fortieth anniversary is at the end of June."

"Big plans?"

Green eyes bright with mischief, she wagged her finger at him playfully. "You're not the only one who can keep a secret."

"My parents have theirs next year, so I'll be taking notes."

"As you should."

He pulled her closer and nuzzled her neck, inhaling her familiar jasmine and vanilla scent. "Speaking of presents, I didn't get you anything for your birthday yet. I was thinking about a vacation to a tropical island. Or a mountain resort. It doesn't really matter where."

"Hmm…a long weekend sounds wonderful."

"I don't plan on leaving the bedroom when I finally have you all to myself. I've missed you."

A soft pink glow crept up on her cheeks. "You sure do know how to make a woman feel beautiful."

"Trust me. You make it easy."

Nick held Ellie in his arms as the songs melted one into another, and he lost track of time.

A tap on his shoulder pulled him out of his reverie.

"May I have this dance?" Jacob gave a little bow, a warm smile on his face.

Nick reluctantly spun Ellie one last time and stepped out of the way.

Jacob cut in, surprisingly nimble for a man of his size. A little shorter than Nick, Jacob's arms were thick with chiseled muscles, his chest wide and strong. He had the body of an MMA fighter and the patience of a saint—he'd lasted the longest of all of Ellie's partners. For six months, they'd patrolled together five days a week. Then when Ellie made detective, Jacob had been promoted to the K9 unit.

Jacob was the only man who knew Ellie as well as Nick did, and he couldn't help the twinge of jealousy that floated to the surface. He pushed it away, opting for a glass of sparkling water from a passing tray and skipping the wine. Now that he wasn't moving, his arms felt heavy, and his body protested being upright so late in the evening after such a long day. Work had started at dawn, and he was running on empty, but seeing Ellie enjoy her party was worth it.

Happy to give his aching feet a rest, he wandered over to a seat near the dessert table. Long legs stretched out in front of him, his eyes followed Ellie as she and Jacob danced. Her thick, curly hair was loose, cascading down her shoulders in tight coils of fiery red. She glided across the floor like a vision, so different from the rough and tumble woman hidden just beneath the classy exterior. Ellie was a walking contradiction in the best way.

He was so lost in his thoughts, he almost missed their secret cue. Another spin around the dance floor later, and her emerald green eyes caught his pointedly as she touched her finger to her earlobe. Nodding, he waited until the two came around again, cutting in so smoothly, Ellie was back in his arms before the next beat.

"You called, my lady," he murmured.

"I need to talk to you."

"We're talking now." He dipped her low, and quickly spun her, cinching his arm tight around her waist.

"Not here. Join me on the balcony?"

"I'd say I like where this is going, but I never know what to expect from you."

She grinned and winked. "I like keeping you on your toes."

He was still laughing when she led him off the dance floor and grabbed her wrap. One of the security guards watched as they approached the heavy door, and he held up a hand, stopping them while he checked the balcony. "All clear." The guard stepped to the side so they could pass through the doorway, but when he tried to follow, Ellie shook her head.

"We'll just be a moment." When he didn't move, she gestured toward the door. "We'll be fine."

The guard scowled but gave a curt nod in Nick's direction. "I'll be just inside the door if you need me."

Her demeanor had Nick's heart racing, wondering what could be so important that she was willing to sidestep security and risk her mother's fury to speak with him alone. She held her tongue until the guard moved to the side, crossing his arms over his chest and standing firm like a concrete sentry. Laughter floated through the open door as they stepped into the rectangle of light that flooded the dark balcony. The thud of the heavy oak door abruptly cut the noise of the party off, plunging the quiet hideaway into darkness.

Placing her hands flat on the cement railing, Ellie leaned forward, face tilted skyward, eyes closed. Her shoulders rose and fell with each breath, lips parted slightly. The pale light of the moon cast a silvery glow on everything it touched. When she turned to face him, her lips were set in a grim line, her fingers threaded tightly together in front of her.

"You're making me nervous." Nick's chest tightened with worry, his elation forgotten. "Is something wrong?"

She shook her head and pulled her thin wrap tighter to ward off the chilly night air. Nick slipped his suit jacket off and wrapped it around her shoulders. Her expression softened, and she gazed into his eyes. "You always know exactly what I need."

"You know me. If I can make life better, I'll do what I can."

"That's why I needed to talk to you. There's a lot going on with work, and I need you to help me with a few things."

Relief flooded through him. He took her hands in his. "I'm glad you're finally ready for a vacation. With everything you've been through, and getting shot twice in the past six months, I'm not surprised you're rethinking things. Stepping away is good. It will give you time to really figure out if this is the right path for you—"

"What?" She pulled her hands from his, taking a step back. "What are you talking about? I can't take a vacation right now."

He pulled back, searching her face. "I thought you were on leave."

"I start restricted duty tomorrow."

Disappointment hit him like a fist. "So, you're going back already? Are you sure that was enough time?"

"I'm fine. I could've gone back to work the same week, but Fortis is such a hard-ass, he wanted me to take more time to recuperate."

"Okay, then I guess I don't know what we're talking about."

Ellie frowned, letting out a quick, exasperated breath. "It's funny. My mom finally starts to see things my way, and then you're ready to whisk me away to some deserted island getaway at the first sign of trouble." She laughed, but the sound held no humor. "It figures, the minute I have my mom in my corner that you would flip."

Her words stung like a slap. "That's not how I meant it."

"Then what did you mean?"

"I just want you to be safe. That's all. Everyone needs a break now and then, and you've been through so much in the past few months." He took a step forward and put his hand on her arm, wishing he'd let her explain before he opened his mouth. By trying to anticipate her needs, he'd made a mess of things. She was upset, and he wasn't sure he could fix it. "Look, I'm sorry. I've been missing you a lot, but I know you can't just leave when things are this intense at work. I was trying to be supportive, and it came out sounding like I'm an ass. Whatever you need me to do, I'm here for you. No judgment. No ulterior motives. And I promise not to try to persuade you to leave your career for a life of leisure. That's not what I'm here for."

Her shoulders visibly relaxed, and she placed a hand over his. "I know that, Nick. I do. But I don't need to be coddled, and if I need to get away, believe me, you'll be the first to know." She inhaled a deep breath, straightening her shoulders, and he could tell she was preparing herself for what she had to say next. He braced himself. "What I need from you is bigger than a last-minute vacation. This isn't the kind of thing I can trust just anyone with, which is why I wanted you out here alone." She gave him a wry grin, blinking emerald eyes up at him. "If I'd known you were bringing me to a surprise party with my whole family, I would've broached the subject in the car on the drive over."

"Whatever it is, you know all you have to do is ask."

"That's good, because you're the only person I can depend on right now, aside from Jillian. I need a favor, Nick, and it's a big one. But you can't tell a soul. Even my family."

She looked so serious that a spider of unease crawled across his skin. "All right."

"No, Nick. I need you to promise that what I'm about to ask you stays between you and me."

"I swear," he said solemnly.

It was an eternity before she finally nodded. "Good, because if I'm going to keep Valerie Price safe long enough for her to testify, I need all the help I can get."

3

Gabe followed a child's squealing laughter down an aisle of the store, looking for a way out of the maze of toy filled shelves. There were board games, both old school and battery operated, even one that seemed to require farting. Stuffed animals of every shape and size filled the area to overflowing. He stopped in front of a teddy bear that reminded him of one he'd once won at a fair.

"Teddy Spaghetti?" Gabe whispered and reached out to touch the bear's fur. Fingers sinking in deep, Gabe smiled at how soft the animal was. How familiar. And how...warm.

The bear's dark brown eyes snapped to life with a sharp blink just as Gabe registered its aliveness. Gabe gasped in horror as the buttons focused in on him. One side of the bear's mouth rose up in a snarl, revealing sharp incisors. At almost the same time that a low warning growl began in the creature's throat, it snapped at him.

Gabe yanked his hand back, falling ass first on the tile floor. "What the hell!" He blinked, unable to believe his eyes.

But he hadn't imagined it. The bear was inspecting his shelf, *clearly looking for a way to climb down. When it found no easy way, it sank back on its haunches, ready to...spring.*

As the bear launched, Gabe scrambled up off the floor, terror and adrenaline giving him speed. When the bear hit the floor and roared, Gabe took off at a sprint, running down the aisle, which seemed to stretch farther the faster he ran.

Around him, the other animals had found life and began to hurtle themselves in his direction, seemingly intent on tripping him up. Heart pounding, he picked up speed. Finally reaching an endcap, he took an abrupt turn, knocking the boxes off one shelf without slowing down.

"Hey!"

Gabe cringed and had no intention of stopping to find the owner of the male voice. But a hand wrapped around his wrist, pulling him to an abrupt stop. Panic lanced through his heart before his eyes found the hand's owner.

Tall. Dark. Familiar.

The man standing in front of him could be his double. Except he exuded sexuality, as if he'd been sprayed with fuckable fairy dust, and it hung in the air, jouncing off his skin and leaving traces of it behind.

"How can you be playing with toys at a time like this?" the man asked, his expression as accusing as his words.

"I'm not—"

The dark man took a step closer, his hand warm around Gabe's wrist. "You were going to leave me here alone."

For some reason, Gabe's eyes burned and filled with tears, so that the man became a hazy blur. "I-I'm sorry."

"Apologies won't get the cows milked."

Gabe laughed, because it was what his grandmother used to say when he slacked on chores.

The man's eyes narrowed, and he stepped even closer until Gabe was breathing in his breath. His body reacted, tuning into the man. He was so beautiful. So sexy.

At first, Gabe didn't understand when a foul stench filled the air between them. He frowned, his gaze falling to the man's full lips. Kissable lips. Lips that moved and bubbled and...sprouted maggots.

His stomach careened, and Gabe stumbled backward, screaming as the beautiful man's face melted, turning into rotten flesh that hung from his jaw and fell with a splat to the floor.

Gabe Fisher screamed, thrashing as he sat up, the vision fading with each beat of his pounding heart. His bedroom came into focus in the dark, illuminated only by cracks of light peeking in around the blinds.

"What the..." Flipping on the bedside light, Gabe wiped his face with his hand. He was sweating, his head soaked. What a nightmare.

But that man.

Gabe had thought about him ever since the doctor had asked him to lock up his office, and he'd done the unthinkable and looked in his scrapbook. The man in the photos, who had resembled himself so much that it was eerie, had struck him as being off.

Remembering the photo he'd snapped in the doctor's office, he fumbled for his phone, opening it and scrolling through until he found its location. In this photo, the man exuded that same sexiness that had held Gabe enthralled in the dream...in the nightmare. Because it had been a nightmare. He shuddered.

He would hate to think a man who looked so much like him had met a bad fate, and he wondered what had become of him. And that got him wondering what had happened with that spur of the moment purchase he'd made on the doctor's computer.

He'd bought a man. A flesh and blood man. On his boss's computer.

After he realized what he'd done, he'd been careful to

cancel the transaction, delete every email, every trace of the sale.

But he hadn't been able to forget him.

Or help but wonder what had happened to him.

Had the man gone back up for sale? If so, what was he being used for, other than the obvious?

Did that sale have anything to do with the man from the scrapbook?

That led him to thinking about the photos in the scrapbook he'd found in the doctor's office and wondering if there were more pictures he hadn't seen. He tried laying back down, but his mind kept wandering back to the dream, then the photo on his phone, and the canceled purchase.

Finally, he rolled out of bed, took a quick shower, and got ready for work. It was early to go in, but he wanted…no. He *needed* to see if there were more pictures of the man.

At the office, Gabe wiped the sweat already beading on his forehead as he retrieved two heavy-duty paperclips from his desk drawer. He'd used them before in his old life in Florida and couldn't believe he was stooping to that low now.

At the doctor's office door, Gabe's stomach clenched, and a wave of nausea climbed up his throat. He was risking everything. The doctor had done so much for him, dragged him up out of a life that made him ashamed to even think of. Still, he couldn't forget the dark eyes in the dream—just like his.

His hands shook as he inserted a straightened paper clip as a pick, bending another for a tension wrench. Feeling around in the lock with it, he concentrated, wondering for a second if he'd lost his touch.

Click! The knob turned, and he was in.

The doctor usually didn't come in early, but Gabe's stomach churned all the same on his way to the desk.

"Dammit." He'd forgotten about the lock on the drawer. He checked the clock, debating on whether he had time, slipping the center drawer open. He hadn't searched this drawer last night. He'd take the time to do it now.

He didn't see them at first, the contents of the drawer were so neat. Stacked neatly and placed under a tablet of paper were the white edges of polaroids. Moving in slow motion, he fished under the paper, pulling them out.

His mouth spread into a slow grin as he stared at the photo, much like one he'd seen before, of the man with his shirt open. Hoping for a new pose, Gabe flipped the photo onto the bottom of the stack, his muscles locking as his brain struggled to comprehend what he was now seeing.

The dark-haired man, this time crouching in a cage. A real cage. Like a large dog would sleep in at night.

Catching his breath, Gabe flipped to the next photo, frowning. This one was much like one of the others, with the man lounging on a couch. Only something was different. His eyes weren't smiling. His coloring was paler, like when Gabe thought about the things he'd done in the past. When they came back to him in nightmares, sort of like last night.

The lips that had burst into nasty larvae last night in his dream had fallen open in the picture, almost as if he were unconscious. Gabe's gaze flicked back to the man's eyes. And it took him a beat to face what his eyesight was telling him.

This man, who'd come to him in his dream, was dead.

Gabe dropped the photos, stumbling back and knocking into the desk chair. The doctor's leather desk chair.

Anger rose up through disbelief.

Had the doctor bought a man, courted him, and killed him? Or something worse? What was the significance of the cage? A prop. Or had he really been kept prisoner, like an animal?

Gabe knew what it felt like to be restrained. He rubbed

his wrists as a tight sensation wrapped around his wrists like phantom ropes.

He'd allowed that then. Because of how far he'd fallen. He was better now, and though he knew his relationship with the doctor wasn't entirely healthy, he'd never thought him capable of something like this.

When Gabe himself had purchased that other man, who also looked like him, on the doctor's computer, had he saved his life by canceling the purchase, or sent him back to something worse?

He knew he would never be able to rest until he found out. He couldn't just walk away. Couldn't forget.

Even if it meant putting his own life on the line.

Straightening the desk drawer and chair, he tucked the photos into his shirt.

4

Ellie knocked on the door to Chief Marcus Johnson's office. Taking a deep breath, she went over what she was going to say one more time.

"Come in."

Chief Johnson sat behind his desk, his brown face clean-shaven, close-cut kinky hair showing more gray than she remembered. He was holding a file in one hand, his glasses perched on the end of his nose, writing furiously, completely wrapped up in whatever he was working on.

Setting the pen down and lifting his head, the chief of police's dark brown eyes crinkled at the corners as his face broke into a wide smile. "Detective Kline. To what do I owe the pleasure?"

She closed the door behind her and sat in the chair across from him, perching on the edge. "I have a problem, and I need your help."

He frowned, pushing the notepad to the side and neatly laying his pen across it. "You should see Fortis about any issues you're having first. It's best to follow the chain of command. Otherwise, people will think I'm doing special favors or that you're going over your superior's head because you think they're inept. It's not good for office morale."

"I knew you would say that, but this isn't about my job."

"Oh?" He leaned back in the chair. "So, this isn't about your duty status?"

She grimaced. "I'm supposed to start restricted duty today."

"Supposed to?" He folded his hands in front of him, a bemused expression on his face. "What does that mean, exactly?"

She shook her head. "That's not why I'm here."

"It's why I'm here," he countered, quirking a brow up at her, clearly inviting her to spar.

Ellie gave a soft laugh and shook her head. "I don't want to see the shrink. I'm doing the mandatory visits after killing Tucker Penland, but—"

"I thought you enjoyed your sessions with Dr. Powell. You seem to be visiting him regularly." The chief's intelligent eyes assessed her, and it was like he could see beneath her skin.

She also felt a little bit like the young teen he'd rescued that dark and rainy night, after she escaped her kidnapper. He'd hit her with his police car, almost killing her but also effectively saving her life.

She'd just discovered recently that her kidnapper had never been found, even though her parents had led her to believe he was dead. Now, she didn't quite know what to believe. She couldn't even trust her own brain since she hadn't even had as much as a flicker of a memory of that horrible experience for years.

That was then.

This was now.

Reminding herself she was a grown woman and that she was there on a mission, she said, "We made headway, but I wouldn't say that I enjoy the visits. More like, tolerate them. Now, Fortis wants to increase the frequency."

She mentally glared at the thought of her boss, Lead Homicide Detective Harold Fortis.

"Seems fair to me." Chief Johnson glanced at his calendar and back at Ellie. "You have been involved in three shootings in the past six months. *Two* of those shootings in one night."

"I didn't shoot Jones. He killed himself because he knew what was coming."

The chief gave her a pointed look. "The jury's still out on what was coming."

Ellie couldn't keep the scowl off her face. "Roy Jones was dirty." She was unwilling to budge, despite the impatient expression Johnson wore. He was going to shut her down, she just knew it.

Chief Johnson pursed his lips. "I'm not saying I doubt you, Kline, but you have to see this from where I sit. I have a duty to everyone who works at Charleston PD to be fair. Every officer, no matter what they're accused of, deserves better than to be tried and convicted in the court of public opinion."

"But this is me, and I'm telling you what I discovered and what I saw. I was there."

Detective Roy Jones was a bad cop who'd recently retired. During his tenure, he had taken money to rig cases, which were then never solved and ended up in Cold Cases. She knew it. She hoped the chief was on her side, but as deep as the human trafficking ring apparently went in Charleston, there was no way to know who was involved.

His dark eyes softened. "I'm not saying that you did anything wrong, but let's be reasonable about this, Kline. I can't appear to be treating you any different than your colleagues, and that includes taking your word as gospel without a thorough investigation, one on a stellar detective whose reputation stands to be completely ruined."

"When the public gets wind of what happened, it won't matter if he's innocent."

"Exactly." Chief Johnson offered a reassuring smile, but the hollows under his eyes spoke of many sleepless nights. "Luckily for the department, the news of a heroic cop who rescued a woman held captive for years in a rich man's basement made front-page news. The media loves you almost as much as it loves a happy ending. Jones's death was mentioned once, and the fact that he was a retired detective was glossed over."

"I read the story. They framed it as a domestic situation that got out of hand."

"And until the investigation is complete, I'm content to leave things as they are." He leaned forward, pinning her with an intense look. "I'd like to keep it that way."

Heat rose from her chest and up her throat, but Ellie fought to keep her emotions in check. "You don't think the media coverage itself is suspicious? Powerful men are involved in this scandal. They would want to bury the story, portray it like Jones was just a random man. That keeps them out of the spotlight."

"Kline, I understand your frustration, but I need you to trust me on this. Let me run the investigation. You keep your head down, do your job, and keep your mouth shut."

"Sir, I thought Fortis was leading the invest—"

He held up his hand, and she clamped her mouth shut as he'd ordered, frustration streaking through her. "Jones was a decorated lawman with a stellar record and more arrests than I care to count. If it turns out you're right about him, every case he ever worked will come under intense scrutiny. You have no idea the chaos that will unleash, so forgive me, but I would prefer to be one-thousand-percent sure an officer is dirty before I move forward. I'm sure you understand."

Taking long, slow breaths, she willed her heartbeat to slow, telling herself to focus on the reason she'd come to Johnson's office in the first place. She wasn't here about Jones and his crooked friends. She had a favor much more important to ask of the chief.

"I see some things haven't changed, namely, that temper of yours." Chief Johnson chuckled. "I'm sorry. I know the past few weeks have been rough on you. For what it's worth, I believe you. I just need to be able to prove it."

It took a second for her to release the muscles in her jaw enough to respond, but his words soothed some of the tension. "Thank you."

"Was there something more you needed to talk to me about?"

Ellie released her fingers one by one from the arms of the chair. She wasn't exactly batting a thousand, and she had to win this one. Valerie's life depended on it. "Valerie Price."

"What about her?"

"I want to make sure she's protected."

"You made that clear when you hired your own guards and paid for a private hospital room." The frown lines in his forehead came back, and his lips pinched into a straight line. "That took a lot of fancy talking to smooth over, but I convince the D.A. it was the best-case scenario."

"Thank you."

"Why do I have the feeling that you're about to ask me to cross another line?"

She swallowed, preparing herself to butt heads with the

chief. "Not cross a line, just making sure that my star witness stays safe."

He scowled. "I've already signed off on protective custody until the trial. She'll be in a hotel with two officers on her at all times, and a unit outside. Her safety is our top priority. Without her, we don't have much of a case despite the mountain of evidence we found on Arthur Fink's computers. I don't have to tell you how much easier it is to get a conviction with a likable witness on the stand."

"As ironclad as that all sounds," Ellie shook her head, "standard protective custody won't be enough. Not this time."

"Why?" He pinched the bridge of his nose and sighed. "I'm afraid I already know the answer, but let's hear it."

"We don't know if Jones is the only dirty cop on the payroll."

"*Alleged*," Johnson corrected, his deep voice more like a father correcting his overzealous daughter than a chief of police.

"Alleged. But if he wasn't the only one involved, then it's too much of a risk to have Charleston PD protecting her."

"I don't see it that way. What are the chances of two officers being dirty *and* on protection detail?"

"Isn't protection detail overtime?"

Johnson nodded. "I'm not sure why that makes a difference."

"Overtime isn't mandatory. So, if you're using officers that volunteer for overtime, how do we know they're not dirty cops trying to get close enough to silence her? You're basically posting a signup sheet to be alone with her. Anything could happen."

"Kline, we've protected witnesses without incident for decades. The system works."

"The system is flawed." She rocked forward in her chair,

forgetting momentarily that she was talking to her boss's boss. He could fire her with a flick of his little finger. "Just because something has 'always worked' doesn't mean it's right for every situation. It's not right for *this* situation."

Chief Johnson closed his eyes, looking weary to his very soul. When he opened them again and focused on her, he spoke slowly. "The city doesn't have the resources to hire outside contractors, and I can't lock her up. What are you suggesting?"

"I want to keep the personal detail on her and move her to a safe house."

"Where?" he shot back.

She shrugged. "I'm still working on that." She hadn't really thought she'd get this far.

"Are you telling me you want to choose a safe house for her?"

Ellie nodded.

"There's no way I can get approval for something like that. Even if I could, the red tape alone would hold it up for months."

"I'll pay for all of it. It won't cost the city a dime." She could feel Valerie slipping out of her fingers, and she couldn't let that happen.

"Absolutely not. You're skating on thin ice as it is, and the last thing you should be doing is inserting yourself deeper into this case while this investigation is ongoing."

"With all due respect, Valerie Price's safety is more important than protocol. She's the only survivor we have who can testify against the people who did this to her. With the information she has, we can take down the entire trafficking ring."

Johnson snorted. "Well, it's in the D.A.'s hands now. Maybe you should make an appointment to see him."

"I'm not asking to be involved in the trial beyond testifying, and I'm not going to do anything stupid like take her to my house and try to guard her myself. I have a plan and the resources to implement it. I just want to be the one to hide Valerie until her court appearance."

She needed to *come up* with a plan…and fast.

"Is that all?" Johnson scoffed, slapping his hand on the desk. "This is a huge request, Kline, and quite frankly, I'm not sure you're in any state of mind to be doing this."

She recoiled, feeling verbally struck. "I'm fine."

"So *you* say."

Still stunned, she lifted her chin. "I'm not sure what you're getting at."

Chief Johnson sighed and rested his elbows on the desk, his expression softening. "Look, Ellie. We go way back, and I guess I've always been partial to you because of that night. You can never quite forget the utter horror of having sworn to protect and serve, and then end up hitting a child with your cruiser. A child of one of our most beloved citizens at that. Still, what you're asking me…" He rubbed the back of his neck. "What you're asking me to do is no small feat."

"Chief, you saved my life." Ellie blinked rapidly when the backs of her eyes burned. "I appreciate the sentiment, and I'll admit I'd rather not, but if it'll help my case, I'll appeal to the beat cop who was patrolling that night. I'm not asking for the city to fund it. I'll cover one-hundred-percent of the cost. There's nothing to get approved."

"That's not the problem."

"Then tell me, please, what is the problem?"

"Your past is making you paranoid." When she started to protest, he shook his head. "Don't try to explain this away. I'm not saying I blame you for wanting to protect this woman. As a kidnapping victim yourself, you're one of the few people who truly understand where she's coming from. That empathy is an asset and makes you a better detective, but at some point, Kline," he pointed a finger at her, "you've let the pendulum swing the other way. *That's* my issue. The trauma you endured shaped who you are today, but you can't let it push you off the deep end."

His words cut deep, and she winced. "I'm not. I haven't gone off the deep end. I'm doing what has to be done. In my position, you'd do the same."

His voice remained steady yet firm as he continued, completely ignoring her last comment. "You believe that one cop is bad, and maybe you're right. But you can't cut off the entire department because you suspect some sort of mass conspiracy."

"I never said that."

"You didn't have to. I can read between the lines. The fact that you went around Fortis *and* Browning to come directly to me speaks to how bad your paranoia is." He huffed, pushing his weight against the chair back, making it squeak. "I'm surprised you trust *me* at this point, the way you've been acting since you found that woman."

Ellie took a deep breath, her chest swelling as her temper rose.

The chief's brown eyes held a spark, like he'd pinned her exactly where he wanted her.

She stiffened, wary, but unwilling to relent. "I'm being cautious, sir, not paranoid."

"Fine, then prove it."

Dammit. She *knew* it. She squinted at him. "How?"

"I want you to see Dr. Powell today. I want you to share your concerns with him and see if you start to see where I'm coming from."

"I can do that."

"I wasn't asking."

Ellie held her tongue and took a breath before she responded. "Anything else?"

"I want you to keep me apprised of everything happening with our witness. You don't have to tell me *where* she is, but I want to know when you move her, how many guards you have on her, where you hired them, and a list of people who know her whereabouts."

"That would defeat the purpose of keeping Charleston PD's involvement limited."

Chief Johnson arched an eyebrow at her. "Are you saying you don't trust me?"

"That's not what I'm saying. But the fewer people who know, the better."

"And if you're the only one who knows how to get ahold of the people who know her location, what do I do if something happens to you?"

Ellie's rebuttal died on her lips, and she frowned. "I didn't consider that."

"That's why I'm here."

"Jillian will have that information," she conceded.

"Fine. Please let her know that she's allowed to give me that information if something happens."

"I will."

Johnson sat back, regarding her over the top of his glasses. "Now that we've settled that, I need to know when Valerie will be released."

Later this week.

"Next week," she lied. "It's still up in the air."

"Good. That will give me time to get things sorted on my end and come up with a compelling reason for why I'm allowing this."

"Thank you, sir."

He gave a curt nod. "In the meantime, I want you to meet with Powell twice a week until he says otherwise. Three times a week would be even better, but I don't know if his schedule can handle that. And I want you to consider how these accusations affect the department and your fellow officers. If he reports that you're not suffering from increased paranoia as a result of the trauma you've experienced, then and only then, I'll sign off for you to take charge of Valerie Price's protection detail."

"And if he doesn't?"

"Then I'll step in and take control of the situation."

Ellie's jaw tightened, but she nodded slowly. "Agreed."

A smile spread across Chief Johnson's face. "Good. I'll see you on Friday, and we'll talk about our options then." He nodded toward the door. "I hate to rush you out, but I have a meeting in five minutes, and it's best if you're gone before Captain Browning shows up."

Eyes widening, she agreed and made her exit. Hopping on the elevator, she got off at the office in the basement evidence room that she shared with Jillian Reed.

Jillian was sitting at the desk when Ellie punched in the door code and strode into the room. "How did it go?"

"He agreed to revisit the idea at the end of the day Friday."

Jillian's brow furrowed, her red-painted lips puckering as she obviously ticked through the calendar in her mind. "Weren't you planning on moving her this week?"

"It's easier to get forgiveness than permission."

Jillian snorted and shook her head. "Chief Johnson won't be happy with you. Did he say anything else?"

"He agreed with Fortis, so I have to meet with Powell twice a week until the good doctor says otherwise."

"Yikes." Jillian wrinkled up her nose, cringing for her. "When does that start?"

Ellie checked the clock and gave Jillian a smile. "If I get there before his first appointment, I'm sure he'll squeeze me in."

"Good luck."

Ellie gave her a little salute before walking toward the

door. "Thanks. I'm going to need it. I bet Chief Johnson has already given Powell an earful about me being paranoid of the entire PD, not to mention that I must have delusions of grandeur to go head to head with the chief like that. I can barely believe it myself."

5

Dr. Phillip Powell pushed his glasses up on his nose with his index finger, eyes darting back and forth across the computer screen as he skimmed his email inbox. Wrapping his hand around the warmth of his insulated steel coffee cup, he inhaled the rich aroma before taking a careful sip. Wincing when the piping hot liquid seared his tongue, he smiled as he swallowed coffee that was still hot almost an hour after he'd arrived at work.

Checking the clock, he settled back into the comfortable desk chair. He had at least an hour before his next appointment, a break in his normally hectic calendar that didn't happen often. But a scheduled block of free time didn't mean much in his line of work. Officers showed up with little or no notice with a haphazard frequency that made any downtime outside of scheduled breaks almost unheard of. He planned on savoring it, however long it lasted.

A knowing smile spread across his face when a gentle knock sounded, right on cue. "Come in."

A familiar halo of red hair pushed through the space as

the door opened, Ellie's face appearing while most of her body remained in the hallway. "Are you free?"

Powell laughed. "You can come all the way in. And yes, I'm free to speak with you." He clicked the mouse to close the email, turned off the monitor, and gave her his full attention. "How have you been?"

Her hand was still on the doorknob, ready to retreat for the slightest reason. Never fully committed to the process. Always wanting to be anywhere but on his couch. As strong as she was, the vulnerability of being his patient was too much for Ellie, and at times, Powell found himself in awe that she managed to find her way there at all.

Her footsteps were muffled by the thick carpet as she took a wary step forward, the doorknob finally sliding out of her grasp. He motioned to the couch and stood, gathering his notepad and pen so he could sit across from her.

She pursed her lips, face paling as she regarded the empty sofa. "I didn't think I would be here again so soon."

"Why are you here, Detective Kline?"

Her head snapped up, green eyes widening slightly. "You haven't heard?"

He stood beside the desk, waiting for her to take a seat first. Giving her permission to change her mind. Letting her be in control of the way things played out. He'd found this was the only way he could get her to open up. "Is it something else about the shooting?" Despite himself, a warm smile split his face. "I know you saved a woman from certain death. That's something to take pride in, is it not?"

Another step forward and the arm of the sofa was against her leg. Closer, but still far from taking a seat and unloading whatever was weighing her down. She shrugged one shoulder, eyeing the couch like an old foe. "I'm still not back to work." Another step and she finally plopped down onto the plush seat, leaning back into the cushions with a heavy sigh.

Head back, she pinched the bridge of her nose as she stared at the ceiling.

Powell took his place on the chair across from her, settling in while she wrestled her inner demons. "Want to talk about it?"

When she finally raised her head so they were eye to eye, the fire was back. "It's crap."

"You don't feel the restrictions are fair?"

She shook her head. "Not one bit. He was going to kill the victim. It was a good shoot. And Jones is another matter."

"This type of leave after witnessing a fellow officer's death, even though Jones was retired, and restricted duty due to your being shot and killing a suspect isn't about the right-eousness of the actions. The time away from duties is about due process and ensuring the health of our officers. It's nothing personal."

"It feels personal."

"Why?"

She blinked, shoulders stiffening, but didn't answer right away.

Powell sat back, pen and paper untouched on the table beside him. He forced himself to relax, consciously releasing the tension from his shoulders, then his jaw, and finally letting his face soften. As he watched Ellie, she subconsciously mimicked his movements until she melted into the back of the sofa, releasing the breath she'd been holding.

Finally relaxed, she said, "I feel like people are just waiting for me to mess up."

"There's often a fine line between an officer being reckless and being determined. Both portray an unwillingness to let go, but only one ends up successful in the end."

"That sounds like one of the new fortunes in a fortune cookie that is actually a saying."

He quirked a brow up at her, overlooking her avoidance

of the topic. "Did you ignore your superiors and follow your hunch?"

She nodded.

"And were you right?"

She snorted. "If Fortis heard you right now, he wouldn't be too happy."

"Then, he'd be wrong."

Her expression softened a little. "Thank you."

"I think it's safe to say that a balance is needed, one that would tip the scales in your favor, making them a little lighter on the reckless." He fully expected her to get up and leave. When she didn't, he took a sip from his water bottle and regarded her with narrowed eyes. "I get the feeling that there's more going on than just your frustration with Charleston PD protocol."

"I wouldn't even know where to start." She rolled her eyes, covering her vulnerability with wry humor as she tended to do.

"Let's start with why you're still sitting here. You've spoken about what happened in Bartlett Woods, but you haven't said a thing about your own kidnapping. Have you remembered anything more?"

"No." She paused, staring off into the distance, and sighed. "Well, not really."

"Let's explore that."

She sat up again, placing her feet flat on the floor. Her muscles tensed, reminding him of a delicate bird perched to run. "There's nothing to explore. That's the problem."

Powell wrinkled his brow. Eyes still locked on hers, he reached for the notepad and pen, crossing his legs slowly. Green eyes followed the movement, her lips in a tight line. "Have you remembered anything? Even if you think it's unimportant."

"Snippets here and there."

"Tell me."

She puffed her cheeks out, blowing out a frustrated breath. "What's the point?"

"You've recovered more memories since we've started working together, have you not?"

She nodded, crossing her arms. Her feet were still on the floor, but now her elbow rested on the arm of the sofa.

"What about the nightmares?"

She stiffened and turned away. "They're bad."

"Not everything you dream is a memory," he reminded her.

"That's good." She flicked her eyes in his direction and away once more.

Powell tilted his head and frowned. "What aren't you telling me? Ellie, what do you see in your dreams?"

"I don't want you to think I'm crazy."

He blew out a soft breath through his nose. "I've recommended that you return to your full duties before, knowing what I do about you. If I were inclined to think you crazy, don't you think I would have brought it up by now?"

She nodded but remained silent for long moments. Powell had almost given up on her elaborating when she cleared her throat. Her voice trembled when she finally found the words. "I see myself, slashing out with something sharp. There's blood everywhere. It's flung in sheets around me, hitting the cement walls and pooling around my feet. More blood than a human being could possibly have in their body. Then the room fills with it, and I try to keep my head above the surface, but it envelops me."

Powell inwardly cringed at the image but didn't dare interrupt.

She closed her eyes, nails digging into the couch cushion. "The blood is hot and thick, and even in the dark room, I can see that it's bright red. Then a light flicks on, and the blood spills out of the room, sweeping me away with it." Her breath caught, and she reached for one of the sealed bottles of water he kept next to the box of tissues on the end table. Drinking greedily, she downed half the bottle before taking a breath. As she gasped for air, her chest heaved as if she'd just surfaced from the river of blood. "The scene always shifts once I'm outside. The light disappears, and I'm in the dark again."

"What happens next?"

"That changes from day to day, but only more snippets that make no sense." She held her hands up helplessly. "Sometimes, the dream is pure blackness, but I can *feel* the dream happening."

Powell scratched some notes on the paper before lifting his head to meet her waiting gaze. "Can you elaborate on what you mean by that?"

"Rather than sights, I'm blind and only pick up on the sensations of the dream." Ellie's green eyes had developed a haunted look, one that he'd seen in too many officers.

"You're pushing too hard."

"What I need to know is there, on the edge of my memory. Then it's gone."

He knew she wouldn't stop trying to get the memory back, and it could only benefit him for her to recover it fully. Still, it would be best if he took her through it as slowly as possible. "We should try hypnosis again."

Long moments stretched while she considered the suggestion. Just when he thought she'd tell him no, she nodded. "All right. But I don't want to go too far under. Last time I felt like I was in a fog for a while after we were done."

His pulse picked up at her assent. "How deep you go is entirely up to you. You're in control."

"It doesn't feel like it."

He flashed her a reassuring smile. "Lean back and relax. Let the memories come at will. Don't force them."

She nodded, relaxing back into the cushions, eyes closing.

Powell continued using his calm, level voice to help soothe her. "Take a deep breath, hold it...now let it out slowly. Start at the top of your head and feel the tension drain out of every inch of your body, from your forehead to your jaw. Now your neck and your shoulders. Your muscles relaxing."

Her breathing slowed as she allowed him to guide her into a relaxed state, then through the chaos that made up what little memories she possessed. She clenched her fists and unclenched them.

When she was fully under, he asked, "What do you feel?"

"Cold metal in my hands. The burning of ropes digging into my wrists." She gripped the cushion beneath her tightly. "Distant voices that seem like they're coming from all around me."

"What are they saying?"

She frowned. "I can't tell. They're so far away and disjointed. I feel hands on me, but their voices sound like they're in another room. I don't know how else to explain it."

Powell leaned forward in his chair, pen poised above the notepad, intent on Ellie. "How many voices do you hear?"

"Two. No. Three."

"Male? Female?"

"Both. One woman and two men."

He was thankful her eyes were closed, because he couldn't keep the excitement off his face if he tried. "Tell me about them."

"I don't know."

"Don't overthink it." The words came out too fast, and he mentally reeled himself back in, waiting several beats before speaking again. "Just tell me the first words that come to your mind about the woman."

Ellie licked her lips and squeezed her eyes tighter, obviously struggling to keep the memory from slipping away. "The woman is young and scared." Ellie frowned. "Not scared. Excited. She's breathless and speaking very fast."

"What is she saying?" Powell jotted down notes so quickly the words ran together. He forced his hand to slow down. "Is she talking to one of the men or both?"

"One. Only one man speaks while she's in the room. They're talking so fast, I can't understand what they're saying."

"None of the words are familiar?"

She shook her head. A second later, she froze.

"What is it, Ellie? Don't overthink it."

"I don't think the other man understands either."

Whatever they were saying, he'd lay money down that it was important. "When the men speak, what do you hear?"

She bit her lip, breathing loudly through her nose. Her knuckles turned white as she fought for the memory. "I can only focus on one word at a time. I feel like I'm wading through syrup."

"Are you moving?"

"No. I'm asleep."

"But you can hear them?"

"Yes."

Powell set the notepad aside and leaned forward. "Ellie, I need you to tell me what they are saying. Block everything else out. Focus on their words."

Ellie's eyes flew open as she sat bolt upright. "No!" Her voice filled the small space, absorbed by the thick carpet and the heavy drapes on the windows. Her cheeks were flushed. "I need to stop." She swallowed hard and licked her lips. "Please."

Frowning at her ability to pull herself from the depths, Powell handed Ellie a tissue and waited for her to wipe away the tiny beads of sweat that had appeared near her hairline. "You weren't resistant to this before."

She cast a glance at the closed door. "I felt like someone was coming for me. Like he was lurking outside the door."

"You're safe here, Ellie."

"Am I?"

Powell blinked. "You've lost me."

"Jones was dirty. Half a dozen people worked closely with him for decades and had no idea he was on the take? I find that hard to believe."

He picked up his notepad again, scribbling what she'd said almost word for word. "They haven't proven he was dirty yet, have they?"

Her expression turned mutinous. "I have all the proof I need."

"That doesn't sound very impartial."

She narrowed her eyes. "Powerful men got away with murder and worse under his watch. We don't need an exhaustive investigation to prove there was a connection between the cases he let slide and..." She stopped abruptly, rubbing a hand over her eyes. "Just trust me on this, okay? I know that he was dirty. He's the one who moved Valerie Price to a new location, arranging her sale to another man when Arthur Fink exposed his own crimes online."

"Miss Price will get her day in court."

"If she lives long enough to tell her story." Ellie rubbed her palms on her pants. "I need to go. Can we pick up where we left off tomorrow?"

"So soon?"

"I have to remember."

"Of course." He sat a little straighter in the chair. "Recovering your memories so you can work through the trauma you've endured has always been the goal, but why this sense of urgency?"

"I want to testify when Arthur Fink goes on trial."

"You're the arresting officer and the detective who discovered Arthur Fink's crimes. Isn't it a given that you'll be testifying?"

"I mean as a victim. Not of Fink specifically, but of the criminals he and Jones are and were protecting. The video of my abduction was on that website, which means that the men involved in capturing and selling Valerie, and others like her, were also involved in what happened to me. Why should Valerie be the one to shoulder the burden of witness testimony alone? I need to remember so I can tell the court what those people did to me. If Arthur Fink comes through with the list of names to save his own skin, and I can recover enough memories to fill in the blanks, there's a better chance of bringing this group to justice."

"Or of making yourself a target." He laced his voice with just enough of a warning tone to catch her attention.

"I've always been a target," she retorted. "I'm not safe anywhere, so why hide when it comes to testifying?"

"Detective Kline, has anyone talked to you about being paranoid?"

She pulled back, scowling at Powell as if he were hurling an accusation instead of asking a question as a mental health professional. "It's not paranoia if I'm right. You said yourself, there's a thin line between reckless and determined, right?"

"But this is different. You've checked the door several times since you've been here, and you've all but accused the department at large of being dirty."

"I don't think everyone is dirty." She threw up her hands, resting them on her temples for a second. "I never said that. But I do think Valerie will be safer if I'm the one to protect her until she's able to testify."

Powell's eyebrows lifted in surprise, but he recovered quickly. "Can I offer a bit of advice?"

"You're going to anyway, aren't you?" she shot at him, her eyes throwing out green sparks.

He chuckled, giving himself a moment to think through his words. "That I am. You need to take a step back from this situation and take a long, hard look at where this is headed. You've taken on a lot of personal responsibility for Valerie and the other victims in the cold cases you've solved, and I believe it may be causing you to imagine situations are far worse than they are." When she opened her mouth, he held up a hand. "I'm not saying that you're not right about Jones. From what you've shared, it's easy to believe that he was on the take. But I believe the stress you've endured recently is more than you realize. You've gone from investigating discrepancies and discovering a dirty detective to proclaiming that no one in your own department can be trusted." He leaned forward as her eyes widened. "I hope you haven't said as much to your colleagues."

She shook her head. "Of course not."

"Good. Perhaps now is a good time to remember why you became an officer and remind yourself that your reasons mirror that of many of your fellow officers. *Most* police officers are good, trustworthy civil servants who got into police work because they love their communities. You can trust them to bear some of your burden and share the duty to protect the innocent at all costs."

"I can't do it." Ellie slowly shook her head. "Not with Valerie. She survived hell, almost died, and came out stronger when most of us would've broken. She deserves to live a long life filled with joy, and the only way I can ensure that happens is to protect her myself."

He held eye contact with her for a long beat, realizing she

was not going to give in on this. The kidnap victim within her wouldn't allow it. He loved that strength.

"You can't do it alone."

Ellie lifted her chin. "I'm not compromising on this."

Powell shrugged. "I can't help you if you won't at least consider what I'm saying. And by ignoring my advice, you'll only be hurting yourself."

"I hear you, and I know you mean well, but my answer is still no." She stood and walked toward the door, clearly eager to end their meeting. "I'm not going to throw Valerie to the wolves and hope no one takes a bite. It's not worth the risk."

"Unless that risk is imagined."

Ellie's hand wrapped around the doorknob, so tight he could see that her knuckles were turning white. "Thank you for your help today, Dr. Powell."

She slipped out the door and let it close behind her before he could open his mouth to respond. Sighing, he tidied up the therapy nook, using what was left of her water on one of the plants hanging from a ceiling hook near the window.

He shook his head and tossed his notepad on the desk. It was going to be interesting to be privy to Ellie taking on another kidnap victim, and possibly wrecking her career by doing so.

6

Jillian schlepped down Ellie's apartment building's hallway, laden down with everything she'd brought from her car, unwilling to make two trips. Her purse strap dug into her shoulder, and the messenger bag that held her work laptop bounced on her hip with every step.

Her arms protested under the weight of a white file box, but she was determined. Her mother would have said stubborn. The plush navy-blue carpet rendered her footsteps almost silent, though her labored breathing made stealth impossible.

"Some private eye you'd be," she mumbled to herself. No one knew, but it was her dream to become a private investigator, and she was as good as living it by helping Ellie solve cases while still working as a file clerk in the basement of Charleston PD.

Stopping and rolling her shoulders, she grimaced and readjusted the strap on the messenger bag so it didn't bang awkwardly against her leg. When she finally reached the front door of Ellie's place, she stuck out her hip, balancing the heavy cardboard file box against her body so she could unlock the door.

Pushing the door inward with her toe, she dropped her bags and the box in the entryway a split-second before a blur of dark fur and wet kisses collided with her. The impact was so hard she stumbled back into the wall, laughing.

"You should've called me to come down. I would've helped you with that." Ellie lounged on the sofa, long legs stretched out. Wearing loose shorts and an oversized shirt, her bare feet crossed at the ankles, she was still damp from a shower, her hair clipped high on her head in a messy pile of tight ringlets. Her favorite thick red robe hung open, the knot keeping it closed barely tied.

It was the most relaxed and the least put together Jillian had ever seen her, yet she somehow looked just as elegant as she did in designer shoes and a dress created just for her.

"I had it under control. Besides, you look like you're in for the night." She consulted her watch with a snort. "At four in the afternoon." Jillian gave Sam another pat, and she extracted herself from the front paws wrapped around her waist before plopping down in the overstuffed loveseat across from her new roommate.

An empty glass with a few drops of dark liquid at the bottom sat on the end table, along with a partially demolished box of handcrafted chocolates. Ellie handed the box to Jillian, taking a piece for herself.

"Rough day?"

Ellie rolled her eyes, savoring the dark square of chocolate one tiny bite at a time before she finally answered. "You have no idea."

"I would be climbing up the walls if I were you."

"I rearranged the furniture."

"Again?" Jillian eyed the room. "Wait, where?"

"I put it back. I didn't like it."

"You need to get out of the house more. At least you're coming back to the office tomorrow. Right?"

"Yeah." Ellie grimaced. "I'll be working the tip line. I think Charleston PD uses it as punishment."

Jillian popped a piece of chocolate into her mouth and groaned as the delightful flavor of gourmet chocolate and red raspberries hit her taste buds.

"Maybe Powell will put a good word in with the chief." Ellie stood, taking her empty glass to the kitchen and returning with two glasses of sparkling water. She handed one to Jillian and sat down again.

Jillian wrinkled her nose. "You've spent a lot of time with the shrink lately."

Ellie snorted, shaking her head. "You're telling me. Johnson made it clear that if I went every day, he'd be thrilled. What a waste of time."

"At least Dr. Powell is nice, right?" Jillian shot her a grimace.

She shrugged. "He's good at what he does. That's not the problem."

"You don't want to be there." Jillian sipped from her glass, the bubbles tickling her tongue, a hint of blood orange flavoring the fizzy drink. As she swallowed, her eyes met Ellie's over the rim of the glass.

"No, I don't."

"If you have to go, you might as well embrace it. Johnson can't dictate what you talk about during your sessions, can he?"

"No, he can't." Ellie fingered her hair, spreading out the clumping curls. "And I took advantage of the time with Powell, but I'm not going to lie, it was pretty intense."

"Did you recover more memories today?"

"Just fragments." She scowled, her eyes going unfocused as her attention turned inward. "None of the pieces seem to fit together, and the parts I remember in large chunks don't make sense."

"Just be patient, Ellie. It'll come to you."

"It's been twelve years." She shook her head. "Actually, almost thirteen years. It happened a few weeks after my fifteenth birthday."

"It's understandable that you feel out of sorts this time of year. Anniversaries have a huge impact on our psyche, even if we're unaware of it."

"That's not it." She bit her lower lip and let out a long, dejected sigh. "I want to testify at the trial."

"You're the lead detective on the case. Isn't that a given?"

"I want to testify as a victim of the trafficking ring that sold Valerie Price to Arthur Fink."

Jillian blinked, setting her glass down on the table so she didn't drop it. "I'm not sure how to ask this without it coming off the wrong way, but why?"

Ellie shrugged, watching the bubbles dance around as she swirled the liquid in the half-empty glass. She didn't answer for a long time, but when she finally lifted her head and fixed her gaze on Jillian, the space between them was heavy with Ellie's haunted memories.

"I don't know why I *need* to do it, but I feel very strongly about it. Maybe it's the only way I can get back some kind of control. I've lived with the fear my kidnapper instilled in me for almost half my life. Every choice I make, everything I do in my life is because of what I went through." She waved one hand in the air in front of her. "Even my career choice is a direct result of my experience."

"I didn't know that," Jillian said quietly.

"We might not catch my kidnapper, but if I can help put most of the evil people behind the human trafficking ring in jail, maybe one of them will rat him out to save their own skin. Then I can stop looking over my shoulder everywhere I go."

Jillian's throat thickened with tears. Seeing her best friend in so much pain hurt, but not being able to make it right was worse. When she tried to speak, her voice caught. She cleared her throat and tried again. "What can I do to help?"

"There's nothing anyone can do if I can't get my brain to cooperate. Even under hypnosis, it's like I'm blocked. I get so deep into a memory, then it shatters into a million pieces. Like running into a brick wall."

"I can't even begin to imagine how frustrating that is for you."

Ellie's shoulders fell, and she jammed her hands into the pockets of her robe. "Maybe it's better this way. If I tip my hand now, the man who kidnapped me might still get away."

"Unless Arthur Fink gives up his name. You know that man probably *knows* who did this to you."

Ellie shook her head, jaw tight. "The D.A. says he's given them a lot of information about other players, but he's scared of the master." She let out a long breath. "Even in witness protection, he's afraid this man will find him and have him killed."

"Do you blame him?"

"Not really. Even if he's rich and powerful, it does seem odd that Fink acts like the guy is some kind of boogieman lurking in the shadows." Ellie slumped back against the sofa and gestured at the box with her chin, changing the subject. "Did you bring work home?"

Jillian sat a little straighter at the mention of the box, eyes widening with excitement. She got up and reached for it as she explained. "Not exactly, but that's what Captain Browning thinks it is."

"Why would he send work home with you in the first place? Doesn't that break the evidence chain of command?"

"It's not actual evidence. He wants all the notes from older case files digitized by the end of the month so they're easier to look up by detail, victimology, and cause of death." Jillian shot her a cheeky grin. "To make it easier for the Cold Case Division to link older cases to more recent ones. He asked me to take home one file box a week and transfer everything to a flash drive, then load it into the database when I'm through. With overtime pay, of course."

"Cold Case Division? So, he's making you type up old notes to make *my* job easier?"

"Basically."

"Did you tell him I've been doing that as I go?"

Jillian shook her head. "Nope. I also didn't tell him I'm already done." She shrugged. "I don't know what he was thinking, but almost everything from the past twenty years is already in the system. I had to transfer some things from older files to the updated format, but I finished at the end of last week."

"So, what's this?"

Jillian slid the box across the carpet to Ellie, and she removed the lid and peeked inside as Jillian explained. "It's a list of all the cases Jones worked after he started getting paid by the traffickers, copies of notes, and a copy of the financial records you obtained so we can use the dates to try and connect the cases."

Ellie's lips spread into an excited grin. "You're a genius."

"I also printed off any information I could find on officers who responded to the crime scenes, Jones's old partners, and anyone else who worked the cases."

"You did all this today?"

Jillian huffed out a laugh. "No. I had to do something with you on leave. It took most of last week to compile everything. I printed most of it today."

"All with Captain Browning's approval."

"His insistence, no less." Jillian snorted. "He loaded it in my car for me."

Looking very impressed, Ellie cinched up her robe as she stood and carried the box into the kitchen, setting it on the long wooden table.

Jillian followed, retrieving two fresh yellow notepads from the small office off the living room and taking a seat across from Ellie.

As Ellie unloaded the papers, she whistled through her teeth. "This is a lot."

"I'm sure there are more, but this is what I've found so far. I thought we could divide and conquer the pile."

"Good idea." Ellie took Jones's financial records out and made a copy, handing one to Jillian. "It makes more sense for both of us to have a copy. We can combine our findings later."

"Are you working half days all this week?"

"I am, but not in Cold Cases. I'll be at the main office. Fortis said the cases aren't going to get any colder while I work through this with Powell." She groaned. "It's ridiculous, and I'm going a little stir-crazy just sitting around waiting for something to happen."

Jillian scoffed. "You'd think they'd give you a medal for saving Valerie and uncovering a human trafficking ring right here in Charleston."

"Right? But Fortis said that's not how it works. So, this week I'm either with Valerie, home, in Powell's office, or PD hell."

Ellie helped Jillian spread the cream-colored folders out on one half of the table as she related what happened in Chief Johnson's office, and the deal with Powell and Valerie's safe house. On the front of each folder, Jillian had written the date, official cause of death, and a couple sentences summarizing each case. There were more than two dozen in total.

Inside the folders, each case was neatly organized. Some were stuffed to bursting while others had little more than a few sheets of paper.

When they were finished laying them out, Ellie planted her hands on her hips, shaking her head. "It's like he victimized them twice."

"I was thinking about that, and how their families are going to take the news. What happens when we prove that Jones was dirty and received bribes for years?"

"According to Chief Johnson, they'll have to assign a task force to go through and investigate every single case Jones touched." She gestured at the stacks on the table. "Not just these cases, but every arrest and court case for his entire career."

"What a mess."

"It is, but it won't be my mess."

Jillian knew her outrage was shining in her eyes and couldn't hold it back. "Why not?"

"The officer who blows the whistle can't rework the cases, for ethical reasons."

"Will you still be in Cold Cases when this is all over?"

Ellie shrugged. "Probably. Jones wasn't the only detective in the Violent Crimes Unit, and there are plenty of victims waiting for justice. It will complicate things, but corruption tends to do that anyway."

Jillian thought that through before saying quietly, "Some won't be able to accept what Jones did."

"I've thought about that. I'll get blamed for things getting shaken up in Homicide, and some people will be sure that I fabricated the evidence."

"There's nothing you can do about that. It's on them if they can't see the truth when it's staring back at them."

Ellie let out a long sigh. "I know that, but that fact doesn't make this any easier." She smiled at Jillian. "I'm glad you're on my side. This is a huge risk to both our careers, and I appreciate you."

"I'm not going to stand by and let the integrity of Charleston PD be influenced by corrupt cops. The people of Charleston deserve better, and so do the honest officers who put their lives on the line every day. Having crooked cops in our midst puts us all in danger."

"You're right, but if you decide at any time that the risk to your personal safety and your career is too much, I won't hold it against you."

Jillian, half insulted at the suggestion that she might desert Ellie, glared at her and shook her head with a wry grin. "You don't think I'm going to let you have all the excitement, do you?" She motioned to Sam, who was sprawled in the archway between the living room and the dining room, just shy of the imaginary line of the kitchen, which was off limits for her. "I have Sam here to keep me safe."

Sam snorted in her sleep, paws twitching as she chased a rabbit in her dreams.

Ellie smiled fondly at the animal. "I'd rather have you working with me, but don't hesitate to let me know if you change your mind."

"I won't. No one else is going to expose the people involved in this conspiracy, and they have no place on the force. Even if we're the only ones left standing when the dust settles, I'm all in."

Ellie pressed her fingertips to her temple. "It's very possible that we won't even be standing when it's all over."

7

"I'm a man of action."

I smiled at Joshua Gibson, even though the twenty-two-year-old man in front of me was disgusting in every possible way. The world would be a better place without him.

"Yes, you are, Joshua," I said in the calm, measured tones that lulled him deep into my powers. "You will show them all that young, successful men must be respected."

"Respected."

"And admired."

Joshua smiled before repeating, "Admired."

"And most importantly, you are a man of action. You will surprise them all by showing them how high you can climb their corporate ladder. You will shock them all by leaping into the unknown, being fearless as you reach your goal...infamy."

"Famous."

The idiot. I'd be glad when he was dead.

"Are you prepared to leap into your destiny, Joshua?"

There was no hesitation. "Yes."

Satisfied, I implanted my suggestions a few more times before bringing him back to reality with a snap of my fingers.

He blinked and sat straighter, his eyes focusing on me. "I feel...different."

I grinned. "That's how fame feels, Joshua."

He grinned back. "I like it."

"And you will seek it?"

"Yes, because I'm a man of action."

He bounded to his feet with all the energy of someone so young. Practically sprinting toward the door, he turned the knob before glancing back at me. "Thank you, Doctor. I'm ready." But he didn't leave. Instead, he hesitated.

"Yes, Joshua?"

"Can I have another of those cucumber waters?"

I considered the request. I'd yet to increase the dosage to such a degree.

Shrugging, I opened my fridge and took out another glass container. I'd learned over the years that glass was much better for the mixture. Plus...plastic. Ugh. One must take care of the planet, after all.

"Please drink it here so I may reuse the bottle." And there wasn't any pesky evidence laying about.

I watched as he drank the mixture down thirstily, not stopping until almost every drop was gone.

"Thanks, Doc."

I kept my smile frozen in place as I took the bottle from his hand, watching him carefully.

"Man of action," I suggested.

He shuddered, his eyes crossing for a moment. "Yes. They'll be so surprised."

Then he was off again, sprinting down the hall and past a startled Gabe.

Gabe looked at me, his brown eyes wide, lips parted

slightly. He'd ditched the green contacts, embracing his natural beauty after I'd commented on the absurdity of covering up such a rich, dark brown with the artificial hue.

"Did he startle you?"

He shook his head, smiling, a self-deprecating laugh escaping his full lips. "Is Joshua okay?"

"Never better." I took a deep breath. "He was excited to put his new plan into action."

Gabe looked relieved. "That's good to see him so inspired." He glanced at the clock on the wall and back to me again. "You don't have your next appointment for more than an hour. Would you like another coffee while you wait? I can bring it to your office when it's brewed, if you'd like."

"About that." I cleared my throat and waved in the direction of the hallway. "Can I see you in my office? I want to speak to you."

Gabe's throat moved when he swallowed. How his heart must've been racing, wondering what I wanted of him. Something inside me stirred, but I pushed it down. I still hadn't finished the scrapbook page for my trip to Detroit, and images of Gabe's doubleganger in a cage plagued my mind. I needed the closure to bring things full circle.

When he didn't move, I arched an eyebrow and turned, striding down the hall in an unhurried manner. I allowed myself a brief smile when I heard him scurrying to follow, too obedient to risk displeasing me. By the time I made it to the door of my private office, he was no more than a few steps behind me.

"Close the door."

"What if a patient comes early...sir?"

I pointed to the monitor on my desk that was devoted entirely to the video feed covering the lobby. "If anyone shows up, you'll be there quickly enough. Close the door, Gabriel."

His nostrils flared when I used his proper name. He did as I asked, shoulders rigid, body slightly hunched as he grappled with uncertainty. I sat with my hands folded on my knee, watching him openly from my chair behind the desk. That seemed to heighten his anxiety, making him appear so small standing in the middle of the room, unsure of whether he should sit or flee. I was tempted to leave him standing there for the rest of the day, but I had a patient coming in an hour. Playtime with Gabe would have to wait.

I motioned to the sofa my patients used. "Please, have a seat."

"I'd rather stand."

Bold, I thought, shrugging. "Suit yourself, but come closer so I don't have to raise my voice across the room."

Taking exactly three steps, he kept the sofa between us. He shoved his hands into his pockets, but his stance portrayed anything but a relaxed employee. Very interesting.

"I called you in here to talk about something that's been on my mind for a while." He stiffened, but I continued. There were things he needed to hear, and I didn't have time to soften them up to spare his ego. "I had certain misgivings about sending you to Florida. A part of me worried that you would slide back into old habits, and I don't want to see you do that."

He placed his hands on the back of the sofa, eyes a little sad. "I wouldn't do that. Seeing the world through clear eyes has changed my life, and I'm not willing to go back."

"I hope not. What a waste it would be if all the effort I put into you was for naught." I lowered my pitch to drive the point home, my gaze unwavering. "I don't think I have to tell you that I've invested quite a bit in you at this point."

His olive skin reddened. "I can pay you back for the trip."

"I'm not talking about the trip, and I don't need you to pay me back. I just need to know that you didn't backslide while you were there. Returning to the place where your demons dwell can be a dangerous thing."

His blush deepened as his gaze went to the floor, shame darkening his handsome features. "I met up with this guy I was close with, and things got..." His eyes flicked up to meet mine for a moment before turning away again. "It was one night."

I let him stand there, his mind conjuring up every worst-case scenario for some time before mercy won out. With a light chuckle, I shook my head. "I'm not interested in a silly one-night stand. As long as you used protection."

He scowled. "Of course I did."

"Then that's of no concern to me." Gabe's lips parted as if to speak, but I didn't stop long enough to indulge him. "What *does* interest me is whether or not you broke your sobriety." I adjusted my glasses so I could look over the rim at him. "I'm sure I needn't remind you that staying off drugs and alcohol are a condition of your employment."

He quickly nodded. "Not a sip, and I avoided the people I used to use with." His fingers tightened on the back of the sofa, and he sighed. "I know that every recovering addict says this, but I refuse to risk falling into that life again. I've existed on the streets and done things for a fix that I can never live down. There's nothing and no one who could ever convince me to give up everything I've worked for, especially in the last year."

"That's good to hear. I invested a lot of money into your transformation, and I expect you to honor that." I motioned to the sofa again, and this time he sat down. "I saved you from a life on the streets. If you can call what you were living any sort of life. Without my intervention, you wouldn't be alive today, if I'm being frank."

"I know, sir. And I appreciate it more than I can say. Like I said, I can pay you back if you need me to."

"I won't hear of it. Your money is yours to keep. I'll take what you owe me in other ways."

He balked, panic widening his eyes.

Laughing, I waved a hand in the air in front of me. "I was referring to your loyalty and your hard work. Being able to trust you is worth more than money."

"I agree, sir."

I decided to give him a reprieve and change the subject. "How many patients are there today?"

Looking relieved at the turn of subject, he visibly relaxed. "You're booked until lunch, then your afternoon is clear."

"Any new patients?"

He shook his head, listing the familiar names.

While he spoke, I pulled up my calendar on the computer. At the bottom corner of the screen, a message icon taunted me. Thirty missed messages in just one day. Scowling, I clicked the button that deleted them, without bothering to open them. I wasn't interested in another purchase so soon and didn't appreciate the aggressive sales tactics. I would buy another toy soon enough. Right now, I was focused on Gabe.

And Gabe was focused on me.

Our eyes met, and he sat there, perched on the edge of the sofa, still looking uncomfortable. The image of him leaning against my desk flashed through my memory. With my hand on his leg and his body so close I could feel the heat radiating from him, it had been hard to pull myself away. Had I pulled back too far? Did he think I was bored with him?

Maybe his feelings are hurt.

The thought surprised me. Feelings weren't something I concerned myself with, unless I was using them to get what I wanted. But Gabe was different, something I'd known since I first laid eyes on him.

I stood, going around the front of the desk and sitting

beside him on the sofa. Turning to face him, I took his hand and lifted it to my lips, holding eye contact when I did.

His lips parted, his nostrils flared, and his chocolate-brown eyes filled with fire. He trembled beneath my touch, the rest of his body rendered motionless by his need.

I lingered, his skin smooth and warm on my face. When I lowered his hand to rest on my thigh, I didn't let go. "There are many things I will tolerate, but dishonesty is not one of them."

The fear that passed through his eyes quickened my heart rate. Young men in their twenties were often arrogant, their egos far too big for what they had to offer the world.

Not Gabe.

He knew his place, and he was eager to please. Knowing that the world he'd become accustomed to could vanish in an instant, there was no request I could make that he wouldn't fulfill in the blink of an eye. In a word, he was perfect. Pliant, humble, and desperate to find a place in the world where he belonged. His desperate need for approval worked to my advantage.

"I don't think I understand, s-sir."

"I'm sure you don't. I know you're keeping something from me, Gabe. There's no reason to hide who you are, and I want you to know that I have big plans for you."

His Adam's apple bobbed as he swallowed. "You do?"

I nodded. "It's going to take some hard work on your part, but if you're willing to push yourself and be upfront with me, I'll give you a life beyond your wildest dreams."

"What are you saying?" His laugh was soft and nervous, his eyes meeting mine for the first time since I took his hand.

I pulled away and stood, unsure of how to answer the question. Could I trust him? And more importantly, what would I do with him if he failed?

I'd brought lost souls into my most sacred space before,

but Gabe was special. I knew that he would serve me without reservation, until his last breath. Unlike Ernest. After fifteen years under my wing, Ernest was distancing himself. The young, eager student now fancied himself a teacher. It wouldn't be long before I had to let him go, and that came with its own challenges.

Gabe's brown eyes watched me still, waiting for an answer he wasn't going to get.

Gesturing in the general direction of the clock, I gave him an apologetic smile and pointed to the door. "We'll talk about this later, Gabe."

He stood slowly, eyes going to the door and back to me, his feet planted on the floor. He opened his mouth, ready to press the issue, but thought better of it. Pursing his lips, he nodded. "Thank you," he said softly and was out the door, closing it quietly behind him.

I listened to his steps fade in the hallway as I went to my desk and leaned back in the large, well-padded chair. My thoughts turned back to Ernest, who had been on my mind a lot recently. Ungrateful and arrogant, he was intent on pursuing his own interests, leaving me to deal with his mess on my own, more often than not. It was time I took out the trash, and Ernest would soon find himself swept up in the garbage.

The only issue was the girl. The anniversary of her escape was coming up quickly, and I'd been waiting for my revenge for thirteen long years. Ernest had waited, too, but I had the feeling that once this chapter was closed, Ernest wasn't planning to stick around. I couldn't risk him exposing me. No. I would have to deal with them both. It was the only way.

Maybe I'll have Gabe take care of Ernest.

The thought brought a genuine smile to my lips. Having my new assistant dispose of my old one was exactly what I needed to clear out the foul energy Ernest would leave behind in his wake. Gabe was loyal and trainable, and he would do anything I asked of him without hesitation. Fate had brought Gabe to me when I needed him most, and now it was time to bring Gabe into the fold. He was ready, and so was I.

The gloom lifted, and I suddenly felt energized. A plan was forming, a perfect plan.

Gabe would play his part.

Ernest would play his.

When everything was said and done, that red-haired bitch would be rotting in the darkness where she belonged.

When I was done with her, no one would ever find her.

8

Valerie Price dropped the single backpack stuffed with everything she owned next to the door before pacing the large private hospital room. Machines surrounding the bed were finally silent after weeks of mindless beeping in a disjointed, chaotic symphony. Once ceaseless, the sounds had eventually faded, becoming as present as her ever-beating heart. Now, the quiet made her uneasy, the absence of constant sound as irritating as the noise had been.

In the last two years, she'd been kidnapped and held in a crazy man's basement, dressed up like a Barbie to fulfill some sick fantasy. After surviving that, she discovered that her fiancé had been murdered and then had been hunted like a sitting duck by his killer.

If it hadn't been for Detective Ellie Kline coming for her that night, when everyone else had given up, she wouldn't have survived Tucker Penland, much less the perforated ulcer that tore as the maniac chased her through the woods with a gun. It was only her pure bad luck that had thrown in a perforated bowel caused by the laparoscopy, which had led to sepsis that had left her hovering on the brink of death for weeks.

Filled with nervous energy after having been confined to a bed for nearly a month, Valerie walked the room once again, opening and closing every drawer, flinging the closet doors wide. Empty hangers swung on the metal rod, the closed loop preventing patients from removing them when they checked out.

She inhaled a deep breath. Even though she'd been through daily physical therapy to get her strength back after her long illness, she was still out of shape, and just walking around her room caused sweat to break out on her brow.

She would fix that. When she was free, she would exercise and run, lift weights to make her strong. She would never be so weak again, she promised herself.

The cute guard who'd become her daily companion watched her with cool indifference, unbothered by her nervousness. Only when she walked too close to the windows did his body language change. A flicker of tension flashed across his face. "Please step away from the window, Miss Price."

Her fingers brushed the stark white blinds, too slow to move the slats to look out before the guard stopped her. She sighed, rubbing her hands together to chase away the cold. "It's freezing in here. I just wanted to let the sun in."

"The time for that will come. Safety first, sunshine later."

When?

She seethed inwardly, irritated with every excuse she'd been given since she'd emerged from captivity, only to be handed off to another monster, one who hunted her before Ellie finally saved her from certain death. That day, by the time the sun brushed the morning sky with orange and pink rays Arthur Fink could never have replicated in her under-ground prison, she was already being loaded onto a stretcher. She'd yet to feel the sun on her skin, and after two years locked away, asking her to wait another moment was torture.

Turning away from the window that beckoned, she crossed her arms and blew her bangs out of her face. They were getting longer, the straight dark brown strands touching her lashes when she blinked. She planned on growing them out now that no one was cutting them back while she slept.

A sudden chill raced up her spine. She shuddered, rubbing her bare arms. "When did she say she was going to be here, Flynn?"

Straight-lined lips that made up his default serious expression turned up slightly in the corners, the closest the handsome, brooding man ever came to a genuine smile. But the light in his deep brown eyes revealed his amusement. "I assure you, she is on her way."

"You've said that."

"And you've ignored me."

Valerie glared at him, rocking forward on the balls of her feet to give her petite frame another inch. "I want a specific time so I know how long I have before I have to be ready."

"There is no reason to know. You've packed everything and checked the room dozens of times. You are prepared, and she will be here when she's here." This time, his lips tilted into what passed as an actual smile, but when a light knock sounded at the door, the smile disappeared as Flynn's hand went to his holster.

Valerie's heart jumped into her throat. She took a step back, ready to hide if he issued the command.

There was a second knock, slightly louder than the first.

This time, Flynn responded. "Who is it?"

"Ellie."

Some of the tension melted from Valerie's body, replaced

by glee. Ellie was finally here, just outside the door. They were leaving the hospital, at long last.

Careful not to open the door too wide, Flynn kept his foot wedged against the heavy metal kickplate. "ID."

A badge slipped through the crack, and Flynn examined it carefully. He peeked through the crack, stepped back, and welcomed Ellie into the room. Ellie tucked her badge into her pocket, giving Valerie a warm smile.

Valerie's feet seemed rooted to the tile floor. Excitement and fear of what lay beyond the safety of the room battled inside her, but she hid the turmoil with a smile.

Ellie tipped her head toward the bag by the door, a pleased smile lighting her face. "I see you're eager to leave."

"You have no idea." Valerie laughed. "Not that Flynn isn't a fascinating conversationalist, but I need to breathe air that doesn't smell like antiseptic."

Ellie wrinkled her nose and simultaneously took a breath, grimacing. "I don't blame you." She grabbed Valerie's bag and slung it over her shoulder. "Let's get out of here before the hospital invents a reason to keep you another night."

Valerie followed Ellie out the door without a backward glance at the bleak, sterile room that had been her home for the weeks since she'd escaped from Tucker Penland in Bartlett Woods. With eyes on her twenty-four-seven and cameras everywhere, the hospital hadn't felt much different than the tiny basement dwelling that had been her prison for so long. She was ready to be free. Ready to live life to the fullest.

Flynn's guard partner, Zeke, led the way. Flynn fell in step behind him, both scanning the hallway and patient rooms ceaselessly as they made their way through the quiet corridors. They passed nurses working at their stations and orderlies collecting dinner trays and placing them on carts.

Zeke abruptly turned into the stairwell, leading them straight across the landing and to a second corridor.

Valerie stayed quiet, used to the way the two men moved with meticulous intention. Everything they did was for a reason, and Valerie trusted them to keep her safe.

They had so far.

They emerged from the stairwell, her nerves stretched tight, stomach tense, and the men led her through an unmarked door that led to the staff elevator. Narrower than the main elevators, they were shoulder to shoulder as they rode down to the parking garage. There, a plain black sedan waited with the engine running.

Flynn opened the rear door, and Ellie slid across the back seat, making room for Valerie. Flynn got in the front driver's seat as Zeke jogged the short distance across the aisle to another sedan identical to theirs. Valerie had just clicked her seatbelt in place when Flynn drove them out of the shadows of the looming cement pillars and into a bright street full of cars.

She blinked rapidly. Even through the tint of the window, the sudden light and the warmth of the actual sun made her eyes water.

"It's rush hour," Flynn explained, smiling at them in the rearview mirror. "It will be harder for someone to keep track of us with so much traffic."

Valerie's heart rate quickened, and she turned to look out the back glass. Zeke and another man she didn't recognize were a few car lengths back. The rest of the cars in the lanes surrounding seemed terrifyingly mundane. There was no way to know what kind of evil the tinted windows concealed.

They could be surrounded by people just like Arthur Fink and Tucker Penland, and they would have no way of know-ing. Valerie's breathing shortened, and after a few rapid breaths, she felt lightheaded. As she had many times, she fell back on the mantra that had gotten her through the worst days of her life.

Your name is Valerie Price, and you will get out of this alive.

The moment of panic passed, and with it, the over-whelming feeling of being exposed and vulnerable.

Ellie squeezed her hand and shot her a reassuring smile. "We're not being followed. This is just a precaution." She reached into her purse and pulled out an envelope so thick the flap barely reached far enough for the adhesive to seal it shut. "Maybe it isn't the right time for this, but my family wanted to give you something to help make the transition a little easier when this is all over."

Valerie frowned, taking the envelope and testing the weight without opening it. "What is it?"

"Money."

Valerie shook her head and held it back out to Ellie. "I already can't possibly repay you for everything you've done. I can't take this too. It wouldn't be right."

"It's not from me. It's from my parents."

"Why?"

Ellie shrugged one shoulder. "Because they want to make sure you're taken care of after this is over. When you have a new life."

Valerie stared down at the envelope. "They don't know me."

"But they know your story, and people are touched by your bravery."

Valerie scoffed. "I'm not brave. I was a victim. I did what I could to make it through."

"You survived, and you found a way to keep your sanity through years of torture and captivity. Most of us can't even imagine living through what you did, but *you* survived and came out stronger. You triumphed over the greatest evil. Never diminish that."

Valerie's chest grew tight, making it impossible to speak the myriad of thoughts running through her head. She cleared her throat, swiping at the tears that spilled over her cheeks. "Thank you for never giving up on me and coming after me, even when everyone else said I was probably dead. I wouldn't be here without you."

"I just wish I would've found you sooner."

The car accelerated when it hit the freeway, taking them north, out of the city and away from the ocean. "I guess we're not staying in town?"

"Not exactly. You have to lay low until the trial." Ellie's lips tightened, and she sighed. "After the trial, I'm sure you'll be put into witness protection, so you can start a new life away from all this."

"Is that a bad thing?"

"No, but until then, it will be unnerving; you won't know where you are."

"What about now? The district attorney said something about protective custody, but I thought that was two cops and a hotel room."

Ellie laughed. "It is, which is why I told them no." Her smile slipped. "Well, not the only reason."

"Do you think the D.A. can be trusted?"

"Yes, I do. But not beyond convicting Arthur Fink for buying you and holding you captive in his basement. Do I trust the D.A. to keep you safe until you can testify? Absolutely not."

"And we can't trust anyone at Charleston PD," Valerie offered.

Ellie shook her head. "I can't believe that Jones was the only dirty cop on the payroll. The only way to keep you safe is to do it myself."

"I don't know what I'd do without you."

Ellie skin flushed a soft pink, but she waved her hand and changed the subject, clearly uncomfortable being the hero. "Until we know who is involved, it's better to keep you close."

The sedan exited the highway, driving three blocks before stopping in front of a gate that protected a private parking garage.

"Can you tell me where we're going?"

Ellie nodded as the sedan slipped through the open gate and around the corner. "Right now, you're getting into another car."

Valerie rolled her eyes, shaking her head. "Funny."

"You'll be there soon enough."

Valerie stiffened. "*You*? Don't you mean *we*?"

"This is as far as I go for now. If they follow anyone thinking they'll find you, it's going to be me."

A silver SUV pulled up beside them, and panic welled up inside Valerie. "I can't do this without you."

"Yes, you can." Ellie forced a smile and handed Valerie's backpack to Flynn. "I'll come get you when it's time for the trial. You'll be safe until then. Trust me."

A tall brown-haired man got out of the SUV and opened the rear door on the driver's side.

Valerie turned to Ellie, eyes wide with fear. "Do you know him? How do we know we can trust him?"

"His name is Nick, and I've known him all my life. You'll be safe with him. I promise."

Valerie nodded, but her stomach was still in knots, and her hands trembled.

Nick waited patiently beside the vehicle as Flynn took up position next to the open door, and Zeke got in on the passenger side, waiting for Valerie.

Grabbing Ellie's hand, Valerie fought the urge to run, and

Ellie's calm eventually broke through her panic.

"It will be okay. You'll be safe with him." Ellie repeated the words, her voice soft and reassuring. "I promise."

Valerie impulsively threw her arms around her new friend, hugging her tight. "I believe you." Valerie's voice shook, giving her away. "But I'm still scared."

Ellie nodded and untangled herself from Valerie's embrace, pushing her toward the waiting vehicle with a smile. "Bravery is not the absence of fear. It's being terrified and doing it anyway. You've got this."

"We need to leave," Flynn urged her, motioning toward the waiting seat.

Valerie bit her lip and nodded, finally getting into the SUV. Flynn closed the door behind them with a muted thud, and Ellie slid into the driver's seat of the still running sedan and drove away. The glass was cold beneath Valerie's hand as she followed the sedan, her eyes wide with uncertainty until she lost sight of the vehicle as it turned the corner.

She leaned back against the leather seat, catching her quivering lip between her teeth.

Nick's bright blue eyes watched her in the mirror as he meandered through the streets of North Charleston before finally making his way onto another highway headed northeast. "It's going to be okay."

"Where are you taking me?"

"I have property on the water. It's only a little five-acre piece of land, but it's surrounded by trees and easy to protect." He smiled, reminding her of a Ken doll. "I bought it as a secret getaway for Ellie and me. You'll be able to go outside without risking your life, and the gentle lapping of the water at the shore is rumored to have healing energy."

She glanced at Flynn. "Are you staying too?"

He nodded. "Zeke and I will be the only ones with you

once Nick leaves. We won't leave your side. You have my word."

Valerie nodded, some of the tension that had settled into her chest fading. "And no one knows where this place is?"

"Just me and Ellie." Nick nodded at her in the mirror. "And now you."

She puckered her lips, thinking she wouldn't mind sitting lakeside. "I guess it's better than staying at a hotel."

Nick grimaced. "I wouldn't want to be confined to a hotel room until the trial starts."

"Do you have a caretaker? Won't they be suspicious if you bring a woman who isn't Ellie?" Valerie chuckled. "Even from far away, it's obvious I'm not a tall redhead."

"I gave the housekeeper a month off, and the landscaper only comes every other week until everything starts growing again." He glanced at Flynn before turning his attention back to Valerie. "Flynn and his crew gave me a list of precautions, and we've got it all covered. I promise, no one will find you here."

He turned off the highway, winding down a long road while Flynn watched out the rear window. "All clear, Nick."

Nick gave a quick nod and turned down a gravel road lined with evergreen trees on both sides. At the end of the long drive, he stopped at a heavy gate, punching in a code and waiting for the gate to lurch open. It closed behind them, and they continued through the woods.

Valerie was already so turned around, she wasn't sure which way led back to Charleston. She hoped that meant their hideaway would be equally hard to find.

When the road widened what seemed like a mile later, and the two-story house came into view, Valerie's jaw went slack. Painted in the same brown and forest green palate as the surrounding woods, the log-cabin-style home blended seamlessly into the landscape. But it was the large windows overlooking the water and the balcony circling the entire second floor that caught Valerie's attention. Beyond the yard, a large lake glistened in the late afternoon sun.

"*This* is your little cottage by the water? It looks like a postcard."

Nick laughed. "Ellie and I thought you would like it."

"I could live here forever." She sighed, the panic that had held her hostage for the past hour slipping away as Nick parked in the garage and closed the door before they got out of the SUV.

"Well, until the trial is over and you figure out what you're going to do with your life, this place is your home." He grabbed her backpack, letting Zeke and Flynn sweep the house before leading her into the modern kitchen and gesturing at a massive fridge. "I hope you're hungry. I bought enough groceries to feed a small army. I didn't know what you like, so I bought a bit of everything."

Valerie yanked open the door, and a wide smile spread across her face. Even after she'd escaped Arthur Fink and survived being hunted by Tucker Penland, her carefully guarded freedom had been no better than living a life of captivity. But Nick had given her something she hadn't had in years. Space to breathe, and a kitchen filled with endless choices. No more bland, restrictive diets for her. She was going to eat like a queen.

And she was going to start with dessert.

By the time the trial date came, she'd be fat as a well-fed hen.

Reaching for a carton of orange juice, her hand paused mid-air. It was wonderful to be staying in a lake house, almost like a vacation. But with everything hinged on the trial, she wondered how she would ever relax.

9

The new pen fit in Dr. Powell's hand like an extension of his fingers, smooth ink flowing over the paper with ease. Through a single earbud in his left ear, a man's voice—thick with a fear he refused to voice—spoke in clipped sentences.

Dr. Powell took down every word in neat cursive, leaving several spaces between each section for his own notes. While many in his field preferred the ease and speed of typing up session recordings, writing by hand gave Powell a chance to absorb every nuance, revealing more than just the words that were spoken.

This time was a chance to dig deep into every moment the patient had spent baring his soul. What the man hadn't said was more telling than the emotions the tough-as-nails officer was trying to hide.

Smiling, he flipped to the next page just as a quiet knock announced his first appointment of the afternoon. "Come in."

Green eyes framed by perfectly manicured reddish eyebrows found him at his desk, her curly hair pulled back into the tight French braid he'd seen her wear so often on patrol. Once she'd made detective, her hairstyle had relaxed a bit, her naturally coiled curls sometimes held back by a single brown clip at the nape of her neck. By the end of her shift, rebellious strands would slip out, her hair as wild and unruly as her own spirit if not tightly contained at all times.

Like her hairstyle, her pantsuit was the same sleek, modern cut she typically favored, but the colors were muted. Even the shirt beneath the suit jacket was far from her usual pop of color. Gray, the shirt provided little contrast against the dark navy suit. The effect was a diluted version of the Ellie Kline he was used to seeing.

She's changed her style to appear more competent.

"It seems you've changed your look a bit since you've returned to work." Powell motioned toward the couch, moving from his desk to the chair he used during therapy sessions. She took a seat, quietly waiting for him to elaborate. "You've made some changes in the past," he flipped through the calendar in his mind, "two and a half weeks since you came back on restricted duty. How are you feeling?"

She shrugged. "I'm fine." She smoothed her hands over her pantlegs in an unconscious gesture, and he hid a smile. "I'm trying to tone it down a little, I'm surprised you noticed."

"I rather enjoyed your occasional hot pink or canary yellow shirt lending a bit of surprise color to an otherwise boring pantsuit. But you're smart to adjust your dress to inspire confidence while you're waiting for full reinstatement." He set the notepad on the table beside him and folded his hands in his lap. "It would be foolish to ignore the fact that unconscious bias exists. There's nothing wrong with using human nature to get what you want."

She nodded, finally leaning back against the cushion. "I

just want to go back to work full-time. I'm ready to get back at it, you know?"

"I understand. Refresh my memory. When are you scheduled to return to full duty?"

Ellie glanced at the calendar hanging on the wall. "Monday, April sixteenth, if everything goes well."

"It won't be much longer, then."

She sniffed, shaking her head. "Maybe to you. To me, that's eleven more long days, and I'm feeling a little stir-crazy."

"But you've managed thus far, *and* after a couple weeks off duty entirely."

Ellie rolled her eyes dramatically. "Barely."

"Surely, there's something positive to come from all this."

"I've gotten really good at making copies." Ellie's shoulders slumped as she leaned back on the couch, letting out a long breath. "I'm not cut out for administrative duties. I've been answering the Violent Crimes Unit's tip line and interviewing walk-ins."

"Walk-ins?"

"Mostly people filing missing persons reports on adults. There's a form they fill out, and I upload it into the database."

Powell tilted his head. "They don't have you working on cold cases? Even if you're not out on the streets conducting interviews, I would think there's plenty for you to do."

"I told Fortis the same thing, but he shot me down, so I've been in the main office. I have a feeling Fortis did it so he could keep an eye on me."

"And how does that make you feel?"

Ellie scoffed, picking at a spec of lint on her pant leg, jaw clenched tight. "Frustrated more than anything. I think giving me thirty days of restricted duty after having leave was overkill."

"You've had multiple incidents in six months, Detective Kline."

"All justified."

Powell noted her answer on the notepad and turned his attention to her once more. "Let's say you're in Fortis's position. How would you handle a situation like the one you're in differently?"

Ellie blinked in surprise, opened her mouth to speak, and closed it again without saying a word.

Powell waited for her to collect her thoughts.

She cleared her throat, thinking about her answer for a few moments before she spoke. "I guess I wouldn't have much of a choice in his shoes."

Powell nodded, trying to keep his pride of her under wraps. "Every officer needs to be cleared before returning to full duty after firing their weapon or being shot. You've experience both in a relatively short period of time."

"And I'm fine." She squirmed a little under Powell's gaze before throwing him a fiery green glare. "I did what I had to do to save the victim. That's what's important here."

"Taking a life is traumatizing, even when it's the only option. There's no shame in admitting that."

Her eyes suddenly welled with tears.

Ahh, there it was. Ellie was hard to crack, but there was a cavern of emotions beneath the surface. Powell grabbed the box of tissues and leaned forward to offer her one.

She took it, wiping away the single tear that had slipped by her defenses. "I became a police officer so I could help people. I never wanted to hurt anyone, but if it's the difference between saving a victim or not, I'd do it again in a heartbeat."

"And that's why you're good at what you do. You were a wonderful beat officer, and you're a talented detective. This will all blow over, and you'll be back to full duty before you know it."

She nodded, balling the tissue tight in her fist. "Eleven more days."

He took a sip of his water, set the bottle down, and gave her a warm smile. "I think you've handled the situation with grace and patience."

"Now, I just need you to tell Fortis that." She laughed as she adjusted the hem of her jacket, uncrossing her legs and crossing them again.

"You're fidgeting."

Ellie cast her eyes to the side for a moment and let out a heavy sigh. "It's not just the restricted duty that has me on edge."

"What's changed? You weren't this agitated Monday, nor were you on edge the prior weeks of therapy." He leaned forward, concerned. "Did something happen?"

She shook her head. "Not yet. But the anniversary of my kidnapping and escape is a week from tomorrow." She paused, and when he didn't react, went on. "Friday the thirteenth. *Thirteen* years later."

He nodded, blinking as he picked up the notepad and his new ink pen to jot down the date. "I'm not surprised that you're feeling a little unbalanced, especially so close to an anniversary." He paused, searching for the right thing to say. "I'm not sure that this anniversary will be any more momentous than the fifth, or even the tenth."

"I can't shake the feeling that it will be."

Another note before he glanced up at her again. She sat stiffly under his gaze, green eyes staring at his forehead so she appeared to be making eye contact. She sat up straighter when he started writing again. "Have you had any contact with anyone you suspect was involved in your kidnapping?"

"No."

"Then what makes you so sure that this—of all the years since you escaped—will be the year?" He tapped the pen on his knee. "If the kidnapper was going to wait this long, why not wait until the fifteenth year? Weren't you fifteen when it happened?"

"I was."

"It seems to me that the fifteenth year, when you'll be twice the age you were at the time, would be a more momentous occasion, don't you think?"

"I don't know." Nervous energy buzzed around her as she leaned forward, resting her chin on one fist. "I just can't help feeling like something is about to happen. I can't explain it."

"And you have nothing to back that up?"

She shook her head. "Just a gut feeling."

"Sometimes, that's all we have in this world."

Her head shot up, and this time, she made direct eye contact. "You believe me?"

"I believe that you have good reason to be concerned, and you absolutely should be vigilant. But I'll also caution you against letting that feeling eat you up inside. You'll end up with relentless nightmares, and if you're not careful, that feeling of dread will overwhelm you. You're no good to the Violent Crimes Unit if you're jumping at your own shadow."

Her eyes flicked to the side.

Surprised, Dr. Powell cleared his throat, pen poised over the paper. "Are you having nightmares again, Detective Kline?"

She nodded reluctantly, her lips pinched tight, a muscle in her jaw flexing.

"Last week, you shared that they were getting better. Is that no longer the case?"

"It's just the past couple days." Ellie clenched her hands tight. When she noticed Powell watching her movements, she unfisted them and took a breath, tossing the tissue in the little trash can by the table. "Monday night was the first bad nightmare I've had in a while."

"After our hypnosis session?"

"Yes. The same wild, pointless visions." She shook her head, a curl escaping its bindings. "None of it makes sense. And most of my dreams seem to focus more on what I'm feeling instead of what I see."

"Your emotions are a valid part of your—"

"Not my *feelings*. Touch. The images move so fast I can't make sense of them, but I feel cold metal in my hand, and my arm aching as I swing through in the air."

"What else do you feel?" Powell leaned closer, his notepad forgotten for the moment.

"The heat of blood spilling over my hand. It's hot, flowing and ebbing with the rhythm of a heartbeat."

Powell winced. "That's a very specific image right there. Is there anything else you can tell me?"

She shook her head, scowling at her hands. One fist was clenched tight as if she were holding a weapon, ready to stab in the air as she had in the dream. "I can't, and that's the problem. It's right there on the tip of my tongue, but it stays out of reach."

"I'm sure that's frustrating for you."

"Very."

Powell glanced at the clock. "We have time for a short hypnosis session."

"I don't think I'm in a good headspace for it." She tilted her neck, rolling her shoulders to illustrate her point. "I'm tense, and my mind is wandering more than usual. I think I'm okay just talking today."

"As the expert, I'm going to disagree. Hypnosis would do you some good right now, and maybe even help you center yourself so you can feel more at ease."

She sat up a little straighter, looking at him in question. "You can do that?"

"No, but I can help *you* do that. Hypnosis isn't about me. You're one-hundred-percent in control, and that includes any suggestions that are left behind to help you cope with the extra stress."

She rolled her emerald eyes. "Extra stress. You say that like I'm a bit overwhelmed."

"Is it worse than that?" He arched an eyebrow, hand already moving for the pen he'd put aside on the table beside him.

She rushed to amend her statement. "Not so over-whelmed that I'm not fit for duty, but this anniversary has been on my mind more than others."

"Maybe because this is the first year since the kidnapping that you have nothing to keep your mind busy." When she didn't answer, he continued. "I'd like to try something a little different today. I've been working with a new technique called Soundwave Therapy. Basically, the tones are curated for a specific activity. In this case, this music, if you will, has been created solely for the purpose of easing one's mind. It should help you drop into a hypnotic state more quickly than you normally would."

"Is it safe?"

"It's just music. I'll have it so low you'll hardly register it."

She shrugged, but her clenched jaw told him she wasn't buying it.

Eager to get going, he dimmed the lights and used his cellphone to turn on a low audio track.

She listened for a moment, sighed, and laid back on the couch. "I guess I expected it to sound more like actual music."

"It's more like white noise than music. Like a fan that lulls you to sleep, except this is only meant to calm your nerves so you can relax." He smiled, reaching into his suit pocket.

Her eyes were already closing, the tension melting from her muscles with each pulse of the quiet, rhythmic beats. He carefully flipped the switch on the recording device in his pocket, turning it so the microphone pointed upward. He didn't dare let Kline see that he was recording their sessions, though the order had come down from the top. Even if she got upset about it, there was nothing he could do.

Orders were orders.

He waited until her lips parted, and her breathing slowed and deepened. "You're safe here, Ellie." He kept his voice even and calm. "You're in my office at Charleston PD, and no one can hurt you here. Do you understand?"

"Yes."

"Good. Now, I want to start with this anxiety you're carrying around over the anniversary of your kidnapping."

She let out a soft sigh. "Okay."

"Ellie, with each breath, you're going to let go of a piece of the fear you're clinging to."

"I can't."

"You can. Listen to the sound of my voice. Breathe in strength, breathe out anxiety." She inhaled and exhaled with his instructions, abdomen lifting with deep belly breaths like he'd taught her. "Breathe in hope, breathe out fear. You control your life, not some faceless monster in the shadows."

This time when she exhaled, her breath was long but shaky.

Powell narrowed his eyes, the dim light casting long shadows over her face. "Ellie, where are you right now?"

"I'm safe." Her voice was dreamy, but her jaw was still tight. Tense. Arms beside her body, her fingers drummed nervously on the couch cushion.

Powell pushed the volume up on his cellphone until the white noise track was almost as loud as his own voice. He waited a few moments to let her adjust. "We're going to walk through your dream, but the most important thing to remember is that you're here with me in this room, Ellie. You're safe, and no one can hurt you here."

"No one can hurt me here." Her fingers touched the upholstery once more before relaxing so her hands lay flat, palms down.

"Good. Take me back to that moment when you feel the metal in your hand. Can you see what it is?"

She shook her head, brows furrowing deeply. "No."

"Look down at your hand. What do you see?"

She inclined her head, going through the motions as if she were in the scene in real time.

Powell held his breath, his unblinking gaze on her.

She bit her lip and gave a small shake of her head. "I just see blood. It's everywhere, and he's on the floor, moaning in pain."

"Come back to the weapon in your hand. Immerse yourself in the sensations you experienced from the moment you saw it. Was it cold when you first picked it up?"

Ellie reached her hand out in front of her, closing her fingers around thin air as if she were picking up the weapon. Her hand turned to the side, as if examining the weapon, though her eyes were still closed tight. Her voice was quiet when she answered. "Yes."

"Hold on to that, feel the icy metal in your hand, notice how it gradually warms against your skin. Tell me about the shape."

Her frown deepened and her eyelashes fluttered.

"Deep breath in and out, Ellie. You're in a safe space."

"I can't do this." Her voice rose higher, chest heaving with short, frightened gasps. Her fingers tapped the sofa again before clawing at the couch cushion in a panic.

"You can do this. There is no danger."

Her eyes flew open, clear and bright, and disappointment

streaked through him. She sat up, shaking her head. "I can't do this right now. I'm sorry. I can feel the weapon in my hand, but when I try to focus on it, I drift out of the memory. And the man." She cleared her throat. "I can see his legs and torso, but my brain is stuck on the blood. I can't see his face."

Intrigued, Powell said, "Can you see where you stabbed him?"

She started to shake her head and froze. "Actually, yes. I stabbed him above the heart. I remember the tip of the blade sinking into his flesh. I hit bone." She scowled, her eyes focused somewhere in the past, though she was staring at Powell. "It wasn't a blade, though. It was something…" She blew out a breath, frowning. "Why can't I remember?" She stood up, eyes flashing with anger. "This is ridiculous. I've been stuck on this one memory, and I can't move past it. Like I'm blocked or something."

When she turned back to Powell, he let out the breath he'd been holding. "Perhaps we should try again another time."

"I told you I couldn't do this today."

"It's okay. You can't force it. I have to ask if the tension is still there?"

She rolled her shoulders, lips parting in apparent surprise. "No, actually. I won't say that I feel better, but that overwhelming sense of dread isn't digging at me the way it was."

Powell leaned back in his chair and smiled. "Well, then I'd say we made a bit of progress today, despite the challenges."

"But is it enough to get me back to work by the end of my restriction? Will Fortis and Johnson see that I've improved, and I'm ready? I need to be back in the field and *doing* something."

"My report will reflect your progress."

She brushed her fingers over her eyebrow, clearly

fighting for patience. "I like how you didn't commit to a yes or no there."

When she went to collect her purse from the table, he slipped his hand into his pocket and turned the recorder off. "There are rules, and I wouldn't be doing you any favors by breaking them." He offered a reassuring smile when she slung her purse over her shoulder and eyed him with barely concealed suspicion. "Everything will work out the way it should, Kline. Trust the process."

She snorted, making her way to the door. "If you say so, Phillip." She blinked, looking surprised at herself. "I mean, Dr. Powell. I'll see you next week. And thanks."

The door eased shut behind her, clicking into place. Powell waited a beat to make sure she didn't turn around and come back in, picked up the phone and punched the keypad. The smooth, deep voice answered on the second ring.

"I need to speak with you."

The man chuckled. "Good afternoon to you too, Dr. Powell."

"We need to talk. I'll head over to your office after my last appointment. Should be around four o'clock."

"I look forward to your arrival."

The line went dead in his ear before he could respond.

Setting the phone back in the cradle, he removed the sheets of paper from the pad that held the notes from Detective Kline's session and put them in her folder. Replacing the file in the cabinet, the metal wheels scraped along the track, forcing him to jiggle it shut. He locked it, smiling as a knock announced his next patient.

He had work to do.

Miss Eleanor Kline's issues would have to wait.

10

Ellie's cell phone rang as she was pulling into a parking space near the side entrance of Charleston PD. She scowled, wondering who could be calling at just before six in the morning.

The number to Fortis's direct line appeared on the caller ID, and her frustration changed to concern. Answering on the third ring, her voice came across as more chipper than she meant it to be. "Good morning, sir."

Fortis didn't bother with a greeting. "I need to see you in my office, Kline."

If she hadn't had coffee already, those words would have jarred her senses to life. "Of course. I just got here, so I'll drop my things at my desk and be right up."

"Now, Kline."

Her stomach clenched. "Is everything all right, sir?"

"We'll talk when you get here." The line went dead in her ear. No goodbye, no explanation.

Reaching for her bag, she paused, grabbing her coffee to take a deep swig. Whatever Fortis wanted to talk to her about, she wasn't about to lug all her things up to his office, then back down again. His urgency had caused tension to begin building in her stomach, so she left her things in the vehicle.

Sipping her coffee as she walked, she skipped the elevator in favor of the stairs to burn off nervous energy before meeting with her boss. Finishing the rich brew while it was still piping hot, she chucked the empty cup in the trash can at the top of the stairs.

Shoving the door open with her hip, she continued down the long, empty hallway that led to the Violent Crimes Unit, where the rest of the detectives worked. Most of the cases were suspected homicides, but many of the more violent assaults found their way into the VCU bullpen, which was headed by Lead Homicide Detective Harold Fortis.

Loud and crowded, Ellie much preferred the quiet space she shared with Jillian on the lower level. The basement room wasn't the bright, open space with a bank of north-facing windows, but she was comfortable there.

In the hallway, she paused just outside the door. The gold letters that announced "Charleston Homicide Division" were peeling at the edges.

She filled her lungs slowly until they were about to burst, but when she exhaled, her muscles weren't any less tense. Fortis typically had a calm countenance, but his tone had been urgent. Mind racing with all the possible reasons Fortis would want to see her before her thirty-day work restriction was up, she turned the knob and walked into the Violent Crimes Unit, ignoring the sudden silence that greeted her as she strode toward Fortis's office. She nodded to anyone who made eye contact with her, keeping her shoulders back, and finally setting her eyes on the lead detective's door.

He waved her in before she had a chance to knock on the glass panel, motioning her toward the chair in front of his desk.

The burnt orange pleather squeaked as she sat down, the two-decades-old foam insert letting air out through a crack in the ancient fabric. The worn wooden arms were polished in uneven splotches by countless detectives who had found themselves under Fortis's watchful gaze for one reason or another, while the rest of the wood was dull and starting to splinter.

Fortis's hazel eyes narrowed on her, his voice serious when he finally spoke. "How are your sessions with Powell going?"

Forcing a pleasant expression on her face, Ellie nodded. "It's going well, I guess."

"How many times have you met with him in the past three weeks?"

She paused, thinking for a moment before she answered. "Seven. I went three times last week."

Her statement earned her an arched eyebrow. "Are you having issues?"

"No, but you and Chief Johnson both made it clear that I'm expected to meet with Dr. Powell as often as possible. He had a last-minute cancelation, so when he called me, I decided to go." She shrugged. "It couldn't hurt, right?"

Fortis nodded, opening his desk drawer and pulling out a file folder. On the label, Powell's neat handwriting scrawled her name in perfectly looped cursive.

Her stomach clenched, but she held her tongue, setting a placid smile on her face, the way her mother had taught her. She knew how to summon an outer calm that hid the questions running through her mind. Her elite Charleston upbringing and being Helen Kline's daughter had assured that. But inside, it was killing her to know whether Powell had given Fortis a reason to believe that she wouldn't be fit for full duty.

He opened the file and slid a single sheet of paper across

the desk, along with an ink pen. "I need your signature right here."

She leaned forward, her eyes widening as she focused on the paper. "Sir, this is a release to return to full duty today."

"I can read, Detective." He grinned. "I thought you'd be ecstatic."

"I am." Grabbing the pen before he changed his mind, she quickly signed her name on the line and dated it. Passing it back to him, she sat back in the chair, almost afraid to let the relief she wanted to feel settle in. "I have over a week before my thirty days is up, so I'm a little surprised."

"We're shorthanded, so I pulled some strings to get your restrictions lifted early. Dr. Powell's support helped, but you need to know that more than a few people aren't happy about it." He glanced up, eyes focused over her shoulder. Ellie turned around to follow his gaze. "A lot of patrol cops would love to be where you are, and there's still some animosity there. I've put a stop to it as much as I can, but I need you to run cases by the book from now on. No heroics, no taking down perps without backup. You understand?"

She nodded. "Yes, sir."

"Good." He dropped her file on the side of his desk in a gesture that told her he was done with it. "As of this moment, you're fully reinstated. Don't make me regret it, Kline."

No promises.

"By the book, sir." Ellie moved to stand when he held up a hand to stop her.

"Good. I have a case for you." He jotted down a case number and a name on a sticky note. "Anderson Duncan. Murder-suicide at an office party downtown."

"Any witnesses?" She took the yellow square of paper from him.

"Dozens."

Her brow wrinkled. "Is it a cold case?"

"Yes and no. The thirteenth anniversary is coming up next month. At the time, it seemed pretty open and shut. Man obsessed with a coworker throws her off a balcony and jumps off after her at a party her coworkers are throwing for her. There were dozens of reports of harassment filed with their human resources department."

"That sounds serious. Why didn't she get a restraining order?"

"*She* wasn't the one filing harassment claims." When Ellie's eyes widened, Fortis gave her a knowing smile. "I figured this would be right up your alley."

"I have to admit, my interest is piqued, but it still seems like a pretty standard case. Why reopen it now?"

"There were details from the case that weren't shared with the media." He paused, his fingers tapping the desktop. "A new case came across my desk that is eerily similar to this one."

"Who caught the new case?"

"Shaw and Decker." She grimaced, drawing a soft chuckle out of Fortis. "Don't worry. I'm not going to ask you to work with them. I just want a pair of fresh eyes on the Duncan case."

She nodded. "How far do you want me to take this?"

"Interview the witnesses and dig into Duncan's personal life. The notes are thorough, but at the time, it was ruled a murder-suicide inspired by obsession and mutual hatred. Now, I'm wondering if we were wrong."

Ellie nodded, taking the file as she stood and turned toward the door. "This wasn't one of Jones's cases, was it? Captain Johnson made it clear I can't touch anything Jones investigated for ethical reasons."

"It wasn't Jones's case."

"I'll get right on this." She was unable to hold back the grin that spread across her face. "And thank you, sir."

Fortis arched an eyebrow at her. "For what?"

"Bringing me back early."

He nodded and cast a quick glance at the detectives working on the other side of his glass before looking back at Ellie. "Between you and me?"

She took a step closer to his desk. "Of course."

"You remind me of a promising young detective who cared more about the victims than keeping the peace in the department. He ruffled a lot of feathers, and a few times I wondered if he was going to live long enough to see retirement. Now that he's older and wiser, he's learned a thing or two."

Ellie glanced at the open office through the wall of glass that separated Fortis's private space from the other detectives, wondering who he was talking about. Coming up empty, she turned back to him. "Which detective are you talking about?"

He laughed, shaking his head. "I'm talking about myself. You don't think you're the only one who's ever pushed boundaries?"

Surprised, it took her a minute to formulate a response. "I guess not."

"But you have to learn to cover your own ass in the process. You're no good to these victims if you get fired for insubordination."

She nodded. "Understood."

"I hope you do understand, Kline. I'd hate to lose a talented detective like yourself. What you have can't be taught." He lifted his chin, motioning toward the door, fingers already poised over his keyboard. "I need your findings on the Duncan case as soon as possible. You're dismissed, Detective."

All eyes were on her again as she breezed through the office, but this time the weight of Fortis's words overpowered their scrutiny. When one of the detectives scoffed, she didn't even flinch. What they thought of her wasn't any of her business. They could stay mad; bringing her back to full duty more than a week early wasn't her decision. They could take it up with Fortis if they were that bothered.

The thought brought on another smile as she retrieved her things from the car and headed downstairs to her shared office. "Good morning," she practically sang.

"You're in a good mood." Jillian smiled, her hazel eyes widening. "I know only one thing that would make you this happy."

"Yep."

Jillian's gaze went to the calendar. "It's a week early."

"Fortis needs me on a case." Ellie keyed in her code and went into the evidence locker room with Jillian right behind her. "Anderson Duncan, almost thirteen years ago."

"I don't remember that one. Have we looked at it before?"

Ellie took a left, heading away from the room that held cold cases. "It's not a cold case." She glanced down at the case number on the sticky note, turning down the aisle that housed evidence of solved cases, looking for May from thirteen years prior. "Here it is. Anderson Duncan and Ellora Rice. Murder-suicide."

Behind her, a soft gasp escaped Jillian. "I do remember that. It was all over the news. Didn't he swan dive into a courtyard fountain?"

The overhead light flickered as Ellie set the white cardboard box down on the nearest table and opened it. A crime scene diagram on the top confirmed what Jillian remembered.

"Looks like you're right. According to the witnesses, they all agreed that he was smiling when he dove off the railing. Judging by the distance and where Ms. Rice's body landed, it was quite a leap to ensure he landed in the water and not the concrete bench around the basin." Ellie handed the diagram to Jillian, picking up the medical examiner's report. "According to the M.E., Rice *could* have survived the fall if she'd landed in the flower bed just two feet away."

Jillian's face paled, and she grimaced at the color photos Ellie spread out on the table. "She landed with her head in the water and her feet on the pavement, bent over the concrete edge of the fountain. Her spine probably snapped on impact. Hopefully, it was quick."

Ellie read the report. "The paramedics arrived within five minutes and marked both as dead on arrival without any treatment. The police were on the scene minutes later, so I would say, yeah, they both died on impact or seconds later."

"How awful for that poor woman. What was the party for?"

"I'm not sure." Ellie shuffled through the individual witness statements until she found mention of the party. She turned the paper so Jillian could read it for herself. "Looks like it was actually a baby shower, but they told Duncan it was a going-away party and suggested he not attend." Ellie pointed out a specific line. "Right there, Virgil Hurst told Fortis they purposely hid the real reason for the party from Anderson to protect Ellora."

"A baby shower?" Jillian's voice thickened with emotion. "Could he have known?"

"The M.E.'s report said she was only twenty weeks, so possibly not." Ellie's gaze met Jillian's. "With the right wardrobe, I've seen socialites hide pregnancy until they gave birth."

"Do you think he realized something was up? She was only thirty-four. If he was obsessed with her, knowing she was about to leave the company would send him off the edge, wouldn't it?"

"But it wasn't Ellora Rice who filed the harassment

claims." Ellie flicked through the stack of papers until she found the printed forms Anderson had filled out in his own words. "I'm not sure who was harassing who here. 'She stares at me when she walks by, whispering one, two, three, four, then she winks.' And here's another one. 'When she passes my desk, she moves my things when she thinks I'm not looking.'"

Jillian's eyes darted back and forth as she read the comment section of a few more of the dozens of claims that Anderson had filed. "These are all petty complaints, but at the same time, how do you even prove someone is doing these things?"

"You don't. It's her word against his."

"Did Ellora Rice ever file against him?"

Ellie shook her head, pointing to a lined area at the bottom of every form. "No, but she had to respond to the claims each time, and she always answered with the same response. 'This is untrue.'"

"That's short and to the point." Jillian frowned. "I'm not sure what to believe here. On one hand, Anderson could've made the harassment up, and there's no way to prove Ellora *wasn't* harassing him. But if Ellora watched him long enough, maybe she picked up on subtle ways to torture him."

"That begs the question, though. Why?" Ellie wrote as she thought out loud. "If she had actually been harassing him and he thought she was leaving, wouldn't he be happy to see her go?"

Jillian shrugged. "You'd think so."

Ellie tapped her pen on the paper and met Jillian's gaze. "And the only two people who can answer that question are gone."

"No matter what the truth is, their toxic relationship made it a horrible work environment for both of them. That's probably why she was leaving *and* why she would hide a pregnancy." Jillian shuddered, wrapping her arms around herself, the misery of Ellora Rice's final moments leaving a haunted look in her hazel eyes. "This is so awful, but I still don't understand why Fortis has a sudden interest in reopening the case."

"Another suspicious suicide came through the department, and there are a lot of similarities that caught Fortis's attention."

"Did he tell you what he meant by that? What kind of similarities?"

"He didn't say much about it." Ellie shrugged one shoulder. "I got the distinct impression that he didn't want to color my investigation with any outside information."

"I'm surprised he remembered this case at all." Jillian motioned to the seemingly endless line of shelves that held hundreds of evidence boxes. "Out of all these cases, why this one?"

Ellie rifled through the stack of papers, eyes darting as she scanned each one. "I wonder who the detective was. He said it *wasn't* Jones, but he never said who it…" Her mouth dropped open.

"What?"

Ellie turned the paper around, pointing to the familiar signature at the bottom of the page. "Harold Fortis."

"Ohhh." Jillian leaned closer. "There's an asterisk by his name. I've seen those a few times. I wonder what they mean."

"It's something the detectives do to mark the milestone. This is Fortis's first case as a homicide detective. That's why he remembered it." Ellie shook her head, staring at the paper in awe. "I'm surprised he trusted me with something like this."

"I'm not. Fortis has never said it outright, but I've heard him put cops in their place when they popped off about you. Fortis has faith in you. He may be the only one who believes

Jones was a dirty cop. It makes sense that he would trust you with this. At least he's on your side."

Ellie nodded, but she couldn't help the feeling of dread that settled on her heart. "Or he knows something we don't know."

"What do you mean by that?" Jillian's voice rose an octave, belying the tension they both felt.

"I don't know yet, but something feels off about this." She met Jillian's worried gaze with one of her own. "This changes nothing. Until we find proof that Fortis isn't dirty too, the only people we can trust in the department is each other."

11

Walking into the office Tuesday morning, the hot South Carolina sun beat down on my head, and it was only the second week of April. I held the *Charleston Herald* up to shield my eyes, annoyed that I'd forgotten sunglasses.

The universe was plotting against me, and I had a feeling as I walked through the entryway and got onto the creaking elevator that the day would be a wash. But I had big plans on the horizon, so I had to focus my energy on making it through the day without killing anyone important.

Gabe was already on a call when I walked into my private waiting room. He flashed me a gorgeous smile, his dark eyes —like the most decadent chocolate—clear and alert. They were his most perfect feature. On a face as gorgeous as Gabe's, that was saying something.

I returned his smile and took the freshly brewed cup of coffee he offered. "You always know exactly what I need."

His eyes crinkled at the corners, but he only nodded, his attention still on the caller. I could hear the pathetic male voice whining over the headset Gabe wore to keep his hands free so he could type. Whoever the caller was, he had a lot of problems. Problems he'd probably created for himself.

I hated him instantly, without even knowing his name.

A quick sip from my coffee cup hid the curl of my lip. I strolled to my office, leaving Gabe to deal with the whining loser. He'd be my problem soon enough. If he was lucky, I'd help him find a permanent solution to his pitiful complaints.

By the time I sat down behind my desk, I was smiling again. Having another prospect for my experiment was an exciting possibility. And planting the seed had taken less and less time with each new subject. Joshua Gibson had been the easiest of all, and I was eager to see if this latest caller would present the challenge I craved.

I set the *Charleston Herald* on the desk in front of me, perusing the headlines for something interesting to pass the time while I finished my coffee. The front page was nothing but sensationalized nonsense and minor events blown way out of proportion with eye-catching photos to sell papers. How half of Charleston functioned from day to day was a mystery to me. What would they do if there was ever a real crisis in the city?

Sighing, I turned the page and froze. A beady-eyed, greased, weasel of a man stared back at me in grainy black and white, his mugshot just another opportunity to schmooze to the camera. Probably completely sure that his status would save him from his own stupidity, Arthur Fink had stared straight into the camera without an ounce of shame on his face.

I wanted to reach through the paper, wrap my hand around his throat, and throttle him until the light drained from his eyes and his body went limp.

His careless bragging had brought attention onto the club that we didn't need, and I'd lost a good business partner in the process. Detective Roy Jones had certainly had his faults, but he'd kept the wolves from the door for over a decade and at only half the price I would've paid someone with half his skill. Now that he was gone, I would eventually have to find someone else to fill that void.

My hand trembled as I skimmed the story on Fink, shaking my head at the arrogance of this one useless man. If we didn't get him handled soon, he would no doubt take us all down with him. There was no way I would just let that happen.

I jumped when the intercom on the phone buzzed beside me. "What?" I snapped before I took a breath and quieted my tone. "What is it, Gabe?"

"I'm sorry to disturb you, sir, but she's adamant that she speak to you now."

She?

"All new clients get a baseline assessment at their first session. Whoever is on the phone will have to wait like every other patient."

There was a brief pause on Gabe's end. "I scheduled the new client who was on the phone already. But this woman called three times while I was on the phone with the other guy, and she is demanding that I put her through or give her your direct line."

"What did you tell her?"

"That if she was someone who should have your direct number, she would already *have* it and wouldn't be calling me in the first place."

His snappy retort tore a laugh from my chest. "Good man. Get her name and tell her I'll call her back at my earliest convenience."

"I have her name. She insisted that I tell you Katarina wants to speak to you now, or she'll show up in person."

An icy chill flooded my veins, setting the hair on the back of my neck straight up. "Put her through," I told him, the laughter gone from my voice. "Hold all my calls too, Gabe."

"Of course, sir."

There was a click, and an almost imperceptible hiss of static before the other line went live in my ear. "Katarina, to what do I—"

"You changed your cell number." Her rage lapped at my ear through the receiver.

"And you've gone back to your old name." I fought to stay level and calm, unwilling to let the rogue woman unbalance me. "I had my reasons. Despite the accusation in your tone, my change of number isn't a personal assault, Katarina. Now, can we cut through this nonsense and get down to why you called, or shall we dance some more?"

"I need money."

"Bold." I stretched my legs out in front of me and let out a soft sigh. "But why call me? Surely you have other contacts with as much wealth and fewer scruples."

"But only you have a vested interest in the information I have."

My pulse quickened, but my voice remained level and calm. "I'll need more than that to part with my money, Katarina."

"I'm not asking for much."

I narrowed my eyes and sat up straight. She was dancing around the question, which was never a good sign with her. "And I'm not running a charity. How much, Katarina?"

"Fifty thousand."

I scoffed at her, flopping back in the chair. "There's nothing you have that's worth that much."

"All right." She paused, clearing her throat softly. "I guess you'll read about Fink's deal in the paper tomorrow."

"What deal?"

"Fink is planning on giving up everyone connected with

the club. Every. Last. Name." She hung on to each word so they echoed in my mind like a threat.

My hand clenched into a fist. "He wouldn't do that. He has too much to lose."

"That's where you're wrong, old man." I cringed at the insult. Fifty was hardly old, but she continued before I could set her straight. "Fink's parents are both gone now that his mother passed away, and he has no siblings and no children. In fact, the only person in this world he ever cared about is somewhere out of his reach, which is killing him."

"Taryn." I scowled. "What's her real name? That sick bastard is always trying to replace Taryn with a new and improved version of the old one. Pathetic."

"Her name is Valerie Price."

"How did you get all this information? I just read the article on him. None of this is in there."

She chuckled, a low sound deep in her throat that was frightening and seductive all at once. "You'd be surprised what a man will tell you between the sheets. It turns out Fink's lawyer is a quick lay with loose lips." She laughed again. "And other talents. Anyway, Fink is prepared to make a deal."

"What's on the table?"

"In Fink's mind, or what his lawyer is working toward?"

I groaned. "In a perfect world, those questions would have the same answer. But not with Fink."

Something snapped and popped on the line. Was she chewing *gum*? "Whoever sponsored him should lose their membership."

I'd had the very same thought more than once. I unclenched my jaw enough to say, "Stop playing games with me, Katarina. What does Fink want, and what is his lawyer trying to get him?"

"Fink wants Valerie. And he's willing to do anything to

get her. But he knows it's impossible, so his lawyer has convinced him to help take down the trafficking ring that kidnapped Valerie. Apparently, the fool hopes she'll be so grateful she'll forgive him for his mistakes and confess that she's always loved him."

Every time Fink opened his mouth, I longed to close it for him permanently. Even hearing Fink's words secondhand from Katarina made my blood pressure rise. I shook my head, disgusted. "He needs help."

"Know any good shrinks?" Her laughter was rich and melodious, and I imagined her throwing her head back with wild abandon, dark hair flying, amused at her own joke.

I smiled in spite of the mess Fink had made. "Very funny, Katarina. This is still not worth fifty grand."

"No. But finding out where Valerie is so he thinks we can give him what he wants is, don't you think?"

Now, she had my attention. "I'm listening."

"He's obsessed with Valerie. Of all his 'dolls,' as he calls them, she was the most like Taryn. He told his lawyer that he often forgot she wasn't the original. He adores her that much."

"Being delusional has been his thing for a long time."

This time, Katarina's amusement came out as a giggle. "True. But as long as he thinks that he'll never see her again, the only thing on his mind is staying out of prison. He's struggling in protective custody as it is, and if he doesn't take a deal, he's probably going to do time. He won't survive." Her tone remained light and jovial, even considering the subject. "Criminals aren't kind to perverts in prison."

My heart clenched. Despite being rebellious, Katarina had always been one of my favorite people. Even when she was on my shit list. And I knew without a doubt that the only reason she cared whether Fink lived was so one of us could exterminate him without bringing down my entire empire. "Let's get down to it. What are you proposing?"

"I'll find Valerie and use her to leverage Fink's silence. For a fee. Then, I'll make sure his death in prison is quick and painful."

"You have friends on the inside?"

Katarina hiccupped a laugh. "Pooh. I have friends everywhere."

"I don't doubt that." It was the truth. Katarina was resourceful on her own, but there was no shortage of people willing to step up and help her when she asked. Those people were mostly men, but even women weren't immune to Katarina's charms.

"Once he talks, it's all over for you and the others." Her tone was still light, but the threat very real. "He'll name names to save his own skin. You can count on that."

Her words rankled. Rage grew inside me, so intensely that my body heated, and I could almost believe my blood was actually boiling. How quickly she'd flipped the switch. Now I remembered why I didn't always like her. "What about you? You don't think he'll turn you in?"

"Sure he will, but they won't find me based off what he knows."

"And what about what I know?"

She laughed. Not the soft, girlish giggle that was more play than anything. A deep, throaty laugh so arrogant my blood pressure doubled. "What you *think* you know and what you actually know is inconsequential. Take the offer or leave it. I don't have time for your mind games."

I considered hanging up, but she had me backed into a corner, and she knew it. Fink was a loose end that Jones should've tied up when he had the chance. But he didn't, and now I was left with an epic mess. "If anyone can find the girl and convince Fink to keep his mouth shut in order to get her back, it's you."

She gave a little gasp of pleasure at the stroking of her ego. "That's more like it. As soon as I see the payment come over, I'll take care of Fink. One way or another, he won't say a word about what he knows."

I relaxed enough to allow a satisfied smile. I had her right where I wanted her again, just that easily. Katarina wasn't the only one who knew how to push buttons to get what she wanted. "And if you can't get him to agree?"

She made the sound of a knife going across someone's neck to slit their throat, like characters in old-timey cartoons often did. "He won't get a chance to talk. Guaranteed."

"Good." I took out my burner phone and accessed a quick transfer app. "Is your username still the same?"

"Of course," Katarina all but purred. She always loved getting her way.

"Should be in there now." I set the burner phone down on the desk, thought better of it, and put it in my pocket so I wouldn't forget to dispose of it.

"There it is." She gave a little laugh of triumph. "Thank you."

"Of course." I paused, letting my voice take on a deeper tone when I spoke again. "And Katarina…"

"Yes?"

I let the silence hang between us.

Her breathing was heavy on the other end, either from excitement or anticipation. Maybe both.

I waited until I was sure I had her full attention. "Don't fail me."

"I wouldn't dream of it."

Gabe waited a few moments after he transferred the caller to the doctor's phone in his office. When the doctor's voice was a soft murmur down the hall, he jumped to his feet and crept down the empty corridor. When he was only a few feet from the doctor's door, he stopped, leaning close so he could hear the conversation. He didn't normally eavesdrop, but ever since he'd stumbled upon the photo album in the doctor's office with pictures of a man who resembled himself, his curiosity had been unquenchable.

Now, he wished he hadn't canceled the transaction. Ever since he'd found the photos in the doctor's drawer and realized his employer must have something to do with a man's death, a man who resembled himself greatly, he'd been eaten up with regret.

His mind had played out different scenarios during which he picked up the man and set him free, like a child would a previously injured bird, or picked him up and got fake IDs for both of them, going into hiding.

But none of those scenarios would play out. It was too late, for one. Second, Gabe's gut told him he'd stumbled into something bigger than he'd ever known. And though he'd done many things in his life he considered wrong, he felt he had no choice but to stick around and see if his instincts were right. Some leftover sense of honor his grandparents had instilled in him, he guessed.

"Very funny, Katarina. This is still not worth fifty grand."

Gabe blinked and pressed his ear closer to the door, wondering if he'd misheard the words. Whoever Katarina was, she was trying to extort a significant amount of money. Even though he was sure the doctor could afford it, why wasn't he railing against the injustice of her request? Gabe waited, dying to know what she had on him.

Rubbing damp hands on his slacks, Gabe forced his lungs to slow their intake of air. He moved closer to the door, eager to hear the rest of the conversation, but the room had gone quiet. The doctor was obviously listening to what the woman was saying, or he'd ended the call. He could be making his way to the door, about to surprise Gabe and catch him in the act.

His stomach clenched, nerves boiling over, Gabe got ready to retreat. He took a step back, and when the doctor finally spoke again, he froze. The volume of his voice told him the doctor was still at his desk, which meant he was safe in the hallway, for now. He leaned in again, wondering what the woman had said on the other end that'd had the doctor's undivided attention.

The doctor gave a short laugh. "Being delusional has been his thing for a long time."

Gabe recoiled. Was he talking about Gabe? Or maybe the man in the photos. Was it possible that the stranger who looked like he could be Gabe's twin was the doctor's lover? Was he wrong about the photo? Did Katarina have proof that the doctor and this mystery man were into deviant role playing. Had the photo been faked? Was she threatening to expose him?

Or had that mystery lookalike died at the hands of a doctor who spent his workweek caring for people who were close to giving up? How could someone who devoted his professional life to taking on the most difficult patients in Charleston cage and then kill a man? And why had the doctor saved evidence of what he'd done in a scrapbook?

Taking deep, quiet breaths through his nose, Gabe tried to calm his racing heart at the memory of the gruesome images. A man who looked exactly like Gabe in a cage in the center of a room, terrified and hopeless. His face showed the telltale signs of a life lost to addiction. Sunken cheeks, dark circles that never went away, and a haze that had made Gabe wonder if the man even knew where he was. Gabe had been lost in the fog of drugs more times than he cared to admit, even to himself.

But the doctor saved me.

Why would the doctor save Gabe, then turn around and harm a man who was Gabe's double? It didn't make sense, and even as he listened to one half of a conversation through the closed door, Gabe couldn't make himself believe that the doctor who'd taken him in when he had nowhere else to turn was anything but the angel of mercy he'd always known he was.

Right?

The photos taken during the doctor's vacation had to be staged. Why, he didn't know. But the doctor was entitled to enjoying his vacation any way he saw fit. He'd earned it.

Another thought occurred to Gabe that instantly had his stomach in knots. Was the photographed man turned on by his own mortality? Gabe had recently stumbled across personal ads of that very nature while perusing his favorite pickup site.

One click on an advertisement had taken him to a website he'd never seen, and he'd been horrified by what he'd found there. People who were desperate to leave this earth but fantasized about torture. There were fancy code words and abbreviations meant to hide the true meaning of their ads, but Gabe had seen right through them. These people *wanted* to die in the most humiliating, painful way possible, and it only took one click to find someone willing to make their darkest fantasies into reality.

Sick to his stomach, he'd scrolled through listing after listing, each one more graphic than the last. If Gabe's doppelgänger wanted this, how did the doctor even find him?

He shuddered. The instant messages on the doctor's personal computer had to be it. When they'd popped up that day, Gabe hadn't thought anything of it. The message had been strange, but so vague Gabe had no idea what it meant. *"I'm glad I caught you in time. I'm not sure this one is going to last the weekend. If I don't hear back from you in an hour, I'll have to put him up for bid."*

At the time, he hadn't intended to violate the doctor's privacy, had only been trying to shut down the computer that had been left on by mistake. But once he saw the message, his interest was piqued. He couldn't just pretend he hadn't seen it, so he'd done some snooping.

Even with his limited knowledge about such things, Gabe decided the messenger had to be a broker; a go-between for people who wanted to experience things no dating site would condone. That was the only explanation Gabe could come up with. Even then, it seemed too outrageous to be possible.

The doctor had been nothing but kind to Gabe. Even giving him an all-expense paid vacation a month ago. And while Gabe was in Florida, showing off the flashy luxury car the doctor had rented for him and enjoying a hotel on a private beach, his boss was on his own adventure, doing things Gabe had never even imagined.

Until now.

"Let's get down to it. What are you proposing?" The doctor's voice was calm, all business, as if he was blackmailed every day.

Gabe grappled with his doubts as they clashed with his loyalty for the man who had rescued him from the street, unsure now if he'd even seen what he thought he had, all overlaid by a healthy dose of fear. Maybe there was an innocent explanation, and it was Gabe's own mind turning an innocent situation into something sinister. He'd heard of people having paranoid thoughts even years after recovering from heavy drug use.

"What about you? You don't think he'll turn you in?" Gabe narrowed his eyes, straining to hear more. This time, the doctor's tone was quiet and ominous. "And what about what I know?"

Gabe's skin broke out in gooseflesh, and he almost abandoned his curiosity right then. What the doctor had said was terrifying enough, but the implicit threat in his tone made Gabe's stomach lurch. If Katarina wasn't scared, she should be.

The outer door to the waiting room clicked open, and Gabe's heart slammed against his ribs. Someone had entered the lobby.

Not now. He'd never get this chance again.

His breathing was fast, his mind racing. He could either walk away and never find out what happened, or risk someone catching him snooping.

On the other side of the door, the doctor chuckled, his tone suddenly light and friendly. "If anyone can find the girl and convince Fink to keep his mouth shut in order to get her back, it's you."

The girl? Gabe stared at the door, his feet rooted to the floor. What girl?

Movement forced his attention away from the doctor's door. Backing up, he tried to compose himself as he set off at a brisk walk toward the lobby, as if he was just coming from down the hall and hadn't been standing in front of an office door eavesdropping. By his second step, a man came into view at the end of the hall.

The placement of the hall in regards to the doctor's office and the lobby was intentional so that guests wouldn't be able to see other patients leaving their session. It gave them several feet to compose themselves or duck into the bathroom if needed. But now that Gabe was the one in the hallway, he couldn't see out into the lobby and had no idea if the man was alone.

Gabe smiled, but he didn't call out. If the doctor heard him, *he* would know Gabe had left his post. The stranger in the lobby had no reason to be suspicious of an employee in the hall, but the doctor would know Gabe was up to something. Another chill passed through him at the thought of what that could lead to. If the tone he'd taken with Katarina was any indication, the doctor was not a man to be fooled with.

The man waiting in the lobby wore a light tan suit jacket with khaki slacks that were more sand-colored than tan. The colors were close but not matching, and Gabe cringed as he approached the stranger. It was an unfortunate fashion choice made by people who couldn't afford a suit, and those who cared more about function than fashion. Gabe had a feeling this man was a little bit of both.

His chestnut hair was a little too long at the collar, the easily touched up patches of gray more messy than dignified. Gabe wouldn't be caught dead letting the early signs of aging take away from the richness of the man's natural hair color. No, this man needed a shave, haircut, and a dye job. In that order. But what was he doing in the office when Gabe wasn't expecting another patient for almost an hour?

"Can I help you?"

The older man nodded, pulling out his wallet. "I'm Detective Daniel Shaw, and this is Detective Jerry Decker. We're with Charleston PD, Violent Crimes Unit. We need to ask you a few questions."

A second man came into Gabe's line of sight as he rounded the corner and could finally see the entire lobby.

He took the card Detective Shaw offered, reading it carefully before shaking his head. "I'm not sure you're in the right place. This is a psychiatrist's office."

"We're aware," Decker offered, his voice raspy. Detective Decker was dressed almost identical to Shaw. Like the first detective, Decker had clearly bought several pairs of slacks and matched them with a single suit jacket to save money. Decker had paired khaki slacks with a navy jacket, a look that somehow worked for him. He was more slender than Detective Shaw, his hair a glossy black.

They looked every bit the part of big city detectives, and after the snippets of conversation Gabe had just heard at the doctor's door, his stomach wanted to cramp. If the doctor was arrested, where would that leave him?

He summoned a vestige of his usual smile. "Can I offer you gentlemen coffee? Any flavor you want." He pointed to the turnstile on the counter, stocked for the clients who rarely used the brewer that made one cup at a time. "I even have one that's donut-flavored."

He grimaced when he realized what he'd said, but Detective Decker snorted. "Good one. Thanks, but we've had plenty of coffee already this morning. We're here to follow up on a case." He leaned over to give himself a clearer view of the hallway, taking a few steps as he spoke. "We were looking to talk to Dr.—"

Gabe stepped into his path, turning up the voltage of his smile. "The doctor is with someone right now. He can't be disturbed. Thank you for understanding."

"How much longer does the patient have?" Detective Shaw glanced down at his watch. "We're not in any hurry."

Still blocking the entrance to the hall, Gabe made sure his voice was polite but firm. "I'm afraid he's on an important call."

"Oh?"

It was clear from his tone that Detective Shaw's interest was piqued, so Gabe hurried to explain with a wave of his hand. "We take only the most extreme cases of mental illness, and many of our patients aren't able to leave their homes. As you can imagine, once we have a patient on the phone, we allow them to talk as long as they can manage." Gabe was shocked by how easily the lies rolled off his tongue. "Today has been one of the longer calls."

"How many patients do you see on average?"

"Three to five a day, and we're open five days a week."

"This is a nice building. Must charge a pretty penny if you can afford the lease on such a limited number of clients." Shaw wandered the lobby as he spoke, admiring a painting on the wall with more than casual interest. "I'm sure insurance pays for it in most cases."

"Like I said, we take severe cases only, so yes, the charge is greater. But many of our patients stay longer than your typical therapy sessions, and we also offer three quiet rooms for them to use after therapy if they're overstimulated." Gabe gave a measured chuckle. "Most psychiatrists don't offer spa-quality nap facilities on site."

"No, I guess they don't."

"I do work with a lot of patients one-on-one before their

sessions, so perhaps I can help you gentlemen so you're not waiting forever."

Shaw turned back to Gabe, an eyebrow arching in question. "I didn't realize this was a group practice. Are you a doctor as well or just a therapist?"

Gabe's hackles raised at what seemed like an intentional jab, but his smile remained in place. He'd dealt with more arrogant men than the detective before. "I'm actually the personal assistant, but I help our patients navigate their insurance and other challenges, like fighting for their right to accommodations for a disability and securing resources they might not know they're entitled to. I get to know most of the patients on a first-name basis."

Shaw turned to Decker, who shrugged. Turning his attention back to Gabe, Shaw said, "Did you know Joshua Gibson?"

"*Did I?*" Gabe didn't like the sound of that. "Of course. Nice gentleman. He's been coming here a little over a year and has made great progress. Did something happen?"

"He's dead."

Gabe gasped, his shock genuine. At the same time, he was aware that Shaw was watching him, and made sure he played the part of dismayed secretary. "Are you sure?"

"He took his life in front of his coworkers," Decker added. "Showed up to work, said he had a surprise for everyone, then took a header out the fifth-floor window."

Gabe's eyes widened in horror. "In *front* of them?"

Shaw nodded. "If he'd been a little heavier set, he wouldn't have been able to fit out the window. It was one of those safety windows that only slides about yeah wide." He held out his hands about eighteen inches apart. "He was so skinny, the manager said he slipped right out before anyone could react."

"I'm stunned." Gabe sat down in the nearest chair, no

longer playing the part, his knees no longer willing to hold him up. "I never would've guessed he would do something like that. He was doing so much better."

"We hear that a lot." Decker's tone was gentle as he glanced at his watch and nodded toward the door.

Shaw stepped toward the exit. "If you could have your boss give us a call ASAP, we'd appreciate it."

"Sure. I'm not sure what he can tell you, but I'll give him your card."

"No worries," Shaw said, giving Gabe a genuine smile for the first time since he'd walked in. "You know how it is. *We* know the guy offed himself, but we have to do our due diligence. We just need a couple questions answered, and we'll be out of his hair."

Gabe nodded, following the detectives to the door and reassuring them that he'd give the doctor the message. When they were gone, Gabe let out the breath he'd been holding and stared down at the business card, which shook in his hand.

Joshua Gibson was dead.

Had thrown himself from a fifth-story window.

He still couldn't believe it.

13

Ellie checked the address, pulling her silver Audi Q3 against the curb when the numbers matched.

The house was a soft primrose yellow with white trim, a one story with a small but inviting front porch. Like many houses in Charleston, in place of the screen door was a white storm door. Pink hydrangeas gave the house a storybook vibe. It was cutest out of all the houses she'd visited since being reinstated full-time last week.

Brianna Harington was the eighth coworker of Ellora Rice and Anderson Duncan's she'd visited, and every last one had been more than helpful. Almost thirteen years later, each was still reeling from the shock of what they'd seen, and so far, everyone was eager to share their grief with Ellie.

She checked her weapon, slinging her bag over her shoulder as she got out of the car and took a deep breath. The day was unseasonably hot and humid for early spring, but there were storms in the forecast that promised to bring one last burst of chilly air with it. Mother Nature was teasing them with a taste of summer, and Ellie was more than ready for the real thing. Everyone complained when the summer was beating down on them, but Ellie loved the way the humidity made the air so thick one could almost drink from it.

The storm door opened before Ellie was halfway up the narrow sidewalk running through the center of the freshly mowed front yard.

A woman in a lavender sundress and tan sandals stepped onto the porch, her curly brown hair pinned away from her face by a single clip at the top of her head, lips painted a deep burnt crimson that shimmered in the sunlight. "Today's pretty hot for April." She stepped aside and motioned to the open door. "Why don't you come inside out of the heat."

Ellie stopped to readjust her bag, smiling at the woman. "Thank you, but I haven't introduced myself."

Her smile slipped. "I know who you are, and I know why you're here." Her eyes darted to the side, but she forced a bright smile. "My neighbors are a little nosey. I'd rather do this inside."

Ellie nodded and followed the woman into the foyer, waiting until the door was closed to show her badge and ID. "I guess someone called you?"

She nodded, curls bouncing. "Virgil didn't think I should be blindsided since we were friends before all this."

Brianna led Ellie to a sitting room off the foyer, passing a table that held a frosted pink vase of cut hydrangeas the same shade of pink as the ones planted in front of the house. The walls of the room they entered were a soft blue, with crisp white trim that looked freshly painted.

"Please, sit. Would you like anything?" Brianna motioned to a frilly floral loveseat in the center of the room.

Ellie shook her head, digging in her bag for her notepad. "No, thank you. I'm just here to interview you because you were there that day. I'll get right to the point and get this over with. You were friends with Ellora before her death?"

Brianna pursed her lips and dragged in a deep breath as they both took a seat. "I was friends with Anderson."

"Oh. I'm sorry, I—"

Brianna waved her hand. "No need to apologize. Everyone wants to demonize Anderson now that he's gone, but I promise you no one was more shocked than I was." She clasped her hands together and stood abruptly. "Are you sure you don't want a drink? Is whiskey okay? I need a drink."

"I'll take a water."

Brianna shuffled out of the room quickly, fingers clutching the flowing fabric of her purple dress.

Ellie sat back, noting the perfectly folded chenille throw on the overstuffed chair, the upholstery of which matched the floral print of the loveseat.

When Brianna returned with a glass in each hand, Ellie took the water with a smile. "Thank you, Brianna."

Brianna nodded, already bringing her own drink to her lips as she sat in the chair. She grimaced at the bite of the alcohol and let out a heavy sigh. "I've been dreading this conversation since Virgil called. I was hoping you'd be here yesterday so we could get it over with."

"I'm sorry. I had planned on finishing up by yesterday afternoon, but everyone had so much to say about Ellora and Anderson."

Brianna grunted, throwing her head back and downing the last of the amber liquid. "No doubt they had plenty of nice things to say about Ellora and nothing but hate for Anderson." Her hand shook as she gestured with the glass in hand, but her deep brown eyes softened as the alcohol took effect. "I hope you don't think any less of me for day-drinking."

Ellie shook her head. "I know reliving that day must be hard."

"You have no idea. I haven't been the same." She ran the

fingers of her free hand through her hair. "I tried to stop him, but it all happened so fast."

Treading carefully, Ellie waited for Brianna to set the empty tumbler down before she spoke. "What made you think you could have stopped him?"

"We were friends. I thought if I could get close enough, he'd listen to me."

"Were you work friends, or did you know Anderson before you worked together?"

Brianna's fingers twisted in her lap. "Before. We met in a support group."

"What type of support group?"

"For OCD. It was the first time in my life that someone really *got* me." She laughed and turned to gaze out the window. "I know this is going to sound stupid, but Anderson changed my life. I grew up thinking I was a freak. You know how people are. They think OCD is a bunch of overzealous handwashing and superstitions about stepping on cracks. But Anderson came from a family that embraced who he was." She scoffed, brown eyes haunted when she turned back toward Ellie. "My mother prayed over me day and night trying to rid me of the demon within. No matter what the doctor told her, she was convinced that she could fix me with traditional remedies and impassioned pleas for mercy. Which just made the symptoms worse."

"Then you met Anderson."

Brianna nodded, glancing longingly at the empty tumbler. "I was younger then. Anderson was thirty-five, and even though he was still struggling with his illness, he had this calming quality about him. I felt instantly at ease. And he was a gentleman, you know?" Brianna blushed. "We were just friends, and he didn't try to take things further. I felt safe with him."

"How old were you when you met Anderson?"

"I'd just turned twenty-one, and I was self-medicating." When Ellie's eyes went to the empty glass, Brianna shook her head. "I didn't go overboard, and mostly just enough to take the edge off."

"No judgment here." Ellie set her pen down and folded her hands over the notepad, giving Brianna an understanding smile. "You were of legal age, and it was thirteen years ago."

"Twelve years, eleven months, and six days." Brianna's cheeks reddened. "Sorry."

"It's fine. So, you met Anderson..."

"At a seminar about taking control of compulsions. He was older than me, but we had so much in common, and we hit it off. A few months later, Anderson helped me get my job."

"What about the person giving the seminar? Do you remember anything about him or her? What was the seminar called?"

She shook her head, fidgeting in her seat, obviously wanting to get up and refill her glass. "We both left early." She laughed. "Everyone else was on the edge of their seats, but Anderson and I saw right through it. It was a money-making scheme."

"There are lots of entrepreneurs who get rich quick selling what amounts to snake oil."

"That's part of the reason we bonded, because we were smart enough to dodge that." Her breath shuddered, and her eyes sparkled with unshed tears. "Anderson helped me so much, and when he died, it hurt to know that people thought so little of him."

"They didn't understand him like you did."

She nodded and took another trembling breath, her forehead wrinkling into a deep frown. "And no one ever said a word about the way Ellora treated him."

"He filed several harassment complaints."

"She teased him mercilessly. Coming into his cubicle and bumping into things so they were out of place, counting out loud whenever she saw him touching his thumb to his fingertips." She demonstrated, touching her thumb to each individual finger on her left hand. "Then she'd cackle and walk off like it was the funniest thing." Brianna's lower lip quivered. "Still, she didn't deserve to die, especially not like that." A tear dripped off her chin. "And especially not the innocent baby she was carrying."

"But you feel she had some culpability after bullying him over his illness?"

Brianna's soft waves bounced as she shook her head. "Not at all. That's what I tried to tell the detective who investigated the case. What happened wasn't about OCD. People with OCD don't just snap and kill their coworkers."

"Maybe it was something other than the OCD that made him lose control. Sometimes people have more than one mental illness."

"No." Her tone fervent, the tears dried up as her focus changed. "He didn't have another illness."

Ellie pursed her lips, choosing her next words carefully. She didn't want Brianna to shut down. "People keep secrets, Brianna. Maybe he didn't tell—"

"He would've told me."

"Then how do you explain what he did?" Ellie kept her voice soft. "A healthy person doesn't do something like that for no reason."

"You didn't know him. He wasn't crazy, but when he showed up that day, he was like a different person. He was…" She groaned, like the memory was a physical pain. "I don't know how to explain it. It was like he was in a trance. He kept saying the same phrases over and over, but they didn't make sense. He was 'a man of action,' and Ellora was 'going to be so surprised.' He repeated those words so many times in this eerily calm tone, but when our eyes met, he looked terrified."

Ellie perked up. "What do you mean by that?"

"I was screaming his name, and he turned toward me." Unchecked tears flowed down her cheeks and neck. She sniffled but didn't wipe them away.

"It's okay, take your ti—"

"No!" Her fingers gripped the hem of her dress, fists trembling against her legs as she relived that day. "I thought he would let her go, but he just held her wrist, his mouth moving with those same words, like a chant. I wanted to run away, but I also wanted to get through the blocked door and make him stop. I was so scared, but there was this moment when our eyes met. He stopped and whispered, 'Help me.'" A sob tore from Brianna's throat, and she collapsed against the back of the chair. Overcome, she wrapped her arms around herself.

Ellie got up from the sofa, plucked a tissue box from the table near the entryway, and handed it to Brianna. Sitting back down, she patiently waited for the woman to compose herself. Her grief was genuine. It was clear that she had cared deeply for Anderson.

"Thank you," Brianna said with a final sniff, gesturing to the box of tissues.

"No problem."

Brianna collected the used tissues, dropping them in a small wastebasket between her chair and the wall. Frowning, she picked up the wastebasket and left the room, returning a moment later with it empty, an apologetic smile on her face. "I've never been able to leave trash in the small bins. I don't know why I keep them around the house. I just empty them into the kitchen trash as soon as I use them."

"You don't need to apologize to me."

"Thank you." She placed the trash can on the floor, moving it until it was parallel to the wall.

When Brianna glanced up and noticed Ellie watching her, Ellie offered a kind smile. "If you're ready to continue, I'd like to go back to what you said earlier. Are you sure he said, 'help me?' No one else reported that."

"Everyone was yelling and trying to get through the door. I don't know how they could have heard him."

Ellie flipped through her notes, skimming through Fortis's neat handwriting to no avail. "I don't see those words anywhere in the detective's notes." Ellie perched on the edge of the sofa, body thrumming with excitement. Passing a single sheet of copied paper to Brianna, she waited for the woman to read it before she continued. "You never said this in your interview. Is there a reason you're just mentioning it now?"

Brianna pursed her lips, nodding. "I thought I imagined it. Like I said, it all happened so fast. Derek was on the phone with 9-1-1 as soon as Anderson dragged her out on the balcony. The paramedics responded within five minutes of the call, but they were both already dead." Her throat caught, and she choked on a sudden sob.

Ellie scribbled down Brianna's words on her notepad.

"I can still hear her screaming, then that horrible silence." She covered her mouth with her hand, her eyes taking on a faraway look.

Ellie waited for her to continue, sensing she was reliving the scene.

"The bodies were still in the courtyard when the detective questioned me, and we'd been there for more than an hour at that point. I was so freaked out, I wasn't sure Anderson had even said it. 'Help me.' Why would he say that?"

Ellie lifted a shoulder, still writing. "I'm not sure."

"I just answered the detective's questions and didn't add

anything. I wanted to get out of there, and I was so shaken, I could barely talk about what had happened." She swallowed hard, forcing herself to take a few slow, deep breaths until she could speak again. "I didn't think the media would paint him as some kind of monster. I avoided the news as long as I could, and I took a leave of absence from work."

"Did you go back?"

She shook her head. "I couldn't do it. No matter how much they scrubbed the concrete, I could still see the blood. Once, I made it as far as the courtyard, and I turned around and went home. By the time I was able to read the article the media put out, the case was already closed, and Anderson was labeled a murderer."

"He killed Ellora, Brianna. No matter how she treated him, it doesn't change that fact."

Brianna lifted her chin, her gaze intent and clearly focused on Ellie's. "Ellora was murdered, but not by Anderson. It was his body, but I'm telling you, as crazy as I always thought my mother was, I learned that demons are real that day."

Ellie opened her mouth but couldn't decide on an appropriate answer to that. Being on the force had taught her that, yes, demons could be real, but she didn't think spirits were what Brianna was talking about.

"Anderson didn't *want* to kill Ellora." Brianna's eyes met Ellie's again, her gaze unflinching. When she spoke, her conviction was unwavering. "I know what I saw. He was possessed. There's nothing you or anyone else can say to change my mind."

JILLIAN MET Ellie at the door when she returned, her hazel eyes sparkling with barely contained excitement.

Setting her heavy bag on her desk, Ellie plopped down in the chair with a sigh. "I'm guessing you found something?"

"I did."

Jillian produced an index-card-sized paper with notes scrawled over every square inch.

Ellie flipped it over, not at all surprised that the back was also completely covered. She frowned, turning the paper over again and scanning the seemingly disjointed words. "I don't know what I'm looking at."

"I was thinking about it, and Jones had complete control over anything logged into your personal case file *here*, but there's no way he could've stopped the media from reporting what they knew. So I decided to look up every article on your kidnapping that was available online."

"How much could they have gotten? Jones stonewalled the reporters every chance he had. He made sure any evidence available was destroyed. My clothes, witness names, all of it."

Jillian pursed her red-painted lips. "You're right about that."

"I know my case isn't the only one where evidence disap-peared, and witnesses were ignored, but…" She shook her head, gaze going to the single box with her name on it sitting beside Jillian's desk. "I can't shake the feeling that Jones went above and beyond to make any useful evidence in my case vanish."

"That's what he was paid to do."

"I get that, but whoever the kidnapper and his assistant were, they must've been extremely important within the circle. Jones scrubbed my case clean and made sure no one would be able to put the pieces together. And it's obvious no one ever looked at the case once it went cold, or they would've been suspicious."

"We can't know if anyone questioned Jones. He could've

paid them off, or worse." Jillian grimaced. "I don't get the impression that taking money to do dirty work bothered Jones that much."

"You're right. I guess a part of me wants to believe that he got into police work for the right reasons, and he was desperate." Ellie turned her attention back to the paper in her hand. Jillian's handwriting was neat, the information she had compiled from her search grouped by date. "I don't remember much news coverage at all. I'm surprised you found this much online."

"The news itself didn't seem overly interested in the story; it was resolved before they got wind of it. A brief article gave a quick rundown of your kidnapping and escape, but even that information was sparse. You were alive and recovering, so there was nothing sensational that would get them clicks. There wasn't much besides the basic facts. In print, the article about you was tucked into the back of the paper with the human-interest stories."

Ellie scowled. "You would think a kidnapping would be a bigger deal, especially since I escaped, and the kidnapper was at large. At the time, I was glad the media left me alone, but now that I know my case was never solved, I wish they'd cared more. It's amazing what a good journalist can dig up."

"Luckily, the tabloids and society pages were all over it."

Ellie rolled her eyes. "Tabloids are hardly reliable news sources."

"That's true, but they have to build their story on something that's true, right?"

"In theory." Ellie laughed. "But I don't think journalistic integrity is high on their list."

"Maybe not, but I found information that was consistent across every publication." Jillian grabbed a highlighter and traced a yellow line across the name of a hospital. "This is the hospital that treated you, right?"

"That's easy to get right, though. There are only so many hospitals in Charleston."

"True. But in this article right here, the *Charleston Star* got a lot right." She produced a printed article with a picture of a patient in a hospital bed.

Ellie barked out a laugh. "That's not even me."

"It's a stock photo, I'm sure, but hear me out. In all the articles, they correctly identified the officer who found you, and not only did they list the name of the doctor who oversaw your physical therapy and recovery…" she high-lighted a name in the middle of the paper, "they had the name of the trauma surgeon who saved your life and an interview with him."

Ellie's lips parted in surprise. Grabbing the article off the desk, she skimmed the words until she found the quote about the doctor. She read out loud.

"Dr. Victor Constantine stated that the young victim came into the operating room muttering incoherently, in and out of consciousness. Her injuries were extensive, causing the doctor to dismiss her ramblings until she grabbed his wrist, looking him straight in the eye with complete clarity, declaring that she'd killed the assistant, but the shadow man was still there." A chill ran down Ellie's spine, but she kept reading aloud. "Dr. Constantine assured her that she was safe and no one could harm her. Her disjointed mumbling continued until the anesthesia kicked in."

Ellie read the rest of the article silently, scowling when she got to the end. "It says here that he didn't call anyone in to take my statement because my life was at risk." She shook her head, air hissing through her clenched teeth as she sucked in a breath. "I wasn't that bad off."

"Are you sure? You were hit by a car, Ellie. By all accounts, you were covered in blood when they found you."

"It wasn't my blood."

Jillian's eyes narrowed. "But a lot of it was, right?"

"I really don't know."

"Too bad they never tested your clothing."

Ellie sighed, slapping the article back down on the desk. "I questioned it back then, but by the time anyone realized I'd been kidnapped, what was left of my clothes had been disposed of. There was nothing to test."

"What about this doctor? Do you think he remembers anything?"

"Maybe." She used her phone's web browser to look up the number to the hospital and hit the call icon.

It rang six times before a friendly female voice finally answered. "Charleston Medical Center. How may I direct your call?"

"My name is Detective Kline with the Charleston PD Violent Crimes Unit. I'm looking for a doctor who worked in your emergency department."

"Worked? Has this doctor retired?"

"I'm not sure." Ellie paused, a bad feeling wrapping its icy fingers around her spine. "If I give you a name, can you see if he still works there?"

"What's the name?"

"Victor Constantine." The line went silent. "Hello?"

"Dr. Constantine died years ago."

Ellie's stomach dropped. "Do you know when?"

"I don't remember, but it's been at least ten years, maybe more. Car accident." Before Ellie could press further, the woman continued. "It was the strangest thing. A single-car accident. No alcohol involved, and they said he was speeding."

"We see that a lot, unfortunately."

"Dr. Constantine drove me home once when my car wouldn't start. He was paranoid about getting injured in an accident of any kind. I couldn't really blame the man. He saw the worst of the worst, and it got to him. I could've walked home faster."

"What are you saying?"

"If you think that man was speeding, I've got a bridge to sell you."

Ellie smiled at the woman's joke. "I understand. You've been very helpful. Can I get your name?"

"Jennifer Wakefield."

"Thank you for your time, Ms. Wakefield," Ellie said, stomach tight with dread as she typed the doctor's name into her search engine. When his obituary popped up, she gasped.

"Is he dead?"

Ellie nodded. "He died twelve years ago."

"*Twelve?*"

"Less than six months after he saved my life." She checked the date on the article, heart racing when her suspicions were confirmed. "And less than a month after he gave the *Charleston Star* this interview."

"Is there anyone else connected to the case we can interview?"

Ellie nodded and groaned when she glanced at the clock. "Just one. Chief Johnson. But he's probably about to leave for the day, and this isn't going to be a quick conversation."

"Do you think he'll tell you everything?"

"I hope so. We've exhausted almost every lead. He's my last hope to find out what happened to me that night."

14

Marcus Johnson leaned back in his desk chair, pinching the bridge of his nose. He let his eyes close for a second, ready for the day to be over. If today was any indication, the citizens of Charleston were already gearing up for Friday the thirteenth.

Sighing, he glanced at the calendar, jaw clenching. He'd been putting out fires all day, and it was only Tuesday, and he knew from experience that the shenanigans wouldn't end on Saturday morning.

He glared at the clock, which seemed to slow down as soon as his attention was on it. Closing his eyes again, he inhaled slowly and released the breath, wishing he could let go of his stress as easily.

One more hour, he thought, and laughed at himself. He was the chief of police and could leave at any time. But part of what kept morale high at Charleston PD was the way he ran his own office. He didn't expect everyone else to work their tails off while he skated along on their hard work, and that made all the difference. Yes, what he had on his plate could wait, but that wasn't how he ran the department, and rough day or not, he was determined to end strong.

When a familiar face appeared in his doorway without a knock ten minutes later, he wished he'd left when he had the chance.

Ellie's green eyes were swimming with frustration she obviously could barely hold in check. Her nostrils flared, and her hands balled into tight fists at her sides as she greeted him.

He waved her in, bracing himself. After she closed the door behind her, he offered her a seat.

She declined, shaking her head. "I can't sit right now."

"Then stand. What can I help you with? Are things going well with Dr. Powell?"

"I'm not here about Powell."

He sighed, feeling his evening slipping away. "Fortis?"

"I want to talk about that night. I need to know what happened. *All* of it."

His stomach dropped, but he wasn't surprised she was here, demanding details. He gave a barely perceptible nod. "Off the record?"

"Whatever it takes to get the whole truth and nothing else. I'm tired of people hiding things from me. Especially you."

Her words hit hard. The memories came flooding back, rushing in as painful as they'd been when he'd first spotted her running through the darkness and right in front of his police cruiser. He didn't want to rehash that night, but he didn't argue. "I suppose I deserved that." He motioned to the chair again. "This will take a while. You might want to get comfortable."

This time, she did take the seat he offered, but she stayed on the edge, perched as if ready for a fight. "Thank you."

"I guess I should've known this day would come. Doesn't make reliving that night any easier, but if that's what you're after, you deserve to know. Where should I start?"

"From the beginning. Where did you find me?"

Johnson nodded, leaning back in the chair, his eyes going to the ceiling as he searched his memory. "Market and Fifth Street. That was the last night I worked that beat."

"Why?"

"When I came back from leave, every time I drove by that intersection, I remembered you flying into the street from between two cars parked on the side of the road." He shuddered and closed his eyes, taking a deep breath through his nose before he continued. "Even now, I can see your face in my headlights an instant before your body hit the front bumper. I tried to stop, but you came out of nowhere, and the road was wet."

Ellie's expression softened. "I know it wasn't your fault."

"Thank you for that."

"What happened next?"

"I got out of the car after I radioed for an ambulance. Oh, Ellie, I was afraid you were gone, but you were awake, eyes wide open, and trying to talk." He shook his head, the horror he'd felt that night coming back to him in a wave. "Covered in blood with an obviously broken leg, and you were *talking*. Not crying, not screaming. I realize it was shock, but you seemed so calm. I went back to the car and checked on the ambulance, but they were too far out. That weekend was crazy. There was a heavy rainstorm followed by a cold snap, and almost constant drizzle all weekend long. The streets were a mess."

"I remember." Ellie cleared her throat, emotions from the memories wanting to choke her. "Well, sort of. When I see myself getting dragged into the kidnapper's car, I was walking in the mist for a long time, but I didn't have a choice, so I just covered my head with my jacket and kept going."

"That was the other thing I was worried about. You didn't have a jacket on when I found you, and there was standing water on the street. Only an inch or two in most places, but I couldn't leave you like that, and the ambulance gave me an ETA of almost twenty minutes. They were overwhelmed with calls at that point. Like I said, there were quite a few accidents. That's the only reason I risked moving you. Life over limb is what they taught us, and I thought there was no way you were going to live twenty minutes without a hospital."

Ellie frowned. "What are you saying?"

"I put you in the back of the cruiser and drove you to the hospital."

Ellie's mouth dropped open. "But everything I've read said the paramedics cut my clothes in the ambulance."

Johnson shook his head. "Your clothes were cut in the ER." He cringed, remembering wishing he could take the girl's place, feel the pain instead. "When you get hit by a car sometimes you bounce, and the road rash—" He stopped abruptly. "Let's just say it wasn't a pretty sight, and they didn't have a choice. Moving you around to pull a shirt over your head would have put you at risk for becoming paralyzed."

"So did moving me to the cruiser."

"True. But luckily, I had help, and we were able to roll you onto an emergency blanket I carried in my trunk. A man helped me load you into the back seat. It was fortunate he'd heard the accident and come out when he did."

"Why is none of this in the report?" She shook her head. "Never mind. I'm sure it was Jones's doing."

"I have my suspicions, especially now that you're saying the information about the paramedics and the ambulance is actually *in* the report. I was honest with Jones, even though it could've cost me my career if something happened to you."

"What about the man? Did Jones interview him?"

"I didn't get his name." His jaw clenched, and he regretted that mistake again for about the millionth time. He'd been thinking about that night a lot since Ellie came on as detective. "I'm not sure where he came from."

"Do you remember what he looked like?"

"Average height, average build. White man. Late thirties, early forties. Honestly, it was so dark, and he was soaked to the skin." Johnson sucked in a quick breath.

"What?"

"He shouldn't have been that wet. It was drizzling, but not the torrential downpour that had happened about thirty minutes earlier. He looked like he'd taken a dunk in the river."

"If he came from the houses, were they far enough away to account for that?"

Johnson shook his head, mentally putting himself back on that street in the dark. "There's no way. That neighborhood has small lots, and all the houses are set close to the street. From the nearest house to where I was standing was thirty seconds, tops."

"Could he have come from farther away?"

"Not a chance. He was there moments after I got out of the car. I thought he was walking or something, or why would he be out in the rain? But he told me he heard the accident and came right out. I didn't question it."

Ellie leaned in, excited. "Did he say anything else to you?"

"No. Wait. Yes. Yes, he did. He told me to keep you safe. That you were a special one. Then he was gone. I turned around to thank him for helping, and he was nowhere to be found. I didn't look for him because you needed medical attention."

Ellie closed her eyes, her expression eerily calm.

Chief Johnson waited, the events of that night churning in his head.

When she finally opened her eyes again, she couldn't hide the fear. "Do you think the man who helped you that night could've been my kidnapper?"

"I'm starting to think that's the only explanation." He balled his fist, the urge to slam it on the desk strong, but he held his temper. "How could I have missed that?"

"You were a rookie, and I'm going to bet it was the first time you'd hit someone with a car. A kid, no less. That would rattle anyone."

"I can't tell you how it tore me up. You moaned all the way to the hospital, and I thought you'd die before I got there. It was the longest eight minutes of my life."

"You did what you had to do, and I lived. That's the most important thing." Her smile was soft and a little sad. "It sounds like you hitting me saved me from the kidnapper. If you weren't there, he probably would've caught me eventually." Her eyes were serious as she held his gaze with quiet ferocity. "And then he would've killed me."

"I don't doubt it. The man seemed shaken, and he was out of breath. I just chalked it up to a typical adrenal response to witnessing a child hit by a car." He forced himself to breathe, his racing heart beating painfully against his ribs.

"Did you notice anything else?"

"Just that your clothes were covered in blood. And I don't mean a typical amount. When I first got out of the car and saw you in the headlights, I was sure you were already dead. There was so much blood; much more than anyone can lose and live."

"It wasn't all mine," she reassured him, her voice faltering.

"I realize that. The man wasn't injured, though."

Ellie's gaze went to the floor, her hands shaking as she collected herself. "I'm sorry. This is a lot."

"Take your time."

She licked her lips, her answering laugh joyless. "I've taken enough time. You've been so detailed, but none of this is jogging my memory. I saw the video, so I *know* most of that blood was from the other victim. He made me watch him torture her until I couldn't take it anymore. Then I told him to kill her."

Kill the bitch. Ellie shuddered.

"It was a mercy."

She bit her lip, nodding, but not really looking like the words sank in. "I know, but that doesn't make it any easier."

"None of this is easy."

She met his gaze, her eyes sincere. "I know that night was hard for you, but I'm glad it happened. You're the only one who has any idea what that night was like for me. Talking to you about it, I don't feel so alone. Isolated."

"I haven't talked about it in so long..." He snorted. "Maybe I should spend some time with Phillip." He held out his shaking hand to let Ellie see what kind of impact it had on him. "You're not the only one who's still struggling with what happened that night."

"Dr. Powell's helped me work through a lot of my feelings. I've been able to let go of the anger I was holding on to."

"I hope whatever anger you had directed on me is resolved."

She tilted her head, eyes shimmering with tears she managed to hold at bay despite the painful memories that sat heavily in the air between them. "I was never angry at you."

"It's a relief to hear you say it."

"Even before I'd confirmed that you saved my life, I was sure you had. The streets were deserted that night, and I ran for so long without seeing another soul. When I saw your headlights, I didn't realize you were a cop. I just ran straight for your car and…" She sucked in a shocked breath.

"What?" Johnson leaned forward, concerned for Ellie.

"I just remembered that." She closed her eyelids tight, lips moving as she struggled to force the memory out. Grimacing, she slammed her fists down on her thighs. "Dammit. It was right there. I can see your headlights bouncing as you went through the dip at the corner. My hair was wet and sticking to my face. My footsteps were loud, but my heartbeat was louder."

"We never found your other shoe." His stomach churned, bile threatening as the memory of the sickening thud of her body hitting the grill of his car pushed its way to the forefront. He swallowed hard, forcing himself to continue, if only for her sake. She needed to know everything, and he was the only one who could help her. "Sometimes, when pedestrians are hit, their shoes end up in impossible places."

"I wasn't wearing the other shoe." She gasped again. "I just remembered that too. I only had one shoe on when I was running, and I was mad at myself for not being able to ignore the pain. I was running for my life, and I still hobbled over the sharp rocks in the gravel driveway." She went still again, rigid and silent before shaking her head and cursing under her breath. "And it's gone again. Why can't I remember?"

"Trauma."

"Shouldn't it be healed by now?"

"Not that kind of trauma," he explained.

She frowned. "I wish I knew how to fix it. If I could just remember what he looked like, or something distinct about him."

"I wish I'd gotten his name, or at least a good description so I could help you with this, Ellie. Anything is better than what I had at that point."

"He would've lied. The fact that he thought to help you

load me into the car speaks to his manipulation. He could've hidden, but he chose to reveal himself to be involved in saving me. It was smart, because why would you suspect someone who was just a helpful bystander?"

His shoulders stiffened, and his jaw clenched, unwilling to accept brushing away the incomplete job he'd done that night. "Don't make excuses for me. I might have been a rookie, but I was still a cop. Interviewing witnesses is part of that."

"When did you have time? I was going to die. Stopping to get the information of a random guy who was at the right place at the right time didn't make sense." Ellie's voice had risen with each statement, her tone tight with frustration. She paused and took a deep breath, and when she spoke again, her voice was calmer, her expression softer than moments before. "You did what you had to do, and no one can fault you for that. Least of all me. You made my survival a priority. I'm grateful for that."

"I can't believe he was right there, and I didn't even consider it. Don't beat yourself up over this. This is my mistake, not yours."

"You couldn't have known. No one can blame you for that." Ellie's braid flicked over her shoulder as she shook her head vehemently, turning her palms upward. "Who would ever guess that the kidnapper ran *toward* the police instead of hiding? He's not your normal criminal. There's no way any of us would've assumed your helper was more than just a good guy in the right place at the right time."

Some of the tension drained from his body. As much as he wanted to blame himself for her kidnapper getting away, Johnson knew Ellie was right. He stroked his chin and sighed, giving her a smile. "I appreciate you saying that. I had nightmares for months after. Once I was sure you were going to lead a full and happy life, they got fewer and further in between, but that first month was hell."

"You're the only reason I'm still here," she said, her voice nearly a whisper. "I can't tell you what that means to me. I was inspired as much by you as by what happened to me. I didn't remember much, even back then, but I remembered that you were there every time I opened my eyes. I felt safe, and that's all that mattered in the days after my escape." Her voice caught. "I can't tell you how important that was."

"I'm glad I could be there for you." His smile turned wistful. "When I saw your name on the list of applicants for Charleston PD, I knew you were going to shake things up. You're the only survivor we know of. If the kidnapper is still alive, he's probably still reeling from losing you that night. I don't have to tell you that most potential victims of serial killers don't escape. You're very lucky."

A dark cloud settled over her face, and he knew he'd stirred up bad emotions again, but it was too late to take the words back. To his relief, she nodded, her quivering lip the only sign that reliving that night upset her as much as it did him. "You're right. I don't always *feel* lucky, but the truth is, I survived when others haven't."

"That doesn't mean you can't still mourn what you've lost. He stole your innocence that day. You'll never look at the world the same again. Acknowledging that doesn't make you any less grateful for being alive today. You survived hell and turned that pain into a calling to serve and protect the people of Charleston. That's something to be proud of."

She was quiet for a long time, face locked in a scowl as she worked through what he knew were heavy emotions. When she finally lifted her head and met his gaze, a renewed determination was in her eyes. "Thank you for telling me about what happened that night. I know reliving those hours wasn't an easy thing to do."

When she stood, and he shook her hand, it disappeared inside his, the reminder of how small and fragile she'd been that night like a punch to the gut.

She'd survived the impossible. If the kidnapper was still out there, biding his time, he was in for one hell of a surprise.

15

Gabe was quiet Wednesday morning when I walked through the office door. My normal cup of coffee wasn't ready and waiting, so I knew immediately that something was wrong.

My assistant's usually bright brown eyes were puffy in the corners, weighed down by a sleepless night and what looked like more than a few tears. I was struck by the way obvious sadness had deepened his already dark features. But instead of looking haggard or worn down, Gabe was a vision of human fragility. I knew him well; something had rocked him to his core, and he was struggling to hold on to his composure.

The need to break him so I could put him back together stirred inside me, but I forced it down again. This was not the place. It would take more than a few therapy sessions to break this particular young man.

I gave him a sympathetic smile instead, a look I'd practiced extensively all through college to convince my peers I cared about their pathetic problems. Then I went to the coffee maker and made my own cup of coffee for the first time since Gabe had been hired. "Would you like some?"

He shook his head. "No. I'm not feeling too well."

I nodded, eyeing him as I took a sip. "You look exhausted. Maybe you should go home. How is the schedule looking?"

He drew in a deep breath, squaring his shoulders. "There were only two appointments today, so I moved them to Monday. I wanted to talk to you before I cancel Thursday and Friday."

"Gabe, is everything okay?"

"Joshua Gibson committed suicide not long after his last session."

My throat clenched and my heart rate sped up. *That was quick.*

I hid my smile behind a sip of coffee, holding the cup up until I could force a frown into place. "Are you sure it was him? He was making such progress." I brought the cup to my lips again.

"That's what I told the detectives."

I froze mid-sip, the impulse to grin fading on its own. "What detectives?"

"You were on that call when they came yesterday. Then you got bogged down with appointments, and I didn't want to upset you while you were trying to work." His chest rose and fell as he sighed. "I know how much you care about your patients."

"I appreciate you taking the extra care, but you should've told me yesterday." I held out my hand for the card he was nervously fidgeting with. He handed it over, and to my dismay, Ellie Kline's name was not embossed on the front. "Detectives Shaw and Decker? Were they here long?"

"No. I told them you were on an important call, and I'd give you their card at a later time."

"Were they expecting me to call yesterday? Gabe, I'm sure

I don't have to tell you that many times, the police require a prompt response. Anything else looks bad."

He shook his head. "They said there was no hurry. They had a few standard questions they needed to ask, but Joshua committed suicide in front of his officemates, so there really wasn't much investigating to be done. I asked that they give you a reasonable time to respond, and they were fine with it." His head lowered slightly, eyes going to the floor in shame. "I should've told you sooner. I'm sorry. By the time I was ready to talk about it, you were already halfway out the door, and you looked so happy. I didn't want to ruin it."

I set my briefcase and laptop down on the table beside one of the lobby chairs and moved closer, placing a hand on his shoulder. When he gazed up at me with those soulful brown eyes, I pulled him close and held him against my chest.

He went stiff for an instant before melting against me. His trembling body and a soft sniff were the only hints that he was overwhelmed with emotion.

My own eyes were dry, but having Gabe so close, the urge to hold him closer had me reeling so that my smile was replaced with a deep frown. Which was far more appropriate for the moment, considering what he'd just told me. But it wasn't the loss of a patient that had me feeling suddenly grim, it was anticipation of the pain I knew I would feel when I finally had to let Gabe go.

"Thank you for being so considerate of my feelings and my time. But you could've told me and shared your grief. Gabe, this is what I do. You don't have to carry your burdens alone."

"They were rude and pushy, even though they said their visit was routine. I wanted to make sure you had some time to prepare before you have to talk to them. They were so callous, and I knew you'd be hurt by the loss of a patient. You deserve that much respect."

His words caught me off guard. My hand went to his back, comforting him as I'd seen others comfort their loved ones. My throat thickened, and I felt trapped in my own skin. It took me a moment to realize that I was experiencing a profound, visceral sense of pride at his actions. He could've let the detectives blindside me, but instead, he'd done everything he could to ensure I had the space I needed to prepare for the encounter.

It was the best thing he could've done. Unsettled and frustrated by Katarina's call, I would've been off my game. By assuming that Joshua's loss meant anything but a victory for me, Gabe had helped buy me valuable time to prepare.

He was so perfect, it was hard for me to breathe. Was this what it felt like to care about another human being? It was almost painful.

I pulled back as if struck by lightning, suddenly desperate to have space between us.

He gave me a sad smile and gestured toward his desk. "I have a few things I want to take care of today before I leave, so if you want to head out, I'll finish up here." He paused, biting his lower lip. "I'm sorry. I should've asked you about canceling appointments first. I just thought it would be the best thing. I'm sorry if I overstepped."

I dismissed his worries with a wave of my hand. "Canceling the appointments was the right thing to do. Next time, ask me first." I gave a short laugh. "Well, let's hope there isn't a next time. I'm not too keen on having detectives knocking on my door."

"What do you want me to do if they come back or call before I leave?"

"Tell them I have the card." My fingers twitched. I was dying to reach out to him but stopped myself. *It's not the time.*

I repeated the mantra, unsettled by my conflicting feelings. This was a first for me. "As far as they know, I'm your boss and nothing more, so they won't expect you to do more than pass the information along, right?"

"Right." He nodded and gave me a smile I could tell was forced. "If they call, I'll let them know you got their message."

"I really appreciate your quick thinking there. It would've been difficult to deal with them yesterday. It's nice to know I can trust you to act quickly and decisively."

"Thank you."

I stood there for a moment, wanting to say something more, but not wanting to ruin the moment. We were closer, more in tune with each other than we'd ever been before. "I think you're right. I'm going to call it a day."

"What about tomorrow and Friday's appointments?"

"If you can move them to next week, do that." I lifted one shoulder, imitating the gesture Gabe used often. "Otherwise, I think canceling them is best."

"What should I tell them?"

"Tell them?" I pursed my lips. "I guess you can tell them I'm feeling under the weather. Use your best judgment. They're not owed an explanation. They won't be charged."

He nodded. "I'll take care of that right away, and I'll see you Monday."

"Don't feel like you have to stay. I can see this death has been traumatic for you. Take time to grieve."

"I will."

I lingered for a few minutes, dumping my cold coffee down the sink and rinsing the cup. Gabe was already on the phone with the first cancelation when I walked out the door, mentally planning my day. Calling the detective from the car seemed like the best thing to do. If Gabe was right, it would be a quick conversation, and I'd have it over with before I pulled into my driveway across town.

Satisfied with that plan, I unlocked my car door. I had one foot on the floorboard as I glanced at the passenger seat, where I always laid my laptop and bag. For an instant, I was sure I'd left them at home, then I remembered the forlorn look on Gabe's face and the strap of my laptop bag sliding down my arm as I laid my things in the lobby. Somehow, I'd completely forgotten them.

Locking my car, I hurried through the parking lot and into the elevator, then down the wide hallway that led to my suite of offices. The doorknob jammed when I turned it. He'd locked the door already.

I fished the keys out of my pocket and slid the office one home, turning the handle and entering.

My things were where I'd left them, but Gabe wasn't in the lobby. Curious, I peeked down the hallway, expecting to see light coming from beneath the bathroom door. If he'd needed to step away from the lobby, it was smart to lock the door. Otherwise, people could come in and take whatever they wanted. But it wasn't the gap beneath the bathroom door spilling light across the carpet in the dark hallway. It was my office.

Careful not to alert him, I made my way down the corridor quietly. The door to my office was ajar, the tiny crack wide enough for him to hear someone knocking on the lobby door, but only if they were loud. I could see the white of his button-down shirt as he shifted, much too close to my private computer for comfort.

I used the toe of my shoe to push the door wider, my gaze locked on him.

He gasped when he looked up, lips parting in shock, eyes wide. In his hand, he held a scrapbook I recognized instantly. It was the book in which I'd placed my mementos from my weeklong getaway the month before, the one I'd luckily not finished filling. If memory served me, I'd printed off the last of the photos and shoved them in my desk drawer, meaning and forgetting to add the final photos to the scrapbook.

We stood on opposite sides of the room, frozen in place.

The ticking of the clock seemed to slow and fade away completely as I focused on the sound of my own heartbeat filling my ears.

Gabe stayed behind the desk, scrapbook clutched to his chest, holding the book so tight the color drained from his knuckles.

We were motionless, eyes locked on each other. I was between him and the only exit. Even if he wanted to run, he couldn't.

But Gabe didn't try to run. He just stood there, unmoving, his expression unreadable. But his heaving chest gave him away. He was scared, though he was obviously trying to hide it. For every breath I took, Gabe took three, but it was what he did next that floored me.

I'd expected him to try to explain himself or talk his way out of trouble. But his generous lips spread into a feral smile.

Every muscle in my body tightened in response.

He brought the book with him as he approached me, page open to the eight-by-ten photo I'd printed on my home computer of my gorgeous captive. Freshly groomed and stripped nude, he stared into the camera, unaware of his fate and sure he could perform his way to freedom.

My heart skipped a beat at the memories the photo evoked, Gabe's hands on the page amping up my sudden arousal.

"Is this where you went when I was in Florida?" There was wonder in his voice.

"Yes."

He touched the man's face in the picture. "He looks like me."

"That's why I chose him." The words tumbled from my lips before I could even think to stop them.

He nodded, eyes still holding mine as he slowly closed the book and set it on the desk. This time, he was the first to reach out.

But I held up my hand, stopping him before he shattered what was left of my self-control. Seeing my muse hold the picture of the man I'd sacrificed in his honor was more than I could bear. His touch would be my undoing. But I couldn't hide my smile at the overwhelming pleasure catching Gabe snooping had brought me.

When he tilted his head in question, I motioned him back to the desk and turned on the computer.

"There's something I need to show you." My voice trembled with excitement, and it was all I could do to wait for the hidden software to open the secret site on the dark web so I could share my passion with him. Then I would see how far loyalty would take him.

And I would know once and for all whether Gabe was the replacement assistant I'd been looking for.

16

Jillian pulled into her parking space, relieved when Ellie appeared from the stairwell a moment later.

Ellie pulled the passenger door open with a wide grin. "I got your text that you were finally on your way home and thought you could use a hand."

"Thank you. This is the last of it. It's not everything, but it will have to do."

"Is Captain Browning getting suspicious?"

She nodded, stepping out of the car and retrieving a box as Ellie did the same. "I think so. I dragged the project out as long as I could, but at this point, *Browning* could've finished this by now, even as slow as he types. Today he asked me to give him an estimate so he could update his records. He's getting antsy."

"Do you think you can buy a few more days so we can get more?"

Jillian shook her head. "Too late. He asked if this was my last box, and I said yes." They stepped onto the elevator, bumping into each other with the large white cardboard boxes, a fake case name and number written in black ink on the labels. "Luckily, I'd already put the other box in my car, but for a moment, I thought he was going to take a peek inside."

Ellie grimaced, using her elbow to hit the elevator button for their floor. "That would've been a disaster."

"I know. But I really think there's enough pieces of the puzzle here to get the bigger picture."

"I hope you're right." Ellie shifted the box she carried under one arm, balancing it on her hip while she unlocked the door.

The living room was dim, a galloping stampede the only indication that Sam was heading straight for them. Ellie set the box down on the table in the foyer, planting her hands on her hips and fixing a disapproving stare on the dog.

Sam planted her feet, sitting down on the tile in an effort to stop her own forward momentum. She skidded across the floor, her body coming to rest a few inches from Ellie's feet.

Jillian snorted, glaring at Sam. "Oh sure. You respect Ellie's boundaries, but when I come into the house first, you run me over like a herd of elephants." Passing through the living room, she set the box on the kitchen table.

Sam sneezed and buried her nose in her paws, one eyebrow lifted so she could gaze up at Jillian through the doorway to the kitchen.

Ellie laughed and shook her finger at the black dog. "Sam, you're such an odd duck."

Sam stood and gave a single bark so soft it was like a whisper. Going to her oversized dog bed in the corner of the living room, she melted into the memory foam padding.

Ellie's lips were pursed tight, trying her best to hold back a laugh. The laugh escaped when Sam moaned and arched onto her back with her legs in the air. "She leads a pampered life."

"I think she loves living here as much as I do."

Ellie joined Jillian in the kitchen, opened her bag, and took out a stack of papers. "I think she likes this place more than you and I combined." She spread the papers across one side of the kitchen table, placing a fresh notepad in front of her. Next, she unfolded a large sheet of paper that was covered in lines and dates.

Jillian moved close for a better view. "What's that?"

"A rough timeline. I used the information Chief Johnson gave me to compile as much as I could about my abduction and everything that happened afterward." She surveyed the spread. "It's not much, but it's more than I had before."

Jillian walked around the table, skimming through each document before she went back to the timeline. "I think I can fill in some of these blanks with what I found this week."

White copy paper ruffled between her fingers as she dug through the first box. She started with a diagram of the street where the accident took place, putting the larger sheet of paper near the top of Ellie's arrangement. Eyes narrowed in concentration as she dug deeper into the papers, she wondered if what she was searching for was in one of the other boxes. No, she knew it was in this one. The call log from that night was one of the last documents she'd printed, so it should be—

She barely suppressed a yelp of triumph when she found what she was looking for. She overlapped the two papers, setting them between the article about Ellie's hospital stay and the notes in Ellie's own writing about the night she was kidnapped.

"These are the dispatch logs from that night. The first one is Chief Johnson calling in the accident at eleven twenty-one p.m. The second is a 9-1-1 call from a Ms. Evelyn Bradford claiming she saw two men shove a woman into the back of a car five minutes later that same night."

Ellie's lips parted, and her eyes widened with excitement. "Was she questioned?"

That familiar pit Jillian got in her stomach whenever she had to tell Ellie she didn't have all the information about her kidnapping opened up, and she reluctantly shook her head. "I'm sorry. She wasn't. Ms. Bradford was a frequent caller, and she lived right here." Jillian used a pencil to circle a house on the farthest corner from the little rectangle Chief Johnson had drawn to show where his squad car was when he hit Ellie. "It was dark, and her vision was so poor she couldn't tell that the vehicle was a police cruiser, so no one paid her much attention."

"Was?" Ellie sighed. "I'm guessing that means she's not alive for us to question now?"

"She was eighty years old, thirteen years ago. She's in a memory care facility near her family in Georgia now."

Ellie nodded, accepting the information easier than Jillian had anticipated. "So, that's one dead end down."

"But it backs up the chief's story, doesn't it? That's something."

"It is, but it doesn't prove that the chief wasn't working with the kidnapper that night."

Jillian's mouth dropped open. "Do you really think that? I know I'm no detective, but I've read his reports, and the notes from the office shrink and Chief Wellesley. By all accounts, he was consistent about the events of that night and sincere about how it affected him."

"I don't suspect him, if I'm being honest, but I can't rule out anyone right now. Fortis thinks I'm paranoid, but I *know* this is more than just one dirty detective."

"I agree." Jillian drew in a long breath. "I just don't get that vibe from the chief."

"I hope you're right. Having him in the hospital with me really changed how I viewed police officers and their contributions to the community. When I woke up, he was there in the chair, uniform wrinkled from staying in the hospital room, watching me. He was nodding off with his hat hanging from one finger, about to fall onto the floor and…" Ellie gasped, her hands going to her mouth. "That's the first time I've been able to remember it that clearly."

"You've been remembering a lot lately. Maybe it's the hypnosis?"

Ellie grimaced, giving Jillian a guilty look. "I don't know. I didn't tell you, but I couldn't even stay under at the last session. It's like there's a wall in my brain, and I can't get around it."

"But you remembered this when you were just talking about the incident." Jillian slid the empty notepad to Ellie and handed her a pen. "Write that down and just keep writing. Talk out loud if you have to but let whatever comes to you come out without thinking too hard about it."

Ellie took the pen, her eyes narrowing. Skeptical. Nevertheless, her pen flew over the yellow-tinted paper so fast Jillian could barely keep up. "Johnson was there when I woke up, and he told me about the accident. He had a scruffy beard at the hospital, and I remember that he was cleanshaven when he came out of the police car."

"Was he wearing his uniform hat? A rain slicker? Tell me about how he looked when he first found you."

"I was in so much pain." Ellie closed her eyes, the pen freezing in place. "He appeared in the headlights and looked so *shocked*. His skin was damp, but even in the pale light, I could tell that he was young. His eyes were so wide, but his voice was very calm. He kept telling me I would be all right."

"Can you back up? Do you remember the impact?"

Ellie started to shake her head and went still. "I do. I was running, and I could hear the man. Jillian, he was right behind me, laughing. I was so tired, and I'd been running without one shoe."

"With one shoe?"

Ellie nodded, the blood draining from her face. "I lost it somewhere. I don't know where. My foot was sore and bleeding, but I still forced myself to run. He was so close I could hear him breathing, so I ran between two cars. There was a light, and I thought I was near a grocery store or a gas station, and I was relieved. Then I got scared again when I realized it might be closed, and I could have just run all that way to die without being found."

Jillian nodded, her heart racing, knowing what was coming next.

Ellie swallowed so hard Jillian could hear the click in her throat. Ellie inhaled through her nose, her hand going to her abdomen as she sat down in a chair at the table. "In the next instant, I was flying through the air. I hit the ground hard and flopped across the pavement."

Wincing at the image of her best friend's body being thrown through the air like a rag doll, Jillian wiped away tears that had suddenly sprung to her eyes. Ellie had been through so much. The fact that she was going through hell trying to piece together the fragments of her memory made Jillian feel worse for her.

"It was surreal." Ellie bit her bottom lip. "I didn't feel anything for an eternity, and then I felt *everything*. It was the worst pain I've ever experienced."

Jillian swallowed the bile that rose in her throat at the image Ellie's trembling words conjured up.

Sitting at the table, Ellie's eyes were closed, and she swayed slightly, her white-knuckled grip on the tabletop.

Jillian decided to push a little more and sat quietly in the nearest chair to Ellie. "You said you could hear the kidnapper. When he was chasing you *before* you saw the light, did he say anything to you?"

"He said that I stabbed him in earnest, but he deserved it for letting me go." Ellie's brow furrowed, her frown deepening as she searched her memory for some elusive fragment. "No. That's not it. Ernest!" She practically shouted the word. "He said he was delighted that I stabbed Ernest, but I wasn't going to fool him so easily. Or something like that."

"Is that the weapon you keep feeling in your hand during hypnosis?"

"Yes!" Ellie said without pause. "Not a knife. It was thick, and I held the weapon by the blade, not a handle, when I swung my arm through the air." She made the motion, still holding on to the table with her other hand. When her arm came all the way down, she cringed as if she were stabbing the man right there in her kitchen. "The weapon was heavy."

"But not a knife?"

Ellie shook her head. "No."

"Where did you get the weapon?"

"A tray of medical instruments."

"That's good, Ellie. Don't think too hard about things, just say the first answer that comes to you."

"Okay." Ellie's voice was distant and almost dreamy, but there was a tinge of panic just beneath the surface. Her lips were parted, and her chest was moving rapidly with tiny, frantic breaths. Eyes still shut tight against the horrors she was reliving, Ellie licked her lips, and a single bead of sweat escaped her hairline.

"Ellie, what did you stab Ernest with?"

"Scissors. Big, heavy scissors." She paused, the sound of her fast and shallow breathing filling the room. "They were silver, no rubber on the handles."

Sam appeared in the doorway, her dark eyes on Ellie, ready to protect her from whatever was causing her harm.

"How many times did you stab him?"

"Once. Right over where I thought his heart should be, but I hit bone, and there was so much blood. As soon as I buried the tip into his flesh, it bubbled up like a spring." Ellie gagged, covering her mouth with one hand.

"Just breathe, Ellie."

When Jillian touched Ellie's arm, she reached out and grabbed Jillian's hand so tight her fingers ached. She winced, but Ellie's eyes were still closed from where she was still clearly stuck between her past and the present. Jillian held fast, taking deep breaths with Ellie until her friend's grip loosened, and the blood rushed back into Jillian's fingertips.

Ellie cleared her throat, eyes still shut. "I tried to pull it out so I could stab him again, but the scissors slipped out of my grip, and I heard the doorknob turning, so I just ran. I slammed into the man and knocked him down. Ernest was screaming, and the man was yelling at him, but I just kept going. I ran into the trees, and I kept running."

Ellie's eyelids flew open, her chest heaving, gaze wild and distant. She turned, staring at Jillian for a moment before she shook off the past. Looking around the room, she slumped farther down into the chair with a desolate moan.

Jillian hurried to the fridge and grabbed Ellie a bottled water. She downed it in loud gulps, and sat in the chair staring at the past, her eyes focused on a memory she'd been trying to uncover for years.

"He's got to be dead, right?" Ellie's voice was low, but the tremor in it was gone. This time when she turned to Jillian, she was in the moment, the lost expression of a few minutes before replaced by the feisty, green-eyed force of nature Jillian knew. "He just left that man there on the floor to die while he chased after me. Could he have lived?"

Jillian was already on her laptop, keys tapping as her fingers flew over them. "If he did survive, that kind of injury would need extensive surgery to repair." She scrolled through several news stories from the night Ellie had escaped and the week that followed and shook her head. "I don't see anything online, and I can't access the department's information here."

"We'd have better luck calling the hospitals."

"And that's going to require a warrant."

Ellie blew out a long breath, glancing at the notes she'd written before the flash of memory had surfaced. "It's still more than we had before. Tomorrow's Friday. We can check the John Does and see if anyone matches up with this man and his wound. If we can find the assistant, we can probably identify the kidnapper."

"Tomorrow's the thirteenth. Aren't you going to lay low?"

Ellie shook her head. "I think Powell is right. The thirteenth year isn't any more momentous than the tenth or fifteenth anniversary. Besides, I can't sit around all day and wait for something to happen."

The shrill ring of Ellie's cell phone split the air, and they both jumped. Jillian's eyes went to the screen of the smartphone beside hers on the table. When the caller ID popped up, Jillian groaned.

"That's one of the Violent Crimes Unit's direct lines." Ellie didn't reach for the phone, letting it ring for a third time before she picked it up. "This is Detective Kline."

Even from where she sat, Jillian could make out the man's gruff voice on the other end.

"Kline," the man said, his tone ominous. "We need to talk."

17

When Ellie answered the phone, she recognized Detective Jerry Decker's raspy voice right away. "We need to talk, Kline."

"What's up, Decker?" She grabbed the pen and notepad, flipping to a fresh page.

"Not sure why I'm catching your calls, but we had a tip come in you need to take."

Ellie's shoulders stiffened, pen hovering above the paper. "I'm not manning the tip line anymore. I've been reinstated to full-time work. I'm not sure who's in charge of it now, but it isn't me."

"Yes, we've all heard you were brought back early, but no, I didn't call you after-hours over a random tip. Believe it or not, most tips can wait until morning. This call is specifically for you."

Her brow wrinkled in confusion. The Violent Crime Unit's tip line was anonymous and available to the general public. Any cold case tips Ellie received came directly to her. Even then, most of the information she got came from interviews, not calls out of the blue. "Is it about my cold case?"

Decker snorted, then coughed and cleared his throat. "I don't know. She won't talk to anyone but you. I asked her for specifics so I could write it down and leave it on your desk instead of bothering you at home, but she refused."

"Oh." Ellie held her pen over the paper, ready to write again. "I'll take her number and give her a call back."

"She's waiting on hold."

Ellie put the phone on speaker and set it on the table so Jillian could listen in while she took notes. "Can you connect her?"

"That's why I'm calling."

Before she could respond to his snarky retort, there was an audible *click*, letting her know he'd transferred the call over to her.

"Hello, this is Detective Kline. Can I get your name, please?"

There was a soft feminine laugh. "I have many names. Which one would you like?"

"You can remain anonymous. If you do, I'll refer to you as Jane Doe in my records. It's up to you whether you want to use your name or a pseudonym."

"You know me as Katarina."

Ellie blinked, writing quickly as her mind raced to figure out why the name and the voice seemed familiar. "Katarina?"

"Having trouble placing me?" Katarina mocked, her tone amused.

Ellie's mind whirled. Was this the woman from the case involving Steve Garrett and a trip to Ghana she'd worked when she first made detective?

"I deal with a lot of cases, Katarina. I'm sorry, but I don't remember where I know you from. Maybe a little backstory would help. If we know each other—"

Katarina's laughter cut Ellie off before she could say a word about the Ghana case.

"Ah yes, the exciting world of Cold Cases. It's a wonder you haven't died of boredom since you were promoted. Who I am isn't important. We've run into each other a few times, but our past isn't the priority right now."

"Why are you calling, then?" Heat crept up Ellie's neck. Whatever Katarina's reason for calling, it was clear the woman was enjoying playing games.

"Because I have information for you."

Ellie decided to play along with the game. "If we have a past like you say, I'm guessing you want to remain anonymous because you're still a person of interest in a case. Maybe more than one. In my experience, criminals aren't the most trustworthy source of information, so why should I believe anything you tell me?"

Katarina's quiet hiss was the only sign Ellie's accusation bothered her. But her voice was still light and happy, as if they were having a friendly conversation and nothing more. "Believe me or don't, I don't care. If Valerie dies, it won't be on my head."

Ellie stiffened, sucking in a quick breath. She cast a frantic glance across the table to Jillian, who was sitting with her elbows on the table, lips parted as she listened in silence. Ellie's heart rate quickened. "How do you know about Valerie?"

"Got your attention now, don't I?" When Ellie tried to respond, Katarina cut her off. "I don't have all day for this. You either want Valerie to live, or you don't. Waste my time, and I'll hang up without helping you."

Ellie's heart was racing now, the pen in her hand trembling. Jillian fidgeted in the chair. Ellie inhaled slowly, trying to calm her frayed nerves. "I'm listening."

"Much better. I knew you were smarter than you looked." Shrill laughter rang through the speaker, filling the kitchen. Ellie's stomach knotted. Would Katarina hear an echo, letting her know she was on speakerphone and end the call right then? But the woman continued without missing a beat. Either she didn't know, or she didn't care. Ellie's money was on the latter. "You've been causing lots of problems for some very important people. At first, they were amused at you, playing detective, but now that you're making things difficult, no one is laughing anymore."

"Which people?"

"The list is long, but only one person matters. The master is tired of you getting in his way, and his patience has worn thin." Katarina paused. "Hmm. And there's a big anniversary coming up, isn't there?"

The master?

Ellie's stomach dropped, but she forced herself to focus on writing down everything the woman was saying, her hand flying across the paper. "Anniversary? You need to be more specific."

Katarina's laugh sent a chill down Ellie's spine. "Don't play games with me, *Detective* Kline. You're much too clever for that. We both know what I'm talking about."

"It's been a long day. I really don't know what you're referring to." Ellie forced a heavy sigh, laying it on.

"The anniversary of your kidnapping and escape. You're the one who got away, you know. Did you think he was going to just let you walk away?"

"There have been plenty of anniversaries since I escaped. What's so special about this one?"

"For me? Nothing. I think the entire thing is petty, but it's not about me. This year is important to the master. Now, *he* has a lot to lose if you keep sticking your nose where it doesn't belong." She chuckled as the terror from that night dumped into Ellie's blood. "I can't imagine why he didn't just finish you off years ago when he had the chance, but it's not my circus, and you're not my monkey."

The pen fell from Ellie's hand. She grabbed at it, aware that her breath was short. Repeating the words that had caught her attention, she avoided meeting Jillian's eyes. She knew all she would see was her own fear reflected back at her. "When he had the chance? What does that mean?"

"He's watching you. He's been watching you since you escaped. It was easy, what with your parents parading their precious daughter around at every charity function in Charleston since you could walk."

Ellie's breath caught, blood running cold. She cast a frightened glance at Jillian, who was staring at the phone with her mouth agape in shock. Ellie's throat felt like it was closing up, her heartbeat so loud that it drowned out everything else. *He's been watching me.* She'd suspected he was still near, but having Katarina confirm it was chilling.

Either Katarina didn't notice Ellie's sudden intake of breath, or she didn't care about her reaction. She kept speaking as if she hadn't just told Ellie that the serial killer who'd kidnapped her was alive and well, watching and waiting for an opportunity to finish what he'd started.

"Once he realized who you were, it was easy." Katarina gave a disapproving huff. "Like I said, not my style, and I haven't given you a second thought since the last time we met, but the master is different."

"When we met? When was that? And why are you calling? If this has nothing to do with you, why get involved at all? It seems like an unnecessary risk for you and for this… this…master."

The word was bitter on her tongue.

"My relationship with the master is complicated, at best. To be honest, he gets in my way almost as much as you get in his. But he confided in me, and I realized that I could use you to get something I've been after for a long time."

Ellie's jaw tightened, her patience with Katarina's game

wearing thin. But Katarina had information on Valerie Price, and she couldn't shake the feeling that whatever this woman had to say was extremely important. Ellie was forced to play the game, whether she wanted to or not. "What are you after?"

"Power. Isn't that what everyone wants? I'm tired of being a pawn in one wealthy man's game. I have my own dreams and plans on how to make them a reality. If you catch the master, then you're getting him out of *my* way too. It's a win for both of us."

"If that's true, why don't you start by giving me his name?" Ellie winced when Katarina let out a loud cackle.

"You're a detective, why should I make it that easy for you?"

"Fine, if you won't tell me his name, can you confirm something I already know?"

"Sure. But you only get one question, so make it good."

Ellie pressed her lips together, considering multiple questions. Her fractured memories did little more than tangle up her thoughts, but one detail popped up over and over. His assistant had kept calling him "doctor." If that were true, and this monster was a real doctor, knowing would narrow the suspect pool down.

She almost groaned. When she *had* a suspect pool. Right now, she had next to nothing. It was worth a shot, so she decided to use her one question on that element. "Is he really a doctor?"

"He is a doctor." Katarina paused for so long, Ellie was sure she'd hung up. "Even if I give you his name and tell you everything I know, you won't find him until *he* wants you to. He's smarter than you, but I have a feeling you care about Valerie enough to give him a run for his money. Maybe."

"If you're so sure I'll fail anyway, why call me at all?"

"Like I said, if you manage to catch him this time, then

he'll be out of my way. If you don't, he'll be busy enough with you to give me time to plan my next move. Either way, I win."

Ellie scowled, scanning the page filled with notes and finding nothing useful despite having Katarina on the phone for several minutes. She decided to try a different tactic. "If it's the anniversary of *my* kidnapping, what does it have to do with Valerie? Why not just take me?"

"The master saw how you put your own career on the line to save this woman, this stranger." She huffed, as if Ellie's bravery was ridiculous. "You risked your life. He knows going after the person you care about is the best way to get to you."

Ellie chuckled, playing Katarina's game to throw the other woman off-balance. "He'll never find her. I'm a much easier mark. Unless he's scared."

"He's not afraid of you."

Ellie smiled, jotting down Katarina's reaction. Instead of amused, she'd been almost too haughty. Was it possible that "the master" *was* scared of Ellie? Had she hurt him like she'd hurt the assistant? Or did he realize, now that she was older, he wouldn't be able to control her like he had when she was fifteen?

If he'd been watching her as Katarina claimed, he had to know Ellie was skilled in self-defense, both armed and unarmed. "Valerie's protected, so he can't get to her. Tell him I said, if he wants to finish this, he can call me personally, and I'll meet him."

"Your arrogance will get you killed someday. Hopefully sooner rather than later, but that won't help Valerie. Protective custody isn't foolproof, and you know it."

"She's not in protective custody. Detective Jones was in the master's pocket, and I can prove that he purposely buried information to protect some very powerful men. I'm not willing to bet Valerie's life that Jones was the only dirty detective. I have her somewhere safe, and no one at Charleston PD knows where she is."

"If you know you can't trust your colleagues, you should know that you can't trust anyone. Even pretty boyfriends." Katarina lowered her voice, her tone dark and threatening. "Even those closest to you aren't safe. Valerie is in danger, and it's all your fault."

18

The line went dead, filling the kitchen with a sudden ominous silence.

Lips parted in shock, Ellie met Jillian's questioning gaze from across the table. "Jillian, what if she's telling the truth?"

"Ellie, *I* don't even know where Valerie is. Katarina is bluffing. You know these people. They like playing games. She's trying to throw you off the scent."

"What if this time, she's not?"

Jillian shook her head. "You said yourself that she's a criminal, and you can't trust someone like that. No matter how convincing they are, you just can't." She pursed her lips, her wheels already turning. "Is this the Katarina I think it is?"

"I'm guessing she's the elusive Katarina Steve Garrett told us about. The way it went down, I wonder if she had something to do with Steve's death. We never found a trace of her. And I think she's called in an anonymous tip before. That, or I'm just overly paranoid at this point."

Jillian pointed to the notepad. "Can I get a copy of that?"

"Sure." Ellie ripped off the top piece of paper and took it to the printer in the small office off the living room to make a copy. She brought it back to Jillian, who was pacing around the table, jaw tight and eyes narrowed, deep in thought. "What are you thinking?"

Jillian shrugged, sinking into a chair. "I don't know yet. I'm going to take your notes first thing in the morning and see if Carl can use some of his forensic tech lab magic and help me track down the number that she called from."

"It was blocked."

"I've seen Carl get around bigger obstacles than that."

Ellie nodded. "All right. I'm not too fond of the idea of bringing someone else into this, but I think we can trust Carl."

"I do too. He could've spread that video of you as a teen being manipulated by your kidnapper all over the office when he found it last month, but he chose to keep it private. If anyone at the office is trustworthy, it's him."

Ellie grabbed her purse, shoving her cell phone into the zippered pocket. "Thank you. I'm going to check on Valerie."

"Right now? It's late."

"I can't wait all night and hope she's okay. Tomorrow's the thirteenth." Ellie laid her hand over her heart, the knot in her stomach so tight she wanted to curl up in a ball. "I've had this nagging feeling that he was going to do something on this anniversary for weeks now. Katarina's call confirms it."

"Why don't you just call Nick or Flynn and make sure everything's all right? You could give them a heads-up and—"

"No!" When Jillian winced, Ellie realized she'd shouted her response. She lowered her voice, giving her a *sorry* look. "No. For now, we have to assume we can't trust anyone."

The color drained from Jillian's face. "You can't mean Nick, Ellie. Nick?"

Ellie pressed her palms to her temples. "I don't know who to trust right now."

Jillian stood, pushing the chair back so fast it tilted on

two legs and hung for a moment before crashing to the floor. "This is insane, Ellie. What if she's playing you?"

"There's nothing wrong with being cautious."

"There's cautious, and then there's this." Jillian gestured to the table. "You're willing to take her word over your own gut. Ellie, you would *know* if Nick was dirty. There's no way he could hide that for so long." Shaking her head, Jillian turned and righted the chair, but she didn't sit.

Ellie's head was spinning as every possible outcome converged into one massive mess. "I just don't know. But I have to keep Valerie safe. She didn't survive hell trapped in Fink's basement for almost two years to die because of me." She brought her fist to her chest to punctuate the statement. "Jillian, I know this is going to piss some people off, but if it saves her life, then it's worth it."

"What are you going to say to Nick?"

"Nothing right now."

Jillian's jaw tightened. "He's going to find out, Ellie. And when he does, he's going to be devastated. I've seen the way he looks at you. No matter what you throw at him, he just rolls with it."

"He'll understand." Ellie's bottom lip quivered.

"You don't even believe that, Ellie. And he won't. In Nick's place, I wouldn't."

Ellie inhaled, straightening her shoulders. "You're not *in* his place. Jillian, you're my closest friend. You know more about this case and what happened to me than anyone else. You heard what that woman said. If there's any chance she's telling the truth, Valerie is in danger. They'll come after someone I care for to hurt me. I can't ignore this and hope for the best."

Jillian glanced away, considering. After a moment, she met Ellie's eyes, her lips pinched into a tight line. She nodded, and Ellie let out a sigh of relief.

"Thank you, Jillian."

"What are you going to do?"

"I'm going to Valerie tonight."

Jillian's body went rigid with worry. She worked her lower lip between her teeth. "Then what?"

Ellie shrugged. Her nerves were so jangled, she couldn't really think beyond her next move. "I don't know."

"Won't Nick be there?"

"No. I hired around the clock security. Nick is going through his days like normal. He has no reason to be there." Ellie took out her phone and powered it down before putting it back in her purse. "I can't risk anyone knowing I'm coming. If Nick can't get ahold of me, he might call you. Promise me if he calls or comes looking for me, stall him."

Jillian scowled. "What in the world am I supposed to tell him? 'Ellie thinks you're one of them, but don't worry, she still loves you?'"

Ellie ignored the sarcasm. "Tell him whatever it takes. And don't answer the door for anyone."

"Ellie, you can't be serious." She threw up both hands. "Just let me come with you."

Ellie's spine tensed. "No, the fewer people who know where she is, the better. You can't go, if only for your own safety." Her hand wrapped so tightly around the strap of her bag her knuckles turned white. "I'm serious. I don't want to believe that he's involved either, but this group, this circle of evil bastards who operate the trafficking ring on the dark web seems to be run exclusively by and for the wealthiest men in Charleston. Nick's family is—"

"Good people, Ellie." Jillian's voice was quiet, a frown cutting deep lines into her forehead. "If you let your kidnapper convince you that the world is a sick, evil place, then he's already won."

"I didn't need anyone to tell me the world is an evil place.

You've seen the cases that come across my desk. Some of the most violent predators were loved by their communities. The BTK Killer was a deacon at his church and a scout leader. I'd be a fool if I didn't consider the possibility that people in my social circle might be part of this." Ellie's breath quivered as she let it out. "Jillian, I need you on my side."

Jillian sucked in a deep breath and closed her eyes. As she let it out, she met Ellie's gaze. "I'm on your side, Ellie."

"Thank you."

Jillian checked her watch, glancing at the setting sun beyond the window. "Part of being on your side is caring about you. So hurry up and get back so I don't have to worry."

"I won't be back tonight." Ellie went to the hall closet, pulling out a plain duffle bag. It was her go-bag, carrying just about everything she needed in an emergency situation. She would never be able to sleep anyway, after that call, unless she knew for a fact Valerie was safe. When she caught Jillian watching her, she smiled and shrugged. "Always be prepared, right?"

Jillian nodded and gestured at the copies in front of her on the table. "I'll text you if Carl and I find anything in the morning." A thin smile spread across her face. "Hope he's a morning person because this can't wait." Jillian went around the table, surprising Ellie when she threw her arms around her neck. "Be careful."

Ellie hugged Jillian back, fighting the tears that suddenly filled her eyes. "I will. I'll see you soon." She forced her shoulders back and pulled away, painting a smile on her face. "I beat him once. I can beat him again."

"I'll see you when you get home."

Ellie gathered up her notes, shoving them into her bag, and grabbed her car keys. On her way out the door, she stopped and patted Sam's head. Glancing back to the kitchen, she met Jillian's eyes and gave her a confident nod, despite the fear welling inside her.

She couldn't tell Jillian, but she was terrified that the kidnapper would get to Valerie before she did. Or worse. He'd waited thirteen years for this moment, and Ellie knew he wouldn't go down without a fight. The clock was ticking, and it was only a few hours until midnight.

April thirteenth. Thirteen years after he'd kidnapped her, only to have her escape.

Everything in Ellie had been certain that he had something big planned. And Katarina's call confirmed it.

She just hoped that when the dust settled, she was the one left standing.

As long as the master was alive, she would never be safe.

No one she loved would ever be safe.

19

The brass handles on the dresser drawer were cold in Valerie's hands. She paused, her chest tightening as she told herself she was being ridiculous. But even so, she eased the drawer open, her eyes glued on the widening gap.

"Is everything all right?"

Valerie jumped, laughing as she turned to face Flynn. "It's fine," she lied.

"I'm sorry, I didn't mean to startle you." A hulking man, Flynn's appearance was deceiving. He was really just a large teddy bear underneath the security guard exterior, his warm brown eyes and hair adding to the image.

"It's okay. I'm still getting used to…" She smiled apologetically. "Freedoms."

"There's no need to rush. It's going to take some time to undo two years' worth of damage."

"I know, it just feels silly sometimes." She gestured to the partially opened drawer. "Like the dresser. I *know* when I open it, I won't see neat piles of lacy underwear or dozens of identical fitted tees and white socks, but a part of me worries that escaping that nightmare was just a dream." She caught her lip between her teeth to hide the quiver and cast her eyes down at the floor. "What if this is all a dream, and I'm still in that basement?"

Flynn stepped into the room, dark eyes never leaving her and filling with something she couldn't dare hope for. "It's not a dream. You're safe here."

"And when the trial's over? Then what?"

"I thought Detective Kline insisted on witness protection."

Valerie turned away from him, not quite able to fathom life after this ordeal. "She did, but I have my doubts."

"About what?"

Valerie glanced at the drawer again, but it wasn't open far enough to get a glimpse inside. Pushing away images of the obnoxiously frilly bedroom that had been her prison in Arthur Fink's basement for almost two years, she forced herself back into the present. "Detective Kline can't trust her officers in her own precinct to keep me safe, but I'm supposed to trust that witness protection is going to be any better?"

"It's a different branch of law enforcement. Federal Marshals run WITSEC."

She frowned, not sure she should voice what she was thinking. Squaring her shoulders, she turned back to the dresser and yanked open the drawer. With lightning speed, she snatched a sweater from the top of the neatly folded stack and slammed the drawer shut. A *whoosh* of air escaped her lungs.

She pulled the sweater over her head to hide her shaking hands and walked past Flynn into the hallway. "I want some coffee. How about you?"

He was right behind her, a constant shadow every day since Detective Kline had hired him and his team. She knew before he answered that he would want another cup or two.

Her private security team went through more coffee in a day than she did in a month. Even late in the afternoon when the sun dipped toward the horizon, the scent of fresh brew still filled the air.

He grabbed two mugs from the dish drainer and held them out with a smile while she poured. "I could use some caffeine."

"I figured as much."

His smile slipped, and he blew out a breath, leaning his hip against the counter and watching her over the rim of his mug as he sipped.

Valerie waited. Flynn had something on his mind, but she'd learned over the past weeks that he couldn't be rushed. So, she mirrored his nonchalant stance, failing miserably at looking even slightly relaxed.

Watching her closely, he set his cup down. "What are you holding back?"

"Nothing." The lie came so easily she almost cringed.

Flynn lifted a single dark eyebrow and took another slow, measured sip. The ceramic made a soft *clink* on the tiled countertop, but his eyes never left hers. He didn't accuse her of lying, but he didn't accept her explanation either. "You started to open your mouth, then you turned and grabbed a sweater so fast you almost slammed your finger in the drawer."

"Did I?"

He nodded. Taking another sip, then another, his deep brown eyes bored into her.

The silence was too much. She shook her head, and her thoughts spilled out. "I've seen it from the inside, and I'm not convinced that this trafficking ring is just in Charleston."

"Of course it's not. It's an international issue, and no major US city is immune." He was so calm, the slight flaring of his nostrils the only sign that this was more than mundane small talk.

His steady, unwavering confidence settled Valerie's nerves even as flashes of the night she was auctioned off pushed their way to the forefront of her mind. The bright light, the auctioneer describing Valerie's physical attributes as if she were livestock.

Scowling, she gulped her coffee, cringing when the hot liquid scalded her throat. "That's not what I meant. It doesn't matter if it's just one officer or all of them, the problem is deeper than Charleston. I know a few of the women I was held with were from other cities and other states." She sucked in a deep breath. "And I know that I heard at least one of our captors mention shipping captives to winning bidders outside the Carolinas."

"I don't doubt that."

"Then why should I trust a federal lawman over a local one?"

"You shouldn't trust anyone." He was still stoic, matter-of-fact.

She held his gaze, stomach tightening. "What about you?"

He shrugged one shoulder, not appearing to be offended by her moment of distrust. "If I was going to hurt you, I've had enough opportunities."

His words rang true.

She relaxed against the counter as tension she hadn't known she was holding on to drained enough that she could admit to herself that he was yet one more person she could trust. Now, she had two. Him and Ellie. "You're right, but that doesn't change the fact that witness protection might be a death sentence for me."

"You don't have to go." Was there something in his eyes when he'd said that? Did he not want her to go?

"I can't stay here. And there's nothing in Charleston for

me." She glanced out the kitchen window, the late afternoon sun sparkling off the clear blue water of the lake. Turning back to Flynn, she gestured toward the front of the house. "You want to sit on the porch for a bit? I need some fresh air."

Flynn took his smartphone out of his pocket, scrolling through the live video feeds of the security cameras he'd installed all over the property. After he'd checked each thoroughly, he nodded, and she hurried outside before he could change his mind.

Valerie sat on the porch swing, and Flynn took his usual chair, which was angled so he had a clear view of the gravel driveway that meandered through the trees and disappeared out of sight.

She used one foot to push off from the smooth wood floor of the wraparound porch and tucked her legs under herself. Her bare feet peeked out from the hem of black yoga pants, toes sporting bright red nail polish. After two years of being forced to wear pink, she couldn't stand the sight of what was once her favorite color.

The knit sweater was itchy against her skin, but the feeling was nothing compared to the joy of picking out a different outfit every day. The sleeves were too long, but Valerie didn't mind. Her fingertips—also painted red—were the only part of her hands that showed. The thick gray yarn provided the perfect buffer between her palms and the hot mug of steaming coffee wrapped in her hands.

She took another sip, admiring the rays of light that peeked through the dense forest surrounding the property as the sun hung low on the horizon. "I need to start a new life, but I'm scared."

"You have every right to be scared. No one will blame you for that."

Her spine had relaxed a smidge more when she nodded. "I just feel so trapped." The wind picked up, lifting her dark brown hair from her shoulders and swirling the strands around her face. She smiled as she tucked the loose tendrils back behind her ears. "It's so nice to be outside and feel the air on my skin."

"Freedom must feel wonderful after being held captive for so long."

Valerie shook her head. "This isn't freedom. I'm still a prisoner here, even if the boundaries are wider. No, I won't be free until this is over, and I can go on with my life." She caught his eye, considering her next move before diving in. "Since you have the cameras and we're in the middle of nowhere, do you think I could be alone for a bit?"

He blinked, obviously surprised. And maybe something else. Hurt? Standing, he nodded. "I'll be in the house if you need me."

Her smile was tight. "I know I won't actually be alone, but I just need a few minutes. I need to focus on something other than this mess, and it's impossible with you sitting there."

He laughed softly, the warm emotion she'd caught in his eyes earlier returning. "I understand. I'll be close, but you take all the time you need."

She finished the last of her coffee, leaning back in the swing and bringing her knees up to her chest so she could pull the oversized sweater over her legs for warmth. When Flynn popped his head out the front door and tossed her an afghan from the living room, she almost asked him to rejoin her. But she needed these moments alone, and she was grateful that he was so willing to give her space, despite the seriousness of her situation.

Detective Kline had chosen the team well. Valerie just hoped that witness protection would be as good.

The sun slipped beyond the horizon, the pink sky slowly being taken over by deep navy. When the first star appeared in the night, Valerie sent up a silent wish. It was the same one she'd wished since the night she and Ben had laid on the hard floor, held prisoner with dozens of other trafficking victims. Separated by gender, they'd moved as close to each other as they could, hands through the chain-link that stood between them. Her heart ached at the hole his death had left.

Star light, star bright.

Smiling, she recited the childhood poem in her head, though she was in her twenties.

I wish for this nightmare to end.

Tucking the afghan up around her chin, she closed her eyes, letting the memory of Ben's soft smile fill her with a warmth the balmiest of breezes couldn't. She could still feel his touch two years later, his voice echoing in her head.

Everything is going to be all right, Val.

He'd been wrong.

He'd died days after he'd said those words, but Valerie hadn't found out until Detective Kline saved her from the same fate two years later. Ben's death was still fresh, and grief overtook her in painful waves in ordinary moments.

But it seemed as if Ben were close now. So close she could almost feel him. His arm wrapping around her shoulder. His nose nuzzling her ear, whispering sweet words of—

A hand clamped over her mouth.

Her heart jumped into her throat as her eyes flew open. Struggling for a breath through her nose, she stared up at the large shadow above her.

"Valerie. Wake up." The voice belonged to Flynn, and she went limp with relief.

Blinking away the fog, she realized she'd dozed off. He held a finger to his lips, and she jumped up, letting him lead her by the hand into the house.

When she walked into the dark room and he locked the door behind them, her stomach clenched all over again.

"What's going on?" Her voice trembled, and she hated the fear that made her whisper in a strangled, raspy rush of air.

Flynn kept moving, brushing past Zeke, who was double-checking all the locks on the windows. "Someone tripped the alarm at the end of the road." He was eerily calm as he pulled his phone out to show her the car rolling down the gravel drive. The bright headlights sent streaks of light across the video as it continued toward them.

Her heart pounded painfully against her ribs. "Do you know who it is?"

He shook his head, leading her through the dark house. "It's too dark to make out anything helpful."

"Maybe it's just Nick."

She caught the look Flynn gave Zeke before he answered. "Nick wouldn't come here and risk giving away your location."

Bile rose into her throat as he pulled her into the room she slept in each night, headed straight for the closet door. But she knew there was no closet behind that door. It was a panic room, installed by the previous owner.

Valerie's breath came in panicked gasps, and she dragged her feet. Flynn tugged on her hand, but she stood in the threshold of the bedroom, frozen in place. "I can't." Her voice was thin, trembling. "I can't be locked in that room alone. Please."

Flynn shot a look back at Zeke and put his hands on her shoulders, the silver glow from the full moon lighting Flynn's face just enough for her to see the pity in his eyes. "I know you're scared, but there are only two of us. We can't keep you safe unless you're in there."

"What if something happens to—"

"We've got this, but I can't be worried that you'll get caught in the crossfire. It's one car. There's a cell phone on the shelf in the back of the room. No texts. I'll call and say the password when it's all clear. If anyone else calls, hang up and call Detective Kline, got it?"

She nodded, body quaking as she took one step after another, until she stood inside the panic room hidden behind an unremarkable closet door.

Flynn nodded at her, all business as the heavy metal door closed between them.

The lock clicked, engaging automatically, and she swallowed, her breath becoming more shallow. On the wall, a keypad glowed, the button labeled *arm* blinking. It was the only light in the dark room.

She closed her eyes, forcing herself to inhale slowly. Hold it for four seconds. Release the breath slowly.

Your name is Valerie Price, and you will get out of this alive.

Hands shaking, she opened her eyes again, calmer. She pushed the flashing button, and the lights turned on instantly as the room went on lockdown.

Valerie breathed a sigh of relief. She was locked in now, safe. Untouchable.

And completely alone.

20

Jillian scowled at the clock, which had only moved thirty minutes since Ellie left to go check on Valerie. Jumping up from the couch, she paced the living room like she'd done several times already. At this rate, she would never be able to sleep tonight. She was too amped up by Ellie's call with Katarina. Each passing minute ticked by as slow as molasses while Jillian waited for morning. Sleep was impossible, so she might as well *do* something.

As she turned to find her shoes, Sam leapt to her feet, obviously mistaking Jillian's actions for dog-walking preparations. When Jillian didn't grab the leash, Sam groaned and flung herself back onto the dog bed dramatically. Whimpering, the dog opened one eye to squint at her owner.

Jillian rolled her eyes at Sam's theatrical display. "Sorry, Sam, but I can't wind down. There's too much to do."

Sam snorted and extended her front paws to the floor, crawling across the cushioned bed until all four feet were on the gleaming wood. Stretching, she let out a huge yawn and smacked her lips together before padding off to the kitchen where Jillian kept the water bowl. Her loud lapping and the resulting bubble of air rising in the large reservoir as Sam drank echoed through the empty apartment.

Jillian opened her cell phone screen and scrolled through her contacts until she found Carl's number. Sending him a text, she set the phone down on the table and went into the bathroom. As she came out, Sam gave a single *woof* to let Jillian know she was ready for her before-bed walk.

"Give me a minute," Jillian mumbled.

Sam chuffed like a dissatisfied client, slunk back into the hallway, and disappeared. The dog bed in the living room let out air as Sam threw herself down and groaned loud enough to be heard in the bedroom. Jillian shook her head and was pulling her socks on when her cell phone buzzed loudly.

Sprinting to the living room, the display was lit up with a message from Carl. *What's up?*

Her thumbs flew across the smartphone keyboard as she answered the forensic lab technician. *I need your help. Can you meet me at CPD?* She hit send and waited, eyes locked on the screen.

Carl answered seconds later. *Now?*

It's urgent. Please?

A frowning emoji appeared, then, *Give me thirty?*

Jillian smiled, so thankful that Carl hadn't even asked for an explanation. All that mattered to Carl was that she'd said it was important. *See you then*, she responded, grabbed Sam's leash, and hurried to put her shoes on. Jillian debated feeding Sam a light meal since there was no telling when she would return. Sam would be far more content with a full belly.

As soon as the kibble hit Sam's stainless-steel bowl, the Lab was wolfing it down, tail swinging happily at her unexpected fortune.

Jillian patted the dog's rump affectionately. "Having your schedule disrupted isn't that bad, is it?" Jillian laughed and ducked into the bathroom to brush her teeth and tie her hair into a loose bun. By the time she came out, Sam was at the water dish again.

Taking Sam outside on her leash, Jillian was careful not to let the apartment door slam. The walls in the Kline family's luxury apartment building weren't as thin as the apartment building Jillian had lived in before, but she liked her new neighbors and didn't want to disturb anyone. Five minutes later, after Sam finished her routine in record time, she was dozing on her large dog bed in the living room.

Jillian headed to her car with her bag slung over her shoulder, her eyes darting from side to side. Nearby, Ellie's parking space was empty, and she didn't like it. Until she called, Jillian would have no way of knowing if everything was okay.

Or if her best friend was being held captive somewhere, alone and scared.

Jillian shivered, breaking stride and easing into a jog. Her footsteps echoed off the concrete, and for a moment, she felt completely and utterly alone as she got into her car and locked the doors. Hurriedly pulling onto the dark Charleston street, she hoped her mission would rid her of the eerie mood that engulfed her like thick fog creeping in from the ocean.

State Street was empty, every light between her and the turn onto Broad Street green. What should've filled her with joy brought more dread. Focusing on the soft glow of lights on inside the old stately homes, Jillian glanced longingly at her favorite donut shop as she drove past. A coffee and doughnut would hit the spot, but they didn't open until four a.m. She'd have to settle for breakroom coffee, and whatever day-old pastry was left at Charleston PD. Her stomach rumbled in protest.

There were only two cars at the far end of the lined parking spaces when she turned into the CPD lot. They were the same two cars that were always leaving when she normally arrived before six, and she knew they belonged to two longtime janitors with friendly smiles that masked their exhaustion. How they cleaned the entire building in just eight hours was anyone's guess, but every morning Jillian was welcomed to work by the scent of lemon cleaner and the squeak of clean tile. She was glad they were still there. She didn't want to be in the building alone.

Bright headlights appeared at the entrance of the precinct parking lot as she slid into her space. She froze and held her breath, but the car turned in, Carl's familiar face visible in the driver's window. She grabbed her things and waited for him on the sidewalk, flashing him a bright smile when he got out of his car.

"Thank you for coming in after hours. I can't tell you how much I appreciate you. I'm sorry I interrupted your evening."

He shrugged as they walked to the precinct doors. "No worries. I wasn't doing anything important, anyway. Just watching ESPN. So, what's so urgent it couldn't wait until morning?"

Jillian used her badge to unlock the side door. "Let's talk in your office."

Carl took the door handle and held it open for her, gesturing for her to enter first. "After you."

They walked the rest of the way in silence, heading down the corridor that led to a wing of mini labs. The building was quiet and empty save for the janitors who worked their way down the tiled corridors behind industrial mops that cleaned a day's worth of foot traffic. The officers patrolling overnight wouldn't return until at least six. For now, Jillian and Carl practically had the entire building to themselves.

Inside one of the labs, Carl closed the door to his private workspace behind Jillian and pulled the blinds. "I'm assuming whatever this is, it's off the record?"

"For now, please."

He made a motion as if zipping his lips.

"Thank you, Carl. I knew I could count on you." She fished the notes from Katarina's call out of her bag and spread them on Carl's desk. "A call came into the tip line tonight. Decker transferred it to Ellie's personal cell phone."

"Is that standard procedure?"

Jillian shook her head. "No, but the caller wouldn't talk to anyone but Ellie." Her eyes widened as a dark thought occurred to her. "Decker transferring the call didn't give the caller access to Ellie's personal cell number, did it?"

Carl shook his head. "That's not how it works."

"Good. I didn't even think of that until now."

"If that was a concern, I would have something in place to prevent it." Carl grinned, rubbing his chest with one thumb. "That's why they pay me the big bucks."

Jillian rolled her eyes. "All right, I admit it, you're amazing, and you're a whiz with technology. That's why I'm here. I was hoping you could trace the call. She gave us a name, and she was involved in a previous case, but we could never trace her or how she fits into Ellie's kidnapping."

Carl's eyes widened. "The tip was about Ellie's kidnapping?"

Jillian nodded. "You should've heard this woman. She was *enjoying* taunting Ellie."

"Are you sure the call was legit?"

"Ellie is." Jillian shuddered, rubbing her arms instinctively as goose bumps rose, even though she wasn't cold. "I don't know what to think, but the woman knew so much."

Carl nodded his understanding and turned to his computer. His fingers flew over the keyboard. Turning the screen toward her, he said, "Only one call came into the public tip line after six. It lasted fifteen minutes."

"That's it."

Carl nodded as he typed the number in on CPD's secure database. "The phone is prepaid, so that's a dead end. No surprise there." There was a soft chime, and a dialogue box popped up on the screen. Carl's eyes widened. "But the burner phone is in our database."

Jillian leaned forward, eyes narrowed as she scanned the text on the screen. "Why is it in our…" She gasped. "Oh. Katarina Volkov. Confidential informant for Detective Jones. Oh boy."

"His name keeps coming up."

"Yes, it does." Jillian pointed at the screen. "What else do you have on her?"

Carl used the mouse to click on her name, frowning when the screen changed. "This is weird."

"That's a pretty small file for an informant. The case number will help." She jotted down the number.

"That's what I was thinking." He scowled, tried to click a few disabled links, and shook his head. "I've only ever seen this happen one other time."

"When?"

"A few years ago. A fraud case that stretched from New York down to Atlanta. The informant was picked up and charged with a host of felonies, then their file was locked down, and they were in the wind. I brought it to Captain Browning, and he told me some criminals are more useful to us on the streets." He shook his head. "I never looked at anything the same after that. This guy was a really bad man, and bodies were piling up, but he was a small fish compared to the people he worked for."

Jillian frowned at the screen, the now familiar anger swelling in her chest. "Justice isn't always just."

"I'm sorry I can't get you more."

Jillian smiled at him, thankful for his help and what he

did find. "This is more than I had, and more than I could've gotten with my clearance. Thank you."

"I'll keep this between us."

"I appreciate that." She grabbed her things and hurried to her office, surprised that the hallways were still quiet and empty. She was so wired now, there was no way she could go home and go to bed. Besides, she had work to do.

She used her code to unlock the door and fired up her computer. Typing in the case number from Katarina's file, she noted the hard copy's location and retrieved it. The cool touch of the metal chair seeped through the thin fabric of her slacks as she sat at the nearest table and laid the contents of the file out in front of her. Ellie's familiar handwriting on the police report caught her attention, but she wasn't surprised.

Katarina and Ellie had a history, and now Jillian knew why.

When Ellie was a beat cop and had rescued young Harmony Jackson, witness cell phone videos had gone viral. From the moment the terrified little girl was pulled from the water until Ellie carried Harmony through the crowd, every harrowing moment was caught on tape. And when Ellie leapt off the dock and onto a boat to capture the fleeing kidnapper, all of Charleston had taken notice of the fearless police officer. Ellie Kline had been celebrated as a hero, and Katarina Volkov, or Katarina Wolf as she had been booked, was arrested for child trafficking.

Jillian's stomach clenched as she read through the file, making notes along the way.

Some criminals are more useful on the streets.

The words of Captain Browning that Carl had mentioned echoed in her head. That Katarina might be tied to the same group that had been operating in the deepest shadows of Charleston made sense. Even before Ellie had found the link between Charleston's elite—Detective Jones and a prolific trafficking ring operating on the dark web—Captain Browning must have known there was something bigger than Harmony Jackson's attempted kidnapping.

What else was he hiding?

Jillian flipped through the pages, reading the terms of release written by the assistant district attorney. Katarina had taken a plea deal and was given a light sentence that was little more than a slap on the wrist. Six months with credit for time served for selling a little girl to a couple with a shady past. She had served three short weeks before striking a deal and was released two days later.

Jillian glared at the paper, anger building at the two-word explanation for her early release. *Prison overcrowding.* It was an excuse often used to give special privileges to wealthy socialites and prominent businessmen.

And Jillian knew it was a damn lie.

Katarina had been released because her freedom served some higher purpose, according to the assistant district attorney. But there was no telling how many lives had been destroyed by Katarina. It sounded like she was a player in the circle of evil that kidnapped and sold kids and young adults like commodities, and the people sworn to protect the citizens of Charleston had signed off on it.

Suddenly, Ellie's willingness to believe that even Nick could be involved in the conspiracy didn't seem so paranoid.

21

E llie pulled off the highway, turning down the narrow road that wound its way through a dense wooded area. When the pavement ended and her tires crunched on gravel, she slowed, squinting into the dark and watching for any wildlife that might dart across the road.

The last light of day had faded long before she got to the private cabin on the lake. As she came around a bend, a fat raccoon lumbered down the side of the driveway. Accustomed to the relative safety of the rural area, the animal glanced over its shoulder when Ellie's headlights spotlighted him and stopped to pick up some treasure without a second look at the vehicle.

At such a slow speed, the gravel drive seemed to stretch on forever, but Ellie didn't want to give herself away. At least, not yet. Going into the situation blind, she had no idea what she would find when she arrived.

She'd almost called Flynn to let him know she was coming, but her paranoia had gotten the better of her. Though she'd handpicked his organization, there were no guarantees. So, she'd donned her bulletproof vest and grabbed her gun, using a light jacket to hide both. Just in case.

She almost missed the house in the distance, until the silver glint of moonlight glancing off the second story window caught her attention. The entire house was dark. Not even the gentle glow of a hallway nightlight reached the black windowpanes.

Her heart raced as she gripped the steering wheel tighter and willed her breathing to slow. They could just be asleep. It was late enough for that. But turning off all the lights?

There were no cars out in the open to help her guess how many people were in the house. The garage, which was at the back, ran the length of the building and could hold at least four cars.

Could they be gone?

Her heart ricocheted into her throat.

Going in blind was an understatement.

It was too late to kill her headlights, and she decided against it in the same breath. Hiding her arrival would look suspicious. It was better for whoever was inside the house to assume that she was coming for a visit, even if it was disrespectfully late at night by Southern standards.

She parked in the open, turning the car so the passenger side was between her and the house. When she got out, she leaned against the closed driver's side door and checked her gun in the fading interior light before it shut off and left her in darkness.

Scanning the yard as she made her way toward the house, Ellie kept her right hand near her pocket, fingers wrapped around her service weapon.

Her right foot had just left the ground, to take the first step up onto the porch, when the hair on the back of her neck stood on end. Ellie dropped to her knee and spun, using the shrubs neatly planted near the porch to guard her back.

A figure moved in the darkness.

"Hands up," she demanded, raising her weapon and getting a bead on the dark shadow.

The man raised his hands immediately, the shadows cast by the house hiding his face from the moonlight. "Don't shoot."

As soon as he spoke, Ellie knew who he was. "Nick? What are you doing here?" Still, she kept her weapon steady.

He tilted his head to the side in question, hands in the air. "Why are you still pointing your gun at me, Ellie? It's me, Nick."

"I know."

He sucked in a quick breath. "What's going on?"

"You first. Why are you here?"

"I got a call."

Her throat tightened. "A call?"

"Y-yes," he sputtered. "Put that damn thing down. Ellie, what's wrong with you?"

She forced down the emotions that threatened to guilt her into doing as he said. "Who called you?"

"I don't know. A woman. She said it was urgent. That you were with Valerie and in danger."

Ellie flicked her gaze to the house, keeping her weapon aimed at Nick's chest.

"Valerie is fine." To his credit, Nick hadn't even shifted. "I've been here for almost an hour. Flynn said everything has been quiet."

"Then why are you still here?"

Nick let out an exasperated breath. "Because it's late, Ellie, and I don't want to drive home. It is my cabin, you know?"

Ellie's hands dropped a fraction, holding the gun before she raised the weapon again. "Where's Flynn?"

"He put Valerie back in the safe room until we were sure

it was you." He took a step forward. "Ellie, put the weapon down."

Footsteps drew her attention to the front door. The screen door edged open, and Flynn stepped onto the porch with his phone screen illuminated. "Ellie, what's going on?"

Ellie turned to Nick then back to Flynn. Her shoulders slumped, and she shook her head. "Someone's playing games."

Nick lowered his hands but didn't move closer. "Ellie, who was that woman on the phone?"

Flynn shifted his weight to his other foot and opened the screen wide. "Whatever it is, no one is safe out here in the open. Let's talk inside. Zeke will keep the perimeter safe while we sort this out."

"After you." Nick gestured toward the door, his perfect Southern gentleman charm turned up, as if she were a stranger.

Ellie holstered her weapon but kept her hand near her waistband as she went into the cabin.

Flynn left the lights off as he led them to the bedroom in the center of the house. It was the only room without windows. Behind the closet door, Ellie knew the panic room was surprisingly big and well stocked in case of emergencies.

Flynn leaned forward and spoke quietly in Zeke's ear. The other man nodded and slipped silently away, closing the door behind him. Flynn turned the bolt and dropped a heavy blanket in front of the gap beneath the door before turning on the light. The deadbolt was shiny and obviously newly installed. Flynn stayed near the door, leaning against the wall with a grim look on his face as his eyes went to Nick and back to Ellie.

"Now," he said after a long silence. "Let's talk about what the hell is going on."

"I got a call tonight." Nick turned to Ellie, his expression tight. Guarded. "The woman didn't give me a chance to ask questions. She said that there were men heading here to hurt Valerie."

"Why didn't you call me?" Ellie folded her arms over her chest. "And are you sure you weren't followed here?"

"Yes, and I tried to call you. Your phone went straight to voicemail. When I couldn't get ahold of you, I came straight here. I didn't want to waste time going all the way to your house first. The woman said you were already on your way."

"I was. I doubled back a few times to make sure I wasn't being followed, so it took longer than it would have."

"I tried to call several times." Nick frowned at her, his jaw ticking.

"She must've called you after I turned my phone off." Both men blinked in surprise, so Ellie rushed to explain. "I didn't want anyone tracking me through the GPS."

"Okay, then why didn't you call *me* first? Or Flynn?"

She pursed her lips, but before she could try to explain, a look passed between the two men.

Nick shook his head, his face darkening with rage. "You didn't trust us." His voice was quiet as he flung his hands into the air. Dropping them to his sides, fists balled up, he began to pace. "Damnit, Ellie, what's happened to you? I can't believe this. It's one thing to suspect someone you hired, but me?" His volume rose with every word. "Me? Ellie, we've known each other since we were *kids*. What the hell?"

"I'm sorry."

Nick stopped pacing, his eyebrows shooting upward. "You're *sorry*? Are you serious? Ellie, you held a gun on me. I've supported you when no one else did, and I've suffered through this paranoia since you made detective last year. But this? Ellie, this is too much. If you can't trust me, what are we even doing?" He shook his head, blue eyes welling with emotion.

Ellie's heart clenched, the weight of his pain more than she could bear. "It's not like that. This criminal enterprise reaches farther than I'd ever imagined. It's not that I don't trust you."

He scoffed. "Right. It's just that you thought I was here to hurt Valerie because you got a tip? That doesn't make this better, Ellie."

Flynn pushed away from the wall, his hands held out. "It's late, and there's been a lot of excitement. You're both exhausted, and whoever this woman is, she's obviously playing some kind of game. I think we should table this conversation until tomorrow." He glanced at his watch. "Go home and get some rest."

Ellie stiffened. "I'm not leaving. And I'm not exhausted."

"Bullshit," Nick shot back. "You have dark circles under your eyes. It's obvious you haven't been sleeping lately. Are you having nightmares again?"

She lifted her chin. "I don't want to talk about this right now. Where's Valerie?"

"She's in the panic room. It's probably best that she stay there until you two sort…whatever this is, out." Flynn shook his head. "And the time for that is not now. Zeke and I will keep watch, then Ellie, if you insist on staying, you can take a shift in the morning while we get some rest."

"If Ellie isn't leaving, I'm not either." Nick glared at her.

A muscle in Flynn's jaw leaped with tension. "Great. Nick, you can take a shift. Then, when everyone is calmer, we'll talk about this."

Nick snorted, stuffing his hands into his pockets. "It won't change anything. She doesn't trust me. You can't come back from that."

Flynn's voice was level, completely unbothered by Nick's outburst. "You both need to cool down. We'll talk about this in the morning."

"Whatever." Nick gestured to the door. "Can you unlock it? I need to get some things out of my car." His glare returned to Ellie. "I'm sure there's a spare room you can make use of. We'll talk later."

He left as soon as Flynn opened the door, angry footsteps heavy as he went down the hall.

When he was gone, Ellie let out a shuddering breath. "Thank you. That wasn't going anywhere good."

"You both need to cool down, and he's right, you need rest. It'll be easier to sleep soundly with us watching your back."

She pursed her lips and nodded, wondering briefly if she should have just brought Jillian with her. If Katarina didn't know where Valerie was, and she obviously didn't, and neither of them had been followed...

But she couldn't even text Jillian, not without giving away her location to anyone who might be monitoring her phone. "I wish Nick could brush it off so easily."

"You can't blame him." Flynn shrugged one shoulder. "You're a client, and I appreciate you being smart enough to be suspicious of anyone and everyone, but Nick is your boyfriend. People outside the business rarely understand that paranoia saves lives."

Ellie let out a bark of angry laughter. "If only he could hear you say that and realize that it's not a reflection of him."

"Get some rest. Things will be clearer in the morning."

BUT FLYNN WAS WRONG.

By the time Ellie woke up, it was nearly lunchtime, and Nick's bed showed no signs of having been used. On top of the blanket, he'd scrawled a quick, angry note. *We'll talk later. I'll call you.*

Ellie held the note in her hands, dropping onto the edge of the bed as angry tears burned her eyes. Nick had never been this mad, and she didn't blame him for being hurt. In his place, she would be angry too.

Flynn and Zeke were quiet as she made her way to the kitchen.

Valerie gave her a warm smile and hugged her tight. "It's going to be okay."

Ellie nodded, biting her lip to stem the flow of fresh, hot tears that threatened. She turned to Flynn. "Do you need me to watch the perimeter so you can rest?"

He shook his head. "Nick relieved us for a few hours after you went to bed. He couldn't sleep."

"When did he leave?"

"Around nine this morning. I thought it would be better to let you sleep."

"I wish you would've let me make that decision for myself." Ellie's tone was snippy, but she didn't apologize.

Flynn didn't react to her snark. "You're at a disadvantage if you're exhausted. I don't know what that woman was up to, but clearly something."

"He's right," Valerie offered. "I don't want you to get hurt because of me."

Ellie's anger dissipated as she looked into Valerie's worried eyes. "This isn't your fault. You were just a little kid when I was kidnapped."

"So were you." Valerie's smile was soft, blue eyes filled with sadness. "Fifteen is just a baby. You didn't deserve what happened to you, and you don't deserve what's going on now."

"Thank you." Ellie sighed. "Except, the only thing that's actually happened is that my boyfriend is pissed at me, and we're sitting here with no idea what the next move is."

"It's only noon."

"Thanks, Flynn. That helps."

Flynn smiled sheepishly, shrugging. "I'm just saying. Don't let your guard down just yet. Maybe you should stay here."

Ellie shook her head. "It's Friday. At some point, I need to call my superior officer and let him know I'm not dead."

Valerie gestured at the fridge. "Can I make you some food before you go? It's been forever since I've seen anyone but Zeke and Flynn."

Ellie smiled as she realized she might be witnessing the Valerie she'd been before she was kidnapped. Had she been the one who always fed her friends? "I'll take a sandwich to go. I have to be getting back."

Valerie opened the fridge and pulled out cheese and sliced turkey.

Flynn caught Ellie's eye, nodded toward the bedrooms, and Ellie followed him to the hallway. "You need to be careful. It's clear that woman was trying to throw you out of your routine for whatever reason."

"I agree."

"I'd feel better if you'd stay here."

Ellie pushed her hair back from her face, using the elastic around her wrist to keep it in place. "I need to get home, get to work. I won't solve anything sitting out here."

"If you change your mind, call first. I know we're all going to be on edge until the trial is over."

She eyed the large man who seemed poised to snap anyone in half who threatened Valerie. "If this is you on edge, I'd hate to see you calm."

Flynn laughed. "I can be both at the same time. Take care of yourself. Do you have a vest?"

Ellie nodded at her go-bag. "You think I should suit up now?"

Flynn looked deadly serious when he nodded. "Vests and as many guns as you have."

Realizing he was right to take the precautions, Ellie opened her bag and pulled on the vest before covering it with an oversized shirt she always carried. Next, she added her ankle and hip holsters, checking each gun to make sure the chambers were filled.

She was ready for whatever came her way. She hoped.

Flynn looked relieved. "Valerie is fond of you, and she'd be devastated if anything happened to you. She's already lost so much."

"I know."

"I'll walk you to your car."

Valerie appeared seconds later with a sandwich, a sparkling fruit juice, and a hug. "Be careful."

"I will."

Valerie pulled away, eyes brimming with tears. She cleared her throat and walked back into the kitchen without another word.

Ellie let Flynn give the all-clear before she went outside, using the remote start button on the key fob to start the engine while she was still a safe distance away. When the car didn't go *boom*, she relaxed and rolled her head on her shoulders to alleviate some more of the tension.

Flynn smiled. "Smart woman. I'd suggest using that feature from now on, if I'm being honest."

"I think you're right."

Getting into the vehicle, Ellie waved once before heading down the driveway and into the woods. She was on high alert, watching the tree-lined shoulder for signs of danger, and didn't relax until she was twenty minutes away, down the winding two-lane road and merging onto the highway. When she'd gone past several exits, she rubbed her shoulder, which she hadn't realized had been so tense that she was now sore.

She was finally far enough away from the safe house to call Jillian without giving away Valerie's location. She'd already disabled the GPS just in case, though she knew it wouldn't do her much good if she was already being tracked. But Jillian had probably spent the night wondering if Ellie and Valerie were all right, and it wasn't right to make her wait longer.

Fishing her cell out of her purse, she used her thumb to hit the button on the side. The phone powered on, loading all the default apps, and finally prompted her for a passcode. Without taking her eyes off the road, she slid her index finger onto the sensor, and the phone unlocked. As soon as her Bluetooth connected, she dialed Jillian's number and held her breath.

Jillian answered on the first ring. "Boy am I glad to hear from you."

"Is Fortis pissed?"

Jillian chuckled like an evil conspirator. "I told him you were sick. He started to call you, and I gave him a song and dance about a stomach virus keeping you up all night. And that I might have to take you to the doctor."

"How did he take that?"

"He told me not to come back after lunch, and to make sure you had everything you needed."

Ellie smiled, a soft laugh escaping. "Thank you for covering for me. Where are you now?"

"Leaving the office." Jillian lowered her voice. "Ellie, is something wrong?"

Ellie let out a long breath. "Everything is fine. But when I went to the safe house, Nick was there, and he realized that I suspected him and..." Her voice caught, and she cleared her throat. "He's not too happy."

"But why was he there?"

"Katarina apparently called him right after she called me. Since I'd turned off my phone already, he went straight to the safe house and arrived before I did."

"She's up to something."

Ellie's hands tightened on the steering wheel, her stomach tied in knots with worry. "I know, but I don't know what. Valerie is safe. Nick left, but I'm sure he'll be fine."

"What about your family? Do you think she wanted you to leave so they would be vulnerable? Have you called to check on them?"

At the mention of her family, Ellie's heart rate quickened. Her father's health was better in the months since the heart transplant, but she still worried about him. And she'd never been quite able to shake the idea that his poor health was her fault. After all, he'd had the stroke that led to a heart attack because of her kidnapping.

She was just glad they'd recently decided that twenty-four-hour protection was a necessary part of life in the public eye. It saved her from having to tell them that her life was in danger, and possibly theirs too. Again.

Ellie let out the breath that had started burning her lungs. "I haven't called yet, but I don't think this has anything to do with them. Going after my parents would be too high-risk. They've had security on the payroll since before my birthday party last month. Flynn's group is the best, and as long as they're at my parents' home, I have no reason to worry."

"I still can't shake the feeling that Katarina didn't call just to mess with your head. There has to be a reason. Keep your eyes open, okay?"

"You're right." Ellie turned up the heat in the car, suddenly chilled. "Waiting for the other shoe to drop has me on edge, but I promise I won't let my guard down."

"All right, well, get home quick."

"I'm fine."

Jillian laughed, but there was very little joy in the sound. "I'm sure you are, but I'm so tired, I can't think. I have news. You won't believe it. And Sam's been home alone since last night. I ended up pulling an all-nighter. After being elbow deep in case files all night, I've about got the creeps. The sooner we both get home, the better I'll feel."

"You and me both." If Jillian had news she was holding back until they were face to face, it had something significant to do with either Valerie or the human trafficking case.

"Hold on," Jillian said. "I'm going to put you on my Bluetooth."

Ellie pressed her foot down on the accelerator, wondering if she'd wasted precious time sleeping in like a lazy child.

Her fingertips tingled on the steering wheel, the same sensation awakening in her gut.

Something was wrong.

Today was Friday the thirteenth. Thirteen years since she'd found out monsters were real.

22

Walking briskly across the CPD parking lot, Jillian unlocked her car and threw her bag onto the passenger seat as she fumbled with the Bluetooth. When she had it in her ear, she connected her phone and set it in the cupholder, snapping it into the locking clip.

"I'm back." She turned the key in the ignition and put the car in reverse to back out of her parking spot.

"So, did you and Carl find anything we can use on Katarina?" Ellie said in her ear.

"She was a confidential informant for Jones, and she wasn't lying about knowing you. You two have quite the history."

"History?"

Jillian smiled, looking both ways before she turned onto the street. "Does the name Harmony Jackson ring a bell?"

Ellie gasped. "Oh my gosh, did Katarina have something to do with that little girl being kidnapped? Why don't I recognize her name?"

"She used an alias when she was arrested."

"Karina Wolf," they said in unison.

Ellie was silent for a moment. "But where does she fit in with Valerie?"

"That's the million-dollar question. Katarina exchanged information for a lighter sentence, among other things."

Ellie groaned. "I knew she pled out to avoid a trial, but I never learned the details. You know how it is when you're on patrol; we catch them, and the courts take it from there."

"No one expects you to keep tabs on every collar you ever made, Ellie."

Ellie let out an exasperated breath. "I know that, but Harmony was special." Her voice caught, and when she spoke again, anger vibrated through the speaker. "What kind of information could a kidnapper have that's more important than her victim getting justice?"

Jillian tsked. "I would like to know."

"Do we know where Harmony was going to be taken?"

"No. Katarina was never asked to divulge that information, or if she was, it wasn't put into any of the reports. But the important thing for Harmony is that you followed your instincts, and now she's safe with her family, where she belongs." Jillian grinned, putting on her blinker to cut through a residential street and avoid a little traffic. "It was a pretty sensational morning, with you diving into the bay to save a kid's life, though no match for the felon crying over the river turtle."

Ellie chuckled at the mention of the chase that had ended up with a perpetrator almost drowning them both when he mistook a turtle for an alligator.

"I guess that video never gets old. Hard to believe that was a year ago. It was my first day with Jacob Garcia as my partner." Ellie was quiet for a moment, and Jillian glanced at the phone screen, sure the call had dropped, but they were still connected. "What's wrong?"

There was a long pause before Ellie finally said one word, "Nick."

"I'm sorry about that. You're right to be paranoid, but I don't blame him for being hurt." Jillian frowned, fatigue weighing heavily on her as she made her way through congested streets. "I would be devastated in his place."

"I know, and I feel awful. The look in his eyes. I don't think I'll ever forget how much pain I caused him. He's been my biggest supporter. When my parents were scheming to get me to quit the academy, he was cheering me on."

"Do you think he'll accept your apology when he calms down?"

"I don't know," Ellie mumbled.

Jillian checked her blind spot and switched to the left lane. As soon as she was over, the right lane started moving, and the left lane stopped. She slapped the steering wheel. It figured. "Why don't you call him?"

"He basically told me not to."

"Ouch."

"I don't know what I'm going to do."

The despair in Ellie's voice tore at her heart. Desperate to offer her friend some hope, she tried to sound upbeat. "You'll figure it out. He just needs a little space."

"That's the problem." Ellie gave a sarcastic laugh. "I think he's been getting more space than he can handle."

"When was the last time you two went anywhere together?"

"The day we moved Valerie to the safe house."

Jillian's eyes widened. "That's not good."

"I know."

"Look, there's nothing you can do about it now." She checked to her right, putting on her blinker in hopes of getting back over. The car just behind her rear fender in the other lane rolled down their window. Jillian smiled, sure they were going to wave her in. They extended their middle finger instead. She sneered, fighting off the urge to sling one back. "Traffic is a mess."

"It's lunchtime."

"I know, I'm starved. I'm just so tired. I forgot about the noon rush hour."

Although Ellie's laugh was soft, it was heavy with sadness. It was the first time since Jillian had answered the phone that there'd been more than frustration in her friend's voice. "You know better."

"How far are you?"

"I should be home a little after one."

The tension melted from Jillian's shoulders. "Good. I couldn't relax last night, wondering if you were okay, so I worked through the night. I should've gone with you."

"Sam needed you."

Jillian snorted out a laugh. "I think Sam is probably a basket case by now wondering where we both are. She probably thinks she's been abandoned."

"As if you would ever abandon that precious hunk of dog. You should get her something special to make up for it."

"Maybe tomorrow." Jillian yawned, waving when the middle-fingered driver was even with her. He flipped her off again, so Jillian blew him a kiss. "I'm over today. Friday the thirteenth is not my favorite day." Realizing what she'd just said, Jillian thunked her forehead with her palm. "I'm sorry, I wasn't thinking."

"It's all right. It's just another day, and we all know people bring out the crazy."

"You're not wrong." Jillian ignored the angry man, who was gesturing wildly, trying to get her attention through the closed window. "Listen, traffic is a mess, so I'd better let you go. I'll see you soon."

"All right. And Jillian?"

"Yes?"

"Thanks for being there, even when my paranoia is pushing everyone else away."

Jillian's heart cracked open and gushed out warmth that made her eyes prick. "It's going to be okay, Ellie. We'll get everyone involved in the trafficking ring, and they'll see that you weren't being paranoid at all. When the dust settles, Nick will let go of his hurt feelings and forgive you."

"And if he doesn't?"

"We'll cross that bridge when we get there. I'll talk to you when you get home."

Jillian ended the call, rolling up to a red light. The angry driver made one last-ditch effort to get her attention before he spun his tires and turned right on the red without stopping. Horns blared, but he escaped without causing an accident. Relieved that he was finally gone, Jillian turned on the radio and did her best to stay awake. She was close to home, and if the traffic ever let up, she'd be there in minutes.

She glanced at the clock and groaned. It was half past noon, and she was running on zero sleep. She was exhausted and starving and wanted nothing more than to eat and crawl into bed, in that order. Skipping lunch and sleeping until Sunday sounded even better, but her stomach growled, twisting painfully. Three cups of coffee and one stale donut wouldn't hold her over forever.

Bemoaning her traitorous body, she went through the green light and turned into the first hamburger joint with a drive-thru she came to. She ordered a cheeseburger and fries, opting for a caffeinated cola instead of her standard ice water. She paid for her order and took a long drag of the fizzy drink, wrinkling her nose when the carbonation tickled her nostrils.

Fifteen minutes and one ridiculously long Friday lunch line later, she was back on the street. She sneaked one hot

French fry from the brown paper bag, then another, eyes going to the clock again. Quarter to one. A smile spread across her face. Even though her car clock was set to standard time, she still thought of one in the afternoon as thirteen hundred hours. It was how her father had taught her to tell time, and it was a hard habit to break.

"If you use military time, you don't have to say a.m. or p.m.," her father had said with a satisfied snort. "Saves time, and everyone understands exactly what you mean. You ever heard someone get confused by twelve? Is it at night, or at lunch? It's asinine is what it is."

Jillian smiled at the memory of her late father lamenting about the inefficiency of civilian time measurement. It had been one of his most common complaints, even twenty years after he'd retired. He was bullheaded and brass, with a heart of solid gold and a gift for turning anything into a dirty joke.

He would've loved Ellie.

A pet store on the right side of the street caught her eye. Tempted to skip it, she thought of Sam waiting patiently for someone to come home to walk her and decided Ellie was right. Sam deserved an extra treat, and the snarled line of cars wasn't going to get better in the next few minutes anyway.

She pulled into the parking lot and got out, eating the last of her fries and rolling the bag up so her burger didn't get cold. "I'll just be a minute," she said out loud. Grabbing her purse, she yawned and stepped out into the warm sun, arming her car. A quick run through the store would wake her up, and Sam would appreciate a special treat. It was a detour that would make them both feel better.

She skipped the carts, heading straight for the aisle that held the massive bones, treats, and colorful toys. Zeroing in on the largest bone, she grabbed it and a box of hamburger-patty-shaped treats. The line was short, and she was back in her car a few minutes later and on the road again. To avoid the bumper to bumper traffic, she took a lesser known route, breathing a sigh of relief at the much lighter traffic.

Her mind wandered as she drove, wondering at Nick's presence at the safe house. She hadn't wanted to ask Ellie about it when she was so upset, but Jillian was suspicious of Nick's sudden appearance there.

Sure, he had a right to be upset at Ellie's suspicions, but his reaction could be genuine, or a way to cover up his guilt. Jillian didn't know Nick well enough to decide which it was. On the surface, everything Ellie had told her seemed legit enough, but there were people who made a hell of a living convincing others that they were sincere. His explanation had sounded like a trip into downtown to check on Ellie would've wasted precious time, but he hadn't even tried to call Jillian. She was sure of it.

Desperate to hear from Ellie, Jillian had checked her phone every five minutes all night. It seemed odd that he would think to save time going to the safe house first, when Jillian had given him her phone number after Ellie had been shot last year, and it had never occurred to him to use it.

He knows I live with Ellie, she thought, scowling. In the same scenario, if she'd called Ellie's phone and got just voice-mail, Jillian would have immediately called Nick. It just seemed like the natural—

The world exploded into a tremendous crash.

A cacophony of sounds.

Tires squealing.

Glass shattering. Spraying.

Tiny tempered shards pelted the skin on the right side of her face and arm.

Head flying to the left, her teeth clanked together as her head connected with the driver's side window. A cloud of white exploded in the same instant, slapping her in the cheek. Her skin burned as a car horn—hers?—loud and constant, drowned out the rush of blood in her ears.

Blinking, Jillian fought to keep her head upright as the airbag deflated and powder filled the air, making her cough.

The car shook, and she winced, pain radiating through her body as she turned her head.

The grill of a large SUV untangled itself from the mangled passenger door as the driver backed up.

She coughed again, tiny droplets of blood spraying onto the limp airbag.

I'm hurt.

Her mind raced as she tried to collect her scattered thoughts. But her head was pounding, and she struggled just to focus on her surroundings.

A hand reached through the driver's window, shoving the gear shift into park. Turning the key, a man with elegant gray at his temples cut the engine and turned it back so the radio and dashboard lights came back on.

Jillian watched him, unable to understand what he was doing. Turning her head slowly, she was trying to figure out how he had reached through her closed window when she remembered she'd busted it with her own head.

"My name is Jillian Reed." Her voice was distant, weak. Automatically, her right hand began searching the center console where her cell phone was securely mounted so it could be found in an accident. A precaution most people never thought to take. Her fingers touched the familiar plastic as her door opened, and someone leaned across her, taking her phone. "My roommate's number is stored in the contacts." Her speech was slurred, her head drumming, and her eyes growing heavy. "The unlock code is nine two…I can't…remember. Jillian. Jillian Reed from the—"

"I know who you are, Jillian Reed." He held the phone in

front of her face so she could see it. "You won't be needing this."

She frowned, sending fresh pain through her head. "What?"

"She's hurt pretty bad." It was a different voice, coming from the mouth of an angel. A gorgeous, dark haired angel.

"Put her in the back of the SUV."

Jillian shook her head, then remembered not to move too much, closing her eyes against the pain. "No. Don't move me. I could be seriously injured. The paramedics—"

"Won't be here before we're gone." The older man laughed.

Jillian forced her eyes open, but the world was fuzzy. The dark angel appeared beside her, but her neck was stiff now, and she couldn't turn her head. Strong arms slid under her, lifting her out of the mangled car. Broken glass crunched beneath the angel's shoes while the first man urged him to hurry.

"The street won't stay empty."

"I don't want to hurt her," the angel said.

The older man scoffed. "She's not important. Toss her in the back, and let's go."

This was wrong. So wrong. But she couldn't think exactly what was off. She tried to speak and pain shot through her head, making her whimper.

A car door opened, and Jillian was floating downward. She winced when her hip hit the seat. Then the strong arms were gone, her head snapped back, and she shrieked in pain. The door slammed shut, hitting her in the back and folding her into an uncomfortable position.

The engine roared as the driver tramped down on the accelerator.

Jillian fought the darkness that crept in around her, but she couldn't focus. Her vision was coming in chunks.

A graying head of hair in the driver's seat.

A face she couldn't place turning to look at her.

The angel.

Someone laughed. A laugh that could only be described as evil.

The black edging into her vision was winning, and her body melted lower into the cushion. The driver slammed the breaks, and she flew forward, slamming against the back of the seat.

"Hurry." The man was agitated.

Sirens in the background, but far away.

"Help." Jillian whimpered. "Ellie. What—"

"Ellie can't help you now," the older man said, sounding very pleased with himself.

Jillian blinked, trying to think through the pain. "You know Ellie?"

"Better than you do, apparently."

Jillian frowned, fighting to stay awake, but she was losing the battle. Laughter taunted her as she descended into the darkness, unsure where the pain that battered her body came from. Something hot oozed over her face and down her arms, and the pungent smell of metal filled the small space.

I'm bleeding.

Eyes closing, she fought to hold on.

Help.

It was her last thought before the darkness won.

23

The petite blonde hurried out of the pet store to her car, balancing a giant dog bone in one arm.

"Keep up with her," I said to Gabe, who drove the souped-up SUV I'd bought the day before. Reinforced and bulletproof, the windows were tinted just a hair shy of the legal limit, making it hard to see inside from any distance. It didn't matter. Although the main streets were busy with lunch time traffic, the blonde was smart and headed down a nearly deserted side street.

We'd been waiting for the perfect moment, and very soon, the time would change over into perfection. The thirteenth hour, on the thirteenth day, of the thirteenth year since Ellie slipped from my grasp.

"Got it." Gabe's slender hands gripped the wheel, tense with excitement. From my place in the back seat, I could see his knuckles turning white. He was ready, body positively humming with glee.

I leaned forward, breath coming quick with anticipation.

Gabe turned down a road that ran parallel to the one

Jillian was on, glancing quickly to the left at every inter-section.

"Speed up and turn up there."

"Yes, sir." He shoved the accelerator down. The SUV rushed forward, smooth as a luxury sedan, and surprisingly quiet.

I grinned, putting my seatbelt on.

Gabe took the left turn with expert precision and floored it, flying down the empty side street, the light ahead of us just turning red.

Perfect.

Gabe didn't slow down, his eyes locked on the road we were about to cross.

Jillian's car came into view, and a laugh of pure joy escaped me. She was looking straight ahead, oblivious to the monster machine barreling toward her crappy car.

I braced myself for impact seconds before the sound of twisting metal and breaking glass drowned out every other sound.

My chest connected with the taut seatbelt as I was thrown forward. My head collided with the doorframe, sending shooting pain down my neck as my head snapped back.

Gabe cried out, the seatbelt doing little to stop him from hitting the steering wheel. The airbags were disabled so we didn't waste valuable time waiting for them to deflate. I hadn't warned him about the missing airbags, thinking it better that he not know ahead of time. Stunned, he sat there for a moment, blinking away tears before shifting into reverse.

Nestled behind the seat in the SUV that was reinforced like a tank, I shook off a momentary wave of fog.

Gabe slammed the gearshift into park, and I unbuckled as

he left the engine running and raced toward Jillian's mangled mess of a car.

I followed, happy with the precision of the hit. The driver's door was largely untouched, broken glass the only noticeable sign of impact. The passenger side had taken the force of the crash, crumpling exactly as it was designed to and leaving Jillian's door usable.

Gabe's eyes flicked in my direction as I smiled and approached the car.

He opened her door and stepped out of my way. "The road's clear."

Knowing I could trust him to keep a lookout, I focused on Jillian. The airbag was a wrinkled mess of white fabric, a spot on her cheek already an angry red from the chemical that kept the material from cracking. Jillian's head was against the headrest, each exhalation a moan of delicious agony. Blood streamed over her cheek from a wound on the left side of her head where it had connected with the window. It had happened so fast, I wondered if she had any idea what had transpired.

"Still clear." Gabe's voice was thin and high, his excitement almost palpable.

My own breathing was ragged in my ears, but I savored the moment as Jillian's injury slowed her movements as she reached for her phone with maddeningly little progress. Licking my lips, I inhaled the sweet aroma of blood, motor oil, and fear.

"She's hurt pretty bad." Gabe, at my side, peered over the door at the woman.

"Put her in the back of the SUV," I snapped at him and stepped back, watching his strong arms as he slid them under her. He lifted Jillian out of the mangled car and held her against his chest. When he turned my way, the sight of him took my breath away.

I was transported back to the quiet room outside Detroit, the quivering man I'd purchased online in the cage. His curls fell over his forehead, eyes dark beneath thick lashes and perfectly shaped brows.

Broken glass crunched beneath Gabe's heavy work boots, snapping me back to reality. I blinked hard to clear my foggy vision. Gabe was watching me, his head tilted with concern. I opened the door behind the driver's seat, and Gabe rushed forward. He let Jillian roll out of his arms onto the seat, and I closed the door so she didn't fall back out. This time, I got into the driver's seat.

Confused, Gabe took half a beat to react, then ran around the car to the passenger side.

"Hurry," I ground out when Gabe paused with the door open as sirens shrieked in the distance. I couldn't chance anyone seeing us leave the scene.

Gabe jumped in, and I sped off before he could get his belt buckled. Jillian moaned from the back seat, and Gabe turned, frowning. "Is she going to be okay?"

I glared at Gabe. "It doesn't matter. I needed her phone more than I need her." I glanced in the mirror at her crumpled form, shrugging. "She'll probably be fine."

"Why her?"

It was the second time he'd asked. "Why not?" I said with a laugh.

He didn't respond. Sitting back in the passenger seat, his leg shook as fingers tapped on his slacks. I blinked, and he was the young man in the cage, holding on to the bars and staring out at me.

Cowering.

His hair, so soft-looking, complemented deep brown eyes that reminded me of...

"Gabe," I whispered. He opened his mouth to speak, but I held up my hand. "Your name is Gabe."

Tears sprung into his eyes, but he nodded. His mouth clamped shut, his jaw tightening even as he trembled. He was angelic, his brown skin radiant. Flawless.

My heart clenched, and my body stirred against my zipper. I wanted to reach out and squeeze the life out of him with my bare hands.

Soft whimpering from the back seat yanked me out of the memory. I glared at the woman's reflection in the rearview mirror, my mouth dry. Why was she back there? Who was she?

Ellie.

The name floated through my mind like an arctic breeze. The girl who'd escaped and nearly killed my Ernest. *She should've killed him.* My eyes went back to the unconscious woman in the back seat. Ellie had been rigid, her blood coursing with Ketamine, but the blonde in the back was soft and pliant, head wound oozing blood.

The damp streets glistened like oil in the night, the labored breathing of the fiery redhead in the back drawing my gaze. Each time we passed under a streetlamp, a bar of light ran across her face. Green eyes glared at me, her anger keeping her conscious though her body was frozen by the drugs racing through her veins. My pulse quickened, and I glanced at Ernest. His face was pinched, but when my eyes trailed down his body and settled on the crotch of his pants, I knew he was just as excited as I.

His eyes darted in my direction, then back on the road. "Why are her eyes still open?"

I shrugged. "She's paralyzed. That's all that matters." I chuckled, a thrill running through me. "Sleep is too merciful for what I have in mind."

A slow smile spread across his face. He licked his lips and sighed.

My hand went to his thigh, giving him a reassuring squeeze. "Soon, my pet. Be patient."

"Are you okay?"

I shook my head, blinking rapidly at the sound of Gabe's voice. "Of course."

"Where are we going?"

"The warehouse, Ernest."

He sucked in a startled breath, air whistling through clenched teeth. "Who is Ernest?"

A low buzzing filled my head, my eyes focusing an instant before the street ahead snapped me back to reality. I jerked the wheel just in time to avoid a parked car. Taking the next turn much slower, I smiled at a bewildered Gabe. "My old assistant. He's nobody now. Now that I have you."

"What happened to him?"

"He grew obsolete."

Gabe drew in another sharp breath, his brows furrowing in concern. "Is he alive?"

I shrugged. "Probably. I don't keep close tabs on him like I did before." I smiled, licking my lower lip. "He bores me."

Gabe nodded.

"I was excited to find someone who looked so much like you." My chest swelled with pride. "I was so lucky he was available when he was. The whim of fate is such a wonderous thing."

"I look like Ernest?"

I scoffed. "Hardly." Tearing my eyes away from the road, I looked at him in question. "What do you know about Ernest?"

"You said he bores you, and that he looked like me."

"I didn't say that." Did I? Gabe's fingers grazed the side of my head, and I hissed in pain. "Don't do that."

"I think you hit your head."

I pushed his hand away, scowling at him. "I'm fine."

"Maybe I should drive."

I stepped hard on the brake, screeching to a halt in the

middle of a brick-lined street. "Fine, drive. I'm not feeling so good." I slid across the seat as he ran around the front and settled in behind the wheel. "Turn left up here and get on the highway."

He put the car in gear, glancing at me every few moments. "Maybe we should get you to a doctor."

I shook my head, regretting it instantly. "I'll be fine. Just a little bump."

"You called me Ernest. I think it's more than a little bump."

"If I called you my bitch, you'd answer, wouldn't you? Who cares what I call you?"

He turned his attention back to the road as he merged onto the highway, and I reclined the seat. "Get off on Clements Ferry Road, and I'll direct you from there."

"Of course, sir."

I closed my eyes, my ears homing in on the labored breathing of the woman in the back seat. *Where did she come from?* I wondered briefly before I remembered. She was going to help me get Ellie.

I turned my head, watching Gabe through lowered lids. He was a vision, but the tension in his neck gave away his anxiety. I'd mistaken it for excitement. I should've prepared him better.

He'd fumbled at the scene of the accident, tripping over every task and almost bumbling my carefully orchestrated timeline. Capturing Jillian should've taken under one minute, but it had taken much longer. We weren't far enough away from the crash site for my peace of mind, but it didn't seem as if anyone had followed us off the city streets and onto the highway. Despite Gabe's ineptitude, everything had turned out fine. Fate was smiling down on me, as she always had.

"You're going to enjoy this, Gabe."

"Sir?"

"There's nothing like having complete control over another living thing. I wish I could've taken you to Detroit." A wistful smile spread over my lips. "Maybe I'll find another, and we'll do it again. You don't have a twin, do you?"

"I-I don't have any siblings, sir."

"It's probably for the best." I focused on my breathing, which had grown ragged. Every breath was torture, and a thick fog hung in my mind, muddling my thoughts. My eyes grew heavy, the smooth road beneath the tires soothing the throbbing ache in my head.

"Clements Ferry Road is the next exit. Where do I go from there?"

His voice startled me. I blinked, turning to the clock and hissing on an inward breath. "Did I fall asleep?"

"Yes, sir."

My head ached a little less than before as I turned to look in the back seat. The woman was curled into a ball on the floor, so limp I was sure she was dead. But she coughed and wheezed, moaning a few times before going silent again.

"There's an unmarked road on the left about two miles down. You'll miss it if you're not paying attention."

"Understood." He cast a worried glance my way. "Are you feeling any better?"

"I'm fine," I snapped. "Just took a hit in the crash, I guess. I don't remember."

"I saw a sign for an urgent care. We can drop her off at the warehouse, and I'll bring you back—"

"No," I shouted, and immediately regretted it as his face fell and he looked wounded. My jaw clenched, causing the pain in my head to swell. "I told you, I'm fine."

"Of course, sir."

I pointed at a narrow opening between two trees that concealed an almost dirt drive. "There's the turn."

Tips of tree branches screeched against the metal roof,

making my teeth vibrate as he turned in, and I cringed. Gabe eased the large SUV through the gap, bouncing through the ruts.

"Take it easy," I growled.

"Sorry."

"Follow this until you get to the end." I closed my eyes again. This time, I didn't doze, every bump and jolt jarring me down to my bones. A few minutes later the driveway smoothed out and took a sharp left turn. "Park around the back."

When the SUV stopped, I forced myself upright and opened the door. The familiar scent of untamed woods that surrounded the dilapidated building quickened my pulse. Memories faded, but scents stuck with a person for most of their lifetime. And this scent; this was the fragrance of fear and power. Of desperate choices and pointless bargains. This was the warehouse I'd taken Ellie to on that dark night and the place I'd killed countless young women who could never hold a candle to Ellie's flame.

Gabe let out a shuddering breath and shifted in the seat. "What about the girl?"

I turned to the back seat, surprised to see she was still breathing. "Take her inside. We'll tie her up like we did before."

My assistant paused before saying, "Okay."

"Ernest, I need you to hurry." I sputtered, realizing I was calling him by the wrong name. I shook my head to try to clear it, then pressed my hands to my temples when it threatened to explode with the movement. "Gabe. Hurry."

"Of course, sir."

Lumbering to the front of the warehouse, I took my keys out of my pocket and unlocked the padlock that secured the rusted metal door. A quick scan of the surrounding area showed no threat, only a sedate country view. I was nervous, which was unlike me. But I chalked it up to bringing the woman here in broad daylight.

I did my best work at night.

I held the door open while Gabe lumbered in under Jillian's dead weight. One hand hung limp, banging against the side of his leg with every step. Her foot hit the doorframe, her shoe slipping off. Kicking it through the opening, smiling as the memory of another one-shoed girl made my pulse hum. I switched on a flashlight and let the door close behind us.

Her constant, labored breathing echoed off the cinder brick walls as I glanced around my old playground. The chair in the middle of the room was crumbling, over a decade old, and well used. But then I blinked, and in its place was the wooden phlebotomist's chair I'd placed there on Monday. A fresh roll of rope balanced on the wide arm.

Rubbing my eyes, I fought the flashes of the past that floated through my mind. They were melting together, making it hard for me to distinguish between now and then.

I stumbled to the sink at the wall and turned the cold water on. The pipes knocked and sputtered, spewing brown iron-stained water for several seconds before it ran clear. I inhaled, and when I was sure the water was safe, cupped my hands together and splashed the icy liquid over my face.

A hand touched my shoulder, and I nearly jumped out of my skin. "Are you all right, sir?"

"I'm fine, just tired. Is the girl in the chair?"

He nodded.

"Good. Help me tie her down."

We made quick work of securing her, the industrial rope strong enough to hold a raging bull. But this captive was docile, still completely unconscious.

"What now?" Gabe asked when we were done.

"I have some errands for you to run."

Gabe glanced at our captive with a worried frown. "Shouldn't I be here for this?"

I smiled at his enthusiasm. "Don't worry, I won't start without you. You won't want to miss this excitement." My laugh echoed in the cavernous room. "You have no idea how much fun we're about to have with Detective Kline."

24

P ain.
  Cold.

A single drop of water *plopped* into a puddle, splashing cold liquid on Jillian's ankle where her sock and pantleg left a small gap.

Eyes still closed, she winced as she lifted her head, and a sharp pain pounded through her brain.

Another droplet fell, adding to the moisture already clinging to her skin. The liquid was icy, lingering for an instant before trickling down into her sock. But it sharpened her dulled senses.

Jillian licked her lips and tried desperately to swallow, but her mouth was so dry. She sputtered and choked, coughing. Her head in agony, the coughing caused the pain to swell exponentially, hot tears squeezed through tightly shut eyelids, rolling onto her cheeks as another splash of cold water found her ankle.

Was she dreaming? Was this a nightmare? Because she couldn't move. And it seemed like she was tied to…a chair.

Instinct kicked in, and she tried to appear as if she hadn't regained consciousness, to regulate her panicked breathing as it echoed in the frigid room, but her head throbbed so painfully she couldn't tell if she was successful.

"Wakey, wakey." The voice was low but giddy. Male. Familiar.

A chill tightened her spine, and her heart quickened. Keeping her eyes shut, she could feel the heat off the man as he leaned in close. Hot breath caressed her face, a pleasant peppermint instead of the rotting stench she'd expected. Her curiosity got the better of her, and her eyelashes fluttered open, the glow of a single bulb hanging from a chain in the middle of the room bringing fresh tears.

"I'm hurt," she managed.

"I noticed." The older man from the car accident straightened with a shrug. "It doesn't really matter. This will all be over eventually."

Eventually? Not soon?

She tried to sort out her panicked thoughts, but fear bubbled up until she was dizzy with rage. She managed to keep her face passive, glaring at him defiantly. He was older than she'd at first thought, maybe fifty, with a not-unattractive touch of gray at his temples. The glint in his eyes, however, told her he wasn't the trustworthy-looking older man his appearance would lead one to believe.

"There she is." He clapped his hands together, delighted. "I knew Ellie's best friend had to be just as feisty as she is." He turned and spoke to someone over his shoulder. "This is going to be great fun, Ernest. Great fun."

Jillian scanned the room, straining to see through the shadows that clung to the dank cement walls. "There's no one there. Who are you talking to?"

He blinked, looking to his right, then left, and scowled.

His mouth opened, and he briefly touched the side of his head. "There was a little accident, and I bumped my head. Nothing major."

"You're talking to yourself." Jillian wished she could take back the words when she realized she'd just pointed out to the madman that he was a madman.

"I guess it could be worse." When he didn't finish his thought, Jillian shuddered. So many implications, and none of them good.

Jillian stiffened when the man slipped his hand into his pocket, and she clamped her lips together to keep from crying out in pain. But he pulled out a simple flip phone. Made of cheap, dull plastic, she knew right away it was a burner phone. Untraceable, anonymous.

The dread in her stomach grew. Did anyone know about the accident yet? Was she missed? And where was she?

Tapping his foot on the bare concrete as he dialed, he held the phone up to his ear with a wide smile plastered on his face. When the call was picked up, he didn't even wait for the person on the other end to say hello. "Have you finished your errands?"

Jillian strained to hear what the other person was saying, but the man's footsteps echoed so loudly in the empty space it was impossible to make anything out.

He nodded, satisfied with whatever answer he'd been given. "I need you here with me. Don't keep me waiting." Hanging up with a triumphant punch of the end button, he turned his attention back to Jillian. "He'll be here soon."

Grimacing, Jillian didn't bother with a response. What was she supposed to say? *Great. Can't wait.* The man was talking to her like he was her friend, and not like he'd removed her from the tangled wreckage of her car in broad daylight. An accident *he* had caused.

Closing her eyes again, reliving the sound of twisting

metal and the pop of the airbag going off in her face, she struggled to piece together the moments leading up to the accident. Had he been following her?

She tested the binds that held her wrists to the sides of the wooden chair. Fiery pins and needles shot through her hands. Hissing through her teeth at the pain, she tried to flex her fingers, but they were numb. "I need to use the bathroom."

He shrugged, taking out a small object and moving closer. Her cell phone. Smiling, he held it up to show the lock screen, which prompted him to put in the passcode.

"I won't tell you the code." She straightened and stared straight into his evil eyes, ignoring the pain still pulsing beneath her skin.

Laughing, he took the final step that separated them.

She wanted to kick him, but her legs were held firmly to the chair from just below her knees to her ankles. There was no way she could reach him. She scowled. "Ellie is on her way home. When she sees that I'm gone, she'll come for me."

He arched an eyebrow, a disturbing smile widening his mouth. "I'm counting on it." He tapped the tips of his fingers together, tittering with excitement. "Ellie needs to know she's not as smart as she thinks she is. She fell right into the trap. I have to admit, you kept us waiting by staying at work all night, but in the end, fate blessed me with her sweet kiss." He looked over his shoulder again and pressed his lips together. "I'll need my trusty assistant, though. Everything has to be perfect this time. This time, we're going to get it right."

Bile rose into her throat as the missing piece clicked. "You ordered Katarina to call us, didn't you?"

"I asked for her assistance. She's quite clever, so I knew that she would find a way to get Ellie out of our hair for a bit." The man began to stroll around the room as he spoke, his gait loose and easy. Relaxed.

"And Nick. They both showed up at Valerie's location after Katarina's call."

He came to an abrupt halt, blinking for an instant before a slow smile spread across his face. "Clever. I'm sure *that* caused all sorts of drama."

"You never planned to hurt Valerie, did you? I was the target all along."

"Bingo." He closed the distance between them until he was only a few feet away.

Jillian pressed her back against the chair, desperate to put as much space between them as possible.

Amused, he chuckled and moved closer. His excited breath came in shallow gasps, eyes wild and nostrils flared. When he grabbed her index finger, she gritted her teeth, hissing in pain. "You know when they first came up with phones that unlocked with fingerprints, everyone hailed it as the greatest invention. But the truth is, it made it that much easier to access private information. Whether you're unconscious or dead, I can open your phone with ease rather than wasting an afternoon trying multiple combinations." He rolled the pad of her finger on the sensor until the phone screen brightened. "There we are." His finger flicked over the screen.

His eyes lit up, and her stomach clenched. "She'll hear me in the background. She'll *know* it's a trap."

His eyes wandered to the right. She followed his gaze, gasping at the syringe sitting on a stainless-steel tray beside three vials. "No. She won't hear a thing."

A flash of light at the far end of the room caught both their attention.

"Ernest!" he exclaimed in greeting. "You're here just in time for the fun."

Hollow footsteps echoed as a man rushed forward, letting the door fall closed behind him. He stayed near the edge of the shadows, his face obscured by darkness. Only his silhouette was visible, but as a sense of familiarity settled on Jillian, her attention moved back to her captor.

He was busy filling the syringe with the contents of each vial. Sitting in a rolling office chair, he smiled and capped the needle, turning it over to mix the liquids. "Stirred, not shaken. Don't want any bubbles," he explained when he caught her watching. "You need to be alive when Ellie comes to rescue you."

"We won't play your game." Jillian pushed each word out through gritted teeth.

"I don't need you now. Gabe, my assistant, is here."

"Gabe?" the assistant asked, his voice confused, but Jillian's attention was locked on the syringe. The crazy man was clearly addled from the accident, slipping between two names without rhyme or reason, but Jillian had more pressing things to worry about.

Giggling almost like a child, her captor pushed the wheeled chair with his feet until he was in front of her again.

She wriggled, but he'd bound her so tightly, only her head and shoulders moved. She lowered her eyes, fighting her bonds as he used a cotton swab soaked in alcohol to clean the skin in the crook of her elbow. Beneath a pink plastic cap, a large gauge needle glimmered. Tapping her skin, he pressed down hard and smiled when her vein appeared.

"Looks like you're an easy stick. My favorite."

Terror streaked through Jillian, and she fought, but her arm was immobilized, giving the man a clear target. He slid the needle into her arm, the *prick* as poignant as the dread that bloomed in her chest. But she didn't make a sound. She refused to give him the satisfaction.

"My, my, you are a stubborn one."

"Is Ellie on her way?" the assistant asked.

"I'll call her shortly. We don't want Jillian ruining the plan we've worked so hard on."

"She won't fall for this." Jillian's words came out sluggish, the room going fuzzy at the edges. Her tongue suddenly seemed huge, awkward as she tried to form words. "She's smarter than you."

"The drugs are taking effect." The crazy man put a Band-Aid on her arm with such care that Jillian's stomach turned. Smiling, his round, pleasant face was warm and welcoming, like someone's kind grandfather instead of a monster.

Across the large room, the door opened again, drawing the attention of both men. A third man, with deep brown hair and olive skin, appeared in the doorway, standing perfectly still for a moment as he took in the scene before him. It was the angel. She vaguely wondered where he'd gone.

"Gabe." The kidnapper waved the young man forward. "You're here."

The world tilted as ice spread through her veins, and heat and a low buzzing seemed to come from inside her head. Her vision was too fuzzy to make out Gabe's features, so she turned her gaze back on the two men closest to her, intent on giving them a piece of her mind as long as she could still think.

But then the first man he had called Gabe stepped out of the shadows and into the light. Lips formed into a tight frown, his tan slacks and beige cardigan that accented his blond hair were out of place in the dirty, musty space.

He met her gaze, and Jillian's eyes popped open wide. She gasped, searching for words as the man's face began to melt, and the encroaching darkness pushed its way past the edges of her vision. She fought to stay awake, her chest heaving with each tortured breath.

Drawing from every remaining bead of strength in her body, she was finally able to form one word before she lost her battle against the poison flowing through her veins and descended into nothingness.

"You."

25

E llie unlocked her apartment door, dropping her purse on the table in the foyer. Her go-bag crashed to the floor as she groaned at the release of its heavy weight. She looked at the package in her hands. The doorman had stopped her downstairs, letting her know that it had been delivered earlier that day.

She gave it a little shake, but the movement didn't clue her in to the contents. There was no return address. Just her name scrawled on the brown paper.

A clink of dog tags announced that Sam was coming to greet her, and the big black dog scrambled around the corner, plunging into Ellie's shins. Jamming her cold nose into Ellie's hand, she licked her and rubbed her face along Ellie's pant leg. She acted as if she hadn't seen a human in a month.

Cooing to the dog, Ellie set the package down next to her purse before patting Sam's head, keeping her fingers in the deep fur as they walked into the living room.

"Honey, I'm home." She laughed at the inside joke, her

voice carrying down the hall. "You were right, traffic was a mess, even for a Friday."

When she was met with silence, she frowned and checked her watch. It had been over an hour since she'd last spoke with Jillian. She'd expected her friend to beat her home, but except for Sam, who was standing by the door wagging her tail as if she needed to be walked desperately, the apartment was empty.

Thinking maybe Jillian stopped to get takeout or got waylaid at the store, Ellie grabbed Sam's leash. If the insane traffic was any indication of how the rest of Charleston was handling Friday the thirteenth, every place was probably packed.

Ellie fished her phone out of her purse, her thumb swiping over the keyboard with rapid precision as she fired off a text to Jillian. *Taking Sam out. If you grabbed food, call me when you get home, and I'll help you bring it upstairs.*

She fastened the leash to Sam's collar and hurried down the hall with the dog pulling her at a fast clip. By the time they made it to the ground floor, Sam was whimpering. She half dragged Ellie to a patch of grass, stopping at the edge instead of the middle like she normally did. Her face was the picture of relief as she squatted and let nature take its course.

"Couldn't hold it anymore, huh, girl?" Ellie frowned, checking her watch again and thinking back to their conversation. Jillian had said she pulled an all-nighter. That meant Sam had been in the apartment far longer than she was used to. It wasn't like Jillian to leave her for so long, and especially strange when she'd said she was coming home to let Sam out.

So, where was she?

Ellie's stomach was twisting itself into knots by the time Sam was ready to head back inside. Digging her phone out of her pocket, she was surprised to see her text had gone unread. She scowled, checking her call log to see if she'd missed a call from Jillian, but there was nothing. Dialing Jillian's number, Ellie stopped in the lobby, waiting for her to answer. Biting her lip, she counted five rings before there was a click as the call was transferred to voicemail.

"You've reached Jillian Reed with Charleston PD. Please leave your message and I'll return your call shortly." Her voice was cool and professional, trademark Jillian.

Ellie took a breath, waiting for the beep. "Hey, Jillian, it's me. Listen, I'm getting worried. Sam hadn't been out yet, and I thought you'd be here by now. Call me, okay?"

Racing up the stairs to her floor, she kept the phone in one hand and Sam's leash in the other, just in case Jillian called back. But she made it to the front door with no text and no return call, leaving her with a growing sense of dread in the pit of her stomach. Jillian was never late, and even when something came up, she *always* made sure Sam was cared for. This just wasn't like her.

She was about to dial again when a phone rang. But it wasn't the one in her hand.

Turning around in a circle, she located the sound. It was coming from the forgotten package she'd left by the door.

Anxiety crawled up her spine as she took a tentative step closer to the box. The ringing stopped, and a second later, her own phone vibrated in her hand, making her jump.

She glanced at the screen. It was a message from Jillian. *Answer the phone.* The message was followed by a picture. Ellie gasped as she found herself staring at a picture of Jillian tied to a chair.

The phone in the box started ringing again.

On legs that felt like water, Ellie lunged for the box and tore off the paper. She knew that she was destroying evidence and she should be wearing gloves, but she didn't care. She had to talk to her friend.

She was being Facetimed.

"Where's Jillian?" she demanded the second she answered the video call.

A low, ominous chuckle vibrated through the speaker. An icy chill ran the length of her spine and settled in her stomach as an eerily familiar voice taunted, "Jillian is fine, Ellie. But she won't be for long." The screen was dark, but she could hear every word clearly.

She hadn't heard his voice in years, but she would know it anywhere. As she stared at the front door in disbelief, she was suddenly fifteen again, tied to a chair, with chemicals being pumped into her body. Controlled like a lifeless puppet. Helpless, completely at his mercy, and paralyzed by her fear.

Shaking her head, she forced the memories of her worst-nightmare-come-to-life aside, focusing on the man on the phone, wishing the bastard would show his face.

"Where. Is. Jillian?" She clamped her jaw tight, wanting to reach through the phone and wrap her hand around his throat, rage bubbling in her veins.

"Such manners. Is that how you greet an old friend?"

"We're not friends," she ground out through clenched teeth.

"That's funny. I have fond memories of you." He laughed, low and evil. "In fact, you're the reason I changed the way I operate. Your resistance, followed by your escape, showed me the errors I'd been making, and I have made it my mission to perfect my technique since then." Through the speaker pressed to her ear, he drew in a breath that shuddered with excitement. "Now that I've had some time to really dig into *why* my foray with you didn't work out, I'm finally ready to give it another go. What a fitting day to do it, don't you think? Happy anniversary."

She recoiled, horrified at the fear that gripped her from just hearing his voice. Holding the phone away from her so he couldn't hear her panicked inhalations, she closed her eyes and struggled to slow her breathing.

You're not fifteen anymore. You're a detective, and he doesn't know what he's up against now. He will not win.

"Ellie? Are you there, my puppet?" He chuckled, a sound that vibrated deep into her marrow. "Oh my, did I frighten you?"

"I'm here." When she spoke, her voice was level, her breathing slowed somewhat, though her rapid heartbeats still pounded in her ears.

He was only human. She could defeat him. She *had* to. Her life had never been the same since that night thirteen years ago, for her, or for her family. His game was about to end, Ellie would make sure of it.

"Show me your face!" he demanded, and although every part of her being screamed for her to run, she lifted the phone until her face appeared on the little screen.

"Happy?" Her voice came out stronger than she felt, and she blinked her eyes, refusing to let the tears threatening fall. "Why don't you show your face too?"

"In good time, my puppet. It's good to see you again. I was afraid you'd run away, and I'd have to come retrieve you." He breathed into the phone, and she could almost feel that breath on her skin. "You can run, if you want, but that wouldn't make you a very good friend, would it?"

"I won't play your game. I don't know how you got Jillian's phone, but Valerie is safe, and you'll never find her. You're a fool for even trying and—"

His sudden laughter cut her off. "It was never about Valerie. I need that woman to testify so Fink can bury himself. But you never could see the forest for the trees, could you?"

Her throat tightened. "Where's Jillian?"

"She's right here."

The phone turned away from the darkness, and Jillian appeared, still tied to the chair. Ellie stared at the screen, trying to take in every detail, but he turned the phone after only a second and the background was darkness again.

He was planning on making her relive the night he'd kidnapped her. Why else would he take Jillian and summon her like this?

He'd waited patiently for over a decade, biding his time until the perfect moment. She'd moved Jillian in with her to keep her safe. And in doing so, she'd done just the opposite. But she'd never dreamed that he would *take* Jillian, and that was exactly why he'd chosen to. Ellie would have no choice but to play along. She would do anything to save her friend, even if it meant reliving the hell she still struggled to remember.

Flexing her fists, she inhaled through her nose and exhaled through her mouth until she had herself under control. She wouldn't let him see the terror on her face. The master wasn't the only one who'd learned a thing or two in the past thirteen years. His was a cold threat, but she'd prepared herself for this every day of her life, since she woke up in the hospital.

"I want to speak to her."

"She's resting right now. But I assure you, she is quite alive and in mostly good shape."

Ellie sucked in a quick breath. *Mostly* good shape? "What have you done to her?" Flashes of syringes and expertly sharpened knifes bloomed in her imagination.

"She had a little accident."

The delight in his voice left Ellie's hands shaking, but she couldn't risk letting him know how scared she was, so she scoffed, hoping he'd be fooled. "An accident? I find that hard to believe. Where are you?"

"Bold. I like that. But there are some rules you must abide by before I give you the address."

"I'll be alone." She knew that's what he wanted, and the truth was, she still didn't know who on the police department she could trust. If she unknowingly brought a traitor with her, she was as good as dead anyway.

"That's a good start. Go to your car, and I'll give you directions."

Filled with indecision, Ellie lowered the phone.

"No! Show your face!" When she lifted it back up, he went on, his tone more pleasant. "You must show your face to me at all times, do you understand?"

"Yes."

"Each time you don't or if you try anything funny, Jillian will pay for your actions. Understood."

Ellie gritted her teeth. "Yes."

"I want you to lay your personal phone on your dining room table, then walk toward your door. I don't want any of your department buddies showing up and interrupting us before I'm done with you."

He's bluffing. But calling his bluff and taking her phone wasn't worth the risk. She shuddered when she realized if he was telling the truth, he also knew exactly where she lived.

Ellie did as he said. "Done."

"Turn the phone in your hand so I can see that you did exactly what I told you to do."

Her fingers shook as she turned the device and pointed the camera lens toward her abandoned phone. "Very good. Now, show your face again and go to your car."

"I need to get my keys."

He sighed. "You have my approval. Your keys and nothing more."

Careful to keep her face in the screen, Ellie grabbed her purse, then dropped her keys to the floor to give herself a reason to bend down and pick up her go-bag too. It was a terrible risk, but she needed the item inside.

"I've got them."

"Go to your car."

Sam was at the front door when Ellie's hand wrapped around the knob. The dog whimpered, as if she knew that Jillian was in danger, and gazed up into Ellie's eyes, her tail motionless, her mouth held tight. Despite her goofy nature, Sam knew when her favorite humans were stressed, and she was ready to act. Chuffing softly so her cheeks puffed out, she nosed Ellie's leg urgently and stared at the door as if willing it to open.

Ellie gently pushed her away. "You can't go, Sam. We'll be back, I promise. I'll bring Jillian home to you."

Sam whimpered, trying to slip out when Ellie opened the door.

Ellie backed out of the apartment, making sure Sam didn't sneak out behind her and locked the deadbolt. A single bark of protest was the only sound Sam made, then she was quiet, resigned to being left behind. The apartment door was cold against Ellie's hand as she gathered her courage, wondering if she'd just lied to Sam.

No. She could do this.

She took a deep breath and hurried through the hallway past her neighbors' apartments, careful to keep her face in the phone's screen. Music floated out from beneath the door at the end of the corridor, accompanied by the scent of fresh cookies in the oven. It seemed cruel that life continued, while Ellie's world was crumbling around her. How could someone be baking cookies at a time like this?

Grimacing, she pushed the grim thoughts away. This man, the master as Katerina had called him, was a human and not invincible. Letting him get in her head wasn't helping. Channeling her fear into anger, she shoved the heavy, fireproof door that led to the stairs so hard it slammed against the wall.

Sweat dripped down her spine as she ran to her car. Once again careful to keep her face in the screen, she tossed the bag and purse into the passenger seat, then got in and placed the phone in the holder located on her dashboard, turning it up until only her face was showing.

"Now what?" she asked as she pushed the button to start the car.

"Turn right out of your parking lot. I'm tracking you, and I'll know if you try to trick me."

"What if I lose you?"

"That would be very unfortunate. If you follow my directions to the letter, you'll have no trouble finding the place. Besides, it should be familiar to you. You've been there before." He gave a delicate snort of laughter. "Sadly, this will probably be my last time using this particular building. I imagine Charleston PD will leave no stone unturned to solve the murder of two of its own. It's a shame, really. So much history here."

Ellie closed her eyes, the faces of several of the women she'd manage to connect to her own case floating through her head. How many more were there? "How many women have you killed?"

"Here? Dozens."

The pride in his tone sent a fresh ripple of dread through her. *Dozens?* They must have been buried somewhere secluded, still waiting to be found, their families wondering what had happened to their loved ones.

Her stomach roiled, sending waves of nausea through her at the reality of what he'd done to so many innocent women. What she'd witnessed him do. Taking the victims in pairs, he tortured one until the other broke and shouted the order for him to kill her friend. Here was a man who not only showed no remorse for what he'd done but seemed to enjoy it.

And he had Jillian.

Unable to curb her curiosity, she blurted the question out before she thought better of it. "Did you stay in Charleston because of me?"

He was silent for so long, she thought he'd hung up. But then he gave a small hum, as if he'd decided there was no harm in telling her the truth. It wasn't like he had any intention of letting either her or Jillian live. He'd made that much abundantly clear.

"Yesss." The word was breathless, heavy with meaning. A single syllable that was so much more.

"And you've been watching me."

"I had to right the wrong and finish what I started. So, yes, you're the only reason I've stayed in Charleston this long. I could have broadened my horizons, but I was reluctant to leave my puppet."

"Was I your first? Is that why my escape bothers you so much?" The longer she kept him talking, the less time he had to torture Jillian.

He laughed, the sound booming through the phone's speaker. "Hardly. But you were the only one who ever got away, and it won't happen again." There was another long pause, followed by a deep inhalation of breath. "As much as I've enjoyed catching up with you, the clock is ticking. If you want to see your friend alive, I suggest you turn left at the light."

With no other choice, Ellie did exactly what he said.

With movements as careful as she could make them, Ellie reached over to the passenger seat and unzipped her go-bag, removing a Glock 19, her personal weapon. She hadn't taken off the service weapon at her hip nor the ankle holster she'd strapped to her lower leg before leaving Nick's cabin. She also still wore the bulletproof vest Flynn had encouraged her to wear as well.

She'd almost balked at the caution, but she was glad now that she had listened to the experienced bodyguard.

The kidnapper would likely frisk her and demand she remove the service weapons on her hip and ankle, but he might miss the Glock she would tuck under her vest. Any upper hand she could give herself was worth the risk. She was at a disadvantage, and she knew the master worked with a partner. If she could get off a shot once she knew where Jillian was and that she was safe, she would take the chance.

Time was ticking away, and Jillian's life depended on her.

Ellie had escaped the master, the monster, once before, but she hadn't been able to save the other girl.

This time, he had her best friend, and there was no way she was leaving Jillian behind.

No matter what.

26

I f it hadn't been for the limbs recently bent and broken above the narrow dirt driveway off Clements Ferry Road, Ellie would've missed the turn, even as the master's eerie voice told her to expect it.

She slammed on the brakes and yanked the wheel to the left, gritting her teeth when a single limb trailed along her window with a loud screech. Her Audi Q3 rocked along the bumpy road, the deep gouges in the earth too numerous to dodge. Hands wrapped around the steering wheel, she scanned the area, noting several small sheds, some in such disrepair only a few withered boards were left standing on the foundations.

In the daylight, without the deluge that had soaked her to the skin the night she'd escaped, the property seemed harmless.

But she knew this place, soul deep.

Knew that beyond the woods and out of sight was the place she'd been held captive with another victim. She could practically feel the thrum of evil coming from the place, like a heartbeat.

She was on the right path. The overgrowth of unchecked vegetation might have altered the landscape unrecognizable, but nothing could erase the presence of evil that hung heavy in the air.

The road smoothed out just before it swung hard to the left, and the dense tree line opened up on an acre of once-cleared land that was now overgrown with saplings and waist-high weeds. Her breath caught when she came around the next curve, and the large metal warehouse loomed on the top of a low hill. Rust-red and dull gray, one side of the building drooped lower than the other. Buried in the soft earth, years of rain and lack of care had left the topsoil to wash away, the corner of the building and the gutter spout had crumpled under the weight of the sinking walls.

"Park and leave your phone in the vehicle."

Ellie did as he said, turning off the car and tucking the phone under her vest before stepping out of the car. A video camera mounted over the entrance swiveled to scan the entire property. Even from across the clearing, she could tell that it was new, and when it stopped, facing her direction, she shuddered, knowing his eyes continued to follow her every move.

"Strike while the iron is hot." She muttered the old Southern wisdom under her breath, smiling at the adage that reminded her to plow ahead. It had served her well, though her bold actions had earned her a reputation for being impulsive and reckless. Now was not the time to second guess herself. She was where she needed to be, and the man who called himself the master was waiting for her.

A large oak tree to her left caught her attention. Transported back to that night, a chill swept over her, the memory of the icy rain that had pelted her bare arms causing goose bumps to form.

Running as fast as she could, she slipped in the mud, wind-milling her arms to hold her balance.

Her hands connected with the rough bark of the gnarled oak tree seconds before a flash of lightning brightened the sky.

She jumped as thunder cracked so loudly, the vibration hurt her chest. Gulping air into her lungs and desperate to get her bearings, she waited for another bolt to light up the night.

Flash!

She took off into the forest, hands up in front of her face to protect it from branches. Her only plan was to put as much distance as possible between herself and the cursed warehouse.

The warehouse was smaller than she remembered, weathered with rusted pockmarks covering much of the siding. A brief echo of that night—rain pelting the metal roof —teased at the edge of her memory, but she forced it back. She'd been terrified, and the spooky warehouse being battered by the raging storm had only amplified that fear. But she'd lived a lifetime since then, and the warehouse was only a building.

And the master was only a man.

Walking around the SUV to give herself as much cover as possible as she surveyed the building, she made her way to the front door and turned the handle.

Unlocked.

Taking a deep breath, she stepped into the darkness of the building, knowing how vulnerable she was making herself. Her footfalls echoed off the concrete floor as she gave in to his demands, letting go of the door. Behind her, the door fell shut, the seal so tight despite the aging metal that it seemed to suck the air out of the room when it closed. The bare bulb in the middle of the dark space did little to chase away the shadows as her eyes adjusted.

Attached to the wall on her right was a water faucet with a deep basin, the steady *drip-drip* from the spout mingling with the fat drops that had collected on a few exposed rafters from a rain shower earlier in the day, falling into puddles scattered throughout the large space. There were no rooms, just one large area with unsealed cement floors that stretched between the four walls.

Ellie took a tentative step forward, hand still on her holster as she peered deep into the shadows.

A metal table with large wheels that resembled a room service cart sat directly beneath the light, but it was the human form taking shape as her eyes grew more comfortable with the dark that drew Ellie's attention.

Blinking, she almost gasped when she realized it was Jillian.

Rushing forward until she was a few yards away, and sure that she'd be walking right into a trap if she went any farther, she paused. Assessed the situation instead of racing in and risking both their lives.

When Jillian didn't call out to her, Ellie realized her friend was unconscious. Head to the side, her eyes closed and mouth slack, Jillian's chest rose and fell with every breath. She was tied to a chair, like Ellie had been so long ago. But it was the rope around her neck that had Ellie's heart leaping in her chest.

"You tripped the switch when you walked in." It was the voice that had haunted her nightmares. The place from those same fevered dreams.

Ellie stiffened until she thought her spine might crack and turned slowly to face the man behind her.

He was beyond the reach of the soft glow from the weak bulb in the ceiling. Only visible from his waist down, his thick but average frame was unremarkable. Black slacks covered his legs, but it was his work boots that caught her attention. Steel-toed and well-worn, they bore a stark contrast to the tailored trousers that were clearly expensive and cut just for him. She blanched when she realized the boot leather was dark with years' worth of blood.

Did her own blood mingle with the rest?

"What switch?" Her voice echoed, eerie and hollow.

He only pointed to Jillian. Daring to take her eyes off the man for a moment, Ellie glanced over her shoulder just as an audible *click* filled the silence. The slack in the rope tightened a few inches, the loop that had been there when Ellie walked in straightening slightly.

"Jillian." She didn't even flinch when Ellie spoke her name. Jaw tightening, Ellie turned back to the master.

His arm raised slightly, and the barrel of a gun peeked out from the shadows. "She's still fighting the sedation. If she can hear you, she can't move yet." He gestured with the revolver. "Take your weapon from your holster and set it on the floor." She did as he asked, squatting to lay it down. As she moved to stand, he laughed. "Backup weapon too."

Pursing her lips tight, she glared at him as she bent lower and laid the smaller ankle gun on the concrete.

His response was another laugh that was far too calm. "The bulletproof vest is a nice touch, though it won't help you if I shoot you in the thigh. Or the head."

Ellie stiffened as he lowered the muzzle, fingers going to the trigger.

He scoffed. "No need for that. Wear the vest or don't, it won't protect you for what I have in store." Chuckling, he sniffed, raising his arm until the gun was pointing at her chest again. "Actually, testing it out could be fun. I've heard the impact packs quite a wallop even with the vest on. Perhaps we can try that theory out and see how bulletproof it really is."

Click.

Dragging her attention from the kidnapper, Ellie gasped when she saw the rope nearly taut.

Her gaze followed the cord up to the rafters, where a large weight dangled above the ground.

Spinning, she fought the urge to rush him right then, but the mechanism that held the heavy weight in the air was a complicated system of levers and pulleys, and the master was the only one who knew how it worked.

Click.

"No!" She scrambled to regain control, wondering if she could retrieve the gun from under the Kevlar vest fast enough to shoot him dead before he did the same to her. "Please, stop it. I'm here, like I said I would be, and I'm alone."

"Every thirty seconds, the weight lowers."

Ellie's gaze was drawn to the pulleys, and her heart sank. She had no defense against this kind of trap, much like the night she was fifteen and on her own in the dark.

Click.

Jillian's head snapped upright, held by the rope, which was now snug.

"I'll do whatever you want, just please, make it stop."

He gestured at the stainless-steel surgeon's tray set up on the table, the single bulb glinting off the metal instruments. "Choose your tool, and I'll stop the timer."

"Come on, Red. Are you heartless? Put her out of her misery."

Her stomach dropped out of her body, and a gaping hole replaced it. This was the room he'd held her in thirteen years before. From the cracked concrete block walls to the rusted aluminum siding that started about ten feet up and angled sharply to form the roof, the space was almost exactly as it had been when she was fifteen. Even the assortment of tools laid out before her was almost identical.

Fighting the onslaught of jumbled memories melding with the present, she tried to stem the panic that bubbled within her. Thirteen years ago, she'd failed, and an innocent stranger had died. This time, if she failed, she'd be sentencing her best friend to death.

"If you stall much longer, dear Jillian will be too far gone to enjoy our little game." He gestured at the table in front of her. "It's time to make your choice."

Arranged neatly on the rectangular tray were a dozen or more instruments of torture. A scalpel, a corkscrew, shears big enough to cut fingers off as easily as the tender branches of young spring saplings, a stun gun, and—

She twisted away from the sight, bile rising in her throat, her rapid heartbeat nearly drowning out the sound of another click. "I can't."

"Then she'll die." He chuckled. "The chair is bolted to the floor. It won't be an easy death." Her gaze went to the guns on the floor, but he stopped her with a gentle clicking of his tongue, as if she were a toddler trying to sneak a cookie from the jar. "I wouldn't do that if I were you. There's a code to stop it." He held up a remote type device as if it was proof. "She'll be snapped in half by the time you figure it out."

You can't outsmart the master, puppet. Choose how she dies or the torture continues.

She gagged. The horror of the memories rushing at her after being buried for so long was more than Ellie could bear. They were still scattered snippets, but with every breath and every word he spoke, the darkness was peeled away to reveal more.

She nodded, taking a step toward the display of torture devices.

"That's a good girl," he cooed. "Already choosing more wisely than the last time."

Anger boiled in her veins, but when the next click came from the general vicinity of his hand instead of across the room, relief spread through her. He'd used the remote to stop the timer. It was a short reprieve, but it was something.

Buying time, she pretended to consider each item, circling the table that held the steel surgical tray with her arms loose at her sides. "Which would you choose?" Her voice was hollow, the words disjointed and emotionless to her own ears. Would he fall for it?

But the master stood a little straighter, intrigued by her question. He took a step closer. The light spread up his body, stopping mid-chest, leaving his face obscured. Hands behind his back, he leaned in to get a good look.

Ellie held her breath, squinting into the darkness as the light spread higher and stopped at his collarbone. So close, but the master knew what he was doing.

"If you start with small cuts, our time together will last longer." He shrugged and stepped forward a half step. "Maybe that will give you hope she'll survive long enough for you both to be rescued. This is always more fun when my puppets have hope."

My puppets.

Ellie forced away the chill that spread through her. Puppets. Toys. Nothing more than strings and joints to be manipulated for his pleasure.

She nodded, holding her hands so they hovered a few inches above the spread of tools he'd so carefully selected and displayed.

His breath quickened, the suspense building his excitement. Out of the corner of her eye, she noticed that he'd taken another step, so close to revealing his face as the light reached his chin.

She reached for the corkscrew, froze an inch from it, as if indecisive, listening for his reaction in the eerie stillness that surrounded them. Flexing her fingers, she moved her hand again, this time stopping above a long steel rod-like skewer with a wooden handle.

The master sucked in a quick breath, so eager for her to

make her choice that he took another step. He was only a couple yards away now.

She touched the stun gun, wishing with every fiber of her being that it was a taser so she could turn it on him, fire up his ass. She picked it up, considering. A stun gun would hurt Jillian terribly, but it wouldn't leave any permanent damage.

"Is that your selection?"

Instead of answering, Ellie frowned and pretended to put the stun gun down. At the last second, she threw it with all of her might, straight toward the bastard's head. While he was busy ducking the device, Ellie grabbed the short side of the tray with both hands and spun, swinging it as hard as she could at the master's face. Tools flew everywhere, into his face before skittering and bouncing across the floor as the tray connected with flesh and hit bone with a sickening crack.

He shrieked in pain, stumbling backward with the remote still in his hand.

Before he could fight back, Ellie swung again, angling the tray this time so the edge caught his cheek with the force of the blow.

He dropped the remote as he retreated, the heel of his boot coming down on the thin plastic device and crushing it beneath his weight before Ellie could scoop it up. Frantic, she turned toward Jillian just as the mechanism lowered the weight again, the rope snug enough to dent the delicate skin of her neck.

The master screamed in pain, hands over his face, blood flowing between his fingers. He was fully in the light now, but the blood covering his damaged face hid any features that would've been recognizable behind the broken nose and the huge gash in his cheek held together with bloody fingers.

Their eyes met before he turned and ran for the door,

leaving her with two choices. Chase him or save Jillian. She couldn't do both.

Jillian's strangled cry spurred her into action. Grabbing the pruning shears from the floor, she leaped a small pool of blood, afraid she might slip and waste valuable seconds.

The weight lowered again, cutting off Jillian's cry for help and leaving her gurgling, desperate for air.

Ellie raced across the space that separated them, spreading the handle wide and aiming for the length of rope above Jillian's head.

The surgically sharpened blade touched the rough fibers of the thick cord.

She closed the handles with all her might.

Click.

27

The shears sliced through the rope like warm butter, throwing Ellie off-balance and sending the tail end of the cord snapping into the air. The tool clattered in all directions, followed by the crash of the huge weight as it struck the floor, shattering the concrete. Long fissures spread outward from the point of impact, now a crater.

Jillian's head fell forward, but the rope was still pulled tight, cutting off her air. She pulled at her wrist bindings, unable to help herself.

Ellie's shaking fingers worked at the slip knot, yanking the rope several times before it finally loosened.

Her friend dragged a loud breath in, choking on a sob. Blinking rapidly, her head tilted forward as if it was too heavy for her neck to hold.

Ellie knelt so she was eye level with her, her hand on Jillian's knee. Her friend's gaze was distant and unfocused even though Ellie was less than a foot away. "You've been drugged."

She gave a slight nod in response. Blinking rapidly, their eyes met, and Jillian's held a glimmer that hadn't been there before. Her cracked lips parted, and she whispered, "You came."

Ellie nodded, putting her forehead to Jillian's. "I wouldn't leave you alone."

The cold from the concrete seeped through the thin fabric of Ellie's pants as she knelt in front of Jillian. Grimacing at the purple hue Jillian's fingers had taken on after hours of being tied too tight, she pried at the knot at Jillian's left wrist first. Her fingers cramped with the effort to move the thick rope a few millimeters. Slipping her finger in the loop she'd created, she pulled until the tension released, and she was able to untie the knot.

Jillian hissed through her teeth when the first of her bindings fell away, and the blood rushed back to her hands.

"Are you okay?"

Jillian nodded, mouth clamped tight, eyes teary.

Ellie nodded and scooted to the other hand, fingering the cord of soft cotton fibers that was stretched taut.

This time when it dropped onto the concrete, Jillian appeared to be ready for the shock of blood flowing all at once. She let out a shuddering breath, rolling her left wrist in wide circles. As she flexed her right hand in small increments, her fingers changed from a grayish purple to an angry red. Silent tears streamed down Jillian's face. When she noticed Ellie's concerned look, Jillian flashed her a gentle smile. "It only hurts. And a lot less than dying."

"I'm just glad you're okay."

Jillian closed her eyes against the fresh onslaught of tears, jaw clenched as she nodded and whispered, "Me too."

The ropes around Jillian's legs proved harder to remove. Tied in several complicated knots, Ellie struggled to grip the smooth fibers. Frustrated and frantic to get her friend to a hospital, she turned, scanning the floor where the tools had scattered.

The door swung open, and her hand immediately went to the gun at her waistband. Expecting it to be the master returning, she aimed at the man's head.

But a familiar voice spoke, throwing her into confusion. "It's just me." Hands up, Dr. Powell paused as the door shut behind him. His gaze ran over Ellie, eyes widening as they went to Jillian. "Is she alive?" When Ellie didn't lower her gun, he froze. "I'm here to help."

Ellie flicked a glance in Jillian's direction. Her friend had passed out again. "She's alive. How did you find us?"

"Something you said about your kidnapper reminded me of a colleague I had years ago who had similar quirks. After that, it was just a matter of following the clues. Once we realized you were here, I knew instantly that my suspicions were correct." Hands still up, he squatted and picked up one of the scalpels that had skittered across the floor when she swung the tray at the monster. "Jillian's injured. We need to cut those ropes off her and get her to a hospital." Powell stood motionless, waiting for her to make the next move.

She searched his eyes, stuck between her own paranoia and the man who'd helped her work through so much of her past with kindness and understanding. Even now, he stood with his hands up, patiently waiting for her to make a decision.

When she finally lowered her weapon, he smiled and nodded, immediately going to Jillian and beginning the painstaking process of sawing carefully through the rope, the blade facing outward so he wouldn't cut her. Ellie watched him for a moment, trigger finger still at the ready, but Powell was focused on the task at hand. "I saw another thin scalpel near the one I picked up."

Her eyes found the blade he was talking about. "We who?" she asked. "You said, 'once we realized.' We who?"

"Chief Johnson. I told him a few weeks ago that I was worried you were in real danger."

Ellie blinked in surprise, walking over to the blade he'd pointed out. She grabbed it, hurrying back to Jillian's left side as Dr. Powell worked on her right. "You said I was being paranoid."

He paused mid-cut and smiled at her. "There's paranoid, and then there's prudent. I thought it best to err on the side of caution just in case." He motioned around the room. "You were right, and I'm so glad I thought to inform the chief so he could have a trace put on your phone."

"A trace?" She tilted her head, a warning bell going off in her head. But this was Dr. Powell, the one who held her secrets. The one who'd helped her when no one else could. "I left my phone at home."

Powell paused, shrugging with a warm grin. "I guess it's good Chief Johnson decided to put one on Jillian's phone too."

"Oh." Ellie was still stiff with tension. "I'll have to thank him for invading my privacy later." She gestured toward the door. "Did you see the kidnapper when you pulled up? He ran out the door, but I don't know which way he went. He's seriously injured."

"I didn't see him." Powell focused on the knife in his hand, carefully cutting away each braided strand until the rope loosened and fell away. "Yes!" he whispered under his breath triumphantly, sitting back on his haunches so he could assess Jillian's wounds. He frowned. "Jillian?"

Her eyelids fluttered, but she couldn't hold them open. Voice weak with the effort, she pushed words out through lips that were starting to lose color. Blood oozed from a wound near her hairline, dripping down her neck and soaking into her shirt. "I'm awake. Just so tired."

"She's lost a lot of blood, and that gash on her head looks

pretty bad." Powell stood and leaned closer, then searched the room. His eyes lit up, and he rushed to a stack of towels next to the sink. Water splashed into the washbasin that was deep enough for a grown man to sit in. Powell took one towel and slung it over his arm, ran a second under the water until it was dripping wet.

The rope finally came loose in Ellie's hand, and she cast it aside, gently holding Jillian's foot and rolling her ankle to get the blood flowing. Jillian's head was against the back of the chair, her eyes still closed, chest rising and falling evenly.

Powell's face was pinched with worry when he handed Ellie the wet towel and took out his phone. "I should've called right away. I was so stressed out, I didn't think to call it in."

Ellie narrowed her eyes. He hadn't seemed stressed for a second, almost as if he'd known what he was walking into.

Phone to his ear, Powell stepped away. "Yes, hello. This is Dr. Powell with the Charleston Police Department. I'm going to need an ambulance." He paused. "Actually, more than one. I have multiple injured."

Multiple injured? Did he think the master was still out there on the property?

Jillian moaned, drawing Ellie's attention away from Powell as he rattled off the location of the warehouse. Ellie stood, leaning close and pressing the wet towel over the gash on Jillian's head. "Dr. Powell is calling an ambulance, it's going to be okay."

"Dr. Powell…" She cleared her throat and licked her lips, eyes half open.

"It's all right, you don't need to talk. We're safe now."

"Not…safe."

Ellie frowned as the door creaked open again, holding the towel in place as she turned. Her heart renewed its violent pounding in her chest.

An unfamiliar young man stood in the doorway, loose dark brown curls framing a cherubic face. For an instant he stood there, mouth slack, eyes darting over the scene.

Powell froze, and the two held each other's gaze for a long second before the phone slipped from his hand.

The stranger raised a gun, squeezing off three shots before Ellie could react.

Powell jerked, then stumbled and tripped on his own feet before slamming into the wall.

Reacting on instinct, Ellie fired off a single shot at the stranger in the doorway.

The young man's eyes widened, and he spread his feet wider in an attempt to remain upright. Stunned, he dropped the weapon, and it bounced off the toe of his shoe and slid across the concrete. Red spread in a perfect circle near the center of his shirt. His chest heaved, pain evident on his face. Stumbling backward, his eyes locked on her. He winced as his back hit the wall as he sank to the floor with his hands covering the wound, as if he could stop the flow of blood.

Ellie kicked the gun out of his reach, then spun and grabbed a towel as she ran toward Powell.

"He shot me." Powell's voice was barely above a whisper. Trembling with pain as he sat spread-eagle against the wall, his breath was thin and rapid, sweat beading on his forehead and collecting until it dripped down his face. He'd taken two bullets to the chest, blood streaming down his shirt.

Heart racing, Ellie took off her jacket and helped him lay down on the floor, slipping it behind Powell's head. "I'm going to put pressure on the wound and try to stop the bleeding."

Powell nodded his understanding, his pale skin sallow. Folding the towel over the wound that was bleeding the worst, she pressed down with all her weight, cursing her carelessness. The master always worked with a partner. She should've expected him, and her mistake might have cost Powell his life.

The younger man was still sitting against the wall near the door, his breath loud and ragged, hands covered in blood. His lips were moving, his voice too low to be heard across the room over Powell's labored breathing.

Powell moaned, and Ellie turned her attention back to the doctor who'd spent so much time and effort trying to help her work through her past. His skin was grayish now, a bad sign. "Stay with me. Keep talking, okay?"

"Hurts." Lying in a pool of his own blood, his head tilted to the side, his eyes were focused on something in the distance.

"I know it hurts." She let a nervous laugh escape. "I've been shot a couple times. The trick is to stay awake. I'm going to ask you a question, and you just answer yes or no, okay?"

"Yes."

"What day is it?"

His lips spread in a half smile, and he grimaced. "You said yes or no."

His attempt at humor gave her hope that he might pull through. He wouldn't be joking with her if he was dying, right? Beside him, his hand flopped near his waist as if he was searching for something. Holding the towel with one hand, she took his hand with the other and squeezed gently. He closed his eyes, coughed, and pinched his lips together.

"You're right, I did say yes or no answers." This time her laugh was forced, but she was trying to keep his spirits up and quell the panic growing inside her. What was taking the paramedics so long?

He opened his eyes but glanced down at his torso instead of at her. His hand moved again, weak and trembling. "It's Friday the thirteenth."

"Good. Next question. Do you work as a barista for Charleston PD?"

He rolled his eyes. "Sometimes."

The fact that he was able to joke was encouraging, despite the shadow of death that clung to him. Frantic to keep him engaged, she pressed on. "You said you knew the man known as the master. Do you know his name?"

"Yes." Powell's head lulled to the side, and his eyelids drooped.

The distant wail of a siren was so soft she thought she'd imagined it, until it grew a little louder. They were close. If Powell could just hold on a little longer, the paramedics would be there to save his life.

He had to live. He was the only one who knew the identity of the master.

28

"Stay with me, Dr. Powell." Ellie let go of the towel long enough to pat his cheek roughly, forcing him awake.

He managed to open his eyes, though his breathing was shallower now.

Moving the towel, she scowled at the fresh blood that appeared. "I need to unbutton your shirt so I can see the wound."

"Paramedics," he managed.

"They're close, I can hear them. But the highway winds around so much they might be another few minutes. Let me help you." Her fingers were slippery with Powell's blood as she worked his top button.

Delirious and fading in and out of consciousness, Powell clawed at her hands, struggling to breathe.

"It's okay."

The first button opened, but the second proved more of a challenge. Frustrated and afraid he would die before the ambulance arrived, she grabbed each side of his collar and ripped the shirt open. Buttons popped off, flying every which way.

Yanking the hem out of his waistband, she spread the blood-soaked fabric, revealing his entire torso and two bullet wounds. The one on his right side had already stopped bleeding on its own, the bullet having gone in at an angle. But the second shot was near his heart, and it was bad.

Ellie grabbed the towel and moved it over the wound that pumped blood out at an alarming rate. Just below a patch of puckered, scarred skin. A raised scar with feathered edges.

Her hand raising. Jabbing downward. The scissors stabbing into a chest.

She rocked back on her heels as the wind rushed out of her.

Powell's eyes met hers, wild and frightened.

The metallic smell of his blood hit her nostrils—familiar —and the weight of heavy surgical scissors was heavy in her hand. Confused, she glanced down at her hand, but there were no scissors, only the bloody towel. The cool metal of a shiny steel instrument in her grip was a distant memory brought back from the darkness.

Jaw clenched, she glared at him. "It was you."

He stared back at her, not bothering to deny her words.

Nostrils flaring, she inhaled sharply, flexing her fingers as horror swelled within her. "You were the one who helped him kidnap me," she spat out the words in clipped, tight syllables, "and *you* were the one—"

This time when his left hand flopped beside his body, she realized he was trying to reach for something, but the bullet wound had done some significant damage, making it hard for him to control his movements. His fingers reached beneath him, clawing at the butt of a gun tucked into his waistband. He managed to pull it out, but it slipped from his weakened grasp and onto the concrete floor.

Ellie slid the weapon out of his reach. Skidding across the

smooth cement, it came to a stop near the sink. Her voice was full of venom. "You were going to kill me."

He didn't deny her accusation. "I couldn't let you ruin everything I've worked for."

The man who'd shot Powell stirred behind her, his breathing so loud now he sounded more like a winded race-horse than a human.

Ellie cast a glare in Powell's direction, stood, and backed away slowly.

A single tear slid down his cheek as his hand clutched at his wounded chest. Blood spurted from between his fingers and cascaded down his arm. He was paler now than he had been, the unrestricted flow of blood causing the pool beneath him to grow.

Ellie stood there for what seemed like an eternity while Powell's breathing grew more shallow, and his eyelids fluttered shut and back open again. Did she leave him there and just let him die? He'd tricked her, earning her trust while manipulating her. Even now, his farfetched story of how he'd come to be in the warehouse in the first place echoed in her mind.

We put a trace on your phone.

When she'd pointed out that her phone was at home, he'd lied so smoothly. *Must've had a trace on Jillian's phone too.* She'd missed it, so focused on freeing Jillian that she hadn't noticed the way he'd explained away her every concern without missing a beat. He'd played her, and she'd walked right into it.

Then there was the man who'd appeared after the master had escaped. Powell had been too far away from Jillian and Ellie when the stranger shot him for him to be hit by mistake. No, the younger man had *aimed* for Powell.

Kneeling just out of Powell's reach, she moved so she was level with his gaze. "I trusted you."

His breath was shorter now, with long pauses between each one. Blinking, he cleared his throat and inhaled once more before he finally responded. "That was a mistake." A long, low groan eased through his slack lips, and his eyes rolled up toward the ceiling.

He was dying, and if the stranger hadn't shot him, Ellie was sure Powell would've killed her and Jillian.

Her choice was clear.

Ellie stood, leaving Powell with his gaze skyward, the light already fading from his eyes. He was too far gone, but the man who'd shot him was alive, and for some reason, he'd risked his life to save her and Jillian. She had to know why.

Powell sputtered and coughed, wheezing as the siren song of the approaching ambulances continued to swell.

She jogged the short distance across the room to the man who'd shot Powell. When she knelt beside him, he forced a weak smile. "I tried to save you from him."

"I get that now."

His face contorted with pain as a wave of agony swept through him. When the moment passed, he continued. "He hurt so many people."

"Try not to talk too much." She used a pair of bandage scissors that had been laying among the scattered surgical tools to cut his shirt open. The wound was above his heart, low on his shoulder. "You're lucky I missed your heart."

He coughed out a soft laugh and clamped his jaw shut against the pain his laughter had caused. "Apology accepted," he managed with a wry grin.

Gently turning him so she could look at his back, she frowned at the smooth expanse of bronze skin. "There's no exit wound, so the bullet's still in there."

"Can't have all the luck." He hissed in pain when she helped him sit back again.

"What's your name?"

"Gabe." He ground the single syllable out through clenched teeth, brown eyes swimming with unshed tears.

"I'm Ellie, but I guess you know that." When she applied pressure to his wound, he arched his back. She gave him a reassuring smile. "You're going to be fine."

He nodded as she adjusted her position, pressing down harder. A soft moan escaped his lips. "Is it supposed to hurt this bad?"

"Pain is good. It means you're still alive."

"That's a relief." He trembled, his breathing ragged and quick. "I'm freezing."

The floor beneath them was cold to the touch, but Ellie knew it wasn't just the chill that was making Gabe cold. He was in danger of going into shock. "I need you to keep talking. Stay with me, okay?"

Gabe nodded, grimacing as he met her gaze. "He's hurt bad."

"Powell? He'll be lucky if he lives long enough to make it to the hospital."

Gabe took a shuddering breath and cleared his throat, working through what she knew from experience was agony. Even a survivable gunshot wound was still taking a bullet. "Not Powell."

"Oh." Her hand went to her gun, but he shook his head.

"He's long gone by now. I caught a glimpse of him running away from the warehouse when I pulled up. His back was to me, but he was moving slow and hunched over."

"Did he leave on foot? I didn't see a vehicle." The sirens were so loud now they filled the hollow warehouse.

"Took Ernest's. It was parked on the other side of the building. You couldn't see it coming through the main entrance. There's a narrow road that winds around until it reaches the highway."

"Ernest?"

"The master's first assistant." He tipped his chin in Powell's direction. "Him."

Ellie's lips went slack as she shook her head, her fingernails digging into her palm. And then she saw it in her mind, the precinct shrink's name stamped on his door.

Dr. E. Phillip Powell.

She shook her head. "All the hours I spent talking to him about my kidnapping, and I never suspected."

Her hand went to her mouth as a memory surfaced. Not a distant, fragmented moment buried for the past fifteen years. *I should've known,* she thought angrily. She'd heard Powell's voice in an early hypnosis session, and she'd let him convince her it was a false memory. In truth, it hadn't been Powell who had spoken the words she'd heard so clearly in her mind, but her subconscious had been trying to warn her, and she'd ignored it. He'd redirected her so effortlessly that she hadn't once suspected him.

Gabe licked his lips, clearing his throat again. "The ambulance is close now, right? I don't know how much longer I can hold on." Eyelids fluttering closed as if to prove his point, he started to lose consciousness but fought and opened his eyes.

"They're here, but they'll have to wait for an officer to clear the scene before they come in."

On cue, a shout came from outside the door. "Charleston PD! Is anyone inside?" It was Chief Johnson.

"It's clear!" As soon as Ellie said the words, Chief Johnson came in through the door, followed by a half a dozen officers.

Johnson stopped, eyes scanning, weapon lowering slightly as the scene before him came into view. "God almighty, what happened here?"

"A man they call the master kidnapped Jillian to lure me here. I was able to gain the upper hand, then Powell helped me untie Jillian." She didn't know what to say about Powell. How did she explain that someone they'd depended on for so long was actually working with the enemy?

Chief Johnson's eyes darted from Ellie to Powell and back again. "Why is Phillip here?"

She blinked, half in shock, her mind wanting to disbelieve what she knew had just happened. "He said you knew he was here."

"No. Why would I send him? He's the department shrink, not an officer."

"He said he talked to you about my therapy sessions and the anniversary coming up. He said you both agreed that I was in danger. Powell even said you had my phone and Jillian's on trace."

"That's not true."

Ellie nodded, turning toward Powell as the chief knelt on the floor, pressing the towel against the wound that had all but stopped oozing blood. "I don't know why I'm surprised. He had me fooled all the way until the moment I saw the scar on his chest." She paused and let out a breath, her hands trembling.

"Scar?" Johnson shouted for the EMS, and they came running in, swarming both Powell and Gabe as he barked orders to his officers.

Ellie stood, her knees shaking. "On his chest, where I stabbed him with a pair of scissors when I was fifteen."

Chief Johnson's eyes widened. "Kline, are you saying—"

"He's dirty," Ellie confirmed. "But he came into the department that way."

Chief Johnson's eyes flashed with anger. Glancing around the room, he moved closer and lowered his voice. "We'll talk about that more later, okay?"

Ellie kept her face passive as she nodded. Chief Johnson believed her without question, and after everything she'd been through, it was a relief to have someone in her corner. Especially someone with as much power at Charleston PD as the chief of police.

"Was Powell unarmed when you shot him?"

"I didn't shoot him."

Chief Johnson tilted his head, gaze narrowing on Gabe. "Who shot him?"

"This guy." She gestured to Gabe, whose face was slack, eyes heavy, as he fought to stay awake while the paramedics prepared him for transport. "Powell was helping me with Jillian, and I had no idea I was in danger. Gabe came out of nowhere and took him out before he could hurt Jillian or me."

Johnson's gaze stayed on Gabe. "Who shot him?"

"I did."

Johnson blew out a quick breath and closed his eyes. Pinching the bridge of his nose, he took several slow, deep breaths before he spoke again. "So, let me see if I've got this straight. You *didn't* shoot Powell, and you *shot* the man who tried to save you?"

"That's the simplified version, I guess."

The chief scoffed. "There's nothing simple about you, Kline."

The paramedics working on Powell already had him on a stretcher. One pulled the stretcher toward the exit while the second continued CPR.

Johnson waved to catch their attention as they passed. "How is he?"

The medic steering the gurney checked Powell's neck for a pulse, jaw tight as his gaze swept over Powell's body. "I can't get a heartbeat, and he's lost a lot of blood. It doesn't look good."

Chief Johnson's lips spread into a pinched, grim line. "Do whatever you can to save him."

The paramedic nodded, and they hurried out of the warehouse to the waiting ambulance.

Ellie cast her eyes to the floor, guilt overwhelming her.

Chief Johnson wrapped her slender hand in both of his, not paying attention to the blood covering her skin. He gave her a reassuring squeeze, just like he had at the hospital thirteen years before.

Despite the comfort his touch brought, Ellie's heart remained heavy.

His eyes were soft when she met his unwavering gaze, a hint of a tender smile on his lips. "It's okay for you to be human." He looked at the paramedics, but they were engrossed in their patients and not paying attention to him and Ellie. "I'm just glad *you're* not the one who shot him."

A clatter of wheels drew their attention back to the scene around them. The paramedics had Jillian and Gabe on stretchers now.

Heart torn, Ellie turned back to Chief Johnson. "Jillian's unconscious, and she won't notice I'm not in the ambulance. I want to ride with Gabe so I can question him now, in case he doesn't make it."

"You can't run this case, Kline. You're a victim."

"I know, but he has information that we don't. I need everything he knows so I can piece together the rest of what happened to me that night and find out if there are more victims we haven't found. I'm afraid if I let someone else investigate—"

"*I'll* be handling this case personally."

"Thank you, sir. But I'd still like to talk to him."

"He's in no condition to talk right now." Johnson shook his head. "In case you didn't notice, he's fading in and out as it is."

"Sir, please."

"You can't ride with him in the ambulance."

"Sir, I—"

"You *shot* him. Even if I didn't think letting you question him crossed a line, I can't let you do that."

Ellie frowned. "It was a good shoot. He shot Powell, and I didn't know Powell was involved."

"Go be with Jillian, Kline. If she wakes up in the hospital and you're not there, she's going to be scared. Take care of your friend and let me handle this, please."

She opened her mouth to argue and thought better of it. "All right."

"I'll be by the hospital to take your statement when I'm done here."

Ellie took one last look around the warehouse before walking through the door and getting into her car. It wasn't until she was alone that she noticed her hands were caked with blood. Powell's. Jillian's. Gabe's. Maybe even the man's she only knew as the master.

Gagging at the thought of having the blood on her skin of the men who'd tortured her as a teen and forced her to watch another girl die, she dug in her purse until she found the travel-sized packet of wipes at the bottom. She scrubbed until the first cloth was dirty, tossing it to the side and grabbing another and another until the bag was empty. With shaking hands, she started the engine and put the SUV into gear, leaving the cursed warehouse in her rearview.

29

The paper-thin hospital sheet pulled at his toes, rubbing against the thick, shapeless socks they'd given him to go with his gown. Using the remote to raise the back, Gabe Fisher shifted in the bed in a futile attempt to get comfortable. His wound burned with every movement.

Taking a deep breath, he gritted his teeth to hold back a moan, fingers clenching the sheet that stopped just below his chest. He shook the thin fabric until it pulled loose from the foot of the mattress and moved it up to his chin, nestled back against the flat pillow, and sighed. His accommodations were far from luxurious, but at least his shoulders weren't cold anymore. He'd take a small victory anywhere he could find one.

The knock on the door was so soft Gabe barely heard it over the constant beeps of the various monitors that were still holding him captive in the stark room. "Come in." He cleared his throat, repeating himself a little louder when no one entered. "It's open, come in."

The door creaked, and a familiar face appeared in the gap. "The nurse told me you were ready for visitors."

He nodded, gesturing to the chair beside his bed. "Sit down. It's not like I'm going anywhere today."

She smiled at his attempt at humor, tucking a coil of bright red hair behind her ear. "Thanks. I'm sure you're bored out of your mind. Jillian was released yesterday, and she was already climbing the walls before that." She dropped down into the seat, her green eyes surveying him with concern.

"How is Jillian?"

"A broken arm that required surgery, but she'll heal in time."

"And her car?" He grimaced as he asked.

"Her car is a total loss."

A flash of himself driving the reinforced SUV, connecting with her passenger door, sent fresh waves of guilt through him. "I know it's probably not the time, but I need to apologize to her."

"She knows you didn't have a choice."

"Why doesn't that make me feel any better?" He bit his lip, eyes wandering to the open window and the colorful buildings that surrounded the hospital. Inhaling deeply, he dragged his attention away from the promise of freedom and back to Ellie.

"Because you have a conscience. She already said she forgives you." Ellie cleared her throat. "If it weren't for you, we would both be dead."

"I keep replaying everything that happened in my mind. I only went along with him out of fear. He's…not what I thought he was." The photos of the man in the cage that he'd found in the doctor's desk hovered in his mind. "I could've stopped him. Jillian could've died. Maybe if I had, things would've turned out differently."

"It's hard not to dwell on the what-ifs, but what's done is done. If it hadn't happened, we wouldn't have found him or you, and I wouldn't know that Dr. Powell was his old assistant. It's valuable information I didn't have before, and that means something."

"How did Powell end up as the police department's psychologist in the first place?"

"I wondered the same thing. When I looked it up and checked the days, I found out that he'd hired on shortly after I graduated from the police academy and received my assignment."

Gabe frowned and shook his head. The motion made his head spin. "He was keeping tabs on you for the master."

"It's the only explanation."

"What a stroke of luck that the position was open then."

It was Ellie's turn to frown. "Actually, it wasn't luck. The former psychologist died. At the time, it was ruled a suicide, but now that we know Powell was keeping tabs on me, it's too much of a coincidence. There will be a thorough investigation. I have a feeling that your boss was involved in it somehow."

"I wouldn't be surprised." A click and a soft beep that was different from the rest interrupted them. When he noticed Ellie's confused expression, he explained. "I'm an addict, so they set me up with metered pain management instead of the button." He wiggled his thumb, trying to explain, but as the pain killers flowed into his IV, his thoughts grew fuzzy.

"The morphine button. I had one the first time I got shot."

Despite the haze that was quickly encroaching on the edges of his brain, he smiled. "The first time?"

Ellie shrugged, suppressing a grin. "I've been shot twice in the past six months."

"Wow. That's some luck."

"Surviving is the lucky part."

Gabe's mood darkened, the happiness at seeing Ellie

fleeing at the reminder of his current situation. He lowered his eyes. "Not for all of us."

Ellie shifted in her chair, her green eyes searching his for a moment before she finally spoke. "Why did you stay with him? You had to have realized he was bad long before he made you help kidnap Jillian, right?"

Gabe's eyes filled with unshed tears as he nodded. He was so ashamed. "I didn't discover that until a short while ago, and then I was afraid of what he'd do to me if I defied him."

"But you were just his employee. Couldn't you leave and never come back to work?"

"No. He took me in off the street, groomed me, and gave me a place to live. A job. My phone, my car. There was no escaping him. If I walked away, he would know exactly where to find me."

Ellie nodded her understanding. "So, you didn't have a choice?"

"It was either play along and look for a way out, or risk ending up dead."

"You did the right thing, Gabe."

Gabe sighed. "I just wish I felt that way about it."

"None of this is your fault." Ellie's hand covered his, offering comfort.

He forced a smile, trying to fight his way past the overwhelming sadness. "Thank you for saying that, but he literally tortured and killed a man because he looked like me." Gabe's jaw clenched as he let out a shuddering breath. "At least one person is dead today because of me. That's a heavy burden to bear."

"How do you know?" Caring green eyes assessed him, making him want to tell her everything.

"It was a fluke. The doctor left his computer on one day, and when I went to shut it down, he had a message. There was this site and these pictures—" A sob tore from his throat.

"I think I know what site you're talking about."

"You do?"

Ellie nodded. "I was on it too. We've been investigating, but it's a slow process. Until we know the identities of everyone involved, it will be next to impossible to stop them."

"Even if you do, they'll just move the operation somewhere else."

"That's the other concern we have." Rummaging through her bag, she pulled out a large tablet and tapped the screen. "I have screenshots of some of the people listed on the auction site. Do you think you could look through them and see if you recognize the man he killed?"

Gabe nodded, and Ellie pulled her chair closer, holding the tablet so he could see it before scrolling through pages of captives, each page containing a dozen photos. Bile burned the back of his throat, but Gabe forced the nausea away. When she flicked her finger across the screen a third time, he gasped and pointed to a photo in the middle. "That's him, right there."

"He looks a lot like you." She took a screenshot, opened the photo gallery, and cropped the picture, so only the man he'd pointed out was left. "Give me just a second to run a search."

Her green eyes were narrowed, lips tight as she worked. After some time had passed, Ellie turned the tablet so he could see the Charleston Police Department seal on the top of the page, the man's soulful brown eyes so much like his own staring back at him. "This is him. His body hasn't been found yet as far as I know."

"Constantino." Gabe whispered the man's name, brushing the screen with his fingers as a dark, heavy sadness settled over him. "What are all these other names?"

"Aliases. It looks like he had a rough life. Drugs, alcohol, and a couple stints in lockup."

Gabe's chest tightened. So similar to his own past, right down to the addiction-ruined life. But the doctor had saved Gabe and killed Constantino. It was a fact that had been keeping Gabe awake at night since he found the scrapbook. "It could've been me."

"It's natural to feel that way, but you don't know why the master kept you alive."

"The master?"

"That's what they call him on the dark web." Setting the tablet aside, she placed her hand over his and gave a gentle squeeze. "You've been very helpful, Gabe, and I know you're tired. But there's something else I need to know, and it can't wait."

Gabe inhaled slowly. "You want to know his name too."

"Chief Johnson told me he tried to question you, but you were in no condition to talk at the time."

His lower lip quivered, the familiar dread welling inside the pit of his stomach. "I've been in and out, but that's not why." He'd already sealed his fate.

"I had a feeling it was something else. If you don't tell me, I can't protect you."

Hot tears burned the backs of his eyes, but he blinked them away. "I'm scared. He's a powerful man, and I wouldn't put anything past him. What if he does to me what he's done to everyone else? He could order someone else to do it, and I wouldn't even know it was coming. How do I prepare for that?"

"You can't." The steady gaze in Ellie's eyes told him she knew from experience.

"I don't want to end up like that man he bought. The one who looked exactly like me. The things he put that man through, and all because of our similarities." He couldn't rid himself of the memory. He thought of the other man, the one he'd purchased on the doctor's computer, who could have suffered a fate even worse by now. Guilt cut through him, nearly shattering his resolve. "It makes me physically ill. I can't bear the thought, and then I feel like an absolute coward for putting my own safety above everyone else. Is that wrong of me? I don't want to be a hero, Ellie. I just want to live my life."

"I understand how you feel, and you're right to be scared. No one blames you for being human, but keeping his secrets isn't going to help you. People like him aren't reasonable. They have no sense of loyalty. Until we catch him, no one is safe."

His jaw went slack. "You haven't caught him?"

Ellie shook her head. "He got away."

Panic stabbed at him, making his pulse leap, and he sat up, pain lancing through his chest. "He's going to kill me."

"You'll be offered protection for the information you have. You're the only one who knows who he really is."

Heart racing, Gabe's gaze darted around the room, and to the window. If he could've gotten out of the hospital bed, he would've jumped up then and closed the blinds, just in case. The view that he'd admired minutes before was ominous now. Could he be out there, watching Gabe right now? Waiting.

"I need you to tell me who he is, Gabe. It's the only leverage you have." Ellie produced a pen and a small notepad that she balanced on her crossed legs.

"I thought you already knew."

Detective Kline frowned. "You can trust me." Holding up the pad so that Constantino's face stared out at him, she said, "Do it for him."

Tears streaked down his cheeks. He straightened his shoulders as best he could, grateful that his mind was starting to clear as the painkiller faded a bit. "I thought they would have...it doesn't matter." He took a deep breath, preparing himself to speak his name again. "His name is Dr. Kingsley."

The pen clattered to the floor.

Ellie scooped it up, wrote the name down, and met Gabe's curious gaze. "Lawrence Kingsley?" Gabe nodded. "I know him. I mean, I met him. Recently."

"You did?"

"My boyfriend, Nick, hosted a fundraiser for mental health awareness, and both he and Dr. Powell were there." She shuddered. "He greeted me. He was within reach of my family."

"It's good to see you, Detective Kline." Dr. Powell took her hand and shook it warmly.

"Please, call me Ellie. This is Nick Connors. Nick, this is my colleague, Dr. Powell."

"It's a pleasure. Thank you for coming."

Dr. Powell gave a half nod. "I appreciate the invite. Have you met Dr. Kingsley, Nick?"

At the mention of his name, a man around fifty with a distinguished feathering of gray at the temples of his dark hair turned and smiled.

"I'm not surprised. He is arrogant and bold."

"But he wasn't worried I would recognize him or his voice?" She scoffed and shook her head.

"It was incredibly bold. But that's the way he is. At no point when he told me about his plan did he act like I might balk at what he was suggesting, he was so sure of himself and my loyalty."

"That's how men like him think. They never consider that people will defy them because they are so sure they're right."

"He was shocked when I hesitated at kidnapping Jillian. Not mad, just disappointed, I guess. I'd been playing the part of the willing participant since he caught me looking through his things. When I questioned him, he behaved like I'd betrayed him." Gabe let out a shuddering breath, feeling better just letting loose of his secrets. "That's why he sent me away once he had Jillian in the warehouse."

Ellie offered him a tender, reassuring smile. "But you came back."

"I went home and got my gun. I bought it after I found the pictures. I was going to kill him and Ernest. I mean, Dr. Powell."

"I didn't think anything could surprise me, but so much of this is completely unexpected. Dr. Powell was so kind to me, and Dr. Kingsley rubbing elbows with people I know. It's all too much."

A knock at the door interrupted them.

Their eyes met, and he saw his own uncertainty mirrored in her expression. "I'm not expecting anyone."

"Neither am I."

30

Ellie was on her feet before the door opened, reaching for her gun. But they were in a hospital, and Chief Johnson had placed three Charleston police officers on protective detail twenty-four-hours a day, despite her trying to hire her own security team once again. Gabe was as safe as he was going to be, and there was nothing else that could be done short of sitting in this room with him.

The door opened, and a lean, muscular man with a dazzling smile stepped into the room. Dark curly hair was cut so close to his scalp that it was little more than a gentle wave. He was right at six feet tall, making him just a hair taller than Ellie.

"You must be Detective Kline." He stuck his hand out, soft brown eyes locked on her. When she didn't take his hand, he chuckled and dug in his back pocket. "I should know better than that. I'm Special Agent Clay Lockwood. I'm with ACTeam."

"ACTeam?" She scanned the credentials he produced and handed them back to him.

"Anti-Trafficking Coordination Team. It's a multi-agency task force committed to ending human trafficking. I'm handling the launch at the FBI field office here in Charleston." His accent told her he was from Texas, though it was slight.

Ellie's back muscles stiffened. "Charleston PD has this handled."

"I'm sure they do. Listen, I know you don't want us encroaching on your cases, and that's fine, but I promise, we're here to provide support. Nothing more."

"Not like we haven't heard that before." She crossed her arms, intent on standing her ground no matter how charismatic Agent Lockwood was. It was hard not to want to like him, as friendly and good-looking as he was, but she knew when the feds assisted that usually meant a complete takeover. She wasn't about to let that happen without a fight. "I've worked far too hard on these cases to just hand them over. How do I know once I give you the evidence I've gathered you won't shut me out?"

His smile remained wide, eyes crinkled slightly at the corners. "I get it, I really do. That's why Chief Johnson asked me to come talk to you personally."

"I work alone."

"I've heard." He placed his hand on his chest in the universal gesture of honesty. "I promise I'm not looking to take over your entire operation. But I know you've got a court case pending, and I'm here to offer resources and support. Local law enforcement is our greatest asset. ACTeam won't risk burning that bridge."

Ellie glanced at Gabe, who'd gone quiet since Agent Lockwood entered. From across the room, he seemed frailer than he had before. Dark circles under his eyes revealed his exhaustion beneath eyelids that drooped every few seconds as he struggled to stay awake. Her duty to protect him won over her resistance to working with the FBI. She couldn't keep him safe forever.

"So, you're just support. Completely hands off?"

This time, Special Agent Lockwood's smile faltered. "Not exactly. There will be some aspects I'll handle, but I'll still need your input."

"What aspects?" The words shot from her lips, rapid-fire.

"Namely the protection of Gabe here. Like Valerie Price, he's privy to information we couldn't get anywhere else." His smile faded completely as he cast his eyes in Gabe's direction and back to Ellie. Gabe had fallen asleep, head tilted to one side. Agent Lockwood lowered his voice to a near whisper. "I don't think you need to be told that people who have seen what they have don't usually live to tell about it."

"I'm protecting Valerie." She straightened her shoulders, daring him to challenge her.

"No one is disputing that, but we can't have both our star witnesses holed up in your boyfriend's lake cabin."

Her stomach dropped. Glaring at him, she expected to be met with arrogance, but Agent Lockwood's expression remained calm and relaxed. His ego wasn't in play here, just the truth. Infuriating. "How did you figure that out?"

"When I asked Chief Johnson if I could speak to his witness in protective custody, he admitted he had no way of getting in contact with her because he had no idea where she was." One side of his mouth lifted, brown eyes glinting with amusement. "I have to admit, that was a first for me. He did give me your name, and after a bit of digging, I found out your longtime boyfriend Nick Connor had purchased a secluded cabin outside the city. The cabin is the perfect setup. Close enough to Charleston to be accessible, but remote and easily protected." He smiled, lifting one shoulder. "In your shoes, the cabin is where I would've put Valerie if I couldn't trust my colleagues with her whereabouts. It was a smart choice."

Ellie shook her head. "How safe is the cabin when you just made finding it sound so easy?"

"Like I said, ACTeam is a task force made up of multiple agencies. I have access to databases I wouldn't have otherwise, even at the FBI. No safe house is one-hundred-percent safe, but you have guards in place to offer another layer of protection. You have a good head for this type of work, which is why I broached the subject of making you the official liaison between ACTeam and Charleston PD. Chief Johnson is on board with the idea."

Ellie's head was reeling. Official liaison? It was so much to take in, but when Clay Lockwood spoke about ACTeam and his work to end human trafficking, he was so engaging, it was hard not to get excited. Still, she had some reservations.

"This all sounds great in theory, but what's in it for Charleston PD? It seems like we'll be sharing information to help ACTeam out. I just want to make sure it goes both ways."

If her blunt nature had bothered him, he hid it well, answering as if she hadn't just questioned his motivation. "There's a lot we can offer this partnership. That includes access to all our resources. The ACTeam database, personnel support, and top-of-the-line surveillance equipment to begin with. I know this might seem like it's coming out of nowhere, but I've had my eye on your work for some time. You're a good fit for this partnership, and I can't stress enough that it *is* a partnership, not a takeover. We can't do this without you." A soft laugh rose from deep in his chest. "Well, that's not entirely true. We can, it's just more efficient if we all work together."

Ellie nodded, then froze, narrowing her eyes at him. "You

said 'couldn't get anywhere else,' not *can't*. Does that mean?" Shooting a glance over her shoulder, she was shocked when Gabe offered a small shrug, a look of chagrin on his face. Ellie closed her eyes and took a slow, deep breath to quell the anger threatening. "You already questioned them both, didn't you?"

Agent Lockwood nodded. "And Fink. Using the information we got from all three, we were able to execute several raids."

Ellie pressed her lips together to suppress a smile since she couldn't decide whether she was in awe of the man or absolutely hated him. "So much for not taking over."

"You're on mandatory paid leave for discharging your weapon, aren't you?" He was grinning from ear to ear.

Loathed. She loathed him. Much worse than hatred. "Funny. And yes, but only for two weeks. I'll be back on duty May first."

"Just in time for Valerie's scheduled testimony. I already promised her you would be there."

Ellie tilted her head, brow furrowed in confusion. "Will they be ready for a trial by then? That's awfully quick."

"She won't be testifying during an actual case. In twenty-eighteen, a bill was introduced to exempt trafficking victims from being forced to testify in court. Especially in situations like these, where we have dozens of players who are all entitled to their day in court. Asking Valerie to testify in every case that pertains to her experience is just revictimizing the victim. So, the prosecution can now make their case on other crimes committed while trafficking. Valerie will still testify, but the court will be closed, and the only people present will be the judge, prosecutor, and someone from our team. They'll walk her through relevant questions and record the proceedings, which can be used in later trials."

"What about Fink?"

Agent Lockwood's smile turned feral. "Fink isn't entitled to those protections. Every time his presence is needed at a trial, he'll be transported back to Charleston to testify. He's under the impression that WITSEC is going to be like an extended vacation, but the next few years will be a different kind of justice."

"He might wish he'd taken jail time instead."

"We can hope."

Ellie glanced at Gabe, whose eyes were closed once again, though she wasn't sure that he wasn't listening. "What about him? Does it matter that he was involved in Jillian's kidnapping?"

"He was pulled from the streets and groomed, and saying no to helping kidnap Jillian put his own life at risk. Gabe is a victim too, even if he doesn't realize it." Agent Lockwood shook his head, letting out a heavy sigh. "If he hadn't come and shot Powell, this could've gone so differently. He'll testify on the same day Valerie does, and he'll never have to step foot in Charleston again after that."

"Good. He deserves a chance at a better life."

"You're just saying that because you shot him." He elbowed her playfully, which surprised her enough that she elbowed him back. "Probably better than throwing him off a bridge."

She rolled her eyes, but the anger had drained away. Yes, he was teasing her, and she'd heard the same thing in the break room at Charleston PD, but his tone lacked the malice she was used to from the other officers. "I didn't throw that man, he jumped. He almost drowned me trying to get away from a river turtle."

"In his defense, I'm not too keen on gators either. Not that I would scream like that and try to climb on your head to save myself, but you gotta feel for the man. He went to prison after that video went viral. There's no coming back from that."

Ellie tried to keep a straight face, but her composure broke and a laugh escaped. "It was pretty funny." She tucked a stray strand of hair behind her ear. "I still get a lot of flak for that day at the PD, like I did it for clout. I didn't even think about it. He jumped, and he was going to get away. Going after him was what I was trained to do."

"Some male officers are still intimidated by a strong woman." He met her gaze straight on, everything about his expression and body language sincere. "That attitude is ridiculous and archaic. They're intimidated by you, it's as simple as that."

Her smile slipped. "You say that like you know me."

"I've done my research." When she recoiled a little, he rushed to explain, his Texas accent coming out a bit more. "Once I realized what an asset you would be to the task force, I did my research about you. Since we're going to be working together, I needed to know everything about you."

She arched an eyebrow. "Everything? I doubt that."

"I know enough."

"Prove it." She tried not to cringe as she threw out the challenge, but she couldn't help herself. She didn't have anything to hide, but she had to know what he'd learned about her personal life.

"You're the only daughter of Helen and Daniel Kline. Three brothers, only one of them is as boisterous as you are."

"I think that's the nicest way anyone's ever described me."

"You're down-to-earth and you think with your heart too much. Your willingness to put your life on the line to save the most vulnerable gets you in a lot of trouble, but I know one little girl named Harmony who will see you as nothing but a hero for the rest of her life." He paused, chuckling. "How am I doing?"

She couldn't help but smile at his flattery, but she shrugged one shoulder. "Not bad. You know some things about me, and I know nothing about you."

He held up his hand, folding down a finger with each statement. "I'm an only child. Originally from Dallas, Texas, I've never lived one place for more than a few years, but Texas will always be home. Cats are okay, but dogs are man's best friend for a reason. I went to college on a baseball scholarship."

"Anything else I should know?"

"I'd rather be outdoors than in, and I don't find strong, smart women intimidating at all."

She huffed at the last statement, amused by his candor. "I guess it won't be *awful* working with you. Being a liaison sounds like a lot of fun, actually."

"I will keep you in the loop on everything we do. You won't be shut out of your own cases."

"I appreciate that."

A quick knock startled Ellie, but Clay Lockwood was unflappable, completely at ease despite knowing that there was a monster on the loose, and the sleeping man across the room was a target.

Without waiting for an invitation, a nurse walked into the room at a near run, talking a mile a minute. "The patient needs to rest, and visiting hours are over." Despite his terse words, he was polite and friendly in a hurried, exhausting way.

Scowling, Agent Lockwood reached for his credentials.

The nurse waved his hand in the air. "I don't care if you're the queen herself, the patient comes first. You can guard his door from the hall."

Ellie arched an eyebrow at Agent Lockwood and gestured to the door. "After you, Agent."

The officers who had been guarding Gabe's room were

gone when they stepped out of the room. Jacob Garcia and Duke had replaced them, along with Chief Johnson, who had settled in a chair with a clear view of the elevator and the stairwell.

Ellie smiled at the lanky police dog whose mostly black coat gleamed. Duke turned away, scanning the hall and everyone in it, too busy to acknowledge Ellie when he was on duty. At Jacob's house, Ellie knew it was an entirely different story, but she didn't take it personally. Duke was there to protect and serve, and he took that job as seriously as Ellie did.

Chief Johnson stood and shook Agent Lockwood's hand. "I see you survived your first meeting."

Ellie shot him a sarcastic grin. "Funny."

"I wasn't talking to you, Kline," Johnson teased.

Detective Lockwood grinned, shaking Jacob's hand next. He smiled down at Duke, but like Ellie, he didn't reach down to pet him. Duke's tail twitched, stopping short of an actual wag.

It was more than he ever gave Ellie on-duty.

She glared at Jacob when she caught him smirking at her sour expression. "I need to head out."

"I'll walk with you." Agent Lockwood fell into step beside her without waiting for her answer. He stepped into the elevator first, making sure it was clear, and he was the first to step out. When their eyes met, he shrugged. "I'm not saying you can't protect yourself, but—"

"Dr. Kingsley is on the loose."

"Exactly." He walked her to her car, leaning against a sleek black BMW X5 parked beside her.

"Is that your car?"

He nodded.

"Nice."

"It's a rental." He pursed his lips for a moment, looking

almost nervous. "I didn't want to say anything in front of Chief Johnson since you're *technically* on leave, but I have some information for you about two of your cases." Opening the back door, he removed two file folders from a rolling suitcase that was stuffed full with documents and cream-colored folders.

She read the names written neatly on the labels. "Anderson Duncan is mine, but I'm not investigating Joshua Gibson."

"I know, but you should. They're related. Both committed suicide after their appointment with Dr. Kingsley." He paused to pull out a photograph. "As you can see, Anderson Duncan rated his own page in one of Kingsley's scrapbooks."

"You raided Kingsley's office already?"

"As soon as Gabe gave us his name."

A deep frowned had her eyebrows knotted together. "If we're going to work together, you can't be going behind my back like this. I want to be involved and in the loop at all times."

He was solemn when he nodded, though his eyes still shone with the warmth she'd seen in him from that first moment. It wasn't an act. Clay Lockwood was just one of those people who oozed positivity. "I had to get approval from your superior officer to bring you into the fold, but now that I have it, you'll know what I do as soon as I know it."

"That's better." She opened her door and set the files on the seat, turned to him and stuck her hand out. "It was nice to meet you."

He shook her hand with a wide smile. Holding her gaze, his soft brown eyes drew her in as they crinkled in the corners. Charismatic and genuinely friendly, he was hard to resist. "I'll be in touch."

"I'm gonna hold you to that."

"Wouldn't have it any other way."

When she realized she was still holding his hand, she pulled hers away, but not before heat began to crawl up her cheeks.

With a wry grin, he got into the car and waited for Ellie to pull out first, as she wondered what she'd gotten herself into. Working with Jillian was one thing, but an entire task force? An FBI agent? It was more than she'd ever dreamt of, and as she pulled out onto the quiet street, she caught her happy grin in the rearview mirror.

Being part of a nationwide task force would be a huge boost to her career, but even more than that, the task force was already making a difference to victims like Valerie and Gabe.

Maybe they wouldn't put an end to human trafficking, but holding the perpetrators responsible for their crimes and making it harder for them to operate undetected was a step in the right direction.

31

Flynn sat in the driver's seat, his back rigid, eyes on the road. Beside him, Zeke had his weapon out, scanning every direction.

In the back seat, Ellie sat beside Valerie, who had her hands stuffed between her knees in an effort to keep them from shaking.

Ellie put her hand on Valerie's arm, trying to comfort her friend. "We'll all be there with you, okay?"

"What if Fink's there?"

"He won't be. Agent Lockwood's team has already deposed him and moved him to protective custody."

Valerie's eyes went wide. "Ellie, what if I'm in the same neighborhood as him? Does WITSEC put everyone together?"

"No, of course not. They won't tell me what city you're going to, but US Marshals have a strict policy against contact between former associates. That includes friends, family, and anyone who has a connection to the case you're involved with." The realization that she wouldn't see Valerie after today hit her like a punch to the gut, but she forced a reassuring smile. "Everything is going to be fine. You'll get into a rhythm, and you'll make friends. You never have to worry about Arthur Fink again."

"Thank you for not telling me it would be like it never happened." Valerie grimaced. "The paralegal they had prepare me for today said that to me, and I almost lost it. He didn't mean anything by it, but it still hurt." Gazing out the window, her breath shuddered when she finally let it out. "Nothing will ever be the same again. Ben is gone, Fink stole two years of my life I can *never* get back, and it's going to be a cold day in Hell before I ever go into a basement willingly."

"I know the feeling." And she did. The bits and pieces she remembered from her kidnapping were still scattered, but there was enough to infiltrate into almost every facet of her life. Her own experience had been traumatizing, but Valerie didn't have the benefit of forgetting all she'd been through. Ellie wouldn't dare diminish her pain, even under the guise of trying to make her feel better. "A fresh start will do you good, you'll see. But I'd be lying if I said I wasn't going to miss you."

Valerie's sudden hug startled Ellie, who had to blink back tears. Valerie sniffed, letting Ellie go almost as quickly as she'd embraced her. "I will never be able to repay you for what you did. If you hadn't followed your gut and come after me, I'd be dead."

In the front seat, one of the men cleared his throat, but Ellie made no comment. She wasn't about to call attention to the thick sound coming from Flynn's throat, giving away the raw emotions he was trying to conceal.

When the courthouse came into view, Valerie stiffened. Her hand shot out and grabbed Ellie's, squeezing so tight she winced. "I don't think I can do this."

"You can."

"Stay with me, please."

Ellie used her free hand to hold up the ID tag hanging from a lanyard around her neck. "I'm already cleared, and I'm armed." Gesturing to the two men in the front seat, she offered what she hoped was a calming smile. "They're armed too. Jacob and Duke will be there, and Agent Lockwood and his team will be on hand. You'll be surrounded by people who would die to protect you. *No one* is crossing that line."

Lips tight and eyes watery, Valerie nodded. "Okay."

"You've got this."

"I wish I was as strong as you."

You're stronger, Ellie thought, but she didn't give voice to her feelings. Valerie was clearly overwhelmed, and any little thing could have her clamming up. The information Valerie possessed was vital to their mission. She was one of the few who had been inside and lived to tell about it.

The cases of Ellora Rice, Anderson Duncan, and Joshua Gibson were wrapped up, only waiting for the doctor to be found so they could be closed. The doctor's escape weighed heavily on everyone, but all they could do was keep their guard up and their feelers out. But at least there had been closure for one family.

Constantino's body had been found and logged as a John Doe. With Gabe's information, the police department in Detroit was able to identify him and release his body to his family. Never a wanted outcome, but sometimes not knowing what happened to a loved one was worse.

Flynn's gruff voice interrupted them. "We're here." He guided the SUV down a ramp, flashing his credentials to the guard at the gate. He waved Flynn through, the wheels of the heavy iron fencing creaking under its weight. It closed behind them with a heavy thud that echoed through the parking garage.

Another guard waited for them at the elevator, checking the interior before letting them on. Flynn and Zeke stood in front of the doors as they slid closed, with Valerie behind them. Ellie brought up the rear, one hand on Valerie's belt, ready to pull her out of the way if they were ambushed when exiting.

If she hadn't been so close, she would've missed Valerie's hand reaching out, fingers wrapping around Flynn's. Motionless, gun in his right hand, Flynn stroked Valerie's knuckles with his thumb, and gave a gentle squeeze. Right before her eyes, Valerie's shoulders sagged with relief, and she stood a little straighter.

Ellie was glad no one could see the smile that spread across her face in the back of the cramped elevator. There was hope in that touch, and a sense that someday things would be normal. Except Flynn wouldn't be going into WITSEC with Valerie. There were specific rules about who counted as family members, and Flynn didn't fit the parameters. Valerie was going into this alone, and nothing Ellie could say would make what she was about to face any less scary.

Special Agent Clay Lockwood waited for them when the elevator reached the second floor. "The courtroom is clear." He leveled his brilliant smile on Valerie. "You're safe here. No one is going to hurt you."

She nodded, and like a well-oiled machine, the four of them fell into step around Valerie.

The courtroom was empty except for the court reporter, judge, prosecutor, and a handful of support staff. A large camera, much like the ones Ellie had seen news crews lug around, stood on a tripod a few feet from the witness stand.

Shoulders straight and eyes locked on the chair, Valerie climbed up the steps and sat down.

She listened carefully as the judge walked her through what was expected of her before the prosecutor stepped in with his slick smile, leaning on the edge of the witness stand to show Valerie just how relaxed the whole thing was. His attempt to put her at ease fell flat, but Valerie was calm and professional, clearly ready to get this over with.

Flynn and Zeke stood near the doors, hovering beside the officers who had been assigned to protect the exits. Like Ellie, they were still suspicious of everyone they encountered, and Valerie's safety was more important than anyone offended by their presence. Clay sat beside Ellie, hands resting in his lap as he listened carefully as Valerie told her story.

None of it was new to Ellie, but she found herself fighting back tears, nonetheless. Valerie had survived being kidnapped to then be sold to a madman who kept her locked in a basement he'd fashioned into a life-sized dollhouse. She recounted the moment she'd learned that her boyfriend, Ben, had died shortly after they'd been captured, and the fear when she'd realized the man who'd bought her from Arthur Fink intended to hunt her like an animal too.

Ellie shuddered at her version of the events they'd shared, deep in the woods with Tucker Penland. But when she locked eyes with Valerie across the courtroom, she knew she'd do it all over again.

Valerie was wrong. Ellie wasn't the one with enviable strength.

THE COURT PROCEEDINGS lasted a grueling three hours, and when the ordeal was over, the courtroom was cleared so Agent Lockwood could coordinate the next step in a secure area.

Lockwood waved them over to the front bench, positioned so he could see them and the doors. When Flynn and

Zeke didn't join them right away, he called both men over. "I need you two as well."

They hesitated, but Agent Lockwood was insistent.

Flynn sat beside Valerie, and this time, they held hands openly, aware that their time together was coming to an abrupt end.

The sight tore at Ellie's heart. She could only imagine how Valerie felt. She'd lost so much, and now she had no choice but to walk away from the only friends she'd had in two years. It wasn't fair.

"Valerie, you did an amazing job, and I'm beyond proud of you. I think we all are." Agent Lockwood smiled, holding a small stack of papers. "I can't tell you where you're going, but I *can* tell you that I pulled some strings to get you in our best setup. I know it doesn't make up for everything you've been through or the people you're leaving behind, but I hope it brings some comfort."

Valerie choked back tears and nodded her thanks.

Ellie's jaw tightened, the cruelty of the victim having to give up everything because of what had happened to her almost too much to bear. She wanted to shout that it wasn't right and offer up whatever amount of money it would take to keep Valerie safe *and* in Charleston. But that wouldn't be practical, and she knew that staying in Charleston would serve as a constant reminder of the past two years of Valerie's life. Valerie was trading one evil for another, and there was nothing Ellie could do to change that.

Agent Lockwood cleared his throat. "After talking with Flynn about some of the challenges Valerie will face due to the widespread prevalence of human trafficking rings in major US cities, and my personal mission to reduce the trauma victims experience at the hands of the justice system, I pulled a few strings, and well…" He handed the papers to Flynn.

The room was silent as Flynn read each line, his lips moving in disbelief. Incredulous, he looked up from the document. "Is this real?"

Agent Lockwood nodded. "It's legit."

"My brother Zeke too?"

Ellie blinked, surprised that she didn't realize the pair were brothers. Some detective she was. "You're brothers?"

"Half. Different last names."

That made her feel a little bit better.

Clay nodded, his voice loud in the room that was still hushed in shock. "Yes. You've done an exemplary job of keeping Valerie safe, and you have the necessary security clearances and training to be named as her handlers." He winked at Valerie, who was struggling to hold her emotions in check as she leaned into Flynn, reading the words on the page. "That's how I was able to get you such a sweet setup."

"I don't know what to say." Her hands shook as she pushed her dark hair from her tear-stained face. "Thank you doesn't seem like enough."

"You did your part to make the world a safer place. It's the least I could do." He cleared his throat and checked his watch. "I hate to cut this short, but you three have a private jet to catch. I wish you nothing but the best."

They stood in unison, Valerie openly sobbing, the relief too much to bear. She threw herself into Flynn's arms, burying her face in his chest. He towered over her petite frame, strong arms swallowing her whole.

Hot tears stung Ellie's eyes, but she didn't bother to wipe them away. She wasn't the only one crying, and it was nice to shed happy tears for once. There'd been far too much pain.

But seeing them together also made her think of Nick. She still needed to talk to him. Soon. She'd do that soon.

Ellie and Agent Lockwood accompanied the trio to the parking garage, where Ellie gave Valerie one last hug, holding on until a light tap on her shoulder let her know it was time for her friend to leave. Nodding through the tears, she held Valerie at arm's length before letting her go and stepping back so she could get in the car and be whisked away to her new life.

This time, Flynn sat in the back with Valerie. His left arm cradled her against him, but his right hand remained free, ready to draw his weapon if needed.

Agent Lockwood nodded to the man in black who slid into the driver's seat. The engine roared to life, and they drove away.

"Thank you for getting Flynn and Zeke in with her," Ellie said as the taillights disappeared around the corner. "You don't know how much it means to know that she won't be alone."

"It was an easy decision, though I did have to pull a few strings to get it done."

Ellie crossed her arms over her chest. "Don't be so pleased with yourself. It's the least you could do after everything Valerie did for your case."

"And yours."

"So true." Ellie inhaled through her nose and sighed loudly. "Shit."

"What?"

"I rode with them."

Agent Lockwood laughed, nodding toward his rental. "I can take you."

"That's good, thanks. This day has been far too long. I'm ready for a vacation."

"You just came back to work."

Ellie narrowed her eyes at him. "Do you always have a punchline?"

"Yes."

"You're ridiculous." She climbed into the passenger seat of

the expensive rental and buckled herself in. "How does your partner put up with you?"

"I don't have a partner." The engine caught, and Agent Lockwood drove out of the parking garage, heading toward Ellie's apartment.

"You didn't ask for directions."

"I don't need them."

Ellie shook her head and leaned back in the luxury seat. "Anything new with my case?"

"*Our* case," he corrected. "And not in the past two weeks."

"What about Jillian's phone?" She turned so she could study his profile.

His smile slid away as he shook his head. "There's no sign of it. And it's been off since Dr. Kingsley used it to lure you to the warehouse."

"She's been beside herself about it. There was so much personal information saved on that phone."

"You learn not to do that."

Scowling, Ellie stared out the window at the stately homes as they passed. Did the owners know how close they were to evil? Would anyone lose sleep thinking about all the ways human beings hurt each other? Or would they sleep soundly, knowing that Charleston PD was there to protect them from the evil they knew, and even the evil they didn't?

"I deleted most of the private information I had stored on my phone, and Jillian already has a new phone. We're both more careful, but even if you only have contacts and phone numbers, there's enough for the right criminal to use."

"You have to choose what risks you're willing to take. It's a tough line to walk, but we're all just doing our best." He pulled up to the curb outside her apartment building. "Would you like me to walk you to your door?"

Shaking her head, she already had her fingers wrapped around the door handle. "I'll be fine."

"I know you will." He waved once as he drove away, headed to the airport, and on his way home.

Home.

The word held so much meaning, but it was different for everyone. For Ellie, home was a quiet apartment with her roommate and a dog named Sam. And for Valerie, home was a fresh start with the man who'd been her protector. Tonight, they would all be *home*.

Tomorrow was a brand-new day. But she wouldn't relax. Couldn't relax. Not until every one of the players in the enormous operation she'd discovered were caught and no longer a danger.

32

The bright noon sun glinted off the blacktop, warming the last of the chill from the air. Windows rolled down and wind whipping through his hair, he pushed his eighteen-wheeler to the speed limit and sailed through the empty forest. It was too early in May for the occasional tourist to stop on the side of the forest-lined road of the Carolinas to take pictures of deer, and too late in the year for the snow-birds who traveled north each weekend in hopes of catching some late-season snow. It was his favorite time of year, and the empty highway made long haul trucking enjoyable.

"What have we here?" he muttered as he topped one of the many low rises, foot instinctively coming off the gas to slow the rig.

The semi's engine roared as Matt Loomis shifted into a lower gear. Ahead, a red Nissan Altima sat on the side of the road, trunk and hood open, the hazard lights flashing. But it wasn't the fire-engine red car that had caught his attention on the empty stretch of Highway 41 North between Huger and Bethera. It was the leggy brunette with red lips and striking blue eyes standing with her thumb out, a wide smile showing off perfectly straight teeth.

Matt slowed, passing the Altima, and pulled onto the shoulder ahead of the car before coming to a complete stop. Before he had the chance to get his door open, the woman slung a backpack over her shoulder, her stride light as she jogged the length of the trailer on the passenger side.

He unlocked the door just as she climbed onto the step and yanked on the handle. "Having car trouble?"

She caught her lower lip between her teeth and nodded. "I've been here for hours. Thank you."

"Are you traveling alone?"

"Yes. Thank you for rescuing me."

He nodded, surprised by her eagerness to get into the cab with a stranger. Most of the women he picked up were wary at first, relaxing as they got to know him a little better. But this woman seemed to have no fear—a dangerous quality in today's world.

"Did you try calling someone? Maybe it's an easy fix."

She shook her head and held up her cell phone. "It's dead. Besides, I can't afford to get it fixed."

"I might be able to help." He twisted toward the storage space behind his seat, where he kept his tools. Before he could grab the black duffle bag, her fingers curled around his forearm. He froze, meeting her eyes, the skin of her palm soft on his bare arm.

"Please. I just want to get out of here. Where are you going?"

"Richmond, Virginia, then on to Louisville, Kentucky."

"That's where I'm going." Giving his arm a squeeze, she lowered her eyelids, pleading, "Can you take me with you?"

His mouth went dry, his nostrils flaring in response. There was nothing he loved more than a damsel in distress, and this woman fit the bill to a T. The sweet smell of freshly washed hair filled the cabin, and her chest heaved with excitement beneath the thin fabric of her shirt.

"Of course," he managed.

Instead of pulling her hand from his arm so he could drive, he guided her hand to the manual gear shift. She wrapped her fingers around the knob, and when he covered her tiny hand with his rough, larger one, she didn't pull away. "So, what's your name, sweetheart?"

"Katarina."

"Katarina." He repeated the name with a smile. "It suits you. Very exotic."

"Thank you. What's yours?"

"Matt Loomis."

"Well, Matt Loomis," she said breathlessly. "I'm so grateful you were here to save me."

His abdominal muscles clenched. Did this woman have any idea how gorgeous she was? She didn't act like the arrogant young women he'd seen so many times on his travels. She was kind, eager, and more than a little naïve. His heart skipped a beat. "Have you ever handled a stick shift before?"

Her dark hair swayed when she shook her head. "No, but I'm a quick learner. Anything you want to teach me, I can learn."

Pressing the clutch, he put the truck in first gear and gave the rig some gas. It rolled forward, leaving her broken down sedan on the roadside. "What are you going to do about your car?"

She shrugged. "I'm looking for a fresh start. I don't really care about the car."

"The state will tow it."

"The state can keep it. I'm going to start a new life for myself, and I don't need my past tagging along. There will be no more working for the man." Giggling, she rolled down her window and pitched the cell phone out. "I won't be needing that anymore, either. The old me is gone. Here's to a new and improved Katarina, starting now."

They rode in silence for a few miles, Matt's attention focused on her tiny hand in his as he shifted to a gear to accommodate a low hill. She was relaxed, completely at ease with him from the moment she'd sat in the passenger seat. He wasn't sure how he'd gotten so lucky, but it looked like the gods were smiling down on him.

He wanted to keep her talking, so he pressed her about her plans. "So, you're starting a business?"

"Of sorts."

His eyebrows shot up at her tone. "What kind of skills do you have?" Swallowing hard, he waited for her reply, his hand still holding hers on the gear shift.

"I have lots of skills." She slipped her hand from beneath his and placed her palm on his thigh.

Even through his jeans, he could feel the heat that radiated from her. Her meaning was clear, but he stopped himself from moving her hand to the crotch of his jeans, which was already feeling tighter. "You don't have to move to be successful. There are a lot of people around here who would pay for your services. Top dollar, even."

"There's a lot to be said for change of pace, and I don't need the money."

He scoffed. "Everyone needs money. You can't buy everything you need with your looks."

"It's worked before."

She was confident but stopped short of arrogant. The more she talked, the more intrigued Matt became. He'd never met anyone like her before. Glad he'd stopped to pick her up, he wondered again if it had been fate that put her directly in his path.

"It's a long drive to Louisville, so we'll have to stop in Richmond for the night."

Her lower lip stuck out slightly. "How far is Richmond?"

Sucking in a deep breath, he imagined her full lip between his teeth. "Almost six hours. We'll stop for food before we get there."

Her hand inched closer to his zipper, blue eyes dancing mischief. "I know a way we can pass the time."

He hadn't imagined her meaning and mentally calculated how far it was to the nearest hotel with semi parking. He didn't think he could make it all the way to Richmond at this point. She was too close, and his need was too great.

Patience, Matt, he warned himself. He wasn't a first-timer, and women like Katarina were to be savored.

"You're too beautiful to waste on just any man. Have you thought about branching out, maybe bringing in a few ladies to work under you?"

"I have. I have a lot of plans. That's why I need to get out of here. The competition is a little too stiff for my tastes, and there are a few cops who insist on making things difficult for me. Well, one cop in particular."

"A woman, I bet."

Katarina flashed him a bright smile. "How did you know?"

"A man would know your worth. A woman will just be jealous of what she doesn't have. You're stunning. It's not hard to believe that someone could be jealous of you."

"You're very sweet, Matt." She rewarded him with a quick kiss on the cheek before sitting back and continuing as if nothing out of the ordinary had happened. "Once I find a place, and I can operate without the law getting in my way, I'll bring more people on. But for now, I'm counting on myself and no one else."

"Smart."

"That's the only way to be successful in this life. I have

dreams—aspirations, really—and involving others just complicates things. I learned that the hard way."

"It sounds like you have a good head on your shoulders. That's a big help when you're trying to forge your own path." He took his eyes from the road long enough to smile at her. Up close, he could tell she was wearing colored contacts, but that didn't matter. It wasn't just her eyes he was intrigued by, but the entire package. Finding out what her natural eye color was would be half the fun when he had her in the hotel.

"What about you, Matt?"

Her question pulled him out of his revelry. "What about me?"

"Is driving a truck your endgame?"

He smiled, shifting in his seat to relieve some of the pressure in his pants. "I get great benefits, and I can afford to spoil myself, so yeah, this is a sweet gig. I'm my own boss, I set my own hours, and I own my truck. No one to answer to and no one to tell me how I can spend my money? It's worked for me for over a decade."

"Doesn't that get lonely?" She dragged her fingers over his zipper, a dreamy expression on her face. "A man has certain needs, Matt."

"I do." He all but growled the words.

"You're such a handsome man. You shouldn't be alone."

He chuckled. "Not to burst your bubble, but I don't spend a lot of time alone. You're not the only one doing what you do."

He'd expected her to pout. In fact, he'd chosen his words carefully in the hopes of getting a rise out of her. But she was unfazed. "I bet you can afford to have a lot of things men want. A woman to warm your bed. *Women* to keep you satisfied at night. The world is yours for the taking, right?"

"Yes."

"What a powerful feeling."

"It is." He swallowed hard when her hand settled over his growing bulge. At this rate, he wouldn't make it to the North Carolina state line. She was too beautiful, the things she was promising too much for him to wait. "A woman needs money to build her empire. I can give you that money, for certain services. Is that something you would like?"

Purring her agreement, she slid closer to him with lust in her eyes. "You're right, I do need money, and there's not much I wouldn't do to get what I want."

"Like I said, you're smart."

"I'm glad to hear you say that, Matt. In fact, I think you'll be my first product."

"Product?" He laughed. "Don't you mean client?"

Her giggle was like rain on a hot summer day washing over him. The joy on her face was pure light, and every breath she took pushed him closer to the edge of reason. He wanted her now, but she was like fine wine—you didn't just drink such a special treat all at once. Maybe he'd take his time with this one. Maybe he'd even keep her around for a few weeks. She was special, and the best part was, she knew it.

A glint of light hit his side-view mirror, the reflection of the midday sun on the windshield of a car moving over the solid double stripe between the lanes to pass him.

Matt scanned the horizon, making sure the road was clear. There was no way he was going to waste time stopping to report an accident today. Katarina had appeared in the exact moment he needed to slake his thirst, and no reckless driver in a no-passing zone was going to ruin it. If they didn't die in a head-on collision, Matt might get out and kill them with his bare hands.

The image made him smile.

When the car was even with his window, he blinked,

surprised to see a cherry red Altima linger for a moment before speeding by them.

He tilted his head to study Katarina, motioning to the car that was quickly pulling ahead of his rig. "Wasn't that your car?"

She lifted a shoulder in a lazy shrug. "There are so many red cars."

She was right, but he couldn't shake the sudden feeling that he'd been duped. For what reason, he didn't know, but he was going to have to keep an eye on this woman. Obviously, she was more than he'd bargained for when he'd stopped to pick her up, and the realization left him bubbling with excitement. Maybe she and a partner had a plan, but they didn't know what they were up against.

Matt had seen more cons than he could count, and this young woman was mid-twenties at most. There was no way she was going to catch him unaware. But the fact that she might try excited him.

If his hunch was right, and someone had hidden in the car and planned to ambush him, he would take care of that and go back to his original plan. Maybe even bring the friend along, if it was another woman, though Katarina would remain his primary focus.

Katarina was special. He could feel it. It had been a very long time since anyone had affected him like Katarina did.

He was glad she was going to be the one.

She was perfect.

He couldn't wait to get to Richmond.

The End
To be continued...

Thank you for reading.
All of the Ellie Kline Series books can be found on Amazon.

ACKNOWLEDGMENTS

How does one properly thank everyone involved in taking a dream and making it a reality? Here goes.

In addition to our families, whose unending support provided the foundation for us to find the time and energy to put these thoughts on paper, we want to thank the editors who polished our words and made them shine.

Many thanks to our publisher for risking taking on two newbies and giving us the confidence to become bona fide authors.

More than anyone, we want to thank you, our readers, for clicking on a couple of nobodies and sharing your most important asset, your time, with this book. We hope with all our hearts we made it worthwhile.

Much love,

Mary & Donna

ABOUT THE AUTHOR

Mary Stone lives among the majestic Blue Ridge Mountains of East Tennessee with her two dogs, four cats, a couple of energetic boys, and a very patient husband.

As a young girl, she would go to bed every night, wondering what type of creature might be lurking underneath. It wasn't until she was older that she learned that the creatures she needed to most fear were human.

Today, she creates vivid stories with courageous, strong heroines and dastardly villains. She invites you to enter her world of serial killers, FBI agents but never damsels in distress. Her female characters can handle themselves, going toe-to-toe with any male character, protagonist or antagonist.

Discover more about Mary Stone on her website.
www.authormarystone.com

Donna Berdel

Raised as an Army brat, Donna has lived all over the world, but no place has given her as much peace as the home she lives in with her husband near Myrtle Beach. But while she now keeps her feet planted firmly in the sand, her mind goes back to those cities and the people she met and said goodbye to so many times.

With her two adopted cats fighting for lap space, she brings those she loved (and those she didn't) back as characters in her books. And yes, it's kind of fun to kill off anyone who was mean to her in the past. Mean clerk at the grocery store...beware!

Connect with Mary Online

facebook.com/authormarystone

goodreads.com/AuthorMaryStone

bookbub.com/profile/3378576590

pinterest.com/MaryStoneAuthor

instagram.com/marystone_author

Made in the USA
Coppell, TX
02 September 2021

61632328R00187